D0505185

ALPHA INSTINCT
KATIE REUS

ETERNAL
ROMANCE

Published by arrangement with NAL Signet,
a division of Penguin Group (USA) Inc.

First published in Great Britain in 2013
by ETERNAL ROMANCE
An imprint of HEADLINE PUBLISHING GROUP

1

Cataloguing in Publication Data is available from the British Library

ISBN 978 1 4722 0080 8

Offset in Times by Avon DataSet Ltd, Bidford-on-Avon, Warwickshire

Printed and bound by CPI Group (UK) Ltd, Croydon, CR0 4YY

Headline's policy is to use papers that are natural, renewable and recyclable
products and made from wood grown in sustainable forests. The logging and
manufacturing processes are expected to conform to the environmental
regulations of the country of origin.

HEADLINE PUBLISHING GROUP
An Hachette UK Company
338 Euston Road
London NW1 3BH

www.eternalromancebooks.co.uk
www.headline.co.uk
www.hachette.co.uk

For my husband, my one true north, my rock. Your unswerving support and wonderful ability to look the other way when things around the house pile up or when we have takeout *again* does not go unnoticed. Thank you for always encouraging me to aim high and for having more faith in me than I do in myself.

Chapter 1

Analena Cordona shoved her hands into the pockets of her thick, quilted down jacket. Not because she was cold, but because for the second time in the past ten minutes she was questioning her decision to meet Sean Taggart without an escort. It was likely stupid—scratch that; definitely stupid—but she couldn't drag one of her sisters or cousins along to meet with him. Taggart was one of the most devious shifters she'd ever met, and she couldn't risk her pack getting hurt. Despite her effort to appear casual, an unwanted shiver skittered down her spine. If need be, she was ready to run at a moment's notice.

The wind howled mercilessly through the trees of Fontana Mountain and when it shifted south she caught Taggart's distinctive, foul scent. He was close. Watching her, no doubt. *Pervy bastard.*

"I know you're there, Sean. Come out now so we can get this over with." She was thankful her voice didn't shake.

To her surprise, a hulking brown and white wolf emerged from a cluster of trees. *What the hell?* They'd agreed to come in *human* form. Glancing around, she saw he hadn't brought anyone else. That tamed her nerves a little but not much. He was still older and stronger and a lot more ruthless. Even though she tried to mask it, he had to smell her fear. "What are you doing?" she snapped, hoping her anger would cover her alarm.

When the animal stood a few feet in front of her, he changed to his human form. Ana looked away but could hear his bones break, shift and realign. Many shifters didn't mind others watching them change, but to her it was such a private, painful thing, she didn't do it in front of just anyone.

She turned back to face him and immediately wanted to wipe the smirk off his face. Of course he'd be arrogant enough to stand naked in front of her when they were supposed to be having a serious meeting. She attempted to keep the loathing out of her voice. "I thought we agreed to come in human form."

He shrugged and had the nerve to grab himself. "I wanted the exercise. Besides, you should get to see what's going to be yours soon."

Mine? Gross. Bile rose in her throat, but she pushed it down. Sure, the man had a nice body, but what lay underneath that exterior scared her. She'd seen the way he treated the women of his pack. He was mean just for the sake of being mean. As Alpha, he should set a better example, but no one had stood up to him yet. "Excuse me?"

"That's why you wanted to meet, isn't it? To proposition me?"

"Not exactly." She cleared her throat and looked around. A light layer of snow had fallen over the normally grassy incline. Other than the wind and rustling trees, she was suddenly aware of how alone she really was. She was at least two miles from her family's ranch.

"We've had a few attacks over the past couple weeks. Some of our cattle have gone missing and I've found a few mutilated cows. And just this morning I found one of my sister's horses dead."

The increasing vandalism against her pack's ranch was a message. Taggart wanted to unite his pack with hers and would stop at nothing to get what he wanted. She was surprised he hadn't done worse.

"And you think my pack had something to do with it?" His voice was monotone.

She noticed he didn't deny it. "I didn't say that. I don't know many humans who venture into our territory, so I just wanted to let you know about it."

He crossed his arms over his bare chest and she forced herself to keep her eyes on his face. It pissed her off that he just stood there naked. He must have known it would make her uncomfortable.

"Fine. I'll keep an eye out, but *we* haven't had any problems. If you had better security, I doubt you would either." His voice was taunting.

"We're doing fine." But they weren't. Not really. Financially they were on solid ground, but with all the males of their pack dead, it was only a matter of time before another pack would think they could move into their territory and force them to assimilate. They might live peacefully among the humans now, but they still had their own laws to worry about. Their black-and-white laws were a lot more primal. As unguarded, unprotected females, they were more or less fair game. It might be bullshit, but there wasn't much she could do about it unless she wanted to take on the Northern American Council. They wouldn't allow a she-wolf to remain Alpha without proving herself. As with males, a true Alpha—regardless of gender—had to prove she was strong enough to protect her pack from anything. If it came down to an actual fight, she couldn't take on Taggart and she knew it. No doubt he did too. And she hated that. Pack law was so different from human rules, and while her animal side acknowledged and understood it, her human side fought against the archaic rules of the Council. Sometimes she worried the eight council members headquartered in Chicago were too out of touch with the changing needs of their kind.

He took a step forward and traced a finger down her cheekbone. Alarm fluttered through her. On instinct, she slapped his hand away. "Don't touch me."

His dark eyes flashed in anger, and instead of moving away he grabbed her by the back of her neck and tugged her against him. She started to fight but contained her rage. Her inner wolf told her he *wanted* her to struggle. She needed to play this right. Among shifters violence against any females was rare, but Taggart was a bastard and nothing he did would surprise Ana. She didn't know much about his parents, but she'd heard his father had been absolutely archaic in his rules with his pack, and it was obvious the apple hadn't fallen far from the tree.

"Soon enough you'll come crawling on your knees, begging to be my mate," he growled in her ear.

I'd rather die first. "Let. Me. Go."

"I think I'm going to have a little fun first." The menacing note in his voice sent up warning bells.

The Cordona women might be small but they were lightning fast. In her shifted form she knew she could outrun him, but she'd have to get away from him first. He grabbed the zipper on her jacket and snapped it down. Adrenaline pumped through her when she realized what he intended.

She kicked at him. He deflected the blow with his thigh. His grip on her tightened for a split second, and then suddenly she was free. Taking her off guard, he shoved at her chest. She hit the ground with a thud.

Shift.

Run.

Escape.

Thoughts of survival overtook her. She rolled over and prepared to go through the change when he dove on top of her, pinning her to the ground. Her throat tightened as she struggled against him.

"Get off of her!" A loud, dominating male voice roared through the woods, reverberating off the trees.

Taggart shifted his weight, and she didn't waste the opportunity. Scrambling away, she put a few yards between them. If he made one wrong move, she was going to shift and take off. Her canines were already extending. They pressed painfully against her gums. Her inner wolf begged to be unleashed.

The need to survive was taking over most of her reasoning, and the only thing keeping her from shifting was sheer willpower.

She wasn't sure where the voice had come from, but she recognized it as sure as she knew her own name. Unless the wind was playing cruel tricks on her. She hadn't heard that soothing voice in about fifty years. Her mouth dropped open when two men she knew and eight wolves she didn't recognize appeared from the thickest part of the trees lining their meeting place. By the large size of the wolves it was obvious they were all part of the warrior class. Where alphas were dominant in disposition, warriors were all that and more. By nature, warriors were born fighters. It was something ingrained deep inside them, and Ana had always thought they were a bit more in touch with their inner animal than other shifters. Warriors could be intimidating, but she'd always respected them. They wanted to protect and take care of alphas and betas alike, not only because it was the pack way, but because the need to protect those weaker was in their blood.

Taggart turned and glared at her. "You think you're so smart, you little bitch. This isn't over." He shifted into wolf form with the speed only an Alpha could manage and darted past her in the direction opposite the newcomers.

As she stared at the two men who'd once been her best friends, she wasn't sure what was going on or why they were there. She truly didn't care. All thoughts of running away dissipated.

Connor and Liam Armstrong strode toward her, of course dressed in all black. Some things hadn't changed.

Before she could contemplate whether it was a good idea or not, she launched herself at Liam, but only because he was closest. She wrapped her arms around his neck in a tight hug. "I can't believe you're here."

He returned her hug in equal measure. "Good to see you too, little wolf." Chuckling, he finally put her down, and she paused for just a moment before wrapping her arms around Connor.

Once upon a time she'd thought she and Connor might be more than friends. Until the day he'd left her without an explanation. Even though he'd taken a little piece of her heart all those years ago, she was still grateful he was with her now.

At first he stiffened under her hold. She started to pull back when he murmured something foreign in her hair—Gaelic, maybe. She couldn't understand his words, but that deep voice of his sent a warm ribbon of awareness curling through her. She prayed he couldn't smell her desire. When he put her on her feet, she was speechless as she stared into his bright green eyes. He still had the ability to take her breath away without even trying.

"Did that bastard hurt you?" His words were almost devoid of emotion, but the flash of anger in his eyes gave him away. His green eyes started to turn almost black as the animal in him prepared to take over.

Though she was tempted to say yes, she shook her head and ran a light hand down his arm. The last thing she wanted was for Connor to go after Taggart. If he did, she'd bring down the wrath of Taggart's entire pack. Considering the Cordonas had no Alpha or male protectors at the moment, she'd be signing death warrants for all her packmates. No matter how much she hated Taggart, she couldn't risk the fallout. She didn't know why Connor was there, but he was a nomad and once he left she'd be stuck defending her pack until she could come to an arrangement with the Council. And that was a headache she didn't want to dwell on now. "I'm fine . . . thanks to you."

"I should hunt him down." This time he didn't bother hiding the rage in his voice. Connor sounded as if he had gravel in his throat as he took a menacing step past her.

She grabbed him and squeezed. "Please don't. It's not worth it."

His muscles flexed under her touch and his breathing was slightly erratic, but at least he stilled.

Looking behind them, she eyed the foreign wolves, then looked back at Connor and Liam. "What are you doing here? And who are they?"

The two men exchanged a guarded look before Connor spoke. "We heard about your pack."

Suddenly wary, she took a step back. "What exactly have you heard?"

"That your father and your . . . mate"—he seemed to choke on the word—"were killed two months ago."

Ana had never officially taken a mate, but she didn't voice that aloud. There was no reason Connor needed to know. "My father and all the males of our pack were poisoned. And all the pregnant females too. My mother wasn't pregnant, but she died anyway." Of a broken heart, Ana was certain. It was as if her mother had just given up the will to live once her mate was gone. Even saying that out loud hurt more than Ana could describe, but she pushed past the pain. As current leader of the Cordona pack, she didn't have time for self-pity.

"How and by whom?" he demanded.

"I don't have answers to either of those." Not that she hadn't tried her damndest to find out who'd killed them. One day all of the males and the pregnant females in her pack had gotten sick, and days later they'd all been dead. Her father, two uncles and their pregnant mates, seven male cousins and their pregnant mates, and Ana's own intended mate. And then her mother was gone too. Twenty-one members of their pack gone. Just like that. It had happened so fast. They hadn't realized what was going on at first and by the time they did, it had been too late.

"What did our Council say?"

She snorted softly. "They're supposed to send someone down to investigate the poisonings, but we're apparently not very high on the food chain. Probably because we don't have a lot of political pull now that we're just a bunch of females." She didn't bother to hide the bitterness in her voice. She'd also been holding off on contacting the Council about Taggart's vandalism. The Council would just view it as weakness and as proof she couldn't run her own pack. If they found out he'd tried to attack her tonight they would no doubt swiftly and harshly punish Taggart, but the entire situation was a catch-22. Their help would come at a price that would likely mean immediate assimilation with another pack not of her choosing.

Connor stared at her but didn't say anything. Silence

descended over them, and she wished she'd kept her big mouth shut. She hadn't seen him in a long time and didn't need to announce her pack's issues to him. Not to mention that she had a hundred questions—like why he was on her land—but wasn't sure where to start.

"You cut your hair," Connor said, breaking the awkward moment.

Self-consciously she raked her fingers through the shorter tresses. Her dark hair barely touched her shoulders now. The last time she'd seen him her hair had been at least a foot longer. She'd also worn bell-bottoms, tie-dyed shirts and tried to emulate Brigitte Bardot. Times had changed and so had she. She shrugged. "It's been half a century. What did you expect?"

He reached out and fingered it. "I like it." When his callused fingers trailed over her cheek, her breath caught in her throat.

Despite her desire to remain immune to him, she could feel her cheeks heat up at the statement. It wasn't even a compliment. Not really. But her traitorous libido didn't seem to care. It roared to life at those words. After years of being dormant, that's all it took for her hormones to wake up. Three stupid words.

His hair was shorter now too. And so was Liam's. Both of them looked liked they'd stepped off the cover of *Soldier of Fortune*. They wore black cargo pants and black, long-sleeved shirts and had military-style crops. But she didn't comment. She didn't want to stand around talking about how much they'd all changed. She needed to get back to her pack. "You said you heard about my pack, but are you just passing through?"

Again they exchanged a look. "Not exactly."

She frowned at the nonanswer. "Listen, I need to get back. Do you have a place to stay tonight?"

They both shrugged noncommittally.

She bit back a sigh. She'd forgotten how infuriating they could be. "I'm assuming those wolves are with you and that they're trustworthy. I've got two empty cabins that should be big enough to accommodate all of you. A couple of you will have to share rooms, but it's a place to sleep." There were more than enough beds and bathrooms for ten wolves.

Back when she'd known them they'd been lone wolves, so it surprised her that they had their own pack now. Connor was definitely an Alpha but he'd never seemed interested in a formal leadership role. And leading a group of shifters was a big responsibility. As she assessed the shifters she realized the smaller wolf hiding behind one of the bigger wolves near the back was female.

"The female can stay at my place unless she's mated. . . ." Her voice trailed off as the reality sank in that Connor could be mated. Hell, he probably was. What sane, single she-wolf wouldn't scoop him up? Still, she didn't scent anyone on him, so maybe not. *I hope not.* She gritted her teeth at the thought. She *didn't* care. If she kept repeating it, maybe she'd believe it.

This time Liam spoke. "Thank you for the offer. Erin's unmated, and I think it would do her good to have some female company. She's had a rough year."

Ana noticed that both Connor and Liam shifted uncomfortably, so she didn't pursue the topic. She motioned back toward the riding trail that led to her ranch. "I walked here, so if you're ready, we can head back now."

Connor nodded and motioned toward the wolves. They paired up in twos and fell in line behind them. Maybe it shouldn't have surprised her that Connor was now Alpha of his own pack. He was a natural-born leader. Broad shouldered and standing over six feet tall, he was almost a foot taller than her. Of course, most people were taller than her. She stole peeks at him as they headed down the trail.

Even though it was shorter, his hair was still a dark chocolate brown. He was 110 in human years, but he only looked to be about thirty years old. He wouldn't have any signs of gray hair for a few hundred years to come. There was a sharper, deadlier edge to him that she didn't remember, but he was still handsome. In a rugged sort of way. And he still had the ability to make her stomach do flip-flops by simply looking at her.

She might be irrationally pleased to see him, but a part of her was terrified over the reason he'd come. It was silly to think he'd hurt her, but what if he wanted to take over her pack? Her family's land? Or claim one of her sisters as a mate? That was probably the one thing she didn't think her heart could handle. The thought of him with someone else—someone close to her—made her ache. Worrying about that wouldn't do her any good now. Soon enough she'd have her answers.

Connor sat on one of Analena's couches and tried to contain the sexual energy humming through him. So many years had passed and he thought he'd been ready to see her again. All it had taken was one look into those espresso-colored eyes and he'd felt himself falling. Fast and hard.

"Chill, brother. You're gonna freak her out if she gets a whiff of that lust." Liam stood by the fireplace with his arms over his chest. He leaned casually against the mantle but he looked tense.

He knew his brother was right, but it was hard to think around her. Pack Alphas talked among one another, and when he'd heard what had happened to the males of her pack he'd known it was time to come back.

He'd stayed away long enough, and he'd be damned if he let some other mutt claim what was his.

The sound of footsteps descending the stairs alerted them. Before she even entered the room, he knew it was Ana. Her scent was so distinctive he'd be able to pick her out of a crowded auditorium. Raspberries and sunshine. That's what he thought of every time she was near.

He automatically stood when she entered the room. Now that she'd taken off that puffy jacket, he could see what he'd been fantasizing about for decades. She was still petite and fragile-looking, but he knew otherwise. The sleeves of her long T-shirt were pushed back, showing lean arms, and her form-fitting jeans did little to hide those tight, muscular legs. The soft curves of her breasts interested him much more.

Liam loudly cleared his throat, jerking him back to reality. He looked at his brother, then at Ana, who hovered by the love seat opposite the couch he'd been sitting on. Instantly he sat back down, and she did the same.

"How's Erin?" The she-wolf he'd picked up months ago was skittish as hell and he couldn't help but worry about her. They all did.

Ana's expression darkened. "I think she's okay. We put her in one of the guest rooms upstairs, but I think Carmen is going to stay the night with her. It's a strange place to her and I don't think she wants to sleep alone."

Connor nodded. "Yeah, when we found her, she'd been . . ."

"Brutalized?"

He nodded.

She clasped her hands tightly in her lap. "Do you know who hurt her?"

He shook his head. If he'd known, whoever had hurt her would be dead. He wouldn't have bothered going to the Council to bring them up on charges. "She won't talk about it."

She looked pointedly between him and his brother. "Where are your other ... friends? I thought you said you wanted to talk."

"We do, but we thought you'd feel more comfortable discussing some things in private. Did you want to invite Carmen and Noel downstairs?"

She shook her head again. "No. My sisters trust me to make any decisions concerning our pack. I'm tired and a little cranky, so let's just get down to business. Why are you guys here?"

"You need protection." He and Liam had discussed things earlier, but now that he was actually sitting in front of her, he wondered how well his proposition would go over.

Her dark eyebrows rose. "Oh, *really*?"

"There are no males left in your pack and you are not an Alpha." She might be an alpha in nature but she didn't have the cutthroat qualities it took to lead a pack. It was one of the things he loved about her. She had a steel backbone but was still soft and empathetic, sometimes letting her heart rule her decisions. Or at least that's how he remembered her. "And if Taggart's attempted attack on you tonight was any indication, I'd wager he's been trying to unite his pack with yours for a while. Am I wrong?"

She shrugged noncommittally.

"It's only a matter of time before someone else comes sniffing around looking to claim control of the Cordona women." He paused, hoping she'd say something. She knew the Council's rules as well as he did, and he didn't want to spell it out to her. Once a pack was officially formed the Alpha in charge was basically supposed to self-govern and deal with internal problems alone. Now that Ana's Alpha was dead, they were still considered a pack, but they couldn't continue much longer without an official leader.

"And you'd like to take on the role of our protectors? Out of the goodness of your heart?" Mistrust crept into those dark eyes, and his gut clenched.

"Over the years Liam and I have ... done well for ourselves. We've formed our own pack—one recognized by the Council—and we're looking to settle down somewhere. Put down roots. All of our packmates are of the warrior class. We have a lot to bring to the table." Years ago he'd had nothing to offer her. At least now he was more than a lone mongrel with no pack and no real money, trying to win her heart.

"What do you want in exchange for your *protection*?"

"A place to live and work peacefully."

"What about the males of your pack? I don't know anything about them. Are they trustworthy?"

He understood what she was asking even though she didn't spell it out. "I respect man's laws and the Council's laws. No female will be forced into any union they don't want."

She relaxed against the couch and absently tapped her finger against the armrest. "I'll need time to think about this."

"There is one more thing. If we do this, you'll no longer be known as the Cordona pack. We will all unite as the Armstrong pack."

Her head tipped slightly to the side and her luscious mouth pulled into a thin line. "Like you said, *if* we do this—and that's a big if—we'll be called the Armstrong-Cordona pack." It wasn't a question.

He looked at his brother, who grinned slightly and nodded. Connor had known she wouldn't acquiesce that easily. Something deep inside him had always told him he'd run his own pack one day. Now he understood it was his inner wolf, his Alpha begging to get out. While he might not have liked her old man, the name Cordona was still hers, and linking their names wasn't exactly a hardship. If it got her to accept his protection, he'd do it. "Fine. I also have another stipulation. If and when we combine, I take the mate of my choosing. Immediately."

Ana's dark eyes flashed with something he couldn't put his finger on, but then it was gone. "I'm surprised you're not mated by now. No one will be *forced*, but my sisters and cousins have all grown into beautiful women. I don't think you'll have any problem convincing—"

"Ana, I don't think you understand what I'm saying. *You* are mine." He hated thinking that she'd been mated to another wolf, but at least they hadn't been bondmates. If they had been, she'd still carry his mark and possibly his scent. Sometimes even death couldn't wipe away a bondmate's scent. Though her mate was now dead, Connor wanted to bury whoever he was all over again. No one else would ever touch what was his.

Her head snapped back up. He wanted to kick himself at the way he'd spoken to her, but he couldn't take back the words now. She *was* his. It was about damn time she figured that out.

"I don't understand. You want to mate with *me*?" The question came out breathy and seductive as hell. And laced with shock. He couldn't ignore the not-so-subtle wave that rolled off her.

Even Liam raised his eyebrows at his bluntness and found a spot on the coffee table to stare at.

Connor ignored his brother. He had to refrain from growling as he stared at Ana. "I want you as my bond-mate."

That got her attention. Her spine went ramrod straight. Plenty of shifters mated but they didn't all bond.

Mated shifters could leave if they wanted to, much like how humans divorced one another. Bonding united their kind for life. Even if one of them wanted to leave, they'd be marked and another wolf wouldn't touch either one of them. It was a big decision and one he knew she wouldn't make lightly. But when he took her as his mate he wanted her completely.

"Bondmate?" The word sounded almost angry.

He abruptly stood. "I don't expect your answer right away. We'll let ourselves out, but we'll be back in the morning to introduce everyone."

Frowning, she nodded.

Once they were outside, Liam punched his arm. And not softly.

He glared at him. "What are you, twelve?" he muttered.

"What the hell was that?" his brother growled.

Connor shrugged and ignored the heated look his brother shot him. "I laid out the stipulations."

"That was not part of the plan. You were supposed to give her a chance to warm up to the idea of mating with you. Then you were going to *ask* that she bond. Not *demand* it. Damn it, Connor. You're such a fucking Neanderthal."

He clenched his jaw. It probably wasn't the best decision he'd ever made, but as far as he was concerned his brother was lucky he'd shown as much control as he had. Ana and her family had rejected him once, but things had finally come full circle. It might be selfish to demand her submission now when she was at her weakest, but he couldn't walk away from her. Not again. "What's done is done. Let's go check on the men."

His brother muttered something about him being a stubborn asshole, but continued walking with him. The memory of Ana's sweet scent and the shock in her wide brown eyes rolled over him. He should have eased her into things, but walking away right now was taking all the restraint he possessed. The wolf inside him wanted to take her hard and rough, then soft and gentle. For hours. Until neither of them could walk or think straight.

The houses and cabins surrounding the ranch fanned out in a circle around the main house. They were far enough apart that the pack members had some privacy, but close enough that they could alert one another if there was trouble. It was like a little village.

Liam nudged him and nodded toward one of the distant fields. "Hey, what—"

They both paused as an orange ball lit up the sky. "Fire!"

Chapter 2

Connor's heart pounded an erratic tattoo against his chest as he raced back for the main house. He banged on the front door, then opened it.

From the entryway Analena glared at him. "What the—"

"Fire. In the west field. Not close to the buildings, but that could change."

Wordlessly she turned and fled up the stairs. Seconds later she came barreling back down with her two sisters, Noel and Carmen. Erin wasn't too far behind.

"What precautions do you have set up?" he asked as they jogged toward the barn housing the horses.

"I've got a stockade of fire extinguishers and blankets in the barn. If the fire gets out of control, we've got vehicles prepared to transport the animals."

"Good. I'm going to get Liam."

Nodding, she didn't break stride as she headed for the barn.

He'd sent his brother to round up the rest of his pack. At least the wind had shown mercy on them and died down. Despite the slightly damp ground, he'd noticed how thick her pasture was. The recently wet weather had probably prevented her from doing contained burns earlier in the year. A fire could still lap up this foliage. And fast.

One shift in the wind and the now small fire could spread out of control all the way to the mountains. He couldn't let that happen. He'd come here to take care of her, and that was what he was going to do.

As he neared the cabins on the south end of the circle, Liam and his seven men streamed out, half-dressed.

"They've got fire extinguishers in the barn. Grab a couple each." He turned on his heel after shouting the order. His guys wouldn't need to be told twice.

He risked a quick glance in the direction of the field as he sprinted toward the barn. Flames painted the field in a bath of orange and yellow, but it didn't look out of control yet. When he raced inside, he found Carmen and Noel passing extinguishers to their packmates.

Wordlessly each female took one and raced out the other end of the building. They were like a well-oiled machine.

"Give me two and give my guys two," he said as Carmen handed him one. Ana wasn't anywhere to be seen, so he guessed she was already at the fire.

Panic bubbled inside him but he forced it back down. This fire wasn't an accident. If he had to guess, he'd say that bastard Taggart had set it. Maybe in an attempt to scare him off, or maybe as punishment for Ana. He didn't know and he didn't care. This type of shit wasn't going to happen under his watch.

Whoever had set it better pray they weren't still hanging around. If he scented anyone who didn't belong, they were going to pay tonight.

His boots pounded over the grass. As he neared the fire, his spirits lifted a fraction. The women had formed a giant half circle and started dousing the blaze. It had grown to the size of a small swimming pool, but it was fairly well contained.

As he raced around to the other side and unleashed a stream of white foam from an extinguisher, he realized Ana wasn't there. He couldn't see in the pitch-black, but thanks to his extrasensory abilities he could see better than humans. Though he didn't want to leave, he set the extinguisher down and hurried away from the fire when he spotted Ana racing across the dark field. Still in her human form, she was full-out sprinting toward the fence line.

That's when he scented it. Someone who didn't belong. Definitely male. And he was close.

Danger.

Something deep and primal inside Connor flared to life. *Protect Ana.* The two words sounded in his head like a gong. He had to protect his mate. At this point semantics didn't matter. She might not be mated to him, but his inner wolf would protect her at all costs.

His canines started to lengthen but he willed himself not to shift forms. Not until he understood the situation.

"Ana!" he called her name as he ran after her.

She glanced over her shoulder at him but barely paused. Now he was thirty yards from her.

Panic surged through him. What the hell was she doing? Didn't she smell the threat? As he covered the distance between them he spotted a pair of glowing amber eyes in the forest. The animal hovered just inside the tree line to the east. It was far enough away that it couldn't attack Ana, but he didn't care.

A feral growl tore from his throat. The sound was foreign even to him.

Twenty yards and closing.

"Damn it, Ana! Stop!"

To his surprise she jerked to a halt. Because of his command? He wasn't sure. As he came up to her, she didn't turn to look at him.

"What the hell are you doing, woman?" he barked.

"Adalita," she said softly, still not glancing at him.

"What?"

"There." She nodded to the west, right by the tree line, but didn't make any sudden movements.

A brown horse whinnied and kept trotting back and forth nervously. Connor had been so focused on Ana and the threat that he hadn't noticed the other animal.

"She's my horse and she was locked up earlier," Ana continued.

The nervous, almost pained note in her voice told him a lot. She truly cared about this animal.

"Stay here," he murmured, and headed toward it.

"No." She grasped his upper arm tightly. "She might run from you."

"Trust me, okay?" He looked into her dark eyes. She opened her mouth once as if to argue but nodded.

It was a small act but it touched him that she was putting her trust in him. "I saw a wolf to the east of us. It's probably one of Taggart's and I think it's gone, but don't go anywhere."

Without waiting for a response he strode toward Ana's horse. Keeping his movements steady but casual, he quickly breached the distance. Adalita pounded her hoof against the ground twice, as if ready to charge, but the closer he got, the calmer she became.

Animals had an innate sense of survival. She knew he wouldn't hurt her. By now she was obviously used to the scent of lupine shifters. Connor murmured soothing sounds until he stood directly in front of her. He reached out his palm and let her smell him. When she didn't bolt, he gently petted her, then loosely grabbed her mane.

Without bothering to get on her back he hurried the horse back toward Ana, who hadn't moved.

"Thank you. I—"

"Ride her back to the barn."

"What?"

"I don't know if Taggart or his wolves are still in the woods. Now *ride.*" He could barely think straight, knowing danger lurked so close to them. To her.

She wanted to argue. He could see it in the stubborn set of her jaw, but she did as he said. Part of him knew he needed to stop with the demands, but he didn't want to waste time worrying about being polite when all he cared about was getting her to safety.

As Ana rode back to the barn, he ran toward the fire. Flames still licked into the sky, but the extinguishers did their job. After what felt like an eternity they managed to douse the flames. Tonight could have gone a lot different if not for Ana's preparedness.

He couldn't help but be impressed by how quickly she and all the women had acted. Even if he hadn't been there the Cordona women would have had no problem taking care of the fire. Of course, it never should have happened in the first place.

The dwindling smoke curled into the cold night air, wrapping around all of them. The chemical scent of accelerant was unmistakable. Whoever had set this hadn't tried to cover it. Even a human could smell the kerosene permeating the air. He stiffened as Ana circled around her packmates, heading straight for him.

His heart beat faster and he had to contain the lust flowing through him. He didn't want to scare her even more.

She stopped a foot away from him. Her dark eyes were expressionless. "I'll do it."

"What?" He frowned, unsure what she referred to.

"I'll mate with you on a temporary basis. If it'll save my pack I'll do almost anything. I just can't agree to be your bondmate. I'm sorry, Connor. We haven't seen each other in decades, and I—" She shook her head and her voice broke on the last word. Her normally silvery voice was distant, remote, and it clawed at his insides.

Not exactly what he'd wanted to hear. And it was his own damn fault. He should have romanced her, courted her, like she deserved. Taken things slow. Told her how he really felt about her and why he'd left all those years ago. Instead he'd barged in like a jackass and made demands. After what had happened she'd probably agree to mate with just about anyone who wasn't Taggart, to save her pack. Shame burned through him like swift, hot lava at the way he'd pushed her into that proverbial corner, but he couldn't take back what he'd said. Demanded. If he was honest with himself, he didn't know that he wanted to. Part of him—a very selfish part—knew that if he pushed her now he could probably get her to agree to be his bondmate. But the human part that deeply cared for her won out and he kept his mouth shut.

Despite his better judgment, he slipped an arm around her shoulder and pulled her close. She didn't look at him, but kept her face against his chest. She felt so fragile in his embrace. It killed him to think she'd been by herself the past couple months, taking care of her pack without any help. And he couldn't understand why she hadn't contacted him. He buried his face in her hair and inhaled her fresh scent. This close to her, it overpowered the smoke.

"Ana, are you sure? I . . ." *I'll protect you anyway.* The words were on the tip of his tongue. He shouldn't have made those demands, but he couldn't squeeze out the words. He was a selfish bastard. He'd wanted her for so long, the need nearly smothered him sometimes. Instead, he wrapped his other arm around her and pulled her into a tight hug.

She stiffened for an instant before slipping her arms around his waist and returning his embrace. That small gesture of surrender turned him inside out. Her fingers dug into his back with surprising intensity, and he wondered how long it had been since she'd let someone hold her. The mere thought of someone else comforting her sent another dagger through his chest.

After a long moment, she looked up at him. There was a flicker of something in her dark eyes that he didn't recognize. Wasn't sure he wanted to. Finally she spoke and her voice was soft. "I'm sure. I'll be proud to call you my mate."

Something foreign pushed up inside him. He was a mongrel who'd been roaming the globe since his parents died more than a century ago. After his father had shamed their family by not protecting what was his, he and Liam had been thrust out into the world on their own and with nothing. She shouldn't be proud, especially when she deserved better. Hell, she was probably saying what she thought he wanted to hear. Swallowing hard, he reluctantly released her. "I'll make the announcement in the morning. Have your she-wolves meet in the barn at seven."

She dipped her head in acknowledgment and stepped out of his embrace. As he looked around the quiet circle of wolves, he realized kerosene and smoke weren't the only things he smelled. Desire and hunger rolled off most of *his* pack.

As long as it wasn't directed at Ana, he didn't care. He might be their Alpha, but they'd all agreed to come here after a vote. His guys had all been loners for decades until he and his brother had convinced each of them to form a new pack. A stronger pack. Settling here and taking mates was the best thing for all of them if they wanted to flourish.

Teresa, Ana's cousin, stretched out on Ana's bed and put her hands behind her head. "You think Carmen and Noel can hear us?"

Ana rolled her eyes as she pictured her two sisters as she'd left them, drinking wine and munching on salty popcorn. "No. They're downstairs, watching one of those stupid reality shows."

Her cousin grinned. "They're worse than my sisters— but that's not what you want to talk about. Since you and I both know we could have handled that fire on our own, I can't believe you actually agreed to mate with Connor Armstrong."

Ana scowled at her as she paced at the end of the bed. "This isn't about the damn fire and you know it. Things have been escalating, so what choice do I have?"

"We could contact the Council and tell them about Taggart's harassment." There was no fire behind Teresa's words and Ana knew why.

"*Great* idea. And then what? They'll send an investigator down here and likely find him guilty. I'm sure there's at least one female in his pack willing to testify against him, in addition to me."

Teresa raised both her eyebrows. "Those females are so weak and brainwashed, I doubt it."

"Whatever. Speaking hypothetically, say he's punished—and probably executed. You know what will happen after that. The enforcer will clean up his mess, but instead of being free we're the ones who will get the shaft. Not right away, but eventually it will happen unless one of us mates with an Alpha." Some days she hated pack law so much she wanted to run screaming to the humans to intervene, but she knew that would cause more trouble. Humans didn't understand anything about their laws and would just make everything worse.

And the Council wouldn't allow her to remain in control indefinitely if she came running to them with every little problem. Even if Taggart was out of the way, she knew another pack would come sniffing around, wanting to take their land under the guise of protection. Most Alphas would take no for an answer and leave her alone. But all it would take was one land-hungry Alpha challenging her for control of the Cordona pack, and there would be no one to stand up for her family. She could appeal to the Council if they didn't want to assimilate with that pack, but they'd have to make a choice on who they wanted as their leader. Or they could just sell their land. Without valuable property, neither she nor her pack would be of any interest to other packs. Absolutely archaic and total bullshit, but that was just the way it was. And while she hated some of the laws, she loved the others. Having the protection of a strong pack meant sleeping soundly at night and not worrying about survival. Their rules dated back thousands of years and though one day they might change, it wouldn't be now. Hell, their own North American Council had been around only forty years, and that semi-unification was a pretty big, civilized step for their kind. They'd been created to keep communication open between packs and to protect packs in positions such as hers. Without them she'd have had no one to turn to in this kind of situation.

"I know," Teresa muttered. "It's just . . . I don't like the thought of you sacrificing yourself to be Connor's mate."

To her horror, Ana's cheeks heated up. Her traitorous body flared to life at the thought of mating with him. Her breasts were suddenly heavy as she pictured what he could do with those strong, callused hands. The mere thought of him rubbing his palms over her breasts and . . .

"Woman, I don't even want to know what you're thinking about." Teresa sat up and brought her knees to her chest, a wicked grin on her face.

Ana cleared her throat and tried to get her lust under control. Now was so not the time for this. And the mating would be only temporary. Her pack needed an Alpha until she could figure out what else she could do. She couldn't keep warding off Taggart forever, and soon someone could truly get hurt because of him. If anything happened to one of her sisters—or any of her pack— she'd never forgive herself if she thought she could have done something about it. "Connor's offer is a good one. At least we know him and his brother, and if the Council has officially recognized them it means they have the financial wherewithal to support all of us."

"Yeah, I guess." Teresa pushed off the bed and stood. "Sleep on it and we'll tell your sisters in the morning, unless you change your mind by then." She gave her a quick kiss on the cheek before leaving.

After she'd gone, Ana stripped out of her clothes and fell onto her bed. *Sleep on it.* Good advice, but it wasn't going to happen. Not with Connor in the same vicinity. Every time she closed her eyes all she could picture was that ruggedly handsome face, his broad shoulders, strong arms . . . Groaning, she turned over and screamed into her pillow. It was going to be an annoyingly long night.

Lounging casually on the bench outside the Native American gift shop, Chuck took a long drag of his cigarette. He savored the smell and taste of tobacco. Darkness had fallen early, but downtown Fontana, North Carolina, was lit up like a fucking Christmas tree. Literally. Twinkle lights were strung up around most of the

light poles in the historic downtown. Everything about
Fontana was quaint, picturesque. Boring. Nestled between the Beech Mountain and Sugar Mountain ski re-
sorts, it was almost identical to the other mountain towns.
Christmas was almost two months away but storefronts
already had holiday scenes in the windows, and joyful,
annoying music blared most of the day. The place was too
damn peaceful, too cheerful. It was like the people didn't
realize a revolution was coming.

What would it take for them to get it? When the
streets were decorated with blood and bodies they
would. Then it would be too late.

Two different packs of fucking shifter *animals* lived
right on the outskirts of town and people didn't care.
Most were even friendly to them. It was insane. Even
more insane than all the interracial couples he saw lately.
That shit just seemed to flood television and movies.
Tainting the pure white bloodline of their ancestors with
filth. People were so immune to it that nothing fazed
them anymore. So why should a group of freaks who
could turn into animals be any different? America had
turned into the land of pussies.

He took another drag of his cig and glanced away
when a young white couple strolled by, walking a yappy
little dog. The dog was a waste of space, but at least they
were dating their own race. All the stores were closing,
so most people were down a few blocks where the restaurants were, but he didn't want to chance getting noticed. Chuck knew he looked casual enough. Wearing
jeans and a dark blue hoodie thick enough to block him
from the icy wind, he fit in perfectly. And the gloves he
wore weren't out of place. It was too cold not to be wearing them.

His phone buzzed in his pocket. When he saw the
number he rolled his eyes. This jackass was constantly

checking up on him. Chuck could barely stand to look at Adler and his nasty burned face, but the older man was technically his boss. He wasn't a high-ranking leader in the Antiparanormal League but he was still one of their local leaders. And if Chuck was honest, the man scared the shit out of him sometimes.

He answered the throwaway phone on the third ring, knowing the delay would annoy Adler. "Yeah?"

"Is it done?"

"No. The bitch is still closing up shop."

"Don't kill her!" Adler's gravelly voice was condescending.

Chuck gritted his teeth. He already knew that. But because Adler's boss was breathing down his neck to grab this woman meant Chuck had to take flack from Adler. "I know. I don't need a fucking babysitter. I told you I could handle this and I can. It's just one old woman."

"This is your first assignment. Don't get too cocky."

But it wasn't. *Not by a long shot,* he thought with a grin. Just his first with the APL. "If you have so many doubts why didn't you do this yourself?" Chuck asked the question even though he already knew the answer. With his scarred face it was difficult for Adler to blend in anywhere. People would remember him. That's why Chuck had been sent.

"Remember who you're talking to, son." The deadly edge to Adler's voice sent an unexpected chill up his spine.

Chuck cursed his fear and he cursed the man on the other end of the line for instilling it in him. He'd seen what Adler did to people who failed him—and to women in general. The man was a misogynist of the worst kind. He didn't even like white women. Something Chuck didn't understand. Women were great, all softness and femininity, as long as they were white. Adler didn't seem to think so, though. He hated them all. Fucking idiot. And he wanted to tell him how to do his job?

He cleared his throat. "No disrespect, sir. I'll call you when I have her."

As they disconnected, the lights to the store dimmed. *Finally.* How long did it take to close up her pathetic little shop? He glanced to the left and right. There weren't any locals or tourists strolling by. Tourists didn't venture into town after dark anyway. They usually spent most of their time at the big ski lodge a few miles down the road.

The Indian woman, or Native American or whatever they called themselves now, flicked a quick glance in his direction as she stepped outside and locked her door. Her long, dark braid hung down her back. His free hand balled into a fist. With hair like that it would be easy to restrain her if she tried to run.

Holding her purse tightly against her side, she hurried down the sidewalk in the direction opposite the restaurants. He'd been watching her for a couple days, so he knew where she usually parked.

Tossing away his cigarette, he stood and kept pace a few yards behind her. His rubber-soled shoes were silent against the icy sidewalk. They'd salted the ground earlier, so it was easy to keep up.

His heart pounded against his ribs as he closed in on her. Withdrawing his KA-BAR, he drew in a quiet, cold breath. He was so close he could reach out and touch her. The old woman didn't even know he was there.

A powerful wave of adrenaline hummed through him. This must be what those aberrations felt like when they hunted someone. Powerful. It felt good, filling him with an almost superhuman strength. Being the hunter was so much better than being the prey.

As she neared the end of the string of shops she started to turn toward him. They weren't going to kill her—at first—but he couldn't risk her seeing him.

Lunging, he slammed her face-first against the brick wall. Pressing his knife into her neck, he didn't say a word. He loathed being this close to her but he didn't have a choice.

To his surprise she didn't cower in fear.

Flailing and struggling against his hold, she screamed. Loud and long. The piercing sound burned his ears.

"Hey!" A hostile male voice from behind him startled him into action.

Shit! Grabbing the back of her head, he slammed it into the wall. Adler wanted her alive, but she wouldn't shut up. This wasn't how it was supposed to happen. She was old and he had a knife. She cried out again so he slammed her again. This time she crumpled.

"I'm calling the police!" This time the male voice was louder, closer. He didn't turn around because he didn't want anyone to see his face.

As the woman slumped to the ground he grabbed her deposit bag and sprinted down the street. Since he'd been noticed, he needed this to look like a robbery, nothing more. Adler would definitely kill him if anything got traced back to the APL. The police reacted fairly fast in this small town, so he had to hurry. As he neared the end of the block he took a sharp left, then stripped off his hoodie and tossed it into some bushes. His long-sleeved orange shirt was a far cry from the dark sweater.

Only now did he risk a glance behind him. No one had followed him, but he kept running. He'd parked his car a few blocks over and he needed to make it there fast.

Adler was going to be pissed that he'd failed. That thought alone caused another surge of panic to hum

through him. Chuck had done a lot worse to stronger
people. Why the hell had he gotten so cocky just because
she was old? He'd been so focused on grabbing her that
everything else around him had funneled out. That
wouldn't happen again. No matter what, he was going to
get his target in the end. He always did.

Chapter 3

Ana stared into her steaming coffee mug as her sisters digested what she'd just told them. She tried to keep her thoughts focused on the conversation at hand but found it increasingly difficult.

Confusion.

Lust.

And more confusion.

Too many emotions bounced around in her head. After the gentle hug from Connor last night and the unmistakable erection she'd felt against her abdomen, her insides were all twisted up. Fifty years ago she'd been young, naive and ready to take on the whole world. She'd been excited at the prospect of sleeping with someone like Connor. Hell, she'd even dreamed of mating with him. Something she'd never told anyone. After he'd left it had been too embarrassing—and painful—to admit her girlish fantasies to her younger sisters. They'd always looked up to her and she hadn't wanted them to see her differently. Then time had passed and it had been easier to lock up those dreams in the deepest recesses of her mind.

Now that the offer to mate was on the table, it felt like more of a business arrangement. Who was she kidding?

It was.

He might have been gentle in his embrace last night, but he'd left her before. He could do it again. Lord knew her pack needed the protection now, but that didn't mean she'd fully submit to him. Ana was positively resolute to keep this temporary. He'd already stomped on her heart once, and she wasn't a masochist. If she could figure out another way to keep her pack together on this land, she'd do it.

Still, the thought of him taking her under the full moon and sinking his canines into her neck, marking her and bonding them together for life, was strangely erotic. The image of their two bodies intertwined flashed in her mind and her face flushed. Obviously it had been too long since she'd had sex. It was the only explanation for her fantasies.

From a logical standpoint she understood why he wanted to mate. She had land, a strong line and a highly probable chance of producing equally strong offspring. It all sounded so awful when she thought about it in those terms but that's the way it was sometimes. To shifters, propagation of their kind was more important than love. Even thinking about their agreement made her want to cry.

Ana took a sip of her coffee and set it back down on the kitchen table. Her two sisters, Noel and Carmen, and her favorite cousin, Teresa, sat around the table with her. Erin was upstairs taking a shower. Ana needed to discuss some things with her pack and didn't want the other she-wolf to hear. Not that she didn't trust her; she just didn't know her.

"We don't need any protectors," Noel, the youngest,

grumbled in response to what Ana had just laid out for them. In human years her sister was sixty, but looked about twenty-two. She acted like it half the time, too. Having grown up on various ranches along the East Coast, surrounded mainly by other lupine shifters for most of her life, she had little knowledge of the outside world.

Their father had always protected the pack and looked out for them. Just because they'd always known that high level of safety and security didn't mean things would always be that way. Ana had to be a realist when it came to her pack's well-being. And staying together on land her father had worked hard to buy was important for all of them.

"Yes, we *do*. That fire is only the icing on the cake. I've been trying to keep you guys in the dark about the other things happening around here, but now I realize that was a mistake." Cattle deaths, horse deaths. And someone had cut a few of their fences, allowing their best cattle to escape. The fire was an escalation, and she knew it wouldn't be long until Taggart's pack did something else. Something worse. She wouldn't let her pack-mates get hurt because she'd been too proud to unite with Connor. She'd seen the way Taggart treated his own females, and after his attempted assault on her, she doubted he'd be kind to her sisters if he trapped one. Even the thought of one of her sisters at his mercy made her see red. "We might be alphas"—she gestured to the four of them at the table—"but none of us are *Alphas* and certainly not of the warrior class."

All true Alphas were also warriors, though warriors weren't always Alphas. They were just damn good fighters. Warrior shifters were so different from the rest of the population. Bigger in human and shifted form, they seemed to be born with slightly different DNA, even from their shifter counterparts. They embraced their animal side a lot more than their human one. It's what made them the protectors of the rest of their kind. Ana might hate it and crave complete independence from outsiders, but she wasn't an idiot. She wasn't an Alpha or a warrior, and if it came down to it, it was better to embrace someone like Connor as pack Alpha than an unknown.

Teresa grabbed her hand under the table and squeezed it. "Your sister is right. It's better she takes a mate now of her choosing than us lose our land to some asshole who challenges her for dominance. Do you really want a crappy Alpha? Someone like Taggart?" She practically spat the last word.

The effect was perfect. A shiver of fear rolled off her younger sisters, so maybe they weren't as blind to the things going on at the ranch as Ana had originally thought.

Carmen finally spoke up. "What about the day-to-day stuff? Are those goons going to come in and take over everything?"

"First of all, they're not goons. They're going to be your packmates soon, so you better get used to it. And second, we could use the help. Now we'll have someone to patrol and keep better security on a regular basis. Do you want to lose another horse? Or more cattle? What if Taggart decides to burn down our homes next time? Or assault one of the betas?" Betas depended on alphas and warriors and, most important, their Alpha, to protect them. They weren't emotionally or intellectually any weaker, just physically. In their wolf form they were as small as regular wolves and had about the same strength. When it came down to brute strength, they were no match for the rest of the shifter population.

"What about our bank accounts? Or our homes? Or

even ourselves? What if they try to force us into a mating?" Noel demanded.

"Your money is yours, our homes are ours and *no one* will be forced into a mating. Do you actually think I would allow something like that? Or that the Council would?" Ana's voice was heated. Connor had given her his word on that and if he tried to go back on it, Alpha or not, she'd kick him off their land and end their arrangement.

"I've heard rumors of it happening before," Carmen muttered, in an attempt to back up Noel's ridiculous question.

"Yeah, from pack Alphas with archaic ideals like Taggart. You both know that's not the norm and that our neighboring pack has no one but themselves to blame for not reporting their Alpha's misdeeds. If Connor tried to implement something like that—and I *know* he won't—we'd report him to the Council and take our chances with finding a new pack."

"I guess some of Connor's packmates are pretty cute," Noel murmured, and Carmen's cheeks tinged pink in silent agreement.

Ana smothered a smile. At least her sisters had noticed the new wolves. It would make her life a lot easier if they were on board with the union. Since Teresa was supportive, her cousin's three younger sisters would be too. And Ana had already spoken to Isabel, one of her other cousins. The oldest of her four sisters, Isabel would have no problem convincing them this was the best thing. She and her sisters were all betas anyway. Whatever Ana decided, they'd go along without argument. They might not like it at first, but betas went along with pack decision because they trusted their leaders to look out for them.

She glanced at the wall clock, even though she already had a good idea what time it was, and tried to quell the nerves fluttering in her stomach. "It's time, ladies."

Silently, they all placed their mugs in the sink. In the foyer, they slipped into their coats and gloves. While they were getting ready, Erin appeared at the top of the stairs. She paused and a wave of fear rolled off her. Most shifters learned to mask their emotions as cubs, but it was obvious life hadn't been kind to this one. Ana doubted she was afraid to go to the meeting, but she was probably fearful of being treated like an outsider.

Carmen had the softest heart of anyone Ana had ever met. Before anyone else reacted, her sister hurried up the stairs and linked arms with Erin. "You stick with me today, okay? I'll show you the ropes."

The redhead nodded gratefully, and a burst of relief coursed through Ana. She needed everyone to get along. At least in the beginning. She knew there would be typical spats among the pack, and a new female always added a strain to the mix, but if this was going to work, their union had to start strong. That was the only way it would weather any future problems.

She'd barely been able to sleep last night knowing she'd be mated to Connor soon. Physically she wanted him. Even if she wanted to, she couldn't deny that. The practical part of her had known something like this was coming. Not with him, of course. As an all-female pack, they'd eventually have to take on a new Alpha or assimilate with another group of males if they were to survive. Their world was a lot more black and white that way compared to that of humans. She'd always thought she'd fall in love first before choosing a mate. Like her parents.

Love was always secondary to survival, though.

Unfortunately her human side ruled her heart more

than most. When her intended mate had died with the rest of the males of her pack, she'd mourned, but her heart didn't feel a great loss. She felt guilty about not missing Alejandro as much as she missed her parents, but there had been no love between them. Just an understanding. They'd been intended mates, not true mates.

Now it seemed she was going to be in another loveless union. In a way, it hurt that it would be with Connor, despite her attraction to him. At one time Connor had been her best friend, even though she'd wanted more. A lot more. She'd thought he did too, but he'd never offered for her. Never asked her father if he could join their pack. Never even kissed her. Instead he'd left without a word. Like she meant nothing to him. One day she'd gone to their secret meeting place, as usual, and he hadn't shown up. For weeks afterward she'd continued to wait for him, until it was obvious he wasn't coming back.

He'd never made any promises to her, so maybe she shouldn't have made any assumptions, but she'd always thought something more would happen between them. He and his brother had been passing through where her pack lived all those years ago, and instead of a brief stay, Connor and Liam had stayed with them for almost seven months. They'd helped around her father's ranch and everyone had seemed to like them. And Connor had seemed happy. Then . . . he was gone.

As she remembered the feelings of anger and hurt at his disappearance, her resolve to keep him at arm's length strengthened. One way or another he was going to tell her why he'd left. She didn't care if it was a petty demand. She deserved to know.

"Have you seen Ana today?" Liam spoke low enough for only Connor to hear.

"Not yet. I saw one of her cousins heading to her

place about an hour ago." Tension hummed through him, but he tried to ignore it. Ana wouldn't go back on her word. She was only five minutes late. He wouldn't read into it. Hell, he couldn't afford to. If his pack sensed any sort of reserve or tension between him and Ana, it could hurt all of them in the long run.

Before apprehension had a chance to set in Ana, her twelve packmates and Erin walked through the entrance of the barn. His guys straightened when they entered, but he had eyes only for Ana. She smiled tentatively and hovered in front of her group as if she weren't sure what the next move was.

All his protectiveness kicked in. He never wanted her to feel insecure when she was with him. He crossed the short distance between them and put his arm around her shoulders as he led her to the front of his group. For a split second she tensed, but it was fleeting. The gesture was meant to be protective, but, more important, territorial. The animal in him didn't care that his pack *knew* she was his. He still needed to claim her.

Soon enough he'd mark her so that everyone would have no doubt about whom she belonged to. When she wrapped her arm around his waist and moved in closer to his embrace, the most primal side of him immediately calmed. He craved her submission and acceptance, whether he wanted to or not.

Keeping his arm around her, he began. "I know we all had a long night, so I won't keep you longer than necessary. My brothers and I are very grateful to you for welcoming us into the Cordona fold. I'm not sure how much Analena has told you, but starting today you're all under our protection. As I'm sure you can tell, we're all part of the warrior class and we take our jobs seriously. The Council will be made aware of the changes, and from this point forward we'll be known as the Armstrong-

Cordona pack." A ripple of unease rolled over the females.

"What will this protection cost us? We're not whores!" A dark-haired woman from the middle of the group stepped out. She looked like she was barely eighteen and had the attitude to go with it.

Connor didn't recognize her, but if she was that young it made sense that she wouldn't yet have been born when he'd stayed with them. Before he could speak Ana stepped slightly forward and out of his embrace.

"Bite your tongue, Natalia," she growled. The unexpected heat from Ana surprised and soothed him. "Your sister and I already told you there would be no forced matings. Don't be stupid enough to think all packs are like Taggart's. Are you calling us liars?"

Teresa grabbed the girl's arm and tried to pull her back, but the young she-wolf shrugged out of her embrace. He guessed she was one of Teresa's younger sisters.

"I want to hear *him* say it," Natalia shot back.

Ana growled again, likely at the show of disrespect, but he didn't blame the young she-wolf. Changes were happening overnight, and these females had been sheltered by their former Alpha for a long time. If all they had to go on as another example of pack life was Taggart's pack, no wonder they were worried. Even if they knew they needed protection, Connor and his brothers were still strangers.

He looked pointedly at the young wolf who had challenged him. "You're too young, but I lived with your pack half a century ago. I'm sure any of the older females can attest to my character. The Cordonas of Girona have a rich history and your heritage won't be forgotten or ignored. It's obvious Ana has been a good leader and she would never let anyone join her pack that she didn't trust. If you doubt that, then I doubt *you* know her well."

The young she-wolf paused for a moment, then bowed her head submissively and fell back in line with Teresa.

His words seemed to have an immediate calming effect on the rest of the females. Even Ana's fingers relaxed. At least he was headed in the right direction. Connor had thought he was prepared for anything, but facing all these she-wolves was more intimidating than anything he'd ever done. The dark-haired women were smaller, slimmer than most wolves he'd come across, but it was obvious their pack was strong and organized. He'd seen that firsthand last night. "There *will* be changes. It's unavoidable. For now, the living situations will stay relatively the same, but the day-to-day operations around here will change. It'll be up to Ana who pairs off with whom, but my men will be following some of you around and learning the ropes starting today. And from now on, the males will be in charge of security. That is one thing I won't bend on. You're now mine to protect."

Ana still hadn't loosened up much next to him. Her back was stiff, and even though he couldn't scent anything, her posture gave away a lot. He briefly glanced down at her. Her eyes were like the ocean. A deep, dark abyss. He could drown in them if he let himself. He could feel his canines start to lengthen and his body prime for sex, so he forced himself to look away. "I want everyone to know they can come to me with any problems, but Ana and I are to be mated. If I'm not here or if you're more comfortable, Ana is my second in command. To *everyone*." He looked pointedly at his men. They already knew it, but he wanted it to be clear. According to pack rules she would be his second in charge the moment they mated, and while the warriors would know that on an intellectual level, all of them had been loners for many years before joining him. Sometimes they had a hard time coming to *him* with problems, so he knew there would be a learning curve for all of them.

Finally Ana relaxed next to him. After he went through the introductions, the pack started mingling, giving him some private time with her. There was a lot they needed to talk about and he knew she had questions. He could see them running through her head every time he looked at her.

Taking her hand, he maneuvered around everyone until they stood just outside the barn. He refrained from touching her further because it was impossible to tell if she'd welcome it and he didn't want to face the rejection. He nearly snorted at the thought. He was now her Alpha and would soon be her mate, and he worried about rejection like an inexperienced cub. Still, he itched to reach out and hold her. "Did that go as you'd hoped?"

She nodded and tucked a dark strand of hair behind her ear. Even though she didn't say anything, when she nervously tucked her bottom lip between her teeth, alarm jumped inside him.

"What's on your mind?"

"You said the living arrangements were going to stay *relatively* the same. What exactly does that mean?"

"I don't think you want to stay in the same house as your sisters, do you? I figured you'd want some privacy. At least . . . in the beginning." Intentionally lowering his voice, he reached out and cupped her cheek to make his meaning clear. A shudder rolled through him as he stroked his thumb across her soft skin. He'd had so many sleepless nights, dreaming about what it would be like to stand in front of her like this and be able to touch her freely. In his fantasies there was a lot less clothing involved.

Her pink lips parted, and for a moment he got a peek into her thoughts. Confusion and lust flared in her eyes but she quickly masked it.

She took a step back from him and cleared her throat. "I guess . . . you want to mate right away, huh?"

He frowned at her words. *Doesn't she?* He actually ached to be with her. The feeling welled up inside him and had only gotten worse since he'd laid eyes on her. "Are you so surprised?"

"No . . . I don't know. It's not that. I just . . . I agreed to the temporary mating, but I wondered if . . ." The Ana he'd known had never stumbled over her words. She'd been so sure of herself. So sure of her place in the world. Nothing had seemed to faze her. Despite her innocence, he'd always felt out of his depth around her. Another reminder that he wasn't good enough for her.

The realization of what she was saying hit him. "You want to wait to *consummate* things."

Wordlessly she nodded, but her cheeks tinged bright pink.

A vise tightened around his chest. Of course she wanted to wait. The rational, human part of him understood why she wanted to. The most primitive part of him roared in disagreement. He wanted all of her, and his inner wolf did *not* care about reason. "How long?" He managed to squeeze the question past his constricted throat. For so many years he'd lived with the knowledge that her family had deemed him unworthy of her. That he wasn't good enough. Some primal part of him he didn't understand and sometimes feared *needed* the union.

"I don't know. It's not like I have a time frame. Maybe

until we get to *know* one another." There was an unmistakable edge of sarcasm to her words. The fire and attitude he'd missed flared to life.

He bit back a smile at her heated tone. "We already know one another."

She shook her head vehemently, her silky dark hair swishing seductively around her face. "No, we don't. Not really. I thought we did; then you left, Connor. Without. A. Word." Ana stared at him expectantly as she gave him an opening.

Her dark eyes seemed to see right through him. She wanted an answer. Deserved one. But he couldn't give it to her. Not now. Maybe ever. Instead he gave her an impassive, bored look. One he knew would annoy her.

She just glared at him even harder. The look sliced through him. She opened her mouth, and he was afraid she'd push him further about why he'd left. He couldn't give her the answer she wanted, so he cut her off before she spoke.

"I'll give you time. But I can promise you that by this time next week, you'll be begging to mate with me." His statement had the intended effect.

Her eyebrows rose in surprise. "Lord, I'd forgotten what an arrogant bastard you were."

"Not arrogant; *confident*." More like terrified that she'd reject him.

Mating with a female who didn't return his feelings would likely rip him apart from the inside out one piece at a time. But he'd rather be with her than watch her mate, or, God forbid, *bond* with someone else. That thought made something dark and fierce burn within him. It was completely primal, completely his wolf side, and it was terrifying. If he'd ever met Ana's former mate, Connor didn't like to think about how he'd have handled it. Somewhere deep inside, he knew he'd have challenged the wolf for Ana. Those practices were ancient, some would say archaic. He didn't care.

He'd put his pride and his heart on the line for her once. Now he was going to take what was his. Eventually he'd convince her to be his bondmate. Once that happened she'd never be able to walk away from him. And vice versa. Hell, he'd walked away from her once. He wouldn't — *couldn't* — do it again.

Her lips pulled together in a thin line. "If it's okay with you I'd like to let my sisters and Erin stay in the main house for now. We have an extra guesthouse that's been unused for a couple years. I'll need to air it out and clean it today, but —"

"We could sleep out in that field and I wouldn't care, Ana." Refusing to give her the space she obviously wanted, he advanced, and this time he didn't stop at cupping her cheek.

He held the back of her head in a dominating grip, threading his fingers through the thick mass of her hair, and wrapped his other hand around her waist. He pulled her tight against him, letting her feel what she did to him. When his erection pressed against her abdomen, her eyes widened.

What the hell? Maybe he shouldn't have assumed she'd known how he felt about her. Years ago he'd thought she was aware of his desire, his need for her. He was so used to keeping his emotions masked, hidden. But he thought he'd let *her* see that part of him.

"Connor," she murmured, her voice a mix of confusion and lust. The sound of his name on her lips was enough to set him off.

When her mouth parted seductively his grip on her tightened. Her tongue darted out and moistened her lips, probably out of nervous instinct, but she wanted him.

There was no mistaking the subtle scent of lust rolling off her. His entire body jolted as the sweet scent wrapped around him. Her eyelids grew heavy and that previously subtle desire turned potent. His throat constricted for a moment. He'd promised to hold off on mating, but kissing was still on the table. Slowly he bent his head to hers, wanting to give her time to stop it. She sucked in a deep breath but didn't pull away. Instead she leaned closer. He almost growled in victory, when the sound of a truck rumbling up the drive made them both pause. "Are you expecting company?"

Her brow knitted together and she sighed—from relief or disappointment, he couldn't tell. "No. And certainly not at this hour. The sun is barely up," she muttered as she turned toward the offending noise.

Ana stared down the long, winding driveway and frowned when she saw the sheriff's Bronco heading up the drive. She didn't know if she should be angry or grateful for the interruption. Sharp disappointment warred with relief inside her. Connor had been about to kiss her. And she'd definitely wanted him to. For so many years she'd fantasized about what it would feel like to have his mouth cover hers. To feel his tongue invade her mouth, her senses. Even picturing it now sent a rush of heat between her legs.

Nope, she decided, *I am definitely grateful for the interruption.* Just because she wanted his body didn't mean anything. It was only the law of physical attraction. Pure and simple. So why didn't anything about the raw heat coursing through her feel simple?

Without looking at him, for fear he'd see straight through her, she motioned toward the vehicle. "Come on. I know him."

She fell into step with Connor when all she wanted to

do was run in the other direction. Pure animal instinct told her to stay and finish that kiss. Her human side told her to run far away from him. *Fast.* The man was a menace to her sanity.

It had been a long time since she'd slept with anyone and the thought of sharing her bed with Connor scared her more than she'd like to admit. She knew he wouldn't physically hurt her, but he was so demanding and that would likely translate to the bedroom. She'd taken a couple lovers over the years but they'd been betas and very forgettable—easygoing in the bedroom, and they'd understood that there were no strings attached afterward. Which was exactly why she'd chosen them. Despite being an alpha, she'd always steered clear of having sex with one. Part of her knew it was because alphas reminded her of Connor, and no one would have ever matched up to the wolf who'd walked away from her. Now she'd be giving up control of her pack, but she couldn't give up complete control of herself to him. She *had* to retain some of that. Whether or not he realized it, Connor had the ability to turn her brain to mush and she couldn't fall into that trap again.

"Does this guy like shifters?" Connor murmured as they neared the metal gate.

"Not exactly." She watched as the sheriff parked, and tried to prepare herself for whatever was about to happen.

When Connor unhooked the chain and pulled the gate back, the sheriff took off his Stetson and nodded politely at her as he strode toward them. "Ms. Cordona, it's nice to see you again."

Somehow she doubted that. "Please call me Ana."

"Okay, Ana. And you are?" He looked pointedly at Connor, no warmth in his expression.

"Connor Armstrong." He held out a hand.

For a moment Ana worried the sheriff wouldn't return it. After a brief pause, the tall, auburn-haired man held out a hand and pumped Connor's once. "I'm Parker McIntyre. You Scottish?"

Connor nodded and a tiny bit of his long-forgotten accent crept into his words. "Born in the Highlands."

The sound of that sexy Scottish brogue wrapped around Ana like a warm caress. When she'd first met him it had been much more pronounced, and it had driven her wild. Now it seemed Connor had all but lost it. She wasn't sure why that disappointed her.

For the first time since she'd met the young sheriff, he actually seemed to relax. Sort of. "That's where my ancestors are from too."

Connor probably knew some of the sheriff's ancestors, Ana thought. She cleared her throat, wanting to get down to business. The last time she'd seen the sheriff had been two months ago, and he'd visited their place only to launch an official investigation after the deaths of so many of her pack. It still surprised her that he'd even opened an investigation. By law he was supposed to, but a lot of law-enforcement agencies treated shifters with rules different than those of humans. "So what brings you out to the ranch, Sheriff?"

His expression darkened. "There was an attack in town last night. A woman was . . . hurt. She was assaulted pretty badly."

"You think it was a shifter?" She didn't know why she asked. He certainly wasn't at the ranch to check on their health.

"We're not ruling anything out."

A surge of irritation spiked through her. If there was a crime, blame the nearest shifter or vampire. It had been more than twenty years since both their kinds had come out of hiding to the world. Time for people to find a new scapegoat. "Just ask what you need to. You want alibis? I don't know what time this attack happened, but around nine last night someone set fire to one of my fields. We were all here and were busy putting the damn thing out." She didn't bother keeping the annoyance out of her voice.

Parker's lips pulled into a thin line. "Someone torched your field?"

"Yeah."

"Why didn't you report it?"

She snorted at his question. What good would that do? "We took care of it ourselves."

The sheriff glanced over her shoulder and frowned. She followed his gaze. The newest male members of their pack were exiting the barn with her sisters and cousins.

"Who are those men? Have they been here long? Do they have alibis?" He fired the questions with barely re-strained hostility.

This time Connor answered. "They're my pack and we arrived last night."

Parker's eyes narrowed suspiciously. "How long are you here for?"

"For good," Ana answered for him. "Connor is my ... fiancé. Our packs are joining." She used the only word the sheriff would understand. If she said *intended mate* or *temporary mate*, he'd stare at her as if she had two heads.

The sheriff put his hat back on. "I'll be checking into your pack, Mr. Armstrong, and I'll probably be back out here to question your men."

"We'll be here. If you're really interested in blaming this crime on a shifter, I'd check into Sean Taggart's pack." There was a deadly edge to Connor's voice.

"I'm on my way to see him right now," he said.

"Be careful." The words just slipped out. She wanted to reel them back in, but it was too late. The humans didn't need to know anything about their relationship with the neighboring pack.

Parker's head cocked slightly to the side. "Any reason you say that?"

She bit her bottom lip, then shrugged. No reason to deny it. "Taggart's an asshole—that's all."

He nodded politely again and left. Connor wrapped an arm around her shoulder as they watched the sheriff drive away. "Taggart's not going to bother you again, I promise."

There was a darkness in his voice that sent a chill down her spine. She'd seen small peeks into his anger, and she was thankful he was on her side. Taggart was a fool if he messed with them again.

Even though she was still a little worried about the Alpha of the neighboring pack, she was much more concerned about what the coming night would hold with Connor. He'd said he'd give her time before they consummated their relationship but the sexual vibes he put off were intense. As his grip tightened around her, a wave of desire emanated off him that was so potent it speared right through her. Her traitorous nipples tingled and rubbed almost painfully against her sweater as she thought about what it would be like to press her naked body up against his. To feel her sensitized breasts against his muscular chest.

Then a new thought snaked through her. Connor was no doubt more experienced than she. Even thinking about him with other females caused an unwanted, almost violent surge of jealousy to rip through her, but she shoved it away.

The few lovers she'd taken had let her call all the shots. Something she *knew* Connor wouldn't do. He'd be dominating and demanding. And what if she wasn't what he wanted in bed? Sure, he wanted her, but that didn't mean they'd be right together sexually. Her skin felt too tight as she thought about that. Swallowing hard, she shrugged off his embrace. The sound was soft, but he growled low in his throat as she pulled away.

Letting him touch her and hold her was stupid and she needed to stop it now, before he got used to it. Who was she kidding? Before *she* got used to it. As they headed toward the waiting pack, she looked over at him to find him staring at her hard. As if he could read her innermost thoughts. And he wasn't trying to hide his. He wanted her in a bad way, and she suddenly wondered if he'd keep his end of the bargain and give her time. Even more terrifying, she wondered how long she could keep her distance.

Chapter 4

Liam cruised down Avalon Street but stuck to the speed limit. He'd had to hike back to the turnoff on Ana's property where he, Connor, and the rest of the pack had left their vehicles. He was thankful to have his Ford back. Connor had told him to do a little recon on the townspeople of Fontana, and from what he could tell it was a quaint mountain town that probably depended on tourism to survive the off-season. From a few of the bustling ski and snowboard shops he'd passed so far, it was obvious the local ski lodge didn't hoard all the business in that area.

All the shops were decorated for the holiday season. Garland wreathes and lights adorned most of the poles lining the main street. The town was an odd mix, though. Half Mayberry and half something else. Not exactly small town, but not big city either. Something in between. Clara's Ice Cream shop, which had probably been there for thirty years, was nestled next to Sala's, a high-end art gallery he'd seen featured on national television a couple years ago.

There was a huge ski resort not far up the road and

Fontana provided the lodging the resort didn't. From what Ana had said, that was a lot.

Ana didn't seem to have much interest in assimilating herself in the town and he knew his brother would agree, but Liam thought that attitude was archaic. If anything, they could bring a lot of commerce to the area. He and Connor had done well in real estate, but if they expanded the ranch, built more stables and opened some of the land to the public for riding and lessons, it would be a smart move on two levels. The Cordonas made a huge profit off their beef sales, but it never hurt to expand and it really wouldn't hurt to make friends with humans. Wasn't his decision, though. But that didn't mean he couldn't meet with a local real estate agent and look at a few commercial properties. Getting to know the townspeople would only help them.

As he steered by a cluster of shops directly off Avalon, he pulled into a parking spot right in front of a bookstore. December's Book Nook.

When they'd left upstate New York, they'd kept their property and homes but had left most of their furniture and other belongings. Including his book collection.

A little bell jingled overhead as he entered the bookstore. The scent of butterscotch immediately accosted him. A few candles lined the window, probably the source of the delicious smell. There was a section roped off in one of the corners with a sign that read THE STORY LADY, EVERY THURSDAY AT 10.

"Can I help you?" A woman stepped out from behind one of the shelves with a smile on her face. Soft red curls framed her face. And not that dark auburn that was so typical, but bright, beautiful red curls. The kind of color a woman couldn't buy from a bottle.

His breath caught as he drank in the sight of her. She couldn't be more than five-four—if that—and with her luscious curves, bright blue eyes and ivory skin, he felt as if he were staring at a bit of his homeland. He wasn't sure where the thought came from but his heart quickened just the same.

When she took a small step backward he realized he was staring a little too hard.

"I was wondering if you had any new releases from Michael Connelly or Jonathan Kellerman." He kept as still as possible when he spoke. He was big and knew that could be intimidating. From what he could scent, she was alone in the store, and he was practically ogling her like a deranged pervert. It was a wonder she hadn't backed farther away.

Her face relaxed slightly and she motioned toward the first aisle. "We just got a shipment of books in last Friday."

She picked a couple books off the shelf and stacked them in her hands as she talked. He tried to listen to what she was saying but all he could focus on was her mouth as it moved. Full, pink and shiny. As if she'd just put on gloss or whatever women used for their lips. He wanted to suck them, nibble them. . . . Her lips stopped moving. Shit, he was staring again.

He focused on her eyes. Regardless of species, women were the most complicated creatures on the planet, but even he knew to *listen* when they spoke.

"Were you listening to a word I said?" There was a slight trace of amusement in her voice.

"No. I'm sorry."

"You don't sound sorry."

"Probably because I'm not . . . Have dinner with me tomorrow night." He sounded like an imbecile, but at least he'd managed to string a couple coherent sentences together.

Her eyebrows rose and she laughed. A loud, throaty

sound that went straight to the ache between his legs. Immediately she covered her mouth and shook her head. "That was rude—I'm sorry. You just took me by surprise. I don't even know your name. And you don't even know mine."

"I'm Liam Armstrong."

She chewed on her bottom lip and he desperately wished his mouth was on hers. Covering and devouring it. Liam wasn't sure what had come over him when it hit him. *Mate.*

He jerked back at the word and tried to reject it. No. Impossible. She was human. That he was sure of.

Mate.

There it went again. The word resounded in his head so loudly he was surprised she hadn't heard it. "Fuck," he muttered.

"Excuse me?"

"Wha . . . nothing. I'm still waiting on your answer. And your name."

"I haven't decided, but my name is December Mc-Intyre."

"I knew you were a Scottish lassie." Over the past century he'd learned to cover his brogue, but he laid it on thick at the moment, hoping it would earn him a smile. He wasn't disappointed.

Grinning, she tugged on one of her curls. "You're a bright one."

She was a smart-ass. Absolutely perfect. And he was absolutely screwed, because she was human. Matings between shifters and humans weren't exactly accepted in all circles. On either side. For all he knew, she hated his kind anyway. His inner wolf didn't care, though. It recognized her on a primal level. When he'd been barely seven, he'd asked his father how he'd known his mother was his intended mate. His father's green eyes had sparkled as he'd explained that some shifters knew immediately but most didn't. And males almost always knew before females did. Liam guessed it was something innate that boiled down to biology. He really didn't care about the science of it; he just wanted to know more about the redhead in front of him.

"So, are you staying at Fontana resort? I haven't seen you around town before."

Resort? Oh, right. "No."

"Not much of a conversationalist, are you?"

"No." And he'd never cared before either. Talking was overrated. It had been a long time since he'd been with a woman, but all his lovers had been shifters and they'd all wanted one thing. Brief companionship. No fuss or complications. December had *complication* written all over her. With a capital *C*.

She tucked a strand of her bright hair behind her ear. "You're not giving me much to go on here."

If he didn't start acting like a normal person she was going to kick him out on his ass and he wouldn't blame her. "I saw an Irish pub up the road a ways. I could meet you there tomorrow. Unless you have to work late." Under different circumstances he'd offer to pick her up, but considering the way he'd been acting, he didn't want to spook her by asking for her address. He could guess how well that would go over.

"Are you talking about Kelly's?" she asked.

He nodded. Kelly's Bar and Grill. That was the place. It looked nice but not too upscale. A place they could relax. He held his breath as she weighed her options.

Finally she spoke. "I'll be there tomorrow at six, but if you don't manage to carry on a conversation, I'm leaving."

A surprising burst of relief jarred him straight to his core. "Fair enough."

She started to say something else when the bell to her store jingled again. She peeked around the shelf, then smiled. "Excuse me," she murmured to him before hurrying away. "Parker! What are you doing here?"

Liam hung back and picked another book off the shelf. According to his brother, Parker was the name of the sheriff who'd come to the Cordona ranch earlier. He continued browsing the shelf but wasn't really seeing anything. As he listened to December's conversation his stomach muscles clenched. It was the sheriff and he was warning her about the new Armstrongs who'd settled on the Cordona ranch. *Great.*

He waited until he heard the bell jingle again before stepping out from the short aisle. December's previously warm gaze was darker, shuttered. She still clutched the few books in her hands but hovered near the door as if ready to bolt.

It shouldn't surprise him, but this time it did. He hadn't thought she'd care about what he was.

Finally she spoke. "Are you . . . one of them?"

Instead of anger, something different settled in his gut. He wasn't sure what it was but it was damn painful. "If by *them* you mean a shifter, then yes. I'm a wolf." He specified because there were so many different species. Not that it would matter to her. To most humans, shifters were all the same. A feline shifter was the same as a lupine shifter.

She swallowed hard. "Did you want to get these books or . . ."

"Yeah," he muttered.

She was silent as she rang him up and the fear rolling off her was starting to piss him off. What the hell did she think he was going to do—bite her? Under different circumstances that might not be such a bad idea.

As she put the books in a plastic bag, he broke the

silence. "Whatever you think you know about my kind, I would never hurt you."

December's blue eyes widened.

"I can smell your fear and it's unfounded." He plucked the bag from her hand. "I'll be there tomorrow at six whether you are or not." With that, he turned on his heel and left.

Ever since vampires and shifters had announced themselves to the world, there had been an almost invisible dividing line drawn through some towns and cities. He didn't understand why. Sure, vampires hadn't wanted to come out to the world, but once all shifters had unified and made a decision, vampires hadn't had much of a choice. Vamps might be a bit more hedonistic in nature than shifters, but they didn't go out of their way to kill humans or incite violence. And shifters weren't violent by nature either. No more than humans. Sure, they were more in touch with their animal side, but with the exception of a few bad apples they weren't prone to senseless violence and they took care of their families. Maybe knowing other beings had the ability to turn into a wolf or a jaguar or even a bear would freak him out if he'd been human, but he didn't understand the *fear*. Twenty years had passed since they'd come out and it wasn't as if they were out in the world, starting wars. And they'd been around since forever. The only thing that had changed was that people knew about them. But friendships had ended over the revelation and some shifters still hadn't "come out of the closet" because of it. He wasn't embarrassed by what he was and he sure as hell wouldn't apologize for it. Not to anyone.

Sean Taggart stepped out the front door of the cigar shop across the street when Liam Armstrong drove away. Until last night he hadn't seen that giant bastard in years. He couldn't believe Ana *knew* the family, and from the look of things, she was going to mate with Connor. Stupid whore. Always looking down her nose at him and his pack yet she was ready to jump into bed with Connor.

He still wasn't sure what had happened to all the males of her pack but he wasn't going to look a gift horse in the mouth. The fates had smiled down on him, and if the Armstrongs hadn't come along he'd be in her bed and on her ranch right now. Where he belonged.

Whistling to himself, he crossed the nearly deserted street and entered the bookstore. Sean rarely came into town—he had people to run errands for him—but he wanted to keep an eye on the Armstrong brothers at the moment. Liam had looked mighty pissed off when he'd left this store, and Sean planned to use anything he could against him or Connor.

A bell jingled loudly and he was tempted to rip it off the hinges.

"Hello. If you need help finding something, please let me know." A pretty human smiled at him from behind the cash register.

Unlike the women of his pack she was softer, a little plumper. And she must be the source of Liam's irritation. *Perfect.* "I just saw my brother leave."

A wave of fear rolled off her. *Good.*

"B-brother?"

"Yeah. Tall guy, dark hair." *Looked like he should be wearing a kilt and swinging a fucking claymore on the battlefield.*

The scent of her fear was evident but she masked it with a bright smile. "If you like mysteries too, check the first aisle."

"I'm not interested in your book collection. I just wanted to check out why Liam left all hot and bothered. Now that I've seen you, I understand."

She frowned but didn't respond.

"Maybe when he's through with you, he'll pass you to me."

"Get the hell out of my store." Her blue eyes flashed dangerously, but she still didn't come around from behind the counter. Smart.

"Your loss." Whistling, he left and had to fight back a laugh at the tension and anger emanating off the red-headed human.

If his father had taught him one thing it was that small victories mattered. He was going to take down the Armstrong pack any way he could.

Ana parked her dusty truck in the hospital parking lot and killed the engine, but didn't make a move to get out. She didn't know why this was so hard for her. Mingling with humans before they'd known what she was had never been a problem. Of course, her pack had never stayed in one place long enough to develop lasting relationships with humans anyway. Her father had drilled that into all of them from a young age. *"Don't mix with humans. They all turn on you eventually."*

When their Council had decided to announce their existence to the world, it was as if things had changed overnight. Decades later she still had problems assimilating. She hated the way people stared at her. Some of it was probably her imagination, but she couldn't help but feel like she was under a microscope sometimes. If she didn't live in such a small town people wouldn't know she was a shifter, but the locals knew what her pack looked like. And they hadn't aged much since they'd settled in Fontana, which she knew freaked out some people. Hence the curious stares. It wasn't everyone and it didn't happen everywhere she went, but it happened enough that she preferred to keep to herself and on the ranch. Her entire pack did. If it had been anyone else in the hospital, she'd have stayed away from town. But when she'd found out it was one of her few human friends who'd been injured the night before, she simply couldn't.

Hooking her purse over her shoulder, she steeled herself for hostility and headed toward the main sliding doors. As she stepped inside the sterile antiseptic smells nearly bowled her over. With her heightened senses, hospitals were one of the worst places for someone like her. The scent of death seeped into her pores without mercy.

Approaching the front desk, she pasted on a smile for the dark haired woman standing behind it. "Hi. I called earlier and was told that Kaya Dunlauxe was well enough to see visitors."

"Of course. Ms. Cordona, right?"

She swallowed nervously and nodded. Maybe Kaya didn't want to see her after all.

"I told Kaya you called and she'd love to see you. Room 203. Head down that hallway and you'll run right into the elevators." She pointed with her pen.

Ana let out a breath she hadn't realized she'd been holding. "Is there a gift shop here?"

The nurse smiled and nodded. "Right on your way to the elevators. You can't miss it."

Once she'd purchased a bag of jelly beans and chocolates—Kaya would hate flowers—she made her way to the room. The door was already open so she half knocked and let herself in.

Kaya's wrinkled face lit up when she spotted her. At sixty, she was still a striking woman. Touches of gray peppered her otherwise long, dark braid. "I wasn't sure if you'd come."

Ana's chest tightened at the sight of the bandage on

the side of Kaya's face and the purple-and-blue bruising along her frail arms. "I would have come sooner but the sheriff didn't tell me it was you. I just found out."

Her dark eyes narrowed. "Was he at your ranch bothering *you* about this?"

"He was just doing his job," she murmured. Ana walked farther into the room and pulled the plastic chair from the corner and closer to the bed.

Kaya muttered something Ana couldn't understand but she guessed it wasn't nice. When the older woman got angry, she started speaking in Tuscarora, her native tongue.

"Have you called your family, or do you need someone to do that for you?"

"My son already called everyone even though I told him not to. I think my sister is on her way here as we speak."

Ana knew Kaya's clan lived in upstate New York, but for reasons she didn't know Kaya and her son had settled in North Carolina nearly fifty years ago. And Ana had known them for thirty. It was a strange thing to see her friend age while she'd stayed relatively the same, but she'd long ago given up any feeling of guilt. She couldn't help nature.

"Good. You'll need family. My pack is here for you, whatever you need. Do you know who did this to you?"

She shook her head. "I was leaving the store and someone attacked me from behind. He roughed me up a bit and took the money I'd planned to deposit. But this"—she pointed to her face—"looks a lot worse than it really is. I'm an old woman and I bruise easily." Her soft chuckle filled the air, but Ana's gut clenched nonetheless. It was obvious that the bruising on her face had to hurt like hell but Kaya was downplaying it for her benefit.

"Was it a shifter?"

Her small shoulders lifted. "I'm not sure. Whoever attacked me was strong, but nowadays, everyone is stronger than me. I screamed, and Mr. Ross, who runs the jewelry store next door, heard me. He rushed out and my attacker ran."

"I'm so sorry this happened to you."

"It's not your fault, dear."

For a brief moment Ana wondered if Taggart had attacked Kaya because of their relationship, and panic surged through her, but she quickly brushed it away. If Taggart had gone after Kaya it stood to reason that she'd be in a lot worse shape than this. Ana held out the plain brown gift bag. "I brought something for you."

"Jelly beans?"

Ana bit back a smile. When her pack had first moved to Fontana she'd been thirty, but that had been before the Council had come out to the world. Back then she'd been so curious about humans and had spent a lot of time at Kaya's store. The older woman had a deep love for the little candies. "Open it and find out."

Her eyes lit up as she peered into the bag. "I better hide this before those nurses get back."

As Kaya pulled the candy out of the bag, Matt, Kaya's son, stepped into the room. Ana steeled herself again for some sort of rejection, wondering if he thought a shifter had attacked his mother, but all he directed her way was genuine warmth.

"Ana! We don't see you in town enough."

She stood as he strode toward her, and before she could react he pulled her into a giant hug. She'd forgotten how kind the Dunlauxes were. Guilt and shame filled her for avoiding them for so long, and unexpected, hot tears pricked her eyes. Not all humans were the same, just as not all shifters were the same. She needed to remind herself of that. Lord, she was a hot mess today. She rarely cried. Not even when her parents had died.

"Hey, why the tears?" Matt pulled a handkerchief from the front pocket of his long-sleeved flannel shirt.

"I don't know what's wrong with me. I just hate that this happened to your mom. There's a chance Sean Taggart did this because of his hatred for me." She didn't know why she was spilling her secret fears to them so freely but she couldn't seem to stop herself. How many times had her father told her to keep her mouth shut around humans? Once they'd come out to the world they'd had to be careful what they said in public for fear of anything being misconstrued. The media had more to worry about than them, but if they got a juicy story about a shifter they ran with it. Today she apparently forgot everything she'd been taught.

Kaya grabbed her hand in a tight grip. "Even if Taggart did this, it's not your fault. You've got to let go of your fears, girl. I'm not going to shun your entire kind because of something *one* did."

Ana swallowed back more tears. "I know." But it was nice to hear. Trusting humans was hard, and after all the years they'd known one another she desperately wanted to trust Kaya and her son. She started to say more, but a nurse chose that moment to pop in.

The woman paused by the door as she looked between the three of them. "Visiting hours are up."

Ana nodded at the woman and picked up her purse. "How long will you be here?" she asked Kaya.

"They're letting me go tomorrow morning, so rest easy. I'll be back at work in no time."

"Yeah, and it wouldn't hurt you to stop by the shop sometime," Matt said.

"I will. I promise."

After saying her good-byes and giving hugs, she

found herself heading back to the elevators once again. She might hate the circumstances but she was glad she'd come. Seeing Kaya reminded her that there were a lot of good people out there. Maybe it was time she started making some changes in her *own* attitude toward the town.

Keeping a careful distance, he held Ana Cordona in his sights as she strode down the hallway. His lip curled in disgust. She came to the hospital under the pretense of caring, but she was just as likely to hurt Kaya as whoever had gone after her last night.

Because Ana was an animal. She might try to hide behind her femininity and softness, but it was all an act. Beneath that pretty facade a monster lurked. As it was for all shifter abominations. For all he knew, she'd sent someone to hurt Kaya, then used it as an excuse to come here and finish the job herself.

Conniving. Deceitful.

Every single one of them.

Kaya trusted her, but that was her mistake. When Ana pressed the elevator button he ducked into the stairwell and hurried to the bottom floor. He didn't want to risk her seeing him following her. She might want to talk, and he didn't know if he could hide his disgust any longer.

Her kind was different that way. They could smell anger or fear. Another unfair advantage of their freakish mutations.

Staring out the long, slim window of the exit door, he watched as she stepped from the elevator. She looked deceptively normal, and it brought the rage inside him bubbling to the surface. No one would realize how dangerous she was. But he knew what her kind could do. He'd seen their barbarism firsthand. His father had been killed by one of them. Mauled and ripped apart. The cops had said it was a bear attack, but after the freak shifters had announced their presence to the world he'd known there had been no bear all those years ago. His father had been too badly torn apart. Ripped limb from limb. There weren't many bears around these parts, and the humans had needed a way to explain the death. No, it had to have been one of those abominations. Now that he knew the truth he'd make as many of them pay as he could while he was alive.

Waiting until she'd passed by the door, he opened it and waited until she reached the end of the hallway. When she turned toward the exit doors, he followed.

His pulse drummed in his ears. Killing her would be a huge blow to her family. When he'd poisoned her pack a couple months ago he'd hoped she'd be one of the first to go, but no such luck. Her sisters and cousins all looked up to her. Her death would have been so much better for him and the world. But the poison he'd created had had a different effect than he'd originally intended. It had definitely worked, but something in it had bonded directly to the testosterone molecules in the male shifters, killing them almost instantly. The pregnant females had simply died because of their weakened immune systems. That was the one thing their species had in common with humans. When pregnant, their females were much weaker and more susceptible to even human viruses. Unfortunately the rest of them had figured out what was going on too soon during his first attempt to exterminate them. Now he'd have to take a different approach. A more hands-on approach. This time he wasn't going to use a poison he'd made. He'd be using silver. It would be riskier because the purchase could be traced back to him if someone dug hard enough, but at least he knew it would work on the rest of the pack.

Reaching into his pocket, he fisted the syringe full of colloidal silver. Any type of silver was a hundred times worse for shifters than a lethal dose of mercury to humans. He'd killed these animals before and he'd do it again. This time he wasn't going to stop with Ana. He was going to finish off the entire Cordona pack and wipe their unnatural bloodline from the earth.

As she weaved her way through the parked cars he closed the distance between them. He hadn't expected to see her today but he wasn't going to pass up this opportunity. Hell, he never went anywhere without a syringe of silver for just this reason. He moved silently behind her, never alerting her to his presence. His father had been a hunter and a damned good one. While he didn't have extrasensory abilities, he could stalk better than her kind.

She was close to her truck now. His heart hammered against his chest but he forced his breathing to stay calm. He needed to keep his anticipation under control or she'd scent him. He was careful to stay downwind of her.

Keeping his movements steady, he picked up his pace. No one was around. He could already see the attack in his mind. One quick jab to her neck and she'd start foaming at the mouth.

An overpowering need to see her writhing on the ground in agony burned through him. Her pretty face would twist in her suffering and those dark eyes would fill with terror. His fist clenched around the cold syringe. He was so close now.

Just a few more yards and he could plunge it into her neck. He tasted the victory, sweet and powerful. Addictive as a drug.

A car door slammed behind him and a woman laughed. "She'll love the flowers," she said to her companion.

Automatically he ducked behind a car as their voices drifted away. They hadn't seen him. *Shit*. That had been close. Too close.

Peering up from behind the four-door sedan, he watched as Ana slid into the front seat of her truck. He gritted his teeth and waited until she'd pulled out of the parking lot, and fought the waves of frustration buffeting him.

This was too public a place anyway. He'd been careful before. He couldn't let his impatience get him caught now. No, he'd stick to his plan. Soon the Cordona pack would wish they'd never settled in Fontana.

Then they'd all be dead.

Chapter 5

Connor's boots crunched across the leaves and other foliage as he stalked across the yard. He couldn't find Ana anywhere and now he'd discovered her truck wasn't in the parking garage.

After he'd gotten back from the bank, he'd been putting out fires between his guys and Ana's packmates. Small, unavoidable spats that were based more on sexual frustration than anything else. The females didn't seem to realize it, but he could see it clearly. Most of his guys had been lone shifters, roaming the globe for decades or longer until he and his brother had convinced them to settle down. Now that they were on a ranch full of single, beautiful wolves, they wanted to mate in a bad way. Their most primal instincts were kicking in and wanted release.

They weren't the only ones sexually frustrated. Right now his thoughts were consumed with Ana and, more important, where she was at the moment. It's not as if he needed a play-by-play of Ana's daily schedule, but he hadn't been able to reach her on her cell and she'd just left this morning without telling him where she was going. After the fire last night, he was ready to send out a search party.

"Hey, Connor." Carmen, Ana's sister, fell into step with him as he walked toward the main house.

He nodded distractedly. "Carmen."

"Ana's not back yet," she supplied in a cheerful voice.

"Oh?"

She shook her head. "Nah, I tried calling her but her phone's still off, so she's probably still at the hospital. Or she already left and just forgot to turn her phone on. Knowing her, that's probably more likely. She hates those things. I've tried to teach her how to text but—"

"Hospital?" He couldn't keep the shock out of his voice.

Carmen's cheeks tinged bright pink. Her hand paused on the front door of the house. "Uh, yeah."

"Why is she at the hospital?" Each word was measured.

"I, uh, I found out that Kaya Dunlauxe was the woman hurt last night, and since they're friends, I told Ana and she headed right over there."

His attention was diverted at the sound of a vehicle pulling up the drive. It was Ana. His heart rate tripled at the thought of seeing her. God, he was no better than a randy cub with his first crush.

"She probably just forgot to tell you. Or maybe *I* was supposed to tell you. Yeah, actually, I think I was," Carmen murmured, guilt lacing each word.

"You're the worst liar, little she-wolf." Sighing, he changed the subject. "How's Erin?"

She shrugged but the concern in her dark eyes was almost palpable. "I think she's going to be okay. She's adjusting well, but . . ."

"But what?"

"I know it's not my business, but tell Noah to back off."

Alarm jumped inside him. Noah was one of his newest pack members, but he'd always been so protective of Erin. Hell, the wolf acted like they were already mated. Connor couldn't imagine him doing anything to hurt her. "What do you mean?"

"I know he means well, but Erin's still dealing with . . . what happened to her. She needs her space, and he can't keep hanging around the house, checking on her like she's an invalid. If she's ever going to heal, she's got to take charge of her life again and that starts with learning to take care of herself." There was a surprising note of authority in her voice.

Shock reverberated through him as her words sank in. "She told you what happened to her?"

"Yeah. We stayed up last night, talking." Carmen didn't expand on the comment. The sadness that rolled off her struck him right in the chest. It was potent, like the harsh winter winds of his homeland.

As far as Connor knew, Erin hadn't told any of the pack what had happened to her. When they'd found her she'd been naked, beaten, bloody and bruised, behind a Dumpster at a truck stop off Interstate 10. If she'd been human, she'd have been dead from the abuse she'd suffered. And no human would have been able to hurt her like that, so that meant one of their own kind had. Which was why he couldn't understand why Erin wouldn't tell him or at least Noah who'd hurt her. That kind of violence was rare, and all it would take for them to punish the transgressors would be for her to either tell him— and he'd mete out his own brand of justice—or call the Council. They might drag their feet sometimes or get too consumed with politics, but they wouldn't stand for anything like that against a female. They'd send the enforcer—Jayce Kazan—to handle whoever had hurt her. That wolf was seriously skilled and would rip anyone apart who got in his way.

"I'll talk to Noah. I promise . . . Did she tell you who hurt her?" Erin might not be willing to tell him, but maybe he could kill the bastard or bastards himself.

Carmen eyed him warily as she nodded. "Yeah, but I'm not telling you who. Sorry—I know you're my Alpha, but she trusts me and I won't break that."

He wanted to demand that Carmen tell him, but couldn't. If Erin had found a friend and someone she actually confided in, he wouldn't take that away from her. "Okay."

"Thanks. And tell Ana that I finished up with the guest house—your house."

He murmured thanks and strode back across the yard. Leaning against one of the giant oak trees, he waited.

After what felt like an eternity, Ana stepped out of the side door of the parking structure. She wore jeans, boots and a thick turtleneck. *Too much clothing,* his inner wolf shouted. She didn't notice him until she was a few feet away. Something must be on her mind for her not to scent him.

She faltered for a moment. "Hey."

That's when it hit him. He scented someone else on her. A human. *A man.* "Where have you been?" The question came out more harshly than he'd intended.

She shrugged, and immediately he sensed her defenses going up. "The hospital."

"Why didn't you tell me where you were going?" The last thing he wanted to do was drill her, but it was as if she were being intentionally difficult.

She bristled at his question. "You didn't tell me where *you* were going to be all day. I didn't realize I needed to check in."

"I'm your Alpha." Not only did he have a right to know, but he also *needed* to know where she was. It was his job to keep his pack safe. Especially her. If an Alpha couldn't keep his mate safe, he wouldn't stay Alpha for long.

She muttered something under her breath as they neared the front steps to the guesthouse.

Our new place. His blood heated at the thought. He might have promised to give her space, but they'd be sharing a bed tonight. He wanted her with him whenever possible. The closeness would prove to be torturous, he was sure. But it would be worth it to have her by his side.

"Have you been inside yet?" she asked.

"No, and don't change the subject." He opened the front door.

The soft scent of orange-oil wood cleaner and some sort of fresh detergent lingered in the air. Ana hooked her purse on the coatrack by the door as he shut it. "I found out the human who was hurt last night is my friend, so I went to see her. It's not a big deal," she muttered.

"So why do you stink like a man?"

"I *stink*?" Her espresso-colored eyes flared.

"That's not what I meant."

To his surprise, she shrugged haughtily and turned on her heel. For a moment all he could focus on was the soft sway of her backside, before a burst of anger surged through him. He trailed after her to find her pulling a beer from the newly stocked refrigerator.

"Want one?" she asked as she casually held one out.

He snatched it from her hand and placed it on the table before advancing on her. He went at her fast, before she could move, crowding her until her back was against the counter. Caging her in with his hands, he flattened his body flush against hers. His canines had started to pulse with the need to extend, and he couldn't hide his lustful scent even if he wanted to. He rolled his hips once against hers. Even though she could no doubt smell his hunger, he also wanted her to *feel* what she did to him.

The pulse point in her neck beat out of control and her dark eyes widened. A trickle of fear—and desire—rolled off her.

"Whose scent is on you?" he asked quietly.

She swallowed hard. The animal in him craved her submission, but his human side didn't want to scare her. Still, he smelled someone on her and he'd get an answer.

"Kaya's son. He hugged me at the hospital. That's all." The truth was in her words and her scent.

He leaned closer so that their faces almost touched. "Why didn't you just tell me that?"

"I don't like this dominating side to you." Her words were barely a whisper.

"Sweetheart, I've always been dominant. I was born to be Alpha of my own pack. You know that." Chuckling, he angled his head and sucked her earlobe between his teeth. It would be so easy to lean down a little farther and rake his teeth against her soft skin. Kiss her, mark her.

She gasped at the contact but pressed a firm hand against his chest. He didn't give her the space she obviously wanted. Her chest rose and fell rapidly as she stared at him. "When we first met you were *different*. You were my best friend, and for a while I thought maybe you wanted ... more. But then you left."

Lifting his head, he looked at her and hated the pain he saw there. He'd left exactly like she said, but ... "I never wanted *just* friendship from you, Ana. And if I'd stuck around to say good-bye ... ." He couldn't finish the sentence. The truth was if he'd waited to say good-bye, he wouldn't have been able to leave her. He'd had to make that clean break and walk away without looking back. It had been for her own good.

But he couldn't tell her why he'd gone. Couldn't risk her knowing the real reason.

Ana's throat constricted as she stared into Connor's green eyes. Even in the bright lights of the kitchen they looked darker. Hell, everything about him looked darker tonight.

Hungrier.

Almost feral. But in a sexy, edgy way. Definitely not scary. Her skin heated under his stare. Why did he have to look so good?

She stared at him, waiting and wanting him to do something to ease the ache she felt inside. She briefly thought about asking him why he'd left, but bit the question back. Maybe there had been someone else. That thought stung impossibly deep and she didn't want to hear the answer. If she pushed harder and he told her there had been another female ... that would be worse than not knowing. With his hard length pressing against her abdomen and distracting the hell out of her, it was hard to think of anything other than what he would look like naked. Yes, she wanted to keep some control, but she was also a female and wanted him to want her as much as she did him.

Finally she broke the silence. "I'm sorry I didn't tell you where I was today." She hadn't meant to make him worry. She wasn't used to checking in with anyone but her sisters. And checking in with him meant she really did have a new Alpha. That the males of her pack were truly and utterly gone and the Cordona women were moving on. In a way they were luckier than humans because they lived longer, but by the same stroke they were cursed. Her entire life was wrapped up in her pack, and when so many of them died it had been like part of her had died too.

Now she was letting Connor into her life. At least when he'd left her she'd been young and had been able to move on, but now things were different. They weren't just friends anymore. He might have agreed to let her wait, but soon they'd be mates. At least temporarily. They were going to know each other in the most intimate way possible. Her resolve to keep him compartmentalized in her life was strong, but she was afraid that once they slept together it would be a whole lot harder.

"The pack has to know you and I are a solid team." Connor's voice broke into her train of thought. "Your sisters and cousins will follow your lead, sweetheart. If you don't respect me, they won't either." His words struck a chord.

She was so used to being the leader by default that she'd forgotten what it was like to have an Alpha. And what was up with him calling her sweetheart? That wasn't part of the plan. He'd never been romantic before. Playful and teasing, yes, but not romantic. She didn't want him to start now, even though the word on his lips made something foreign inside her chest twist with an emotion she wasn't sure she wanted to define.

Right now she needed to build up a resistance to his charms. If she could keep some sort of control between them, she'd be okay.

He raked his teeth along her jaw, sending desire straight to the building heat in her belly. It blossomed, waiting for someone to give her the release she desperately needed. All her thoughts short-circuited. Why was he nibbling against her neck? This was *so* not part of the plan either.

An alarm bell went off in her head. His hands were at the hem of her sweater. Pushing up. She could practically feel what it would be like if he kept going and cupped her breasts. Held them in his callused hands. Stroked and teased them until she was so hot she could burst into flames. *Stay in control.* She repeated the words in her head and frantically grabbed his wrists. "What are you doing?" she blurted.

He stepped back and out of her embrace. His breathing was harsh and uneven and his canines had lengthened slightly. "Shit," he muttered. "I'm sorry. I know I told you I'd give you time, not take you on the kitchen counter." His eyes seemed to bore right through her.

"You don't want me?" Sharp disappointment punched through her chest even though she was the one who'd stopped things. What the hell was wrong with her? This was supposed to be a good thing. He was giving her what she wanted. She had control back, but all her body seemed to want was his hands *back* on her body.

"I . . . shit." He turned and stalked out of the kitchen, then out the front door before she could move.

An icy fist clasped around her heart. She might have wanted to wait until they mated, but she *wanted* him like she'd never wanted anyone else. On a completely physical level, she hungered to feel his naked body against hers. To feel him slide his hard shaft into her. It had been so long since she'd even thought about sex, but with Connor in her life, it seemed her familiar fantasies had flared to life once again. Only this time she'd be able to live out her fantasies if she wanted.

At that moment she'd never in her life felt more like a fickle woman. Even though she'd thought she wanted to wait, all he had to do was put his hands on her and she wanted to strip off her clothes.

After she ascended the stairs and entered the master

bedroom, she quickly changed out of her sweater and jeans and into a long pajama set. Normally she liked to sleep naked or in just a shirt, but that wasn't happening tonight. Not if she wanted to stay sane.

Her sisters had done a good job of cleaning the house. Everything in the room looked perfect. Crisp, clean towels were folded on the rocking chair in the corner of the room. The wrought-iron, king-sized bed had a new, luxurious sage-colored comforter, and Carmen had no doubt added the tea-light candles on the nightstand. Everything else was fairly spare. Antique furniture pieces littered the house, but it lacked a female touch. If they were going to be living there for a while, she was going to make some changes. But for now, she lit the candles and slipped under the covers.

Now all she could do was wait.

Connor stalked by house after house until he reached his brother's cabin. Most of it would be empty because his guys were out patrolling the perimeter, but Liam wasn't on duty tonight.

He started to open the front door when it swung open. A tired grin played across his brother's face. "Thought I smelled you. What the hell are you doing here? Thought you and Ana would be tearing up the sheets—"

"Damn it, Liam," he muttered. He knew his brother was just messing with him, but he didn't like anyone thinking or talking about Ana in those terms. Connor glanced past him and into the cabin. No one else was there, so he felt free to talk. "I don't know why I'm here."

Wordlessly Liam stepped outside and leaned against the wood railing of the porch. And waited.

Connor scrubbed a hand over his face. "I was ready to take her right on the kitchen counter."

"And that's a bad thing?" Amusement laced Liam's words.

"She's not ready."

"Ana's a big girl. She made the deal."

"Because she had no other choice. I *gave* her no other choice." He slammed his fist against the railing and winced when he saw a new indentation in the wood. Everything had seemed so clear before he'd arrived at Cordona Ranch. He'd come in, sweep her off her feet and offer the protection she needed. But he didn't want her gratitude. He just wanted her.

Willing and all his.

Mind and body.

"So go back over there and get creative."

The last thing he wanted to do was take advice from his younger brother. Liam hadn't stayed with a woman longer than a week. Then again, neither had he. "Creative?"

His brother grinned wickedly. "Get your mind out of the gutter. Not like that. Show some restraint, man. Show her that you're not a fucking animal—even though that's exactly what you are. You want her to trust you? Give her a reason to. *Restraint.* Repeat it."

"You're probably right," he muttered.

"No *probably* about it. I am. And if you want her to trust you, you've *got* to tell her about the cubs."

"I know. *I will.*" Bringing a wolf cub into a new pack was one thing, but bringing in a new she-cat was something else entirely. Felines and lupines didn't exactly get along. Well, he had no problem with them, but right now he and Ana were still feeling each other out and he was on shaky ground with her. She might have accepted him as Alpha but this was still a temporary arrangement to her. He could see it on her face every time he looked at her. He didn't want to spring one more change on her so soon.

"Don't be an idiot. She's going to find out about them sooner than later, so if I were you—"

He growled low in his throat. "One thing at a time. I need to feel her out first."

Liam snorted. "Feel her out or feel her up?"

Connor sighed as he stepped off the front porch. "Let me know if there's a problem tonight."

Liam nodded and stepped back inside.

Connor stared at the two-story home that would be his and Ana's for a while. It loomed before him like a dungeon. *Restraint?* He'd been dreaming about Ana for the past fifty years, and Liam wanted him to show restraint.

In the kitchen he'd been ready to turn her around, mount her, and mark her, taking her as his bondmate. *Despite* the promise he'd made to her. He'd felt his most primal side taking over and if he hadn't stopped, he'd never have forgiven himself. Worse, she'd have hated him for life.

Restraint, restraint, restraint. He repeated the words over and over as he opened the front door.

All the lights were off downstairs and Ana's scent lingered on the stairs. Okay, she was in one of the bedrooms. He could show restraint.

He hoped.

A soft light illuminated the hallway through the only open door along the long hallway. He stepped into the room to find Ana sitting in the middle of the giant bed with a sheet clutched tightly against her chest.

And she was completely clothed. His inner wolf sighed.

"I'm sorry I left." His voice was hoarse.

"Why did you?"

"I needed to think. I realize I might have come on a little strong last night with my . . ." He couldn't say *re-*

quest because it would be a lie, and he didn't want to say *demand* because it made him feel like a bigger jackass than he was. "With our deal."

"Might have?" She snorted loudly, and for some reason the irreverent sound put him at ease.

It was natural. The way she'd acted around him when they'd first met. Laughing and comfortable all the time. He strolled over to the rocking chair and moved the towels onto a bench by the window. He needed to keep his distance while he talked. Ana tracked his movements.

"Do you remember the first time we met?" he asked.

Her cheeks tinged pink as she nodded. "How could I forget? Two naked strangers surprised me while I was out riding."

He and his brother had been swimming in one of her family's ponds on their ranch in upstate New York. It had been a much different time then. Simpler. And at the same time more complex. He and Liam had been aimlessly roaming around the United States, trying to figure out where the hell they belonged. Before the Council had officially formed in North America and before they'd come out to the humans. He understood the Council had had no choice but to come out to the humans. With technology advancing so rapidly, it would have been a matter of time before their existence was discovered. Sighing, he shook those thoughts away. He didn't care about that right now. All he cared about was the woman in front of him.

"You were so young then," he said quietly. Young, full of life and ready to embrace anything.

Her shoulders tightened at his words. He wasn't sure what he'd said but maybe it had been the wrong thing. "I've thought about you a lot over the years."

She relaxed a fraction. "Really?"

"Yes." More than he cared to admit. All he had to do was conjure up her face and he got hard. It was embarrassing, but he'd known from the moment he met her they were intended mates. Something she still didn't seem to realize. One of the memories he carried of his father was him telling Connor that when he met his mate, he'd know. *"Na worries, wee wolf. Whin ah met yer ma, ah knew she wis th' one for me. Ah felt it in mah gut th' moment our eyes locked. Some dinnae ken richt awa' but we Armstrongs have a history o' just knowing. Ye will tay."* And Connor had. Without a doubt. Every fiber inside him had come alive when he'd met Ana. His human side had understood that it was biology. At first. Which is part of the reason he'd resisted his original attraction to her. He'd wanted to be with her because *he* wanted her and she wanted him. Not because his body ordered him to mate with her. Then when he'd gotten to know her, his feelings had become something more. Deeper. Stronger.

Then he'd been forced to leave.

She hadn't said she'd thought about him over the years, but he brushed past it. "I told you I'd give you time and I meant it."

"Really?" she asked, her voice unsure.

No. "Yes. We're going to take things slow." He stood and took off his shirt and shoes, but left his pants on. Normally he preferred to sleep naked or in his wolf form, but tonight he'd have to stay clothed. That extra barrier was necessary to hold on to his tiny shred of restraint. Hell, it was slowly dissipating as he stared at her luscious, parted lips.

She scooted over as he got under the covers with her, but he didn't miss the way her dark eyes hungrily roved over his bare chest. Damn, she really was going to make this hard for him.

"What does *slower* mean for someone like you?" she finally asked.

"Someone like me?" He wasn't sure if he should be offended.

Her cheeks stained an even darker shade of pink. "You know what I mean, *Alpha*. I'm sure you have a ton of experience with females, so I don't know if this slow thing is something you can even do." There was a blend of sarcasm and uncertainty in her words that was tempered with a hint of jealousy when she'd said the word *females*.

He wouldn't deny he'd had a lot of experience before her, but after was a completely different story. And also not something he wanted to talk about. Ever. Right now was about the two of them. "I can do *slow* and soft." He lowered his voice as he leaned closer. "And fast and hard, or a mix of the two. Whatever you want, Ana."

She didn't say anything as she stared, but her breathing had increased and her eyes were dilated slightly.

He bit back a grin. "We need to do this in steps. Kissing is the only thing on the menu for tonight."

"Kissing?" One dark eyebrow rose and the heat he'd witnessed moments before was replaced by pure skepticism.

"That's right." It pained him to think, let alone *say*, the words, but if he wanted to do this right he had to gain her trust first. That meant hands off. For the most part.

She eyed him warily until he reached out and cupped her cheek. Holding her like this, touching her in this way, was almost too much. His hand actually shook as he caressed her soft skin. And they hadn't even kissed yet.

He slid his fingers through her thick hair as he leaned forward. Raw hunger flowed through him as her tongue darted out to moisten her lips. Taking him off guard, she covered the short distance between them. It took a moment to register that when their lips clashed, so did their bodies. She was half draped across him. Her sweet scent wrapped around him, enveloping him completely. They might not be mating tonight, but he planned to make sure his scent covered her.

Through her top her nipples rubbed against his bare chest, and he didn't bother to bite back his groan. The feel of her moving against him tested the stupid promise he'd made. Her tongue met his, almost shyly, in an erotic little dance. It wasn't the hungry way he'd imagined. It was somehow better.

She tasted minty and fresh, and as their tongues intertwined he could feel the tension leaving her. It was subtle, but she trusted him. At least with her body. That was something.

Reaching between them, he freed the first three buttons of her long-sleeved top. She didn't even seem aware of his movements until he cupped one of her breasts. It felt almost heavy in his hands, though it wasn't much more than a handful. He hadn't gotten a good view of her breasts yet, but he planned to change that. Soon.

A surprised moan escaped her as he rubbed a lazy thumb over her hardening nipple. She started to pull back, but he tightened his grip on her head. If she'd insisted, he'd have let her go. But she sighed into his mouth and a shudder rolled over her.

Gripping her hips, he rolled her onto her back and moved so that he was nestled between her thighs. Even with his jeans and her pajamas as a barrier, there was no denying how much he wanted her. His cock pressed painfully against the denim, begging to be freed.

When his hips surged against her, she pulled her head back a fraction and seemed to be shocked. "What are you doing?"

In response, he nibbled along her jaw, raking his teeth across her skin. "What do you think?"

"You said kissing only," she whispered.

He wasn't exactly sure why she was whispering but he decided to go with it. "Kissing covers a lot of things, love."

Moving lower, he continued kissing her, even though he felt her tense when he hovered over one of her breasts. Her top was splayed open, perfectly revealing both her breasts. In all his fantasies he'd had to wonder what they looked like. He'd imagined, sure, but nothing was better than the real thing. Soft, perfectly rounded. Not too big; just enough for him to hold. To kiss. And her nipples were a light brown. Many nights he'd lain awake wondering what color they'd be.

Lightly he blew on her exposed skin. "Do you think you'd like it if I kissed you here?"

Her breath hitched in response.

Smiling to himself, he started to lower his head. Before he got the chance, lightning fast she jerked her top together, covering all that smooth, satiny skin and denying him what he wanted.

"We . . . need to stop." Her voice was ragged and unsteady but her jaw was firm.

She was hot and ready for him. Even if he hadn't been a shifter, he'd be able to scent it. He wanted to argue, convince her to keep going, but he was an Alpha. He had some pride. Sort of. With how he felt, he'd sell his soul for one more taste of her. Then she wiggled out from underneath him and started buttoning up.

"Fucking restraint," he muttered through gritted teeth as his head fell against the pillow.

As he cursed the cold for the hundredth time that night, Chuck glanced at his watch again. December's bedroom lights had gone off half an hour ago. She should be asleep by now.

After the last incident, he couldn't afford to fuck up this kidnapping. If he somehow forgot how important this was, he had the bruised ribs and sore jaw to remind him. Adler might be a nasty-looking bastard, but he knew how to fight. Something Chuck wouldn't forget anytime soon.

Going after the sheriff's sister was stupid, but one of Adler's contacts had heard December arguing with the sheriff about going to dinner with one of the new shifters in town. At this point Chuck wasn't sure if she was a shifter whore or not, but either way she was still the sheriff's sister. Chuck had tried to make a case with Adler about his decision to target her, but that's when Adler had clocked him across the face.

Apparently Adler had also heard that the big shifter, Liam, had been talking to a real estate agent in town and he'd shown more than passing interest in the bookstore owner. Once Adler heard the shifter had a definite interest in a human female, he'd called his boss at the APL. Chuck wasn't exactly sure who Adler's boss was, but the guy was obviously high up in the food chain and he wanted December kidnapped. He seemed to get Adler worked up enough every time they talked, and that was a pain in the ass for Chuck. Nothing he said could convince the other man that this was too big of a risk.

Adler's plan to use the female to lure the shifter, Liam, into a trap was actually good, even if it was risky. He wanted to see how much the shifters would sacrifice to save a human female. It would go a long way in telling the APL exactly what buttons they could push with these animals in the future. There might be more to the plan but right now Chuck didn't know. His boss told him stuff only when he felt like it.

Instinctively he rubbed his jaw, then winced at the painful contact. "Bastard," he muttered.

His cold breath curled in front of him. Glancing around the quiet street, he rose from his hiding spot across from her house. December's neighbors were out of town for a couple weeks, so he'd used one of their giant oak trees as cover.

Adler was parked a block over, waiting for his call. Once he knocked the girl out he wouldn't have to drag her far. Not like she weighed much anyway. And she was pretty. Soft, white skin he wouldn't mind running his hands over. Hell, he might even break his rules about not touching their captives. It didn't sound like she'd actually fucked one of those animals yet, but he'd wear a rubber just in case. After the beating he'd gotten from Adler, fucking the sheriff's sister would take off the edge. His cock started to harden just thinking about it.

He smiled to himself as he crossed the street. This job might be chancy but at least it would have a perk afterward. Every house on her block was quiet. After midnight most people would be dead to the world. His shoes thudded lightly as he walked across the frosty asphalt, but once he made it to her front yard he was silent again.

She'd parked in the driveway instead of pulling into her garage and he wasn't sure why. He wasn't going in that way so it didn't matter. Stupid bitch left a "hidden" key on her back porch.

Not in plain sight, but it hadn't taken much searching to find the hide-a-key tucked into one of the dried-up potted plants. Using the key, he twisted the lock and opened the door. He pushed out a quiet, relieved breath when an alarm didn't sound.

Adler had told him she didn't have one, but Chuck hadn't been entirely sure he'd been telling him the truth. It was like that prick wanted him to fail.

Chuck pulled his black ski mask down over his face. The stairs were right next to the kitchen. He inched his way up them. A floorboard creaked halfway up and he paused.

His heart thumped against his chest in a staccato rhythm. After a moment he continued. The stairs creaked a few more times but he hurried up the rest of the way. When he reached the top he waited again.

From the street earlier he'd seen a light upstairs in the window to the far right. It had to be her bedroom. Out of habit he patted the side of his belt. His knife was there but he wouldn't be using that tonight. He'd become accustomed to using his knife to scare people, but after the other night he wasn't going to risk dealing with another screamer.

Withdrawing the medium-sized stun gun, he started toward the bedroom. Raw adrenaline hummed through him. He was doing to enjoy this. Pausing at the door, he listened. When he heard muted movements he froze. Blood rushed loudly in his ears as he took a small step back. Had she heard him? Before he could move, the door swung open.

It was dark but he could make her out well enough to see the terror on her face when she spotted him. The sight of it made him smile. This bitch was definitely coming with him tonight.

She shrieked and at the same time swung out with her hand. He easily ducked her attempted blow. She tried to kick at him but he tackled her to the ground. A surprising surge of lust coursed through him as she struggled underneath him.

She screamed again. This time louder. Not bothering with the stun gun, he knocked her across the face. Not as hard as he normally would. He didn't want to break her bones. But he wanted her stunned into submission. "You like it rough, shifter whore?" Now he used the weapon to jolt her system. Her mouth opened but no sound came out as her body started to spasm.

She went slack, her head lolling back on the floor.

"December!" A male voice carried from downstairs.

What the hell? Chuck pushed up. There wasn't supposed to be anyone else here unless . . . her brother. *Shit.*

He shoved up from the floor. His options and time were limited. Killing a cop wasn't something he ever planned to do. It brought too much heat.

Still on the ground, December mumbled incoherently. *Screw it.* He wasn't getting pinched for this. Fleeing the room, he escaped back down the hallway. As he reached the end, the sheriff arrived at the top of the stairs. Wearing boxers and a T-shirt, he looked slightly disoriented but he had a gun.

Chuck lunged at him, slamming him against the wall. The action took the cop off guard for a split second. Chuck didn't waste the opportunity.

Sprinting down the stairs, he rushed out the side door. A shot splintered close to his head, urging him on. He heard shouts behind him and risked a quick glance as he ran across the yard. The cop hadn't followed. Probably checking on his sister instead.

Chuck pulled out his cell with a shaky hand and dialed Adler as he raced down the sidewalk.

He picked up on the first ring. "You got her?"

"Shit, no. Her brother was there and he caught me. I'm about to turn onto Magnolia." He tried to keep his voice low as he ran.

Adler cursed. "I'll pick you up."

As Chuck rounded the next street he immediately spotted the dusty green Chevelle rumbling toward him. Adler slowed down but didn't completely stop, barely giving him a chance to jump into the front seat. "That fucking cop was there." He slammed his fist against the dash then ripped off his mask and threw it on the floorboard.

Adler was silent as he steered down another side street, farther away from December's house. Chuck didn't know who the car belonged to but he knew Adler had stolen it earlier that night. They'd stashed another car a mile away and planned to ditch this one in case anyone had seen them leaving December's house.

"I told you it was stupid to try to take her."

Adler sighed heavily. "My boss is not going to be happy about this."

"Fuck your boss. Why isn't he here doing something if this is so damn important?" Chuck turned around to see if they were being followed, but they weren't.

"I fail to see why it's so hard for you to see the bigger picture." Another sigh. This one more annoyed.

Well, Chuck was annoyed too. Annoyed he was always kept in the dark. He hadn't lived in Fontana long, and Adler had only recruited him recently. Chuck wasn't sure how long the other man had been with the APL and until recently the group hadn't been very vocal about anything. Now he occasionally saw members on various talk shows discussing the danger of shifters, but they never admitted any violent actions. Everything was so hush-hush with them. So why the hell should he know what the bigger picture was if no one told him? "You never tell me shit so maybe that's why I can't see the bigger picture," he spat.

Adler shook his head as he made a left-hand turn.

His stomach knotted with tension. "Aren't you going to say something?" He knew another lecture was coming and he'd rather get it over with now. At least Adler couldn't punch him while he was driving. Maybe his mood would cool by the time they got back to his place.

"There's not much to say. You are useless." Adler's voice was calm, emotionless.

That's when Chuck saw the knife. The blade glinted wickedly under the moonlight as it slashed toward him.

He held up his hands in defense, but Adler slammed it into his chest. In shock, Chuck stared at the black handle protruding from his ribs.

A bitter, metallic taste filled his mouth. His own blood.

Agonizing pain ripped through him. He tried to breathe but choked instead. Liquid filled his nose and airway. The son of a bitch had stabbed him. He stared at Adler. He wanted to lunge out at him but his body wouldn't obey.

Adler's dark eyes barely flickered with any emotion. "Fucking die already," he muttered.

Chuck clutched the handle of the knife. To do what, he didn't know. He was a dead man even if he pulled it out. The reality barely set in when blackness engulfed him.

Chapter 6

Ana stared into the darkness of their room. Moonlight bounced around, creating shadows of the furniture along the wood floor. When she shifted, Connor's grip on her waist tightened. She wasn't exactly sure how much time had passed, but with each minute that ticked by, the worse the ache between her legs grew.

All she could envision was what it had looked like to see Connor about to take her breast in his mouth. It had been almost surreal watching him. As if it hadn't really been her. She still couldn't believe she'd managed to stop him. Her fingers had trembled as she'd buttoned up her top but he hadn't seemed to notice. She tried to scoot a little farther away but his grip simply tightened even more. By his steady breathing she was pretty sure he actually was sleeping. Sighing, she stopped fighting him. She might be more than a little sexually frustrated, but for the first time in ages she felt safe.

Ironic, considering Connor was more or less the Big Bad Wolf. Still, it was a relief to hand over some of the responsibilities of the ranch. Especially the protection part. Though she hadn't admitted it to her sisters, ever since the males of their pack had died, she'd lived in a state of fear. It hadn't affected her on a day-to-day basis, but in the back of her mind she'd worried that a group of warrior shifters would come in and just take over. Connor's wolves were different from any males she'd met before. Even different from her father's pack. They had a lot of respect for females, as most shifters did, but they were obviously more hardened to life. It was subtle, but she'd seen it in the way they'd talked to and acted around her packmates.

She closed her eyes and forced all those thoughts from her head. For once she wanted a good night's sleep. As blessed darkness started to take over a distant, foreign sound greeted her ears. Before she'd even sat up, Connor had jumped from the bed and was pulling on a sweater.

"Is that a vehicle?" she asked, her voice thick and tired. So much for a full night of sleep.

He nodded. "Sounds like it."

The bright red numbers of the digital clock told her it was almost three in the morning. Anyone coming to see them this early would only be bringing bad news. She scrambled from the bed and quickly shoved her legs into her discarded jeans. By the time she'd tugged on her turtleneck, Connor had disappeared from the room.

She found him downstairs, waiting by the front door, talking on the phone. He acknowledged her with a nod but continued speaking. "All right. Radio the men and round them up. Whatever it is, we'll need them here."

"What's going on?" she asked as he disconnected.

"I don't know, but look for yourself." He pulled back the curtain blocking the small window next to the front door.

Red and blue lights flashed in the distance but they were coming up the drive fast. The dirt drive stretched on for miles but it would only be a matter of minutes before they reached the gate. "What are we going to do?" Ana looked at Connor.

His jaw was set in a firm line and his beautiful green eyes had darkened to almost midnight black. It wasn't a trick of the light either. He was pissed and likely fighting not to change.

She placed a hand on his forearm and almost immediately the natural color returned. "Are you okay?"

He nodded, but took a moment before he spoke. "I'm fine. I'd forgotten how often humans jump to conclusions without having any facts."

"We don't know why they're here," she murmured.

"It's three in the morning and I count two squad cars. They probably have more backup waiting. This is *not* a friendly visit."

"I know." She sighed and automatically went to open the door, but he beat her to it.

He stepped out first, then turned and nodded for her to follow. She'd been opening her own doors for so long, she'd forgotten what it felt like to be protected. Male humans had a funny tradition of opening doors for women and allowing them to enter a building first. One never knew what was on the other side of a door. It didn't make sense to let a female step into possible danger without assessing the situation first.

Connor placed his hand on the small of her back as they strode across the yard. She wanted to shrug it off but decided to let him keep it there. Even if she wouldn't admit it, his presence reassured her. The cops visiting twice in one day was bad for their pack. By the time they'd reached the gate, everyone had filtered out of their houses or cabins and stood by expectantly. A few of the males on protection duty were coming in from the fields too.

Ana spotted four men in tan-and-brown uniforms and a redheaded female she vaguely remembered seeing in town before. It was dark, but the light from their homes, the nearby barn and the pale moon overhead gave them more than enough illumination.

Connor opened the gate and he, Ana and Liam greeted Sheriff McIntyre and two of the uniformed officers. The other officer hung back with the woman. Connor could sense the rage coming from the sheriff and fought his own.

Tempering his anger, he stepped forward in an attempt to block Ana. "How can I help you, Sheriff?"

"I need to see all of the newest members of your . . . pack." He directed the demand behind Connor to Ana.

Connor could feel his canines start to extend and had to control the dominant need to protect her. And to put this guy in his place. This was his land, his pack, and the beast inside him didn't care that the sheriff was the law. It only cared that he was encroaching on his territory. "You don't speak to her. You speak to me. I'm the Alpha of this pack now." The man might not understand what *Alpha* meant, but he sure as hell understood Connor's tone.

The sheriff averted his steely glare back to him. "Fine. I need to see all your men. Right now."

"Why?"

"I don't need a reason."

"Yes. You do. Unless you have a warrant, shifters have rights too. Or have you forgotten that?" Connor's heart rate sped up.

The man stepped forward menacingly. "You son of a—"

"Parker!" The redhead stepped away from the other officer and hurried toward the sheriff.

The family resemblance was unmistakable. Even

though she was a bit shorter and definitely a lot softer, they both had the same bright blue eyes. She must be his sister. And she was sporting a nasty-looking black eye. Fresh too.

Connor frowned when he saw her, his protective nature kicking in, but before he could speak, Liam stepped past him. "Are you okay?" His voice was low.

Wide-eyed, the redhead nodded. Her fear was apparent, but at least she didn't run away screaming from him.

"What happened?" Liam asked, his voice barely above a whisper.

"Why don't you tell me?" the sheriff asked with venom.

Liam pivoted toward the man. "What the hell does that mean? You think *I* did this?"

"Someone broke into her house tonight. Luckily I'd fallen asleep on the couch and stopped him before he could hurt her worse than he did."

Connor didn't understand how his brother even knew the redhead, but he grabbed his arm and pulled him back. He didn't want the cops thinking Liam was making any aggressive overtures. Past experience told him they'd use any excuse to hurt a shifter. "And you think someone in our pack hurt her? What possible reason could we have?"

Before the sheriff could answer, his sister placed a calming hand on her brother's arm and looked at Liam. "After you left the store today your brother came in and made some nasty comments to me. The person who broke into my house tonight was wearing a mask, but he was the same height and he called me a shifter whore. I don't know if it was the same person but . . ." She trailed off uncertainly.

"Wait. My *brother* talked to you today?" Liam turned to look at Connor, not accusingly but in shock.

Connor shook his head at Liam, then cleared his
throat. "I'm sorry, ma'am, but I think you're mistaken. I
was in town today but I only stopped at the bank. We've
never met."

Her eyebrows knitted together as she looked back
and forth between them. "Not *you*. He had dirty-blond
hair, dark eyes. Almost as tall as you both. Maybe another brother?"

"We don't have another brother," Liam said.

It had to have been Sean Taggart. Connor wasn't going to say it aloud because he planned to take care of
Taggart on his own, but Ana muttered the vile wolf's
name loud enough for everyone to hear.

The sheriff turned to his sister. "You told me he was
his brother."

Her blue eyes spit fire. "That's what he *told* me. It's
not like I asked for ID or anything. I just wanted him out
of my store. And I still don't know if he was the one who
attacked me tonight. He wore a freaking mask. I don't
know why you insisted on dragging me out here when I
told you—"

"Go wait in the car," he said.

She looked at Connor, then at Liam, and her gaze lingered longer than necessary on him before she did as
her brother said.

Connor held up his hands. "I'm going to reach into
my back pocket, so tell your boys to keep their weapons
holstered." He wasn't sure if they were trigger-happy or
not but he wasn't taking a chance. Even if they didn't
have silver-coated bullets, regular bullets still burned
like a bitch.

He fished out the business card he'd been hoping he
wouldn't have to use, but this man was going to be a pain
in Connor's ass. That much was obvious. "This is the
number for my attorney. You need something from me

or anyone else in my pack, call him first or get a fucking warrant before setting foot on this land. He represents every single one of us." It was petty, but he felt smug as he shoved the card at the sheriff.

When the man saw his attorney's name his eyes widened, but he didn't comment. Just tucked it into his front pocket and turned on his heel and left. Connor would have much preferred to make peace with the humans living in Fontana, but he wouldn't stand by while law enforcement harassed his pack. If he let it slide now, it would only get worse with time.

Once the vehicles turned around and headed back the way they'd come, he looked at his brother. "I take it you know the redhead?"

"I met her today in town. I should go talk to her . . ." Liam's voice had taken on a possessive tone Connor recognized well.

"Ana, will you go check on your sisters?" Connor asked without looking at her.

Wordlessly she headed toward one of the groups of women.

Connor waited until she was out of earshot. "You think getting tangled up with a human now is the best idea." It wasn't a question.

Liam didn't respond, just glanced down the drive, even though they'd disappeared from sight. He growled softly in his throat.

"Stay away from her."

Liam glared at him. "She's my mate."

A headache was starting at the base of Connor's skull. "She's human."

"You say it like I have a choice."

His brother's words took a moment to sink in. *Mate?* "You're sure?"

Liam nodded, his expression grim.

Shit, shit, shit. "You've got to stay away from her. Especially now."

"What if someone told you to stay away from Ana?"

"I've stayed away from her for the past fifty years!" If anyone knew about sacrifice it was him, and he wasn't going to take shit from his brother.

Liam shrugged casually and that pissed him off even more. "That was *your* choice."

"And you would have done differently in my shoes?" He took a step toward his brother, hot rage filling his veins. He loved Liam more than anything, but he'd still kick his ass.

"You did what you thought was best." His answer was monotone and that only infuriated Connor more.

He hadn't done what he'd *thought* was best. He'd done what *was* best. For Ana. Leaving hadn't been about him or his needs. It had been for her. Something Liam couldn't understand. He might know December was his mate on a primal level, but he didn't *know* the woman. Didn't care for her the way Connor did for Ana, and his brother's attitude pissed him off. "You don't know shit, little brother."

Liam muttered a few choice words in Gaelic, then turned and jogged down the drive. Connor knew that once he was out of sight he'd lose his clothes and shift. He was going to track her, then watch over the red-headed woman until he was certain she was safe. Connor knew what Liam was doing, because he'd do the same thing in his position.

As Alpha, Connor could force him to stay, but that wasn't a battle he wanted to get into. Not now. Not ever. Coming between a wolf and his mate was bad news. Especially since that wolf was his brother. It seemed impossible that Liam's mate was a human, but Mother Nature could be a nasty bitch when she wanted.

*   *   *

Taggart looked up from his desk as Vince, his second-in-command entered. "They gone yet?"

"Yeah. Local assholes. I don't know why you won't let me do something about them."

Taggart slammed his fist against the desk. "Because we don't want any problems with them, idiot." They needed to keep their noses clean. At least as far as the outside world was concerned. The local cops were harassing his pack and apparently the Cordonas too from the sound of it. As if he'd be messing with some humans right now. They had more important things to worry about.

Under Taggart's intense scrutiny Vince looked at the floor. "I couldn't get to Ana's grazing field like you wanted. Connor has his guys patrolling the property pretty regularly. I was thinking, you could just offer to buy some of her property or something," he muttered.

Taggart gritted his teeth. "You think Armstrong will let me buy any of that bitch's land? He'd tell me no out of spite."

"If someone else made the offer, it might work," Vince said quietly.

Vince had a soft spot for one of the Cordona women. Taggart just didn't know which one. It might explain his resistance lately to vandalism.

Maybe he should have just offered to purchase the land two months ago when Ana had been in mourning, instead of trying to unite their packs. But he'd wanted Ana in his bed. He still did. The bitches in his pack were nothing compared to her. Pretty yes, but they were all weak. He needed a strong and smart mate. Ana might have an acerbic tongue, but she had a good head for business. And he needed that right now. Especially if he wanted to get the second part of his operation off the ground.

Selling meth was lucrative at the moment, but in the long run marijuana would make him more profit and his clients would have longer life spans. Not to mention the law didn't have much of a problem with pot. Meth, coke, heroin—that kind of shit *always* brought trouble sooner or later. The Feds could get involved and that would be a nightmare. Dealers—human or shifter—couldn't be trusted. No, he had to be smart this time around. He'd nearly gotten busted in California years ago, so he'd relocated.

And Ana had the *perfect* spread of property for his future endeavors.

The curvature of her mountain would protect them from prying government satellites and, more important, she had fertile, rich soil. He could grow during the spring, summer and early fall. "Forget making any offer. We kill Connor and Liam, then take what we should have two months ago."

"What about the rest of his pack?"

Taggart shrugged. He didn't know much about them yet, but from what he'd seen the other night, the new males were warriors. Didn't matter. He had his own share of warriors and he relished the challenge. "If they're resistant, we'll kill them too. I don't think we'll have to, though. Everyone needs an Alpha." Whether alpha, beta, or warrior, most wolves yearned for a strong Alpha to lead them. It was in their blood.

Chapter 7

Ana placed her hands on her hips as she looked up at Ryan, one of the new wolves. He was tall and broad, even for a lupine shifter. Taller than Connor. "Is there a problem here?"

"Yes, there is," Teresa interrupted. "He wants to change how I stock *everything*."

Ryan's jaw clenched once in frustration. He appeared to be in his early thirties by human standards, but Connor had told her he was almost 150. Older than most shifters she knew. Shifters might not age at the same pace as humans, but their eyes gave them away every time. Right now he was tempering his annoyance. "I just thought it would make more sense to move the saddles in where the halters and leads are stored. It'll clear up some space, and then we can move the feed so that it's in a less damp area, which will save more money in the long term."

"There's not enough room to move everything around." Teresa's voice was heated.

His gaze snapped back to hers. "If you'd let me finish what I was saying before you bothered Ana, I would

have told you that I planned to build and mount a wall
rack for your saddles in addition to building more storage shelves. That'll clear up all the space you need."

Teresa's cheeks turned bright pink. "Oh."

Ana bit back a sigh. The barn was so thick with sexual
tension, even if she didn't have extrasensory abilities
she'd be able to see it. "Have you worked on a ranch
before, Ryan?"

He nodded. "I owned one many years ago."

When it was obvious he didn't plan to explain, she
continued. "If you see anything else around here that
could use some improvement, run it by Teresa first and I
promise she'll be willing to listen." She tilted her head in
her cousin's direction. "Isn't that right?"

"Yeah," Teresa muttered.

Shaking her head, she started to leave them when a
gray wolf cub tumbled past her. "What the . . . ?"

A second later, a female *jaguar* cub followed hot on
his tail. The spotted animal raced past her so quickly, it
took a moment for her to digest what she was seeing.
Ana turned and started after them, to find Ryan scoop-
ing them up, one in each hand.

"What the hell is going on?" She hadn't meant to
shout but the words flew out.

The few horses whinnied nervously. By now they
were used to wolves, but the scent of a jaguar was something else entirely. A new predator—tiny as she was—
would take some getting used to.

Both cubs buried their faces against Ryan's neck. He
grinned and held out the tiny jaguar. "This is Vivian."
She tried to scramble away but he held her tight. Then
he held out the gray wolf, who attempted to wiggle out
of Ryan's hand. "And this is Lucas."

Her heart instantly warmed at the sight of the two
cubs. Even the jaguar. It had been a long time since their

family had any little ones running around. Most of her packmates were younger than her and weren't interested in settling down yet. And all the pregnant shifters, with the exception of her mother, had died from the poisoning. Almost on cue, an ache sparked in her chest at the thought of her mother dying from a broken heart, unable to live without her mate. But Ana pushed past the pain as she eyed the little ones. Seeing them somehow made the ache inside easier. Life was treasured among her kind and, well, the cubs were totally adorable. "This might sound like an obvious question, but who are they and where did they come from?"

"Uh . . ." Ryan looked down and for the first time since she'd met him, he seemed uncomfortable. His neck turned a dark shade of red.

Behind Ana, Teresa chuckled at his obvious discomfort, which earned her a glare from Ryan.

Okay, if he wasn't going to answer, she'd try another tactic. "Were they with you guys the other night in the woods?"

He shrugged and the jaguar tried to burrow deeper against his neck. "Sort of."

"That's not an answer," she said through gritted teeth.

"I think you should talk to Connor about this."

"Well, he's not here, is he?" He'd gone out with some of the men to scout their property. And if he knew what was good for him, he'd stay gone for a while. Ryan didn't respond, which only infuriated her more. She was Connor's mate—almost—so he should be answering her. "Where have they been sleeping?"

"Our cabin."

She glared at him but softened as she looked at the cubs. "You guys want to come with me and get cleaned up?"

The jaguar turned her head around and stared at Ana. Almost instantly, the little feline jumped at her.

Muddy paws and all. Something warmed inside her when the cub curled up and rested her head on Ana's shoulder. Cubs were so trusting sometimes. They just wanted someone to take care of them. "Do they have any clothes?"

"Yeah." Ryan shook his head as Lucas dove for the ground and scampered off.

Ana was tempted to run after him, but he'd been fine by himself for the past day so she let him go.

Ana nodded at her cousin. "Grab this one's belongings and bring them to the main house. I'm going to move her in there for a while. She shouldn't be stuck with all those males."

"Man, I'm glad I'm not Connor right now," Teresa muttered as she walked away.

She should be. Connor had a lot of explaining to do. Hiding this from her was just stupid. As she headed for the house, she held the she-cat away from her. "You're Vivian, huh?"

In response, she licked Ana's face and her heart melted. No wonder Connor had taken them in. Even though she was pissed he hadn't told her about them, looking at this one's cute face was enough to melt most of her anger. But not all of it.

Liam shifted against the booth and discreetly wiped his damp palms on his jeans. He'd been watching December's store all day from across the street—and trying not to feel too much like a stalker—and no one had bothered her. Unless a couple of yuppie-looking assholes in ski jackets hitting on her counted. Or they might have just been buying books. Either way it didn't matter to him. The most primal side of him didn't want any males talking to her. Barbaric, yes. Just the way it was.

He checked his watch again, even though he knew

barely a minute had passed. He'd told her he'd be at the pub today, waiting, and she was only five minutes late. Maybe he should have expected her not to show. Especially after what had happened earlier that morning. Still, she hadn't seemed like she had a vendetta against shifters.

Unlike her brother.

Something familiar tickled his nose. He looked across the sea of tables and booths. In the darkened atmosphere, booze, cheap perfume, and stale smoke drifted around him, but one scent nearly knocked him over.

He stood when he saw her. December tucked a bright curl behind her ear and glanced around at everyone. Her nervousness nearly overpowered the soft, fresh scent she emanated. He wasn't sure what it was, but it almost smelled like fresh linen. Crisp and clean, just like her. She wore a button-up cardigan underneath her thick down jacket. And her dark jeans were loose. Instead of showing off her delicious curves, it seemed she was intent on hiding them.

Not that it bothered him. He didn't want anyone else looking at her anyway. Still, he'd give anything to put his scent all over her.

"I wasn't sure you'd come," he said when she stood next to the booth.

"I almost didn't." Self-consciously she turned the bruised side of her face away.

On instinct, he reached out and touched her chin, forcing her to look at him. "I'm sorry this happened to you." If he'd been there, the person who'd hurt her wouldn't have gotten out of her house alive.

She shrugged, but he didn't miss the flare of fear in her eyes. At least she didn't pull away and that surprised the hell out of him. "It could have been a whole lot worse if my brother hadn't been there. He wasn't even supposed to be there, but his washing machine died so he was at my place doing laundry. After dinner he ended up falling asleep on the couch, watching television. I don't know what I'd have done if . . ." She trailed off as a shudder overtook her.

Unlike her brother, Liam would have ripped the guy's head clean off his body, but he didn't voice that out loud. No need to scare her before dinner.

A surprisingly violent urge ripped through him as he thought about what could have happened to her. He'd been keeping those thoughts at bay all day so he wouldn't go mad. As unwanted images flared in his mind, the lock he'd kept on his thoughts popped open. Immediately he wanted to kick himself for putting off those pheromones. When shifters exuded too much emotion they didn't hide it well. The nearby humans might not understand exactly what was going on, but they'd be able to sense the shift in the air.

"Are you okay?" December asked softly.

"I should be asking you that. Do you want to sit?" He motioned to the booth.

Hope bloomed inside him when she slid in and dropped her purse next to her. She shrugged out of her coat. "I don't know why I'm here, but I wanted to see you. I feel like you did something to me."

His eyebrows rose. "Did something?"

"Put a spell on me or something," she muttered as her cheeks flushed.

He tried to hold back a bark of laughter, but failed. "That's called chemistry, baby, but I'll *do* anything you'd like me to. All you've got to do is ask."

The stain on her ivory skin flushed deeper but at least she wasn't running out the front door. Once the waitress took their drink orders, he relaxed against his seat. If she was ordering a drink, it meant she planned to stay.

Liam just hoped he could carry on a decent conversation. He swallowed hard and focused on her bruise. "Did that bastard do anything else to you?"

"Ah . . . no. And I'm sorry my brother dragged me out to your place earlier. I'd told him about what happened in the store with your brother—the guy who *said* he was your brother—and he jumped to conclusions."

"That happens to us a lot."

"It shouldn't." She reached out and placed a comforting hand over his. She looked just as surprised as he felt by the contact.

For a moment he forgot to breathe. As he stared at her delicate hand covering his, his chest constricted when the image of that hand covering another part of his anatomy flashed in his mind. He shook his head. If he let his thoughts stray in that direction, he was going to be in serious trouble. She snatched her hand back before he could read into it.

"This is a nice place." Lame small talk, but he had to think of something to say when all he wanted to do was reach out and touch her.

She nodded and a real smile played across her lush mouth. "I love Kelly's. The bar and even these booths were shipped over from Galway more than twenty years ago."

"Have you ever been there?" he asked. The way her voice softened when she said *Galway* was interesting.

"No. One day, though." Her voice was wistful, hopeful.

Damn, if it would make her smile he'd take her there himself. For a monthlong vacation. As a rule the Irish didn't have problems with shifters. Or any supernatural beings, for that matter. Except maybe vampires. He and December would stay in bed-and-breakfasts dotted along the coast. Maybe hop on over to Scotland. It had been too long since he'd seen his homeland. That was the one nice thing about the mountains of Fontana: lush, rolling hills.

"How old are you?" Her abrupt question brought him back to reality.

"Excuse me?"

"I've heard that you age a lot slower. I just wondered how old you were—that's all." She idly ran her finger up and down the condensation on the outside of her beer bottle.

For a split second he thought about lying to her because he didn't want to freak her out, but knew he'd regret it. "I'm a hundred and eight."

Her blue eyes widened. "So what happens if you . . ."

"If I what?"

Her face flamed. "What if you want to settle down with a human or something? I mean, I've heard of humans mating—is that the right word?—with shifters, but I've never actually known anyone who has. Do they just grow old and you don't?"

Damn, the woman was inquisitive. Not that he blamed her. Shifters didn't share their mating process with those they weren't intimate with. He chose his words carefully. "When humans and shifters bond, the humans' aging slows to match their mates'." Liam was sure there was some scientific explanation behind it, but all he knew was that Mother Nature had a way of working things out. He wouldn't know how to explain it to her even if he could. It was like he knew planes could fly, but he sure as hell couldn't explain how they stayed in the air. Once that bond was in place between a couple, the two were linked for life as bondmates. It probably had something to do with the biting claim the males gave to their females, because simply mated couples didn't link the way bondmates did. If there was no official bond, the female's aging didn't change. Well, unless the human female got pregnant. Or at least that's what he'd heard. It had been centuries since he'd even heard of a human and shifter bonding.

Her eyebrows knitted together even tighter. "Bonding? Is that different from mating?"

They were edging into dangerous territory.

She shook her head before he could brush off the question. "I'm sorry. I can't believe I'm asking you all these questions and we haven't even finished our first drink."

"No worries. It's only natural you'd be curious. Do you think we could order dinner before delving into the secret shifter handshake?"

His lame joke brought out a bright smile and laughter from her. Which was exactly what he craved from this woman. He simply wanted to get to know her. Find out what she liked to do when she wasn't working. What she liked in the bedroom. The other shit could work itself out later.

He gripped his beer tighter in his hand and scooted closer to the back of the booth. That shifter was so wrapped up in December, he doubted he'd sense him nearby but he wasn't going to take any chances. And he really didn't want December to see him. He knew her and her brother and didn't want to get caught in a conversation with her. Not with a shifter so close.

He'd heard that their kind could sense fear and loathing and everything else in between. If he wanted to kill the rest of the Cordona pack, he'd have to tread carefully. Going after Ana the other day at the hospital had been a stupid mistake, but now he planned to finish what he'd started.

It was only a matter of time. And planning. These new males on the ranch added a wrench into his plans.

"Can I get you another beer, darlin'?" the waitress asked, jarring his attention away from the booth across the bar.

"Wh ... oh yeah. One more, then bring me the check, please."

"You got it."

As she sauntered away, his eyes were drawn back to December and that hulking shifter. He wanted to go over there and empty his gun into that abomination's heart. Not that it would do any good.

Silver bullets were damn near impossible to come by except for in law enforcement, and even then humans had to register their purchases. If he was caught with silver bullets on his person he'd be in a shitload of trouble. Unfortunately he didn't know how to make them himself. Months ago he'd briefly entertained the idea of searching out some APL members, because he'd heard a few of them had moved to the area, but he didn't want to work with a bunch of redneck hillbillies. Even if they likely knew how to make their own bullets, he still couldn't do it. They had ties to those neo-Nazis and he wasn't a racist. He was better than that, and he liked to work alone.

As he watched the shifter across the bar he narrowed his gaze. Shifters were freaks. Animals. They should be the ones in hiding. Or better yet, exterminated altogether. He could feel the rage starting to burn through his veins so he pulled out a twenty and dropped it on the table.

The other beer forgotten, he slipped out of his booth and out the back door. Soon he'd wipe out the Cordona women; then he'd take out Taggart's pack. Shifters would realize their kind wasn't welcome here, and things would go back to the way they used to be.

*   *   *

Connor slid off the horse and loosely handled the reins as he led the giant animal toward one of the stables. It had been years since he'd gone riding and he'd forgotten how much he enjoyed it. The past few decades he and Liam had been busy buying and selling real estate and everything else had taken a backseat. After he'd left Ana he'd decided that the next time he saw her, things would be different. *He* would be different. When he'd first met her he'd had enough to live on—only what he needed, which hadn't been much—but it hadn't been enough to take care of her the way she deserved. Now he could take care of her and their pack indefinitely. It wasn't just a matter of pride but a matter of survival. While he'd be happy living in the woods with nothing more than the fur on his back, Ana deserved a hell of a lot better than that.

Some of the horses whinnied as he strode into the barn, but didn't make too much of a fuss. He'd separated from his men earlier and they'd each ridden to different points along the property. There were still a few places he needed to check out, but he planned to do that with Ana. He wanted some alone time with her and if he remembered correctly, she was most at ease when she was riding. He'd use any advantage he could get to loosen her up.

As he pulled open the door to the empty stable, Ryan stepped out of the neighboring one. "Hey, Connor."

Before he could respond, Lucas peeked out from behind Ryan, wearing jeans and an oversized jacket. The blond-haired little boy had a scowl on his face.

"What's he doing out?"

Ryan shrugged. "He and Vivian decided they didn't feel like being cooped up anymore."

Connor scrubbed a hand down his face. "Has Ana met them?"

Ryan nodded and his lips curved up slightly. "Yep."

Shit. He'd wanted to wait until tonight to tell Ana about the cubs. Bringing in potentially unwanted cubs could cause problems, but he hadn't been willing to abandon Lucas and Vivian.

He didn't think Ana would truly mind, but he remembered how prejudiced her father had been. Convincing her to join with his pack was one thing, but adding a jaguar cub to the mix was something else entirely. Cats and dogs didn't exactly blend well, and ideals about species separation ran deep among a lot of shifters. In that respect, they weren't much different from humans. "Where's Vivian?"

"Cooking with Ana," Lucas grumbled. "And now she doesn't want to play with me anymore."

"She's *with* Ana?" He couldn't contain the shock in his voice. The jaguar cub didn't warm up to many people.

Ryan nodded again. "She's glued to her side. Oh, Ana wanted me to let you know that we're all having dinner in the main house tonight. Seven sharp. If I were you I wouldn't be late." Chuckling under his breath, he ruffled Lucas's hair. "Come on. You can help me brush down Connor's horse."

Connor pulled off his Stetson as he headed toward the house. Before facing Ana, he needed to clean up. And he figured it wouldn't hurt to let her cool down. He'd promised to be honest with her, and then she found out about the cubs this way.

He should have known better. Hell, he *did* know better. His lie had been destined to bite him in the ass. Worse, Liam had been right. He should have just sucked it up and told her. Sighing, he pushed open the front door and was immediately accosted by her subtle scent. She might be in the main house at the moment, but her essence surrounded him here.

Scenting her, seeing her every day was something he could quickly get used to. Half a century of pent-up sexual frustration was about to come raging to the surface, and he feared he'd already screwed things up. In the darkest part of his mind, the place he kept locked up tight, he wondered if Liam was right.

Maybe he shouldn't have walked away from her. He could have let her choose. She'd been so young then. So happy and deeply immersed in her pack. So very secure of her place in the world. He could have asked to mate with her, but if she'd said yes her father would have banished her.

She could have chosen her family over him, though, and he wasn't sure he could have lived with that. The not knowing was better. At least he had *something* to hold on to: the dream that she would have picked him. Hell, even if she'd chosen him, she'd have resented him in the end. Taking her away from everything she'd ever known. Her sisters, cousins, parents.

He shook his head as he ascended the stairs. It was time for a shower. A cold one. He'd had a hard-on the entire ride back to the stables, thinking about her. He'd planned to take things to the next level tonight but he had a funny feeling he'd be sleeping in the doghouse instead.

Of course, that was if she didn't kick him out of her life entirely.

Chapter 8

"Press the cookie cutter like this, Vivian." Ana motioned with the rounded cutter and pressed it into the thick dough.

The dark-haired girl used both hands to mimic Ana's actions. "Like this?"

"You got it. Think you can finish the rest of them?"

She nodded, then ducked her head shyly and focused on her task.

As Ana pulled the roast from the oven, Carmen strode into the kitchen. "You need any help?"

She shook her head and motioned toward Vivian. "Help her with the *polvorones*."

"Yum." Carmen's eyes lit up as she sat at the kitchen table and started talking to Vivian. The girl mumbled a few words, but Carmen talked enough for three people and she seemed to understand Vivian's quiet nature.

Vivian had said only a few words. Ana guessed she was probably about ten years old in human and shifter years. She didn't know much about feline shifters, but she was pretty sure they developed at the same pace as wolves. Vivian was a tiny thing, even for her age, but she seemed to be well-adjusted. *A kitty cat living among a bunch of wolves.* Ana grinned to herself at the thought. If she'd been that age she'd have likely been scared out of her mind. No, she knew she would have been. Especially without her sisters or family around.

As her thoughts drifted, she frowned. She didn't understand why Connor had kept the existence of the cubs from her. Maybe he'd fathered one of them and hadn't wanted to tell her. Did he think she'd shun him because of something like that? If he did, then he didn't know her at all. That stung almost as much as the blatant lie. He could argue that it was simply an omission, but to her it was a lie. And a big one.

She heard the front door open and shut. No one bothered locking doors on the ranch during the day. Well, except bedroom doors. Front doors didn't matter much. They scented each other coming long before anyone reached the front stoop. Sometimes she hated that ability. Like now, when she knew Connor was likely making his way through the house, toward the kitchen.

Her fingers clenched around the bottle of wine she'd grabbed from the cupboard but she forced herself to relax. If he was lucky, she wouldn't toss it at his head.

"Something smells good." Connor's deep voice enveloped her, but she refused to turn around.

Carmen saved her. "Yeah, Ana's been working all afternoon. Well, Ana and Vivian. I can't believe you didn't bring this adorable little cub around sooner."

Connor cleared his throat. "Ah . . ."

Carmen wasn't through with him. "Why is that, Connor? She's been such a big help around here already with these cookies. I don't think Ana could have made them without her. And I'm pretty sure *you* are not going to get any tonight."

Vivian giggled softly, so Ana pushed aside her fear

and turned to face them. Like a total chicken, she averted her eyes toward the table. Away from where Connor hovered in the doorway.

"I helped set the table," Vivian said proudly as she slid from her seat and came to stand next to Ana. For the first time since she'd met her, the little she-cat beamed.

"Yes, you did. You're a much better helper than my sisters." She winked at Carmen. When Vivian grabbed Ana's free hand, her heart squeezed. She hadn't said anything but it was obvious her mother wasn't around. Or worse. As someone who had just lost both her parents, some part of Ana wanted to do everything she could to protect this cub. "You want to help me by telling everyone upstairs that dinner is ready?"

Vivian nodded but didn't let go of her hand. Instead she looked up at her with big brown eyes that could melt snowcaps.

"You want me to go with you?"

She nodded again.

Ana looked at Connor and shoved the wine bottle into his hand. "There are two more in the cupboard. Would you mind putting them on the table?" She kept her tone civil, bordering on saccharine sweet. Only because she knew it would bother him.

At least he had the decency to look uncomfortable. "Of course. Do you want to talk before dinner?" His voice was low, but Vivian was inches away, practically attached to her.

"About what?" She lifted a mocking eyebrow.

"We'll talk *after* dinner, then." His jaw clenched tightly, and a perverse part of her took immense pleasure in it.

In response, she snorted loudly, which earned her a quiet giggle from Vivian. *Talk after dinner, my ass.* But what did he expect? He was the liar. Not her. And she wasn't going to have this conversation in front of anyone else, especially not a cub.

Still holding Vivian's hand, she strode through the attached dining room, where two long, rectangular tables held more than two dozen chairs. Some of the men would be patrolling and she was pretty sure Liam was still in town, so there should be enough room. If not, they'd add more chairs.

As they reached the top of the stairs, Vivian clenched her hand tightly. "Will you read me a story tonight?"

Surprised, she looked down at the girl. "Sure. What kind of stories do you like?"

"I have a lot of books but I like the one about the princess and the frog. My mommy used to read it to me."

Used to. Those two words answered her earlier worries. Ana's throat clenched, but she crouched down so that they were at eye level. "Where's your mommy now?" It was extremely rare for a shifter to abandon their young, but it did happen on occasion.

Vivian looked at a spot on the floor. "She's part of the earth now."

Ah, dead, then. "I'm sorry she's not here."

"Me too . . . You look a lot like her."

That explained why Vivian had been so attached to her. Ana's heart warmed even more. She didn't care where this cub had come from or the fact that she was a feline. She'd do everything she could to make sure she fit in. Clearing her throat and fighting back the lump in it, she stood. "Come on. Let's get everyone for dinner."

Connor stabbed a piece of beef with his fork. Ana had been effectively ignoring him all through dinner. Not in an obvious manner. She was civil, sweet even, when he asked her a question, but she'd kept her attention on her sisters and Vivian all night.

He doubted anyone else could sense the dissension, but he knew her well enough that she was just waiting to let loose on him. When some of the pack started to get up, he reached out and placed a hand over Ana's. The movement was slight but she tried to pull back from him.

He tightened his grip and turned her hand over.

Her lips pulled into a tight smile but she didn't struggle against his hold. "I need to help clean up."

"The others will take care of it. You cooked." He kept his voice low but there was no denying the subtle order.

"Yeah, we got it, Ana. Me and Carmen will bring out the cookies later." Vivian jumped down from her chair and balanced her plate in her hands as she headed for the kitchen.

"What do you want?" Ana asked quietly through gritted teeth.

"To talk." He lightly stroked her wrist with his thumb.

Her cheeks tinged pink at the gentle caress, but her eyes didn't soften. *Damn, I'm in trouble.*

"Fine. Back porch?"

Nodding, he stood and pulled out her chair. With a straight back, she marched past him with her nose held high. The haughty angle of her chin made him bite back a groan. Even pissed off, she got him hotter than anyone else ever could.

He walked outside first, and when he was sure they were alone he stepped back and let her onto the porch. She leaned against the wooden railing and crossed her arms over her chest.

Connor gave her space and sat on one of the rocking chairs. "Vivian seems very taken with you."

"And I'm very taken with her. She's easy to love."

"I should have told you about her."

"Yes, you should have. You should have told me

about her and Lucas." Her voice was tight and her eyes spit fire.

He searched for the right words. "I'm sorry."

"For what?"

"For not telling you about the cubs."

"You mean for *lying* to me?" Now there was no denying the heat in her voice.

"I didn't—"

"Yes, you did! Don't try to sugarcoat it. You lied to me. After everything I've agreed to, I don't understand why you'd lie about something so stupid. *So trivial!* It makes me wonder what else you've been keeping from me. Are you the father of one of the cubs? Or both?"

"No, I'm not."

It was slight, but she let out a sigh of relief at his answer. She pushed off the railing and took an angry step toward him. "Then why? Explain yourself, or I swear I'll back out of our arrangement right now and you can get the hell off my property."

An icy fist clasped around his heart. *Back out?* He couldn't—wouldn't—let her. "Vivian is a jaguar." He said the only thing he could think of.

"And?" She spread her hands in front of her questioningly.

He closed the distance between them until he'd caged her in against the railing. It was dirty to use his size against her but he needed her to be a little off balance. The thought of her backing out of their deal was enough to rip a hole in his chest. "I know you consider this arrangement temporary. I can see it in your eyes. None of this is temporary to me or my pack. We want to be here, and I want to take care of you. I thought if I dumped too much on you at once you'd have more ammunition to say no to the whole thing. And I wanted to ease you into the idea of letting a jaguar join our pack."

"Why?" Her dark eyebrows knitted together. Most of the anger had left her voice, only to be replaced by confusion.

"We were already bringing in a new female with Erin, and Vivian is a jaguar. I thought . . ." He shrugged as he let the unspoken words hang in the air.

Big mistake.

Her eyes flared again with anger and something worse: hurt. "I get it now. You thought I'd *actually* care that she's a different species. Do you really have such a low opinion of me? You think I'd abandon a little girl because of what she is? Why would you even want to mate with me if you think so little of me?" Her voice cracked on the last word.

Shit. When she said it like that, he knew she was right. He wished the floor beneath him would split open and swallow him. He reached for her, but she jerked away. His inner wolf howled in frustration. Every part of him wanted to comfort her. "I hadn't seen you in fifty years, Ana. I thought if there was a chance you'd . . ." He sighed. Any excuse was pathetic and she deserved better. "You're right. I shouldn't have lied and I should have had more faith in you. I made a stupid choice, but damn it, Ana, I really am sorry. Please don't let this come between us."

Her face deadpanned. "Where did you find them? Vivian told me her mother is dead, so I'm assuming her father is too."

He was surprised by the abrupt question but he answered truthfully. "Vivian's parents were killed in Colombia. I was friends with her father, and when I found out she was going to be placed with her maternal grandfather's pack, I . . . liberated her."

"You kidnapped her?"

He shifted his weight. "Not exactly. Her mother left

her pack for a reason, and I made a promise to Roberto— that was her father—that if anything ever happened to them I'd take care of Vivian and any future cubs they might have. I've got the necessary paperwork if anyone comes after her, but I doubt it'll ever come to that."

"That's a pretty big responsibility to take on." Despite her stony stare, her voice softened.

He shrugged, mainly because he didn't want to get into the details. Asking a wolf to take care of feline offspring was almost unheard-of, but Vivian's grandfather was a piece of shit who liked to abuse little girls, and Roberto hadn't had many friends. Hell, Connor hadn't had many friends around the time they'd met either, but he'd been doing business in South America and Roberto had helped him out on more than one occasion. Even if they hadn't been friends, he'd respected the feline shifter for his honesty and wouldn't have been able to say no to the request anyway.

"What about Lucas?"

"Ryan found him in Montana a few years ago when he was barely four. He'd been abandoned as far as anyone knows, though I find that hard to believe. It's possible his parents were killed, but either way, we don't know who his parents are—or were—and Lucas doesn't remember anything. Lucas has been with Ryan since before joining my brother and me."

She was silent as she digested his words. More than anything he wanted to wipe the hurt off her pretty face. Ana was completely right. He should have trusted his instinct when it came to *her*. He should have come clean about the cubs right away. Instead he'd acted like a coward.

A lead ball sank into his stomach. If she decided to back out of their arrangement, he couldn't stop her. They hadn't mated and he had no claims on her. But he wouldn't let her go without a fight. Even if he had to play dirty. After having a taste of her last night, walking away was unthinkable. "You promised to give us a shot."

"Says the man who's been lying to me," she shot back immediately.

The dominant animal in him wanted to throw her over his shoulder and simply claim her, making it impossible for her to kick him off the ranch. His humanity won out. "Where does this leave us?"

She paused, but finally spoke. "I'm staying here tonight. I need some space."

Every primal instinct inside him wanted to argue with her, but the human voice of reason told him to shut the hell up. He'd already pissed her off enough. Forcing her to stay at their place would only make things that much worse between them. "I'll see you in the morning."

"You're not going to fight me?"

"You'd prefer I did?"

She eyed him warily. "No. You just seem to be accepting this too easily."

"I fu— messed up. I can take responsibility for that."

She paused for a long moment, then nodded. "Okay."

Without touching or kissing her—even though he desperately wanted to—he headed back in the house. As the door shut behind him he couldn't shake the feeling of dread that settled over him. He might have ruined their relationship before it ever had a chance to start.

He opened the trash bag and pulled out his camouflage jacket. He'd kept it in the plastic bag with a bunch of pine boughs for two days to mask his scent. There was no way of knowing how many of those abominations would be patrolling the Cordona land but he knew they'd be out there. And they'd be able to smell him if he didn't cover his tracks.

Their security would be better, but he'd gotten onto their land undetected before and he'd do it again. Soon the Cordonas would be dead and so would the Taggart pack. They were trickier to get to, but he'd recently come across some information that would help him deal with that problem soon. If he couldn't kill them, he was going to make sure they got locked up and kicked off their land for drug running. Unfortunately the Cordonas were above reproach, so he wouldn't be able to pin any illegal activity on them.

After slipping on his jacket and skull cap, he shoved the bag under the seat of his truck and got out. He'd turned off the dome light so he wouldn't attract any more attention than necessary. Staring at the edge of the woods, he glanced around, but didn't feel like he was being watched.

He patted his jacket pocket even though he knew what he needed was still there. The bulge underneath his hands reassured him. His boots made minimal noise as he skirted through the woods. He'd grown up here, knew this land as well as the animals. It was simply a matter of making it—and getting back to his truck—without being caught.

Once he traveled a few miles inland toward the ranch, his heart started to pound mercilessly against his chest. He was so close. Despite the cold, he wiped sweaty palms against his pants, then cursed himself. He couldn't afford to emit too much body odor.

Even in the dark he could see the cluster of homes surrounded by fences. Their garden was dormant now so he couldn't poison their fresh food, and he couldn't poison their wells like he had last time. They wouldn't be using them so soon after the poisoning. But he could break into one of their storage sheds and contaminate their bottled water and canned foods.

Keeping low to the ground, he inched his way until he reached the shed farthest from the barn and parking structure. Right in the middle of enemy territory, he'd never felt more alive in his life. Terror forked through him, but so did an exhilarating sense of power. Their lives were in his hands and he planned to make them suffer and die. With his glove-covered hand, he tried the metal knob once, but it was locked. He picked the lock as quickly as he could.

Once inside the small storage facility, he glanced around. Cases of bottled water, flavored water and juices were stacked against one wall, and a small amount of canned food was on the other. Not bothering with the food, he headed for the beverages instead. He pulled a syringe from his pocket, bypassed the plain water and bent to the first case of flavored water. Quickly and carefully he injected bottles in each case with colloidal silver. The colored liquid covered any traces of the color of the silver. As he continued injecting, he kept his focus on the cases closest to the door. Those would get used first.

Now all he had to do was wait for them to get sick again. Once their defenses were down he'd be able to strike harder. This time he wasn't going to stop until every one of them was dead.

Connor gritted his teeth as he faced off with the older wolf. "No disrespect, Alpha, but—"

"You disrespect me by even coming here. I see the way you carry on with my daughter. It is disgusting. Now you dare ask to mate with her. Unthinkable!"

"I've shown her nothing but the respect she deserves." And restraint. He hadn't even kissed the innocent she-wolf, though his inner wolf howled at him all the time, demanding just a small taste. A little nibble. But he knew he'd never stop once he'd held Ana.

"She's promised to another." The man's words sliced through the air with arrogant finality.

Connor's eyes narrowed. *"She's never said anything to me about that."*

"And why would she? You're a passing fancy. You will be nothing but a small memory to her soon."

Did Ana even know her father had promised her to someone? She would have told him, wouldn't she? *"I think she has the right to make that decision, sir."*

"Fine. I'll allow her to decide. You or her pack. If she chooses you, I'll banish her forever. You and your mutt brother have no place in my pack. I've given you shelter, and this is how you repay me? You go too far coming here tonight." The truth of the old wolf's words hit Connor square in the chest.

He meant everything he said. He'd banish sweet Ana from the only family, the only life she'd ever known. Her sisters and mother were her entire world.

"You would do that to your own daughter?" His throat tightened painfully.

"If she chooses a mongrel with a dirty language over her own people, she's no daughter of mine."

"She's your daughter!" The reality of the situation rolled over him. Deep down he knew that no matter what he said, the old Alpha would never change his mind.

"She's also a member of my pack. I have a duty to my people to protect them from outsiders."

"I don't want to harm you or your pack. I just want the freedom to be with Ana. I know she feels the same way about me. Don't you care for her happiness?"

The old wolf laughed sharply. The harsh sound grated against Connor's ears. *"I know what is best for my daughter and you are not it. You have a decision to make."*

He opened his mouth to offer another argument but stopped. It didn't matter what he said. He could see the *resolution and loathing in the other wolf's eyes. Connor hadn't noticed it before—likely because he'd been so wrapped up in Ana. All he'd cared about was what she thought of him. Now he was in too deep to climb out of the hole he'd dug for himself. No matter what he did, it would hurt Ana in the end. He couldn't ask her to make such a big decision. She was too young.*

Connor turned and strode from the house. Anguish burrowed deep in his chest like a sharp, silver-pointed arrow, making it difficult to breathe, but he continued walking. And kept walking . . .

Connor jerked upright in bed. Immediately his eyes were drawn to the empty spot in the bed. Growling at the empty room, he punched his pillow. He hadn't dreamed about *that day* in years. The memory of Ana's father's words and obvious disdain rolled around in his head. If only the old wolf could see him now. He'd not only taken over his pack, but he was going to mate with his oldest daughter.

The bitter thought tore at his insides. He shouldn't give a shit what that old man thought. And he didn't. Or at least that's what he told himself.

He shifted against the sheets and stared blindly at the ceiling. Ana would be next to him tomorrow night.

Chapter 9

Ana quietly shut her bedroom door behind her. For some reason she almost felt like a stranger in the house. Which was stupid.

She'd been living here for decades, but sleeping here last night had felt almost wrong. It's not that she'd missed Connor's strong arms embracing her—because she hadn't. And it's not as if she'd missed the feel of his mouth on her lips. Because she *hadn't*. Or at least that was the lie she told herself. So why had she woken up aching for his touch? His strong embrace?

She rolled her eyes at her thoughts as she headed downstairs. A steaming cup of coffee would ease her mind. Since no one else was up, she'd get to make it exactly the way she liked.

When she pushed open the door to the kitchen, she froze. Connor sat at the table in front of his laptop, sipping from a coffee mug. His brown hair stuck out in a few places, as if he'd just woken up. He looked adorable and sexy at the same time. He fixed those stormy green eyes on her and her knees went weak. A man didn't have a right to look so good at this ungodly hour.

"What are you doing here so early?" The question came out harsher than she'd intended.

"Good morning to you too," he murmured as he raked an approving, heated look down the length of her body.

When his eyes zeroed in on her breasts, her covered nipples peaked under his scrutiny. They rubbed against her sweater with painful awareness.

She gritted her teeth. It wasn't fair that he had such an effect on her body. No doubt he knew it. The only thing that made her feel better about that was the lust she scented from him. "Sorry, I . . . never mind." She grabbed her favorite purple mug and poured herself a hot drink. Inhaling, she savored the rich French-roast aroma and tried to ignore him.

"How'd you sleep?" he asked as she took a seat across from him.

"Perfect." She doubted he'd believe her lie.

"I didn't," he growled.

She lifted an eyebrow. "Is that right?"

"You should have been next to me."

She shrugged casually even though she felt anything but. "And you shouldn't have lied to me."

Instantly his eyes darkened. "I missed you last night."

The abrupt admission made her pause. No doubt the words were sincere. He was hard to read sometimes, and forget about revealing any sort of emotions. The fact that he'd admitted something so simple shouldn't matter, but it touched her in a way she wasn't sure she was ready to come to terms with.

Still, she didn't say anything. Her parents had never been big on outward affection, and while she'd respected them she wanted something different for herself. She wasn't willing to take that risk with Connor, though. If anyone could break her heart, it was him. That wasn't going to happen. She wouldn't let it.

He continued staring at her. There were so many promises in his eyes, it made her abdomen clench with need. She could practically envision what he was thinking. Probably because she was thinking the same thing. Right now the thought of their naked bodies intertwined while he took her on the kitchen table sounded wildly right. Her nipples peaked even harder against her sweater, and Connor cracked a knowing grin.

"You all right?" he asked, his voice heated.

The question dragged her out of her fantasies. "What are you doing on the computer?"

"Business."

Could he be a little more evasive? "You never told me exactly what you and Liam do."

He shrugged. "Decades ago we sold some antique items that gave us enough to live comfortably, and recently we've made a few real estate investments."

Antiques and real estate? "Hmm."

His eyes narrowed. "What does that mean?"

"Nothing. It's just all very vague. And I don't see you out antiquing with your brother. That's a little too metrosexual, especially for someone like you."

He frowned. "Metrosexual?"

She shook her head and bit back a smile. Of course he wouldn't know what the word meant. "Never mind."

His frown didn't disappear. "I didn't say I went antiquing. I said I sold some *antiques*. You think I can't take care of our pack?"

Where did that come from? "Uh, no. I just wanted to know . . ."

He snapped his laptop shut and leaned back in his chair, all his attention focused on her. "What is it you want to know? I'll answer anything."

Everything you've been doing the past fifty years. She wanted to ask but was afraid of the answer. What if he'd left her because he'd found someone else? And what if the reason he'd come back was because she was his second choice? A weird ache burned in her chest. That kind of knowledge would sear a hole inside her that she didn't think would ever heal. She rubbed her sternum as if it could dull the intangible pain before pushing her chair back. She cleared her throat as she tried to think of something semi-intelligent to ask. "Uh, I wondered if you were a boxers or briefs kind of guy." The comment popped out so fast she couldn't rein in her big mouth. She hadn't meant to ask it—even if she *did* want to know the answer—but at least it had the intended effect on Connor.

He blinked once as he stared at her. His green eyes filled with not shock exactly, but mild surprise. His mouth parted slightly, and she smiled inwardly that she was able to take him off guard and hopefully push him off-kilter just a little. She felt unbalanced this morning and didn't want to be alone in that.

Her tiny victory was short-lived when a grin spread across his face. "You want to find out right now?" he asked playfully.

She couldn't help the smile that pulled at her lips. He'd been the first male she'd ever flirted with, and she found she'd missed the light flirty banter that had once flowed so freely between them. Even if she didn't want to admit it. Still, it was tempting. "Sorry. No time this morning."

He stared hard at her for another long moment before standing. "What are your plans for the day?"

She placed her cup in the sink. "I'll be doing what I do every Monday: riding along the south end of the property. Checking on the cattle and the fences. We all take turns and—"

"Good. I'll go with you."

Alarm jumped inside her as he took a few steps toward her. "That's not necessary."

"I want to see what you do and get a better feel for the day-to-day workings." He leaned past her as he placed his mug in the sink. When he did, his arm brushed against her shoulder and she had the sudden overwhelming—very annoying—urge to kiss him.

Looking at his lips, she licked her own.

"Keep looking at me like that and we're not going to get anything done today." There was a seductive promise in his deep voice. One she very much wanted to find out if he'd keep.

She averted her gaze. Suddenly light flirting didn't seem so harmless. Not when so much sexual tension hung between them. So many unspoken things. She could feel her self-control slipping away and that scared her. If she gave in to him right now he'd hold all the power. She knew eventually they'd cross that line of physical intimacy, but it couldn't be this morning. Not until she got her equilibrium back. "We should get going."

"You sure about that?" The question was a seductive growl.

Am I? "Yeah," she muttered.

"Then stop staring at me like that." He laughed softly as he headed toward the door.

At least one of them had control.

"How did Vivian sleep last night?" he asked.

"Okay, I guess. She tossed and turned a lot, but after waking up once she didn't stir the rest of the night. Or if she did, she didn't wake me." Ana had let Vivian sleep in her room last night. It couldn't turn into a habit, but the little girl had practically begged, and big brown eyes were apparently Ana's weakness. She hadn't been able to say no.

As they stepped outside the crisp, clean morning air rolled over her. A light fog had descended across the ranch. Patches of ice littered the ground and icicles hung from the outside of the barn. They'd melt off once the sun was fully up, but for now they created an icy decoration.

"Why am I surprised you like Bear?" Ana shook her head as Connor opened the stall door to the hulking Irish Draught stallion.

"I didn't pick him. He picked me." Connor slowly entered and led him out.

She nervously waited while he saddled and mounted him. The stallion was a well muscled, beautiful animal. In the sunlight his coat gleamed a shiny black. The stubborn thing usually bucked men, but by his submissive trot, it seemed he'd picked a new owner. Interesting. Bear hadn't even let her father ride him.

Ana strode down a few gates and opened Adalita's door. She always rode the same purebred Andalusian, and the chestnut animal rarely let anyone else touch her. Ana murmured soothingly to her as she petted her soft coat and saddled her.

Once they were past the first two gated fields, the grassy hills stretched out before them for miles. She pushed her feet into the stirrups and squeezed her legs together. Her horse responded immediately and increased its gait to a faster walk. She didn't have to say anything to Connor, as he sped up and kept pace with her.

She was thankful he didn't seem to want to chat this morning. Riding Adalita was usually her only alone time on the crowded ranch, but Connor was a good riding companion. The man never made idle chitchat. She shot him a quick glance. "Are you okay if we go faster?"

He raised an insulted eyebrow. Before she could signal her horse, Connor pushed his into a trot.

It was easy to feel like they were the only two people on the planet on such a quiet morning. With the exception of their horses, everything was eerily silent as they headed across the property. Her thighs were starting to burn when Connor abruptly stopped.

Pulling tight on the reins, she stopped and turned around. "What is it?"

"Do you smell that?"

She wrinkled her nose and shook her head. She only scented typical earthy smells. "What do you smell?"

"Danger."

The one word answer sent a chill skittering up her spine. Her father had been the same way. He'd often scented things the rest of the pack couldn't. It usually wasn't something tangible in the air, but more of a feeling he had. Maybe it was an Alpha thing. And it wasn't something Connor would joke around about.

He held a finger to his lips and pointed toward a cluster of trees. Quietly she followed as he turned Bear around and headed for the woods. They dismounted and tethered the horses to a fallen log.

"What's going on?" She kept her voice low.

"It could be nothing. Something in the air just smells . . . off." His green eyes had nearly turned black, and she knew he was ready to shift to his wolf form at a moment's notice.

"We're close to Taggart's property line. Maybe that's what you're scenting."

"Maybe . . . Stay here," he ordered. Without giving her a chance to respond, he stalked back toward the thinnest cluster of trees.

Ana looked at the horses, then at Connor's retreating back. Adalita whinnied quietly, but neither animal seemed bothered by anything. Still, she didn't like the thought of Connor heading into something without any backup. Shedding her jacket, she draped it across her saddle, then pulled a silver dagger from her pack.

There weren't many things she feared in life except her own kind and maybe faeries—and the fae didn't venture into North America often unless they had a damn good reason. They lived mainly in Scotland and Ireland. If she ever thought about feeling sorry for herself in regard to shifter rules, she reminded herself she was glad she wasn't part of the fae. Talk about draconian rules. If it was a human Connor scented, then she wasn't really worried. It was difficult for humans and even vampires to hurt shifters. Vamps were fast, but unless they were ancient, they usually weren't fast enough. And it's not as if they came out during daylight hours. No, if Connor really had scented something, it was likely another shifter.

Probably lupine, but maybe feline or ursine. Though she doubted it. The majority of feline shifters lived in South America, and ursine shifters usually congregated farther up north. Of course, it could be a coyote shifter. There weren't any of their packs in at least a hundred-mile radius of the ranch, and if they tried to encroach on their land without announcing their presence first, the coyotes' council would be harsher on them than her own Council. Ana glanced around and tried to calm her nerves. She could stand there all day wondering *what if?* but it wouldn't do Connor any good.

Trailing after him, she paused when she reached the open field. He was gone but his sweater, boots and jeans were discarded by a tree. Her fingers tightened around her dagger as she took a few steps out into the open. Inhaling deeply, she scented something foreign. He'd been right.

Inhaling again, she tried to focus on the new scent. It was to her left.

Walking along the line of trees, she moved closer and closer to the edge of her property and Taggart's. She still had a couple hundred yards to go but that knowledge alone made her heart beat faster. She didn't want to get anywhere near that bastard. Connor didn't know Taggart's pack the way she did. Taggart was ruthless and didn't care about the Council's laws. If he challenged Connor, he'd fight dirty. The thought of him hurting Connor had her tightening her grip on her dagger.

Sudden movement from the trees made her pause. She crouched down next to one of the longleaf pine trees, and as soon as she did a squirrel let out a loud chirp. Glancing up, she spotted a gray squirrel and cringed. His tail twitched wildly as he continued chirping. The territorial alert was either directed at her or something else. Either way, he was likely to give away her position. Before she had a chance to move, a mangy, pale-gray lupine shifter emerged from the woods about twenty feet in front of her. It was skinny but still huge, almost her human height on all fours.

It jerked to a halt, then narrowed its glowing crimson eyes in her direction.

Her heart thumped erratically. Red eyes meant one thing.

It was feral.

By its wild eyes, she guessed it was diseased. Probably recently. Unless it had once been a human and turned against its will. She dismissed that thought as quickly as it entered her brain. Shifters didn't turn humans for sport. Most didn't undergo the change well and it was too dangerous anyway.

Clutching the weapon tightly, she took a wide step to the side. If she didn't provoke it, it might not attack. But she wasn't counting on that and was going to protect herself.

It growled deep in its throat. An eerie, whiny sound that sent icy chills spooling through her. By the look of it, the deranged animal hadn't eaten in a while either. Its ribs were visible and when it snapped at her, she got a view of nasty, sharp yellow teeth.

With her feet hip distance apart, she crouched and got ready for an attack. Normally she'd shift and run from such a large opponent. There wasn't enough time, and she'd be able to take him on better in her human form.

If he hadn't been feral, she wouldn't try to fight. But feral wolves didn't think like skilled hunters. They just wanted to kill and eat. Which made them weaker. All she had to do was stab him through the heart with her dagger.

Bracing herself, she waited for him to make the first move. He growled, then ran right at her. The thing had no strategy whatsoever. It just wanted to kill.

He was only a few feet away now. As he lunged, he bared his neck and underside to her. Dagger out, she leaned back, ready to strike. Before she could drive it into his chest, a mass of fur and muscle hurtled through the air.

"Connor!" Pure black fur and strong, muscular legs flew past her as he tackled the feral animal. When he stood on all fours, he was almost five feet tall. Terrifying and majestic at once.

For a feral wolf, the gray one was surprisingly agile. He took the hit from Connor and rolled across the grass before pouncing back to all fours.

When it lunged at Connor, Ana knew the fight was over before it started. Snarling wildly, it came at him with no regard for protecting its neck.

Connor easily ducked the strike. As the animal sailed past him, Connor turned lightning fast and caught it from behind. In one giant bite, he snapped the gray wolf's neck.

With a thud, it hit the soft earth. Still clutching her knife, Ana stared at the limp, lifeless animal. Its neck was bent at an awkward angle and blood pooled around its head, soaking the ground beneath it.

Before she could move, Connor shifted back to human form.

Connor could think of nothing else but Ana as he underwent the change. Pain ripped through him as his bones broke and his tendons and ligaments realigned. He tried to focus on the rush of rapture that would inevitably follow once he was back to his human form, but thoughts of Ana being hurt overrode everything. That was a special kind of agony all by itself.

Losing Ana . . . He cried out in pain as his bones shifted back into place. He blinked a few times as the world came into focus. His fingers dug into the earth beneath him.

"Connor, are you okay?" Ana crouched next to him and rubbed his back in soothing little circles.

Every part of him loved the feel of her hands on him. Still on his knees, he turned his head and stared at her. "Did he hurt you? What were you *thinking*?" Ignoring the dirt on his hand, he blindly reached for her and grasped one of her hands.

She raised a dark eyebrow and held up a silver dagger that gleamed wickedly under the rising sunlight. "I was thinking I'm almost seventy and know how to take care of myself. He was feral, not a warrior. I could have handled it."

"I told you to stay put. . . ." He frowned as he stared at the dagger. "Is that what I think it is?"

"It was blessed by the fae hundreds of years ago. It belonged to my father." The rare dagger would have plunged the feral wolf into a comalike state almost immediately. Fae magic was incredibly powerful and rarely used, and it surprised him she had something like this.

He warily eyed the weapon. Years before the Council had come out to the world and years before he'd moved to North America, his parents and first pack had been killed by faeries looking to expand their land in the Highlands of Scotland. He and Liam had been out playing and his father had telepathically warned them to stay away. At the time, he'd been ten and Liam eight. They'd waited hours in the woods for some kind of message from their father but none ever came. Eventually Connor had ventured back toward their land and had found the entire pack slaughtered. Blinking, he shook the images of the carnage away and focused on Ana. "Where did your father get it?"

"I don't know. I never asked. And who cares?" Dismissively she set it down and stroked a soft hand down Connor's back. "Are you sure you're okay? I've never seen anyone move so fast."

He didn't answer because he couldn't make his throat work. It didn't matter that Ana would have likely been able to protect herself. The vision of seeing her facing off with that mangy animal would forever be seared into his brain. If he could, he'd kill the thing all over again. Swallowing a curse, he leaned forward. She let out a small gasp before he covered her parted lips with his.

Hungrily he kissed her. Like a wild animal he ate at her mouth, afraid she'd somehow disappear.

There was a lingering taste of cinnamon coffee on her tongue. When she moaned into his mouth, his hips surged forward. He wanted to finally consummate their relationship, right here and now. Hell, he'd been ready for years. Forever, it felt like. And she wanted him. The knowledge urged him on.

The voice of reason shouted loudly in his head. Now wasn't the time or place. They had a dead, bloody problem lying a few feet away and another one he needed to tell her about.

He could feel his inner animal start to take over. He wanted to claim Ana so badly his body ached, and it had nothing to do with the fight.

Somehow he pulled his head back. As he witnessed the hunger in her dark eyes he had to remind himself why he'd stopped kissing her. "I have to get dressed; then we've got to get out of here."

She shook her head slightly, as if she'd forgotten where they were. Glancing over his shoulder, she frowned. "What about him?"

"I'll come back later with Liam to burn him."

"But we can't just leave him. What if he's one of Taggart's wolves and that monster comes looking for him?"

"It was a justified kill. He was on your property and he was feral. I did Taggart a favor."

"Taggart won't care. He'll try to use it against you. Trust me—he doesn't care about rules. We need to do something about this now."

The desperation in her voice made him growl. She'd been taking care of her pack for too long. Why couldn't she let him do his duty as Alpha? "Don't worry about that bastard. He's *my* problem, Ana. Besides, we've got other things to deal with."

"What are you talking about?"

"I've got something I need to show you." He grabbed his discarded clothes and shoes and quickly dressed. As he zipped up his jeans, he was mindful of his almost painful erection. No matter what else happened today, he and Ana were mating tonight. They wouldn't bond, of course, but he had to mark her. The world needed to know she was his. He couldn't take it any longer. She might have told him she wanted to wait, but every time they were together she acted otherwise.

When he started heading southeast, Ana grabbed his arm. "What are you doing? That's toward the property line."

"I know."

Quietly she fell in step with him. It was obvious she wanted to say more but she held back. Which was more than he could say for her earlier actions.

As Alpha it was his responsibility to protect his entire pack. "Why didn't you stay put like I told you?" He kept his voice low as they trekked across fallen leaves and dry grass. Many of the trees were bare because it was winter, but the forest was still relatively thick.

She looked at him guiltily. "I thought you might need some backup."

"Damn it, Ana. What I need is for you to stay safe. If anyone else had disobeyed a direct order—"

"Well, I'm *not* anyone else. I'm going to be your mate." She lifted her chin a notch higher in that haughty, sexy way he loved.

"That doesn't mean you get to pick and choose what you listen to."

"If you really want to mate with me, then you should know I don't take orders very well."

"Then I'll just have to come up with unique ways to *punish* you."

"P-punish me?" She faltered slightly.

He smothered a smile and dropped his voice even lower. "Mm-hmm. I think tonight I'm going to show you exactly how I punish disobedient she-wolves."

She didn't respond, but he scented her desire. Tonight he'd dominate her, but he'd also show her how much she meant to him. He didn't care what his brother said about restraint. Ana needed to know how he felt about her, and the only way he knew to show it was between the sheets. He planned to worship her the way she deserved.

As they neared the ledge, he stopped and motioned for her to crouch on the ground. There was a steep drop-off on her property that delved into a valley and right onto Taggart's land.

"What is that?" she whispered, even though they were more than a hundred yards away and a lot higher up. Shifters had sharp hearing. Two of Taggart's men stood guard outside a ranch-style, one-story house.

"You smell that?" he asked. It was a faint chemical odor. If they'd been humans they'd have to be much closer to scent it.

"Barely. It's like ammonia and burning plastic or something."

"I think they're cooking meth in there." He'd only seen a meth house once before, but it fit the profile.

"What?"

"Look at the windows." Despite the cold, they were all open, probably to ventilate the house. And there was a huge pile of smoldering embers to the south of the structure. No doubt where they'd been burning their trash. If Taggart was running a meth lab, he wouldn't take his trash anywhere or leave evidence of it. This far off the beaten path they'd be able to keep their drug production hidden.

"I know Taggart is an asshole, but selling hard-core drugs?" She scooted back a few inches from the ledge and turned on her side to face him.

"Might explain the feral shifter." For a shifter to turn feral, it was usually from disease or because a human had been turned against his will. That rarely happened. Drugs were the only other reason for a shifter to turn. There was a lot they didn't know about the aftereffects on their kind of all the new drugs that were available, so more than likely meth use had turned the wolf feral.

Her lips pulled into a thin line. "Even so, that doesn't explain the attacks in town. Why would he go out of his way to attack the sheriff's sister?"

"He wouldn't." Connor might loathe the other Alpha, but Taggart wouldn't bring unnecessary heat if he was selling drugs. It didn't make sense. So far the two attacks had been against one woman loosely connected to their pack and another whom his brother was interested in. The attacks on the ranch were just personal bullshit because Ana had rejected Taggart. At least those had stopped. Either way, this drug business was going to stop too.

Out of the corner of his eye he caught a flash of movement. "Look at that," he murmured.

Ana inched back up to the ledge. "Oh, my Lord."

Taggart walked out of the house and stripped off a surgical mask. He might not be using the drugs, but he sure as hell knew what was going on. He was probably checking on his production.

All Connor's protective instincts kicked in. If that was a cook house, there could be more feral wolves roaming around, and he didn't want Ana anywhere in the vicinity of that asshole Taggart. Wordlessly Connor placed a hand on her shoulder and nodded for her to move back.

Once they were almost back to the horses, Ana finally spoke. "I can't believe I'm saying this, but we should notify the police."

He shook his head. "No. The humans will lump us all into the same category. That shit is too close to your property and Taggart might try to claim that it's your meth house."

"But if we tell them about it, they'll have to believe us."

"We'll take care of this our way. I'll contact the Council and ask them to send an investigator." Or maybe the enforcer. Connor didn't like to bring in someone whose main intent would be to "clean house," but he'd learned a long time ago that humans had to be watched carefully. He wouldn't depend on their law enforcement when shifters had their own way to deal with problems.

The first five years after shifters and vampires came out of hiding had been tense. Out of necessity, the North American Council of lupine shifters had convened with the other councils around the world and for once, feline shifters and lupine shifters had worked together. Technology was advancing too rapidly and hiding from humans was becoming all but impossible. Vampires had been pissed when shifters had made the decision to announce their existence to the world, but they'd had no choice but to deal with it. Surprisingly the humans hadn't gone to war with them, though many had more or less expected it. Humans fought each other enough, and most civilized governments preferred to wage war in other countries anyway. With so many shifters and vampires living in all countries across the globe, a world war wasn't an option anyone wanted. Still, in smaller towns, if there was a problem it was so easy to blame any and all shifters. He'd seen it happen before and he wouldn't let anyone in his pack get railroaded. "I mean it, Ana," he growled. "No police."

She held up her hands in mock surrender. "I'm not going to do anything," she muttered.

"So far you haven't exactly shown you know how to listen."

"And you haven't shown you know how to tell the truth." Sarcasm laced her words—something he found he'd missed immensely.

He preferred any mood of hers over her anger. Smiling, he shook his head. "Don't change the subject."

"Fine. I swear I won't do anything stupid." She grinned playfully and nudged him with her hip as they walked.

When she smiled at him like that, it was hard to breathe. Her dark hair fell around her face in soft waves, and as his eyes traveled lower he had to bite back a groan. The woman rarely wore a bra and today was no different. It had nearly driven him crazy when they'd first met. He'd quickly realized she hadn't been doing it to tease him. Though that's what it felt like sometimes. Her nipples were visible through her sweater and all he could think about was running his tongue over her breasts and of the delicious moans that would come out of her. Tonight he wouldn't stop there.

His cock strained painfully against his zipper. He needed to get her naked and fast. "Want to go for a run before we head back?" His voice was hoarse but she didn't seem to notice.

She frowned. "You think we should?"

He shrugged. "That dead wolf isn't going anywhere and it's a ways from the property line."

She bit her bottom lip nervously, and he guessed it was because she'd have to get naked first. He wasn't sure why it should matter but something told him it did. "I'll turn around while you shift."

When she relaxed he knew he'd been right. "There's a creek about half a mile north of here. It's probably half-frozen, but we can leave our clothes with the horses and get a quick run in."

He resisted the urge to turn around as they undressed. Shifters had naturally higher body temperatures, so even though it was cold, it wasn't nearly as uncomfortable as it would be if they'd been human. Once he was in wolf form, he started to turn around, but Ana nudged him with her nose.

He'd forgotten how small she was. Because she was an alpha, compared to regular wolves and beta shifters she was still bigger, but with brown patches covering her white fur, she was cute and almost unassuming. He knew better, though. While she wasn't part of the warrior class, she could fight if she needed. And she was fast.

She yipped loudly and nudged him again. Before he could react, she bounded away and raced through the thicket of trees. He followed not far behind. The ground was soft beneath his paws. At least in her shifted form Ana was more at ease with him, and it was refreshing. If he could get her to let her guard down, their mating process would be much smoother. Once—if—they bonded, they should be able to link telepathically in human and wolf forms. Some packs could and some couldn't. It was just a matter of genetics. He knew her sisters and cousins couldn't, while his former pack had been able to, and he and his brother still could when they wanted. But bonded mates were different. They could almost always communicate that way.

It scared the shit out of him that she'd be able to read his thoughts freely, but he wanted to claim all of her. His own father had become a shell of a wolf when his mother had died. Some days Connor wondered if that's why his father had been killed in the attack against their pack a year later. His father had been strong, one of the toughest Alphas of his time, but he'd been easily defeated. Maybe he hadn't cared enough to fight back. Connor knew that by letting Ana into his head and heart he'd be opening himself up to that kind of pain, but he couldn't stop himself. The need for her outweighed everything else, even his fear.

When they neared the grassy bed by the creek, he shifted back to his human form. Normally he liked to get in a longer run but his adrenaline was still high and he didn't want to wait until tonight to see Ana naked. He stretched out on the cold grass and enjoyed her confusion.

She crouched down on her belly and growled softly. He propped up on one elbow and turned to face her. "I want to see you, Ana."

She actually barked at him. Then she covered her face with her paw.

It took a moment for him to understand what she wanted. "Fine. I'll turn around." Rolling over, he turned his back to her while she shifted. Most wolves didn't care about undergoing the change but Ana was so private about it. Hell, she was private about everything. He hated that she was that way with him too.

"What's so important that you needed to talk now? It's freaking cold out here!" He turned to find Ana sitting a few feet away with her knees pulled up to her chest and her arms wrapped around her knees. Completely blocking everything he wanted to see. Well, almost everything. With her legs in that position he got a nice shot of her—

"Connor!" she snapped.

"It's not that cold," he said as he stalked toward her. The wind barely bothered him as he drank in the sight of her. Just looking at her, his blood heated.

Without releasing her grip around her knees, she leaned back a few inches. "What are you doing?"

"What does it look like? I told you I wanted to see you." As he crouched in front of her, he placed his hands on her arms and pulled them away from her knees.

"Wait. *See me*, see me? You don't want to talk about anything?" Her voice slightly shook.

"Talking is the last thing on my mind, love."

"We're in the middle of the woods," she sputtered as he pushed her knees down.

His abdomen clenched as he drank in the sight of her. The flat plane of her stomach was bunched tightly and her nipples were rock-hard points. From the cold or because she was turned on, he couldn't be sure. The look in her dark eyes was a mix of lust and hesitancy. The erotic combination had him clenching his hands into fists to keep from grabbing her and taking her hard and rough. The way his body demanded.

He skimmed his fingers down her thighs to her knees, then gently pressed them apart. He wanted to see what was his. The scent of her desire hit him with startling intensity. No doubt about it now. The sweet perfume was all the confirmation he needed. There were some things she couldn't hide. The soft, dark hair covering her mound was trimmed into a perfect strip.

"Connor." Her voice was barely above a whisper as she reached out and placed her hands on his shoulders. For a brief moment her fingers dug into his skin, but then she scrambled away and drew her knees back up, covering herself. "This is crazy. You said you'd give—"

"You time. Yes, I know," he growled. *How much more time does she need?* He started to say something else when his brother projected to him.

Connor, get back to the ranch now! Something's happened to Teresa. We think she's been poisoned.

He clutched his head at the abrupt intrusion. Why now, of all times? "Shit."

I'm on my way, he projected to Liam.

Ana raised her eyebrows. "What's wrong?"

"We've got to go. Teresa's hurt."

She looked around in confusion. "Teresa? What are you talking about?"

"Liam just told me he thinks she's been poisoned."

"What do you mean he *just* told you?" Disbelief laced her words.

"We communicate telepathically." It's what had saved his and Liam's life. His father had warned them away the day he'd been killed.

"In wolf and *human* form?" Her dark eyebrows rose. Some related shifters could communicate in their animal form but it was much rarer to do so as a human. Connor's line had just been genetically blessed. "Yeah."

"Wow . . . Did he say anything else about Teresa? Is it serious? What happened?"

"All I know is that we need to get back."

Without a word Ana turned over and shifted to her animal form. Connor pushed back the acute disappointment that forked through him and the surprise when he noticed a tattoo on her shoulder before doing the same.

He was worried about his packmate, but soon enough he'd get Ana exactly where he wanted her, and nothing was going to stop him.

Chapter 10

Ana clutched Teresa's chilled, sweaty hand tightly in one of hers and held her cell phone against her ear with the other. "Thank you so much, Doctor ... We'll see you in a few minutes.... No, the gate will be unlocked. Just come to the main house."

"He's coming?" Carmen asked as Ana snapped her phone shut.

She nodded. "He'll be here soon. Luckily he was on his way home from the hospital, so he's nearby."

Teresa stirred against the sheets and her eyes flickered open. "What are you all doing in my room?" she muttered.

Ana brushed back a few strands of her cousin's sweat-soaked hair. "Sweetie, Dr. Graham is on his way. And you're at the main house now, okay?"

"Doctor? What are you talking about? Don't need a doctor," she slurred before her eyes drifted shut.

"Is this what it was like before?" Standing behind her, Connor squeezed Ana's shoulder in a comforting gesture.

Ana looked up at him. "Yeah. It started with one,

then spread. It moved through the males and the pregnant females like wildfire. Once we realized what was going on we managed to stop the damage, but . . ." She tore her eyes away. Talking about it brought up too much agony inside her. It had been an unthinkable time. Watching her father and so many of her male cousins die within hours of one another had been awful. Then to see the pregnant females, some in their third trimester, die—that had truly been the hardest thing she'd ever had to watch. She'd never felt so helpless in her life and she hated the feeling. If she hadn't had her two sisters by her side she didn't know that she'd have held it together for so long.

Connor sat on the edge of the bed next to her. "What about their blood? Was it ever tested?"

She nodded. "I sent it off to a local clinic that's shifter friendly, and each sample tested positive for some kind of poisoning."

"Why didn't you ask the Council for help? They have doctors."

"It all happened so fast, we didn't have a chance. By the time we figured out our wells had been poisoned, it was too late for the males and pregnant females. The lab we sent the samples to confirmed that most of us had been poisoned—including me—but for some reason the poison interacted worse with the males. The man I spoke to thought it had something to do with testosterone or the higher metabolism of the males. And you know how weak pregnant females are. It's no wonder they died so quickly. I contacted the Council afterward and sent them blood samples, but by then we had things under control. Now we all drink bottled water, most of our food is from whole food stores and we provide our own meat."

"So why do we need an outside doctor for this?"

"Do you want to wait for the Council to send someone?" Without waiting for a response, she continued. "Dr. Graham was there for our pack when we needed him. When he found out what was going on he offered up his services immediately when a lot of those at the hospital would have scoffed at us. He's one of the few humans we trust."

He didn't respond. Just frowned.

Ana narrowed her gaze at him. "I know you don't like bringing in outsiders but we don't have a choice. And I trust him."

"I'm still calling the Council. About the feral wolf *and this*. They need to know what's going on."

"Feral wolf?" Carmen asked from her seat on the other side of Teresa's bed.

Crap. Ana hadn't had a chance to tell anyone about what they'd found.

Connor answered before she could. "Ana and I found a feral wolf on the south side of the property today, but he's been taken care of. I'm going to call a meeting later tonight, but make sure you spread the word that no one is to wander off anywhere by themselves, okay?"

Wide-eyed, Carmen nodded, then returned her attention to Teresa.

Ana pushed up from her seat. "The doctor should be here by now. I'm going to go meet him."

Connor followed her out into the hall. As they descended the stairs, he said, "I've sent Liam and Ryan to take care of the wolf's body."

"When did you have time to tell your brother about . . . never mind." She'd forgotten about the telepathic-mind-link thing. She should have figured it out anyway. The two of them had always looked at each other like they *knew* what the other was thinking. Now some things made sense.

As they stepped outside she spotted the doctor walking through the gate. Her heart twisted as she thought about what could happen to her packmates. Watching her parents die had been hard enough. She didn't think she could bear to lose her sisters or cousins. Or Connor. That thought brought a rush of unexpected tears to her eyes. She wanted to protect her heart against him. And she would. Still, the most primal—and apparently masochistic—part of her was damn happy he was back in her life.

She quickly blinked, but Connor didn't miss a thing.

"Hey," he murmured. Stopping in his tracks, he lightly brushed his thumb against her cheeks, wiping away her tears. "You're not going to lose anyone. I promise."

"What, are you a mind reader now?" she asked, semijoking.

He shook his head. "No, but I can read you."

Before she could respond, the doctor interrupted them. "Ana, I'm so glad you called me." The blond-haired man in his late forties rushed toward them, carrying a medical bag. Even though he smoked regularly, he was aging well.

"So far Teresa's the only one affected. We're not even sure what kind of poisoning it is, but the symptoms are similar."

The doctor nodded politely at Connor, then focused his attention on Ana. "I want to test her blood immediately."

"Of course. Doctor, this is Connor Armstrong. He's the new Alpha of this pack and my mate." He was one of the few humans who had a minor understanding of shifter dynamics, so she was free to talk in their terms.

"Pleasure to meet you." The doctor held out his hand, and to Ana's annoyance Connor hesitated before grasping it.

"She's upstairs." Ana motioned to him and led them.

Once they were in Teresa's room Ana hung back with Connor and Carmen as the doctor checked her vitals and took a sample of her blood.

After a few minutes of working in silence, he finally spoke. "I won't know for certain until I have the tests back, but she looks the same as the others. I'm sorry."

"Can you tell how she was poisoned?" Connor asked.

He shook his head, his expression grim. "Unfortunately, no."

"Then why is no one else sick?" Connor spoke again.

"I can't answer that. She appears too incoherent, but I'd like to monitor her food intake from this point forward. If we can stop this now it might not spread like it did before."

"We've already started checking our food," Connor said.

The doctor paused and eyed Connor curiously. Ana knew he was used to dealing with her, and maybe he was nervous around Connor. Lord knew the wolf could be intimidating when he wanted. Finally Dr. Graham spoke. "Right now that's the best thing you can do. Make sure everything is clean and keep a running list of the items that are silver-free."

"Thank you, Doctor. Is there anything else you need?" Ana asked.

"No, but I want to keep an eye on her for a while."

"I'm going to stay too," Carmen murmured.

"Okay." As Ana and Connor left they nearly stumbled over Vivian, who sat directly outside Teresa's bedroom.

Ana crouched down next to her. Vivian was so young; Ana didn't want her around any of this. "Hey, sweetie. What are you doing? I thought you were playing with Lucas."

"Is Teresa going to die?" Vivian's voice shook.

Ana paused and tried to choose her words carefully. She didn't want to lie, but she didn't want to upset the little girl. "The doctor is going to do everything he can to keep that from happening."

"But you can't know he'll save her. What if you die too?" She suddenly pushed up from the floor and raced past them.

Ana's heart lodged in her throat. She started after her, but Connor placed a hand on her shoulder. "Let me talk to her, okay? She gets upset if anyone even talks about dying. I know how to calm her down."

Ana wanted to argue, but he'd known the little cub longer. "You sure?"

He nodded and placed a soft kiss on her lips. There was nothing hungry or urgent about it, but her heart rate ratcheted up instantly. When he pulled away he dropped another kiss on her forehead. "Start scanning the food in our house and I'll meet you back there."

Mutely she nodded and forced her rubbery legs into action. A hundred different worries raced through her mind, but if she let herself focus on what *might* happen to her cousin or the rest of her pack, everyone else would sense her fear. Even if she didn't want to, she had to stay strong for them and for herself. Pack life wasn't so different from the lives of human families, she supposed. They all depended on each other to get through hard times.

"It looks like they're burning Mike's body." Vince handed the binoculars to Taggart.

He peered through them and squinted at the two men standing in front of a controlled fire. The wind wasn't in their favor today, so they had to keep their distance. "I think you're right."

"You think they know *why* he went feral?" Vince asked.

Taggart shrugged. "Doesn't matter. They won't be able to prove he was feral now."

Vince frowned. "But he was."

Taggart bit back a sigh at Vince's obvious statement. "We know that and whoever killed him knows that, but they won't be able to *prove* it."

"So?"

"Someone in their pack killed one of our pack members, and they're going to pay for it."

"What are you planning?" Vince's voice was cautious.

"I'm going to demand a piece of their property in exchange for Mike's murder." Taggart had gotten the best end of the deal and he planned to capitalize on it. With Mike dead and burned, there was no proof that one of his wolves had turned feral because of meth use. He'd been a fucking idiot using that shit, then shifting to his animal form. Taggart had planned to kill him anyway, but now he didn't have to worry about it. Since that problem was out of the way, he was going to take that land. Hell, he might even be willing to give up Ana for it.

"Connor won't go for it. He was probably the one who killed Mike."

The wind suddenly shifted in their direction and he scented Ana. It wasn't fresh, but she'd been there recently. "You smell that?"

"Yeah. *Ana.* You think she killed him?"

"No. Her mate wouldn't have let her out of his sight. If she was here, so was Connor." But if she'd been there too and she knew without a doubt the wolf had been feral, she'd fight tooth and nail against parceling some of her land to him.

Which meant he'd likely have to use force and intimidation against them. He smiled to himself. He'd probably lose a few of his wolves if they went to war with Connor and Ana's pack, but it would be more fun that way.

Liam steered his truck into an empty spot in front of December's bookstore. Maybe he should give her some space, but after dealing with a dead wolf and possible poisoning at the ranch, he wanted to see her again. Hell, he needed to see her, regardless of all the other bullshit. If only to reassure himself she was safe. After dinner last night it had taken all his willpower not to kiss her.

But she hadn't been ready. Unlike shifter females, the curvy redhead was very easy to read, and while she was attracted to him, she was still nervous around him. Not scared, which would have driven him crazy, but he hated the skittish vibes she put off.

The little bell jingled overhead as he entered the store. Her eyes widened when she saw him but she was helping another customer. She smiled shyly at him and returned to ringing up the woman at the cash register. He ducked down one of the aisles and flipped through a couple books until he heard the bell jingle as the woman left.

Before he could search her out, December appeared at the end of the aisle. And today she wasn't wearing those bulky clothes. She had on a sweater dress that hugged her curves in all the right places and leather knee-high boots that wrapped around her calves like a second skin. His entire body heated as he drank in the sight of her. What he wouldn't give to peel off those boots and start kissing her feet. He'd work his way up her ankles and legs to her inner thighs—

"What are you doing here?"

"I wanted to see you."

Her eyebrows lifted in surprise. "Oh."

"Is that okay?" He covered the few feet between them so they stood inches apart. He desperately wanted to touch her but refrained.

"Yes ... I ... What exactly is it you want from me?" She twisted her hands nervously in front of her.

He frowned at her question. "I don't understand."

She flushed. "What are your intentions toward me?"

"I want to date you." He said the only thing that would make sense to her. If he admitted he wanted to make love to her until neither of them could walk or think straight and eventually claim her so that she'd be his and no one else would ever touch her again, she was likely to kick him out on his ass. Or run screaming in the other direction. Neither option was appealing.

"Listen. I think you're really sweet, Liam, and—"

"Are you breaking things off with me before they've even started?" Suddenly the little store was suffocating.

"I just don't want to give you the wrong impression or lead you on."

"You want me." The statement was bold and took her off guard.

Her cheeks tinged bright red. "Excuse me?"

"I can smell your desire, and even if I couldn't, I can see it in your eyes every time you turn that hot gaze on me. You. Want. *Me*." He reached out and trailed a finger down her soft cheek. Something in his chest loosened when she didn't pull away.

"That doesn't matter." Her voice was tight. At least she didn't deny it.

"What's the problem, then?"

Her shoulders lifted slightly. "I don't like wasting my time."

"Neither do I. I'm not looking for something casual." Man, those were words he'd never thought he'd utter.

"That's not what I meant. I just ... This thing with us

can't go anywhere, and something tells me that if I get involved with you it'll hurt like hell when we end things." The raw truth of her words cut him and he still didn't understand what her problem was.

"What makes you think things would end?" Then it hit him with the intensity of a silver dagger slicing through his chest. "You don't want to get involved with me because of what I am."

Her cheeks darkened again and he knew he was right. She cleared her throat. "It's just too complicated. My brother—"

"I don't want to date your brother," he growled. "I want you."

Before she could respond, the bell to the store jingled and in walked her brother. *Perfect fucking timing.* It was like that guy had a GPS tracker on Liam or something.

"You should probably leave," she murmured low enough for only him to hear.

Like hell.

"Weren't you just in here?" the sheriff asked as he strode toward them.

"Is it a crime for shifters to shop now?" Liam didn't bother to hide the anger in his voice.

"If you're not buying anything, then get the hell out of here and stay away from my sister." The sheriff's voice was low and threatening.

"Parker! What's the matter with you?" December took a step toward her brother and put a placating hand on his arm, but he shrugged it off.

If it had been anyone else Liam would have stayed and stood his ground, but it was obvious how upset December was so he forced himself to leave. "I'll see you later." And he would. No doubt about it. He didn't care what the sexy redhead said. They had a lot more to talk about.

At the door he paused and turned back to face the sheriff. "Did you ever stop by Sean Taggart's ranch?"

"None of your business."

Liam bit back a sharp retort. "I don't care what your beef is with me, but you better stay with your sister tonight. If Taggart has it out for her, he won't stop until someone is hurt. Or worse." Before either of them could respond, he shoved the glass door open and strode out into the cold.

His heart pounded erratically against his chest and he could feel his canines start to extend. The animal inside him wanted free in a bad way. He practiced his breathing exercises—something he hadn't done in about a hundred years—until the urge to shift subsided.

As he steered out of the parking lot, he projected to his brother. *How do you control yourself around Ana? Being in the same room as December is enough to make me crazy.*

Are you in town? Connor asked.

Yeah. The feral wolf is burned.

I know—Ryan told me. Why did you leave without telling me where you'd gone?

Because I knew you'd give me grief about seeing December, and I can't stay away. Her brother showed up and—

Damn it, Liam! I'm in the middle of a meeting and the entire pack is staring at me as if I've lost my mind. Get out of my head."

Liam chuckled to himself. *Everyone's there?*

Silence.

What's Ana wearing? And what would you like her to be wearing?

You're lucky you're my brother. The growl of Connor's voice echoed loudly in his head.

Liam knew when to leave well enough alone but it

didn't stop the short-lived grin on his face. Anything to take his mind off the redhead who'd suddenly consumed his every waking thought.

Ana shut the door to the house and resisted the urge to collapse onto the floor. She hung her coat on the rack and trudged up the stairs. After Connor's meeting they'd methodically checked everyone's home for signs of silver poisoning. As Alpha he had a duty to personally see to the well-being of the entire pack. And as his mate, she had to share in his duties. Not that she minded. This was her family. But her feet ached and, worse, the fear that the poisoning was starting up again had settled deep inside her.

They'd split up to cover more ground, and from the quiet of the house it looked like she'd beaten him back. She intended to take advantage of the downtime. After starting a hot bath, she stripped out of her clothes and pulled her hair up into a clip so it wouldn't get wet.

Steam drifted up from the oversized tub, but when her feet hit the water she sighed in relief. It was hot but not scalding. Tingles raced down her arms and up her back as she descended into the tub. As she sank deeper under the rising water, she heard the front door open and close.

Barely a few seconds passed before Connor stood in the doorway of the bathroom. His eyes darkened as he zeroed in on her exposed breasts. Her already hard nipples peaked under his heated stare. The water was rising but not fast enough. She gripped the side of the tub to stop from covering herself. Whether she was ready or not, tonight was the night. She knew it. He knew it. Physically she wanted him and she wasn't going to deny it. Spending another night in the same bed as him and feeling sexually frustrated wasn't something she planned to do. Maybe if they finally slept together she could get him out of her system. Get a grip on her emotions. Anything was better than living with all this pent-up craziness.

She spoke to break the growing silence. "I just got back a few minutes ago. I couldn't find anything in any of the houses I checked. Even though the scanner tested negative for silver, I checked for tampering of any unopened food and didn't find any of that either."

"I found something," he said grimly.

Her heart raced at his tone and matching dark expression. "What?"

"One of the storage sheds has been broken into. It looks like a lot of the flavored water has been contaminated with some sort of liquid silver. I found a bottle in Teresa's recycling bin. She must have recently grabbed a case from the shed."

Ana started to push up, but Connor shook his head. "I've removed the rest of the water from her house, and thankfully only one bottle was missing from the new case."

Frowning, Ana settled back against the tub. "Someone broke into one of our storage sheds?" That was a bold move.

Connor's jaw clenched. "Somehow they got past our security. I'm having new locks installed, and in addition to increasing security, we're throwing away everything inside the shed. Tomorrow I'll buy more bottled water."

"I'll do it," she said. Her cousin had been poisoned, and while she trusted Connor, it would make her feel better to actually be the one to purchase the water. To see with her own eyes that it was safe. "What about the rest of the houses?"

"I didn't find any other signs of tampering."

They were both silent for a long moment and she guessed he was thinking the same thing she was. Someone had managed to get onto their land undetected. Definitely not impossible, but it was a scary thought.

Finally Connor spoke again. "I stopped by the house to check on Teresa, and whatever the doctor is doing seems to be working. She has a little color, even if she's not awake."

She shifted against the tub in a strategic effort to cover herself with some of the rising bubbles. "I know. I stopped there too. As long as she doesn't take in more silver she should heal normally. Quickly, even . . . Did you see Vivian while you were there?"

"Yeah, why?" he asked as he leaned against the counter.

Ana shrugged. "I don't know. I think I might have hurt her feelings when I told her I wasn't staying over there tonight. I read her a story and Carmen said she could sleep in her room, but she seemed unhappy."

"She's had a lot to deal with over the past year. Getting into a routine will be good for her."

Ana knew that but it still bugged her. She started to say something else when Connor seemed to zone out. Even though he was looking directly at her, his eyes had glazed over and she knew he wasn't seeing her.

She stopped the running water with her foot. The sudden quiet jerked him out of his thoughts. "What's bothering you?"

"Two months ago, did the others start getting better before they got worse?"

Ana fought back the memories as she shook her head. "No. It was *bad*, Connor. Like a plague just swept through here, mowing down everyone in the way."

"Do you think Taggart was involved?"

She shook her head. "No. When he found out what was going on he wasn't helpful, but he was truly surprised."

"Who *was* helpful?"

"What do you mean?"

"I wasn't here, Ana, and I don't want to make the same mistakes as last time."

"Mistakes? Are you saying this is our fault?"

"No!" He strode across the room and crouched next to the tub so they were eye level. "That came out wrong. I want to know what we're up against. I promised I'd protect you and I can't do that unless I have the whole picture."

A thick lump settled in her throat and she racked her brain, trying to remember. "Dr. Graham was here and so were Matt and Kaya Dunlauxe. She's the woman I saw at the hospital."

"Anyone else?"

"Sheriff Parker was out here a few times. I know he doesn't seem to like you and Liam much, but when everyone was dying he was surprisingly helpful. Well, helpful but still wary. It was obvious he didn't trust us, but he launched an investigation and actually did his job."

Connor muttered a curse under his breath about the sheriff. "Anything else you can think of?"

"We threw away all our food, started drinking bottled water instead of from the tap or the wells and then we started testing everything on a daily basis. But it was too late for my . . ." Her voice broke on the last word. She understood he needed answers, but she'd locked up the memory of her parents' deaths for so long, she was afraid if she let the tears out, she'd never stop crying. Not being able to mourn had taken its toll.

"Don't cry, Ana," Connor murmured.

She frowned when she realized her cheeks were wet. "I'm not," she whispered.

He didn't respond as he stared at her, but it was as if a switch flipped. His dark eyes went from being concerned to hot and hungry. Being so close to him, while she was naked no less, dried her tears. He wasn't looking lower than her face, but she could practically feel his eyes devouring her. Her breath caught in her throat and time seemed to stretch on. They might not be telepathically connected yet, but she could read everything he wanted to do to her in his eyes. They were full of dark, erotic promises. What she saw there made her shiver.

Connor had to remind himself to breathe as he looked at Ana. Leaning forward, he kissed one of her cheeks, then the other. Pecks, really. He tasted the salt of her tears and she smiled under his kisses. And he could actually feel some of her tension abate. A sigh tore through him when she began to relax. This was what he'd been waiting for.

He wanted her at ease. Hell, he needed her like that. If he didn't want to screw up their first time together, she needed to be as turned on as he was.

Searching out her mouth, he covered it with his. Her lips opened willingly and she tasted a sweet and minty flavor. As he probed with his tongue, he dipped one of his hands beneath the water. Running his hand along the flat plane of her abdomen, he stopped when he cupped her mound. He thought about working up to this, but he *had* to touch her here. Had to claim her.

Ana spread her legs a little wider, so he dipped a finger inside her. She was wet but tight. Too tight. He needed to prepare her for him. He knew he was big and it wasn't something he'd thought much about since he was a young cub. It was a part of who he was.

Even though she was wet, he wanted her panting and begging for him because she *needed* to feel him inside her so bad, she ached.

Blindly he leaned over and reached for the tub stop. He tugged the chain free, then grasped her under her arms. She let out a gasp as he helped her to stand. Unable to stop himself, he leaned closer and nipped the top of her shoulder, near the tattoo he'd seen on her earlier in the woods. It was a small outline of a wolf howling at the moon. And it was sexy as hell. "This is new," he murmured.

She smiled almost mischievously. "I got it about a decade ago. Probably my only rebellious act."

As she started to step over the tub, he scooped her up and headed for the bedroom.

"I'm all wet," she protested weakly.

"I know." He grinned when a light flush of pink stained her cheeks. The almost-shy reaction surprised him. As he laid her on the bed, he reached behind her head and pulled her hair clip free.

Her dark hair tumbled around her face and pillowed onto the bed beneath her. Stretched out before him, she was everything he'd been fantasizing about for years, and better than he'd built her up to be. Hell, his fantasies seemed like black-and-white photos compared to reality. Staring at her now, he didn't know how he'd walked away from her before.

While he wanted to keep part of himself hidden from her, he didn't know how that could be possible. After seeing how his father crumbled after his mother's death, Connor knew that once he'd been with Ana he couldn't lose her or walk away from her. Even if she deserved better than him, he wouldn't leave her.

He couldn't survive it. As quick as humanly possible, he stripped out of his clothes and stood by the edge of the bed.

She stared up at him with wide eyes, but the heat burning in those dark depths set him on fire.

All his instincts told him to take her hard and fast, but he wanted to work her up to it. Fighting his inner wolf, he climbed onto the bed and grasped her foot. She let out a startled gasp when he lifted it to his mouth.

Damn, even her foot was sexy. She'd painted her toes a soft pink. Unable to resist, he kissed the delicate arch of her foot. "You know you used to drive me crazy when we first met," he murmured as he worked his way up to her inner ankle.

"What are you talking about?" The question was a breathy whisper, and it rolled over him like a caress. Her fingers clutched the sheets underneath her.

"I thought you were intentionally trying to tease me." He had to keep talking or he'd throw restraint out the window and thrust into her like his inner wolf demanded.

She spread her legs wider as he worked his way up to her knee. Her sweet scent grew stronger the more he kissed her. A knee shouldn't turn him on, but hers did. He ran his tongue over her soft skin, then followed with a light scrape of his teeth. She jerked a little under the action but she let out a soft moan.

"Always running around without a bra. It was enough to drive any male insane." He zeroed in on her inner thighs. Dropping light kisses, he avoided her soft, inviting folds and the perfect strip of dark hair covering her mound. The heat emanating from her was enough to knock him on his ass.

"For years the thought of what your nipples looked like tortured me." He inched closer to her heat.

Ana tugged on the back of his head, gripped his hair and forced him to look up. "So is this payback? Are you trying to torture me?"

"Torture *you*?" He sounded like he had gravel in his throat.

Her eyes turned to a mercurial, smoky storm. "I want to feel you inside me."

The quiet declaration set something off inside him. His throat tightened as rational thought melted away.

Wordlessly Connor pushed up and repositioned so that he was nestled between her legs. He didn't bother testing her. The scent of her arousal was potent. Even a human would be able to smell it. Positioning himself at her entrance, he plunged into her hard and fast and stayed there, buried inside her without moving.

Her lips parted, and he caught her gasp with his mouth. Their tongues danced with an unspoken urgency. Ana ran her fingers down his back, digging into his skin with surprising strength.

Her inner walls expanded and tightened around him like a satin glove. Tight and wet, her body accepted him, but he didn't make another move to push into her. He wanted her to adjust to him first, and if he was honest, he didn't want to pull out. The feel of her around him was too intoxicating.

He lifted his head so that their faces were inches apart. The rest of their bodies meshed together perfectly.

Like two pieces of a puzzle.

Her legs stretched around him and she locked her ankles together across his upper thighs. The angle was perfection, allowing him to move inside her if he wanted.

"Are you okay?" he whispered.

In response, she rolled her hips up to meet his. The stroke was firm and insistent. *Okay, then.* She wanted it faster.

Ana's mind was too jumbled and her body was too over-sensitized to make a coherent sentence. *Am I okay?* The ache between her legs was almost unbearable and if he did something to ease it, then she'd be okay. *Better than okay.* Maybe not tomorrow morning, when the gravity of her actions set in, but for now, she felt amazing.

Telling him what she wanted in bed was something she couldn't do just yet, so she spoke with her body. The fact that this was Connor on top of her, his cock inside her, giving her so much pleasure, was a lot to compute. When she rolled her hips, he got the message.

Loud and clear.

He pulled back once, then slammed into her. Hard.

The shock sent waves of ecstasy to nerve endings she didn't realize she had. She could actually feel her vagina pulsate. It fluttered around him as her body familiarized itself with him. Letting her head fall back against the pillow, she reached her arms up and grabbed on to the iron bedpost. She wanted him to ride her.

"Look at us," he ordered. The command in his voice made her nipples tingle in awareness.

Her head snapped down as she stared at their two joined bodies. Both of their stomach muscles were bunched tight. The planes of his were more defined, muscular, where hers were flatter, softer. Even though her skin was olive in complexion, he was still darker, tanner. The erotic differences in their bodies made her clench tighter around his shaft.

His hips moved as he pulled out of her, inch by inch until he was almost completely free of her and the head of his shaft only nudged her opening. The rest of his penis was visible and it was thick and hard. Involuntarily her inner walls tightened, wanting to feel him inside her again. Filling her completely.

Before she could voice what she wanted, he rocked into her. The motion was smooth and startling at the same time.

He was bigger than she'd expected, but she knew her body could handle him. The intrusion bordered on painful when he pushed in completely, but the pleasure overrode everything else.

He wasn't stopping now. Fisting the sheet next to her head, he slanted his mouth over hers as he drove into her. His tongue was demanding and harsh as he invaded her mouth. Moaning into him, she tightened her legs around him, opening herself further.

His strokes weren't controlled, but wild and animalistic. When he tore his mouth away from hers she wanted to protest, until he raked his teeth over her neck. She knew he wouldn't bond them. He couldn't. If she accepted him as her bondmate, he'd have to take her under the full moon. He would take her from behind, and as they joined together he'd sink his canines into her neck not only to mark her, but bond them together for life. Only then would they link telepathically.

He was marking her, though. Making sure she was officially his. As he was hers. His scent would twine around her, letting the world know they were mated. Technically she could still walk away from him if she wanted, even after they mated, but some primal part of her scoffed at the thought.

A tiny voice in the back of her head whispered that they could have been doing this for the past fifty years if he hadn't left her, but she silenced it and dug her fingers into the firm skin of his back.

When she did, he sank his canines into her skin. Not deep, but enough to mark her. The sharp action pushed her over the edge. She hadn't realized she was even standing at the ledge, but she surged into climax.

His pelvis rubbed over her sensitive bundle of nerves each time he ground against her. The rubbing action over her clit combined with his thrusts was too much. Like a fast-breaking wave, she peaked, then descended into free fall. Her vagina tightened around him in a vise-like grip as a shout tore from her.

She wanted to bite it back, show *some* control, but she

couldn't. The scream ripped from her lungs as the orgasm overtook everything, including coherent thought.

If Connor's life ended at this moment, he'd die happy. He lifted his head so he could see Ana's face. Her dark eyes had glazed over and uncontrollable shudders racked her body. Her thighs tightened around him and her fingers sank into him. The way she held on to him was as if she never wanted to let go.

He'd worried he wouldn't be able to hold out long enough before coming. All his muscles were pulled taut, but now he could let go. Ana was like a package of dynamite. She hadn't needed much stimulation before exploding. That moved him, knowing how reactive she was for him.

Once he'd had her, oh, a hundred times, he'd want to take it slow. Savor kissing and teasing every inch of her delicious body. Now wasn't the time for slow and sensual. And it seemed she didn't want it that way either. As he thrust again, a flood of emotion burst inside him and he tried to ignore it. A kaleidoscope of colors flashed before his eyes as he came.

He couldn't hold back any longer. Grasping her hips, he thrust, emptying himself inside her in long, hot streams. Her hips continued to meet his stroke for stroke, until finally her ankles unlocked and her legs loosened their death grip around him.

His cock had a mind of its own, though. Blindly, his hips made small jerking motions until he gained control of himself.

Panting, he propped up on his elbows and stared at Ana. A soft smile lit up her face. Since he'd been back he'd found her smiles to be a rare, wonderful thing. When he'd first met her, she'd given them out all the time. As if she'd had plenty to spare. Now she had more responsibility. More sorrow in her life. Sometimes it showed so clearly in her eyes.

And he wanted to take away her pain any way he could. He leaned down, closing the short distance between their faces, and lightly kissed her lips. She still tasted sweet.

When he gently tugged on her bottom lip, she smiled and traced her fingers down his back until she reached his backside.

He chuckled when she grasped him. "You seem to like that part of me."

She grinned and clutched tighter. "You have a very, *very* nice behind."

Hearing her praise—however small—caused his erection to lengthen again. It had been at half-mast and now it was quickly rising to full salute again.

Her eyebrows rose as she felt the change.

"We're not finished yet, love," he murmured against her soft cheek. Reaching between their bodies, he rubbed his thumb over her clit, and she jerked against him. Her inner walls trembled around him in response. He didn't bother to hide his groan. "Not finished by a long shot."

Chapter 11

Ana opened her eyes and rolled over. Connor's side of the bed was empty but it was still warm. Smiling, she ran her hand over his pillow and inhaled his earthy scent. Then she frowned. She shouldn't be smelling him like some lovesick cub. It was pathetic.

Angry at herself, she shoved off the tangled sheet. The sound of running water in the bathroom greeted her ears.

After their first time last night Connor had woken her two more times. He'd tried to wake her up a third but she'd feigned sleep. The man was a damn machine. Not that she was complaining. She couldn't remember the last time she'd slept so peacefully. Certainly not in the past couple months. The orgasms he'd given her had the ability to knock her out. Unfortunately her hope that she'd get him out of her system hadn't exactly worked. She wanted more of him. *It's just physical,* she thought. *Nothing more.*

She swung her legs off the bed. The wood floor beneath her feet immediately cooled her. She brushed her teeth in one of the other bathrooms, then started to head downstairs. At the last second she grabbed Connor's discarded shirt from the floor and slipped it over her head. Since she and Connor had revealed their intent to mate she figured pack members would announce themselves before coming over, but she wasn't taking a chance. Most shifters didn't mind a little nudity, but she knew Connor was dominant and possessive, and it would grate on his nerves if anyone else saw her naked. And she wasn't keen on the idea of anyone else seeing her in the buff either.

As she ascended the stairs, she scented a familiar male. "Liam?" she called out before entering the kitchen. She found him leaning against the counter, coffee mug in hand. And a scowl on his face. "I take it you didn't sleep well?"

He set his mug down with a thud and a bit of coffee sloshed over. "And I can tell you did," he grumbled.

Despite the fact that he was family, she could feel her face flame. Now no one would have any doubt about the unification of her and Connor. His scent covered her, and any male who came near would know she was marked. If they didn't bond it would fade with time but only if they stopped sleeping together. Ana knew that wasn't going to happen. "Connor's in the shower, if you want to wait for him." She grabbed a cup.

"Actually I wanted to talk to you."

"Really?" Her eyebrows rose.

"You're a woman."

Ana bit back a grin. "Uh, yeah. Thanks for noticing."

"Remember the woman from Sunday?"

"The sheriff's sister? *Oh yeah*. I think even her brother could smell your intent toward her."

"Did Connor say anything about her . . . ?" He trailed off.

She shook her head.

Liam cleared his throat. "She's my mate."

She couldn't stop the gasp that escaped. "But she's human."

"It doesn't matter. She's *mine*."

Good Lord, he got the same intent expression on his face as Connor when he wanted something. They were definitely cut from the same cloth. It wasn't impossible for humans and shifters to mate, but it was rare. Ana didn't actually know any shifters who had mated with humans. "So what's the deal, then?"

His lips pulled into a thin line. "She doesn't want anything to do with me."

"I don't know about that." She'd noticed the way the redheaded human had stared at him. It had been hard to miss. She'd been a little fearful, but Ana had also sensed curiosity and blatant lust emanating from her. Humans didn't hide their emotions as well as shifters, and the redhead was no different.

"No, she *wants* me and she doesn't even deny it. That's not the problem. She just doesn't want a relationship with me because of what I am."

Ana bit her bottom lip. If he was coming to her for relationship advice he was out of his damn mind. Even at her age, her experience was limited. And right now she had no clue where she stood with the sexy wolf showering upstairs—and they were mated. They might have had hot sex—lots of it—but her mind and body warred with each other. The closer she let Connor get to her, the more she opened herself up for heartache. *Talk about relationship-challenged.* "So?"

His scowl deepened. "So help me out. How do I change her mind?"

"If I'm your only hope you're out of luck, Liam." The frustrated growl he let out sounded so much like his brother's, she smiled.

"What's funny?" he demanded.

She shook her head. "Nothing. She's interested in you, right?"

He nodded.

"Then give her time. You two are from different worlds. We might know a lot about humans but she likely doesn't know anything about our kind."

"I don't want to give her time." He looked like a young cub pouting because his favorite toy had been taken away.

"Spoken like a true Armstrong," she muttered.

"What's like a true Armstrong?" Connor appeared in the doorway wearing only a pair of worn jeans. He raked a heated look over her face, then dipped lower, drinking in her entire body, straight down to her toes.

An involuntary shiver curled through her. He'd asked a question but all she could think about was the heat growing in her belly. After last night she should be too tired. Should be too sated. All it took was one look from him and her temperature ratcheted up about a thousand degrees. And it didn't hurt that he'd strolled in without a shirt on. She wanted to run her hands over all that muscle.

"You two are disgusting." Liam set his mug in the sink and stalked past Connor. The front door slammed behind him a few seconds later.

Silence descended and she hated the sudden awkwardness that threatened to take over her. "Hi." The way she said it sounded as if she were talking to a stranger and not the man she'd just spent hours making love with. The man she'd just mated with. She knew how much he wanted her physically, but after last night their relationship had most definitely changed.

His lips curved up slightly as he crossed the room. "Hi, yourself." Placing his hands on the counter behind her, he ran right into her personal space and leaned down to kiss her.

Not a hot, searing, claiming kiss, but a sweet, lazy, good-morning one. She ran her hands up his chest and locked her fingers behind his neck. The area between her legs dampened as his tongue flicked over hers.

When he sensed the change in her, the kiss went from sweet to scorching in an instant. He fisted the bottom of her shirt and started tugging it upward. Air rushed over her, but her nipples were already hard.

Suddenly he jerked back. "Son of a . . ." He shook his head.

"What?" She stared at him in a daze. *Why did he stop?*

He tapped the side of his head. "Liam just informed me we've got company. We better get dressed and check it out."

She didn't bother hiding her sigh. He was right, of course. They also needed to check on Teresa, and she needed to go shopping for backup cases of water. And she still needed a shower. Still, disappointment forked through her like a bolt of jagged lightning. After last night their relationship balance had shifted. She'd given up all her control to him in the bedroom, and while she knew he'd never hurt her, she felt as if she needed to gain back some of that emotional control.

When she was younger she'd been able to brush off her heartbreak as puppy love when he'd left. This was different. The foreign feelings blossoming inside her were more. She wanted him so much it frightened her. She was thankful for his presence and his support at the ranch, but she knew she could grow to depend on him so easily. Too easily. She couldn't allow that to happen. He'd left once. What was to stop him from doing it again? The reality was sobering.

"Where'd you just go?" Connor's voice was low, guarded.

She shook herself. "Sorry. I spaced for a second. You're right. We need to get dressed." She quickly side-stepped him and hurried out of the room.

Connor glanced down at Ana as they headed across the yard toward the main house. He wasn't sure what had happened in the past few minutes to make her turn back into herself and shut him out, but he didn't like it. After last night things had changed between them.

He was sure of it. Each time they'd made love he'd seen her emotions clearly in her eyes. Each time he'd pushed deep inside her and each time she'd called out his name—

Ana gave him a curious look. "Do I need to hose you down with a fire extinguisher?"

"I was just thinking about last night."

"Yeah, I kinda guessed that. If you don't want every-one else to know that, then tone it down, *Alpha*." There was a trace of humor in her voice.

He'd been in control of his emotions since he was a pup, but now that he'd actually tasted her, held her, been inside her, it was hard not to think about it. Fantasize about doing it again. "It's hard when all I can think about is what you looked like last night as you rode me. I don't even have to close my eyes to picture the way you rose on your knees and—"

"Jeez, Connor. You weren't very talkative last night, so let's not talk about that *now*, when we can't do any-thing about it." She nudged him with her hip and grinned.

The last thing he wanted to do was talk about it be-cause it only got him that much hotter. And she was right. He didn't talk much in the bedroom and neither did she. It was like their bodies were already attuned to each other.

Reaching out, he grasped her hand and held it as they walked. It was a small thing, innocuous, but he'd never done it with another female before. Never wanted to.

Her eyes widened in surprise. For a brief moment she tried to pull away, but he held tight.

As they neared the main house, the front door opened and Carmen stepped out with a man Connor didn't recognize. His long, dark hair was pulled back in a clip and he smelled familiar. *The man Ana must have seen at the hospital.* Connor's inner wolf growled protectively.

Next to him, Ana dropped his hand and hurried forward. "Matt, is your mother okay?"

"She's fine." The dark-haired man embraced her lightly.

It was a quick hug. He didn't hold Ana too long or inappropriately, but the beast inside Connor wanted to lunge at him for touching what was his. The violent urge shouldn't have surprised him, but the intensity of his need to assert dominance was almost overwhelming. As Alpha he knew how to control himself, but this feeling was entirely new. He'd heard how newly mated wolves reacted if others got too close to their mates, but he'd never imagined such a burning need. He actually wanted to hurt this stranger and protect Ana. Clenching his fists at his sides, he savored the pain of his nails digging into his palms. Anything to distract from the sight in front of him.

Ana gave him a sharp look—no doubt because she scented the change in the air—as she stepped out of the man's embrace.

"Hi, I'm Matoskah Dunlauxe. You can call me Matt." He held out a friendly hand.

Connor paused for a moment before grasping it. He experienced the juvenile urge to squeeze with more pressure than necessary but stopped himself. He nodded once. "I'm Connor. The new Alpha."

"He's also my mate," Ana said.

The man's dark eyes widened as he turned back to Ana. "Congratulations. It's about time you found someone."

"I know, right? Now Noel and I can settle down," Carmen interjected, and shot Matt a shy but flirty smile. There were no rules about the oldest having to settle down first, but obviously Carmen was interested in Matt and was not so subtly trying to let him know she was available.

Ana rolled her eyes at her sister's statement. It soothed Connor that she'd told Matt they were mated, but it didn't stop him from wrapping a protective arm around her shoulders.

Matt glanced back and forth between Ana and Connor. "I'd like to speak to you privately, if possible."

Carmen cleared her throat, and it was hard to miss the disappointed look on her face as she took a step back. "I'll be inside."

Once the door shut behind her, Matt spoke. "What's going on at your ranch?"

Beside him, Ana stiffened. "What do you mean?"

"I've been having dreams lately. Dark dreams." Matt's expression was grim

"About what?" Ana asked.

"You."

The word sounded ominous and it sent a foreign sensation twisting through Connor. His chest tightened painfully. "What the hell does that mean?"

"My dreams don't always make sense, but they're *always* a warning of what's to come," Matt said.

"I don't understand. Are you talking about visions?" Ana asked.

He nodded. "My father was a dream walker, but he used meditation to enter the dreamworld. I...can't control what I see as easily. These images and dreams only come to me when I'm asleep."

Ana moved into Connor's embrace. "What did you dream about exactly?"

"The first few dreams I wasn't sure what to make of until I saw you at the hospital the other day. Then I realized they must be about you. Are you brown and white in your animal form?"

When Ana nodded, he continued. "I keep having visions of you running. Sometimes it's across a field; other times it's through the woods. Wherever you go a dark cloud follows. Up until now the dreams ended with you being swallowed by the darkness, but in my last vision you were confronted by a coyote. You need to be careful, Ana." The warning hung in the air, a thick, heavy shroud.

Next to him Ana shuddered, and Connor wanted to kick the man's teeth in for upsetting her. Especially now, of all times. One of their packmates was sick and this asshole wanted to cause trouble.

"That's it? You came here because of some *dreams*?" Connor didn't bother keeping the skepticism out of his voice.

"*Connor,*" Ana muttered his name through gritted teeth.

Matt's dark eyes narrowed slightly, and Connor had to give him credit. The human didn't back down. "You shift to animal form yet you scoff at *my* visions? Talk about arrogant."

"What does the coyote mean?" Ana asked, trying to keep the focus on what was important.

He shrugged noncommittally. "It could mean a number of things. Sometimes what I see is literal; other times it's symbolic. Coyotes are tricksters, troublemakers. Someone wants to hurt you and they won't stop until they do. I sensed a powerful rage inside the coyote. It wants to see you suffer. Maybe not you personally, but your pack."

"We've been experiencing some problems with Sean Taggart's pack, so maybe that's what you're seeing."

Connor wanted to cut her off. He didn't want this stranger knowing anything about their lives.

Matt nodded, then motioned toward the house. "I saw Teresa a few minutes ago. I'm truly sorry about your cousin."

"Thank you."

"I remember how bad it was last time. If you need any help, call me."

"We have it under control now. If you have any more dreams, call first." Connor didn't keep the deadly edge out of his voice. He wanted this guy off their property and away from his mate.

Ana dug her fingers into his side, but he didn't flinch.

Matt sighed heavily, then nodded at Ana. "I'll see you soon. Just . . . stay safe."

"Thanks for coming," she said, as he turned away.

Once he was out of earshot, Ana shrugged off Connor's grip and glared at him. "What's the matter with you?"

"He could have called before coming over. All that could have been said over the phone."

"Is this about a general dislike of humans or is this about you being a jackass?" She placed her hands on her hips.

"*Jackass*?"

"I can practically taste the testosterone coming off you and it's disgusting. You *know* he's not interested in me. It was kind of him to visit, especially when his mom was likely hospitalized because of her friendship with me. We still don't know if it was Taggart behind the attack on Kaya, but my bet is that it was. Matt and his mom don't owe us anything yet he came out here to warn us anyway. I've never even heard him mention his father before or anything about dream walking, so I imagine it's not something he freely broadcasts to people. We should be thankful he took the time to see us."

She muttered something else under her breath, turned on her heel and stalked through the front door.

An apology on his lips, he followed after her. The moment they stepped inside Vivian collided with her and latched on to Ana's side. "Carmen fell down!"

Ana's eyes widened. The panic he saw there pierced him, but he focused on the little cub. "Where is she?"

With an unsteady hand, she pointed. "Kitchen."

He could feel Ana and Vivian close behind him. His heart jumped in his throat as he entered the large room. Carmen was lying by the small table, eyes squeezed tight, curled into the fetal position, shaking like she'd been submerged in Arctic waters.

Reaching underneath her, he scooped her up. Despite her shaking she was burning up. They had much higher body temperatures than humans, but the heat radiating from her was scorching and unnatural.

"Did she have anything to eat?" he directed his question to Vivian, who still hung on to Ana's leg.

"She was eating a muffin." The little girl's voice shook.

On the table there was a half-eaten, crumbled mini muffin. "Did you find her like this?"

She shook her head. "No. We were talking about making breakfast for you and Ana and that human man and she just fell down."

Ana reached out and felt her sister's face. Her own

complexion paled as the heat touched her fingertips.
"Oh, Carmen—"

"Ana, check on everyone and bring Vivian with you.
Don't let her out of your sight." He didn't like barking
orders at her, but if she didn't stay busy, he worried she
might lapse into shock. There was nothing she could do
for her sister at the moment. If they wanted to stop what
was going on, they all had to keep a level head. Though
the truth was, if something happened to Ana, he knew
he wouldn't be able to stay rational.

"I need to help Carmen." A tremor laced her words.

"Ana, you need to check on the pack. Let *me* help
your sister."

She looked torn, but she nodded and grabbed Vivian's hand on the way out the door.

As he rushed up the stairs, panic washed over him
when Carmen started shivering even harder. He needed
to bring her temperature down fast. Without bothering
with her clothes, he turned on the shower in her bathroom and held her under the lukewarm water. He didn't
want to throw her into shock, so he gradually worked
the water until it was colder. Her eyes flared open briefly.
Confusion fluttered across her face before she passed
out again.

At least she clutched his arms as he held her up. If she
hadn't lost the use of her basic motor skills, she still had
a fighting chance. The knowledge that they'd just
checked the food and water the night before clawed at
his insides. Unless someone had broken into the house
overnight, no one had access to it. Carmen didn't have
any puncture wounds on her skin that he could see, so
he doubted she'd been injected with anything. Connor
wasn't sure how she'd been poisoned, but he was going
to exchange more than words with Matt very soon. He'd

been in the house before Connor and Ana had come over, giving him plenty of opportunity to lace their food with poison.

An invisible pressure weighed on his chest as he hurried across the yard, using trees as cover. He'd seen one of Ana's female relatives leave through the side door of her home, carrying a trash bag, and he wasn't going to waste the opportunity to get the young she-wolf alone.

Since he couldn't poison the pack simultaneously like last time, he was going to take them out one by one, any way he could. And high doses of silver should do the job since the poison he'd created hadn't. It should kill them all. Unfortunately he'd have to get a lot closer to these creatures for the silver to work. They'd discovered he'd broken into the storage shed and were now being even more careful.

The time for patience was over. He'd poison those he could, but he was going to have to take a more direct approach this time. If he could take the females off guard, he could kill them quickly and efficiently. The males would be harder, but with the females dead these loners might leave anyway. They weren't from around here and had no ties other than the women. From what he understood about shifters, males went where the females were.

Either way he'd continue killing as many of them as he could. They owed him more than they realized.

It was early. Too early for most of the pack to be awake. Still, if he got caught sneaking around it would raise suspicion. Something he couldn't afford. His breath curled in front of him like smoke rolling out of a chimney.

The morning air was quiet and the sky dark and overcast. A warning of what was to come. Gripping the syringe in his hand, he forced himself to take a deep, calming breath as he rounded the back of the house. They'd be able to sense his fear or agitation.

If they did, they'd no doubt kill him if they figured out what he'd done. He refused to be killed by these animals. Not after they'd killed his father in such a brutal manner. *A bear attack.* That's how the local assholes had ruled the death. But he knew better.

His heart thumped against his chest like a drum when the young girl—no, animal—closed the lid of the over-sized garbage bin.

When she spotted him, she smiled, revealing a perfect row of white teeth. "Morning."

He envisioned those teeth growing as she turned into the animal she was. He nodded politely. "Good morning."

"What are you doing here?"

Ignoring her question, he frowned, and with his free hand motioned to her face. "You've got some sort of smudge there."

Her hand flew up and she rubbed the imaginary spot. "Did I get it?"

"No." He shook his head and stepped closer. She wouldn't view him as a danger anyway since they knew each other, but he kept his movements unhurried and unthreatening. "It's right here—"

Reaching up with his other hand, he jammed the needle into her skin and shot the liquid silver directly into her vein. Her eyes widened and her pretty mouth opened to scream, but nothing came out other than a choking, gurgling gasp.

The poison worked instantly. Once it hit her bloodstream it moved with lethal speed. Unlike imbibing it, this method was the most toxic for their kind.

Her eyes stayed unnaturally wide as she hit the earth

with a soft thud. Something dark inside him urged him
to stay and watch the life leave her body, but he couldn't
risk it.

Adrenaline roared through him. He'd succeeded so
quickly. He only wished he'd done this the first time.
Though it probably wouldn't have worked with so many
males. The females, on the other hand, would be easy to
kill if this was any indication. It didn't seem to matter
the species; they were always more trusting. Weaker.
Glancing around, he found he was still alone.

But that would change fast. The sun started to peek
up now, pushing through the dark clouds and bathing
the ranch in warmth. It would be only a matter of time
before someone found her body. And he needed to be
gone when they did.

Chapter 12

Ana looked down at Vivian as she opened the front door. "You didn't eat anything in the house this morning, did you?"

The little girl shook her head.

"Good. Don't run off. Okay? I want you to stay with me while we stop at all the houses. After we check the food, I'll get you breakfast, but I want to test it first." She shut the door behind them and started to ascend the steps.

"Silver won't hurt me anyway."

Ana frowned at Vivian's quiet declaration. "What?"

The little girl's shoulders lifted. "I'm a jaguar."

"Oh . . . right." She was embarrassed she'd forgotten that silver didn't affect felines. If Vivian was going to stay with them, Ana realized there was a lot more she needed to learn about her. "You still stick close to me anyway. Okay?"

"Is Carmen going to die?"

Ana's throat seized at the question. She couldn't lose her sister. Not either of them. The fates had been cruel the past couple months but they wouldn't be brutal enough to take her younger sisters away. Not now. Not when their lives were finally starting to turn around. They had a new Alpha, and Carmen was finally looking to settle down with a mate. That thought warmed her more than she'd imagined. She just wanted her sisters to be happy and safe. Ana shook her head sharply. "No one is going to die." If she said the words enough and believed them, maybe it would be true.

"Ana!"

She turned at the sound of her cousin screaming her name. "Come on," she murmured to Vivian. They jogged across the grass toward Isabel.

Though they were the same age, her dark-haired packmate looked as if she'd aged overnight. "It's . . . it's—" She broke off sobbing. The sound was raw and uncontrolled and pierced Ana's heart.

Isabel was a beta and didn't handle stress as well, but Ana had never seen her like this, not even when her parents and brothers had died. A frisson of cold fear curled through Ana. She hooked her arm around Isabel's waist to steady her and held her packmate tight. By the way Isabel shook, she feared her cousin would collapse. "Come on, Isabel. Talk to me." She kept her voice low and soothing.

"Behind . . . house . . ." She pointed an unsteady finger toward their brick home.

Ana looked around and realized a few more members of the pack had exited their homes. She also noticed Noel exiting the barn with one of the males, but she brushed the detail aside. Gently, she unhooked her arm from Isabel, then looked at the little cub. "You stay here with Isabel and watch out for her. Okay? Don't go anywhere."

Vivian nodded solemnly. "I promise."

With everything going on she didn't like letting the

cub out of her sight, but they were on a ranch surrounded by shifters, and besides, she wasn't sure what was actually *behind* the house. Even though she knew Vivian should be safe for a few minutes, her sister should have been safe in her own home and now she was ... Hell, Ana didn't know what was going on with Carmen either, and she hated that Connor had taken over. She should be the one taking care of her sister. The knowledge rolled around in her stomach like a lead ball. But if she'd stayed and argued, it would have wasted time. As she rounded the corner of the house she jerked to a halt.

Alicia, the quietest, sweetest beta wolf, lay flat on her back, unmoving. By the gray pallor of her skin, Ana knew Alicia was dead before she reached her. The she-wolf's head rolled to the side and her eyes were open unnaturally wide. An expression of shock covered her face.

Crouching down, she took the young girl's wrist. The warmth of life was already receding and she had no pulse.

Hot tears pricked Ana's eyes. *How could this have happened?* Reaching up, she brushed the young girl's hair back from her face. Also losing warmth.

"Shit." Connor's deep voice cut through the air.

Without getting up, she looked over her shoulder to find Connor standing behind her. For a brief moment, fear sparked through her that he'd left Carmen, but she knew he wouldn't have done so if her sister wasn't in good hands.

Ana hadn't even scented his presence. All she'd been able to focus on was her dead packmate. Her mouth went dry as she stared at him. She didn't know what to say. *Shit* about summed up everything going on right now.

She started to lift Alicia's body when Connor stopped her.

"Wait." Crouching next to her, he brushed the girl's hair away from her lifeless face. "Look at this."

Ana frowned as she focused on what he pointed to. There was a faint puncture wound, and the area around her neck was swollen and irritated. Not overtly, but when she looked close, the girl's skin was puffy and raised. "Someone *injected* her?"

"Looks that way." His voice was grim.

"Who could have gotten past our security? Aren't your men patrolling the grounds?" Their ranch and surrounding area were big, but she didn't understand how someone could have snuck past their security, then gotten away without being seen. Of course, someone had managed to poison the water in their storage shed too. Whoever it was, he was a skilled tracker or hunter.

"What do you know about your friend Matt?"

"Wait. You think *he* did this?" She shook her head vehemently. There was no possible way.

"I'm trying to look at this objectively, Ana. If it wasn't for you, I'd have already hunted him down and made him talk." His voice was harsh.

An unwanted shiver snaked through her. She knew Connor was a predator. Hell, she was too. But this was a different side to him, and the wrath coming from him was potent and scary. Connor didn't make idle threats. She racked her brain, thinking of everything she knew about the Dunlauxes. "Kaya moved here with him when he was little. I don't think he was even five at the time. Uh, they own a store in town and sell jewelry, art, pottery, rugs—stuff like that. They're two of the few humans who welcomed us immediately. Connor, I've literally watched Matt grow up. His mom used to bring him out here to go horseback riding all the time when he was younger. I can't imagine him being involved in this."

"What about his father?" Connor's green eyes were growing dangerously dark.

She knew he was fighting his inner rage, forcing his animal back down, so she rushed to continue. "I don't know. Kaya mentioned him only once. She said he was Sioux, which is where I think Matt got his name from. She's a descendant of the Tuscarora, though—I do know that. I wasn't kidding when I said I'd never heard him mention his father until today."

Connor's expression was resolute as he lifted Alicia's small body. "Stay away from him."

"He did *not* do this." Though her heart ached at the sight of her lifeless cousin, Ana was positive that Matt wasn't involved in any of this. She wouldn't blindly blame him as an outlet for her anger.

"Ana." There was a warning note in Connor's voice.

Now wasn't the time to argue with him. Isabel and Alicia's other sisters would need the comfort of the pack. "I'll stay away ... We should lay her in the barn until the burial ceremony." *God, another death.* A tight cord cinched around her heart, making it difficult to breathe, but she tried to push past it. She couldn't afford to let anyone see her weak. Still, a few tears escaped as she looked at Alicia.

When they walked around the back of the house, Ana spotted Isabel and her three remaining sisters huddled together. Noel stood next to them with her arm wrapped around Isabel in support. Most of the male pack members stood by too, their expressions dark and dangerous. Vivian had latched on to one of Ryan's legs, and little Lucas had latched on to the other. For that Ana was thankful. At least she knew both cubs were safe.

Ana could feel the air change. These men wanted blood. They might not have been pack members long, but when someone killed one of your own, it didn't matter. Especially not to male warriors. The wolf inside her wanted justice but not blind revenge. Innocents got hurt that way. And then the town would turn against them. She'd seen it happen before and she didn't want it happening to her pack. They'd be hunted down and it would only be a matter of time before they had to relocate. Again.

As she looked around at the men, she didn't see Liam. "Where's your brother?"

Connor growled something indistinct low in his throat. Almost as if on cue, Liam's truck rounded the bend and steered up the dirt drive.

As they entered the barn, Connor held out Alicia's small body and handed it to her. "Can you take care of her?"

Pushing past the lump in her throat, she nodded. "Of course."

Connor reached out and cupped Ana's cheek for a moment. His eyes were dark and she could see the conflicting emotions running through them. "Ana, we're going to find out who's doing this. I promise."

Still not trusting her voice, all she could do was nod. She took Alicia to one of the empty stalls and laid her on a soft strip of hay. Soon they'd need to cleanse her body, then wrap her in the traditional ceremonial burial veil, but for now this would have to do.

"I can't believe it." She turned at the sound of Noel's voice.

Her younger sister's face was unusually pale. Noel had taken it the hardest when their parents had died. Ana reached out for her, and her sister immediately wrapped her arms around Ana's neck. Noel might be alpha in nature but she needed comforting right now.

"How's Isabel?" Ana knew it was a stupid question. It just popped out.

Sniffling, Noel shrugged as she pulled back. "Not

great. All her sisters are supporting one another, but I think this hit them harder than when . . ."

Ana didn't need her to finish the thought. It was harder than when most of the pack had died. Those deaths had been sudden and swift. They'd all been able to lean on each other because of the unexpectedness. Even though they still had pack support it shouldn't be happening again. Despite her desire to believe in Matt's innocence, Connor's warning about Matt played in her head. "Are you planning to go into town soon?"

Noel shook her head, and a few tears rolled down her cheeks.

Ana's heart ached watching her sister's pain. "Good. Don't. And stay away from Matt Dunlauxe."

Noel frowned. "Why?"

"Don't worry about that. Just do what I say. Okay? And will you please stay here until I'm back? I don't want Isabel or any of her sisters tormenting themselves by looking at Alicia."

"Of course. Where's Carmen, by the way? Why didn't she come outside?"

Shit. Ana cleared her throat. "She's with Teresa. I'll be back in a few minutes." As she hurried from the barn, she brushed off the guilt. She hadn't exactly lied, but an omission of the truth was just as bad. She didn't want Noel worrying yet. Not until she knew how sick Carmen was. If she could keep her sister unaware for a while it was worth a little guilt. Now she just needed to find Connor.

When Ana walked back into the main yard, almost everyone had dispersed. A few of the men still stood around and the rage and anger she'd scented before was actually stronger. They might be part of the same pack now, but she didn't know them well, yet she could tell these men definitely wanted blood.

Connor was the Alpha so if he made it clear he wouldn't stand for blind revenge, they would listen. Or she *hoped* they would. And she really hoped Connor *wouldn't* stand for revenge. What she knew of him she admired, but he was like an onion. Every second they spent together, more layers peeled back. He was darker, more dominant than she remembered. A true Alpha.

She nodded at the men and when she spied Ryan on the front porch by the main house, she hurried over to him. "Where are Connor and Liam?"

He tilted his head to the left. "At your place."

"Thanks." She started in that direction, but he stopped her.

"How's Teresa?" Before she could answer, he continued. "Lucas keeps asking about her."

Sure, cowboy. I'm sure he's not the only one worried about her. "She's doing better. Why don't you go upstairs and see her for yourself? She needs all our support now."

He nodded solemnly but didn't make a move from the porch. Just looked at the house longingly.

She didn't understand why Ryan wouldn't visit Teresa when it was obvious he was smitten with her. Shaking her head, she jogged toward her and Connor's place. As she opened the front door, she heard shouting. The voices came from the direction of the kitchen. Instead of walking in, she hung back. They might be able to scent her, but their own anger likely masked her presence.

"I'm not just your Alpha—I'm your brother! This is *our* pack now," Connor growled.

"And December's my *mate*. I have to protect her." Liam's voice was just as heated.

"Her brother's the sheriff. I think he can handle it."

"Not if a shifter is after her. No human can protect her."

"Why would shifters care about her?"

"I'm not saying they do, but someone broke into her home and tried to hurt her. And I don't care if it's a human or a shifter. I have to protect her."

"I feel like I don't even know you anymore, Liam. One of our packmates was murdered this morning. *Murdered*. You should have been here!"

"You might be my Alpha, but December is my mate. I'll do anything to protect her, even if it means defying you. Just because you were a pussy where Ana was concerned doesn't—"

Crunch!

It sounded like someone's fist slammed into something—or more likely someone.

"Bastard," Liam growled.

There was a crash, then the sound of more fists pummeling into skin. They wouldn't do any lasting damage to each other, but the last thing the pack needed now was dissension. Especially between Connor and Liam.

Leaving her hiding place by the front door, Ana hurried through the foyer to the kitchen and found Connor and Liam rolling around on the floor like two adolescent cubs.

"Stop it, both of you!"

They didn't even flinch, just continued pounding on each other. Connor reared back and slammed his fist into Liam's jaw. Without pause Liam turned sideways and came back with his elbow, smashing it into Connor's face.

She hurried to the sink and pulled the sink sprayer from its holder. Aiming it, she flipped on the faucet and pressed down hard. Water spewed from it, spraying first Connor, then Liam.

"What the hell?" Liam batted at the water and sat up.

Connor rolled away but still crouched on the floor

near his brother. He looked pissed and ready to take another swing at Liam. Or he might be waiting to lunge at him again.

She didn't stop spraying.

Finally Connor held up a hand in defeat. "Damn it, Ana. We stopped."

She let go of the sprayer and glared at them. "What the hell's the matter with you two? One of our pack-mates is *dead*. My cousin is fighting for her life, and now my baby sister is sick! All those betas and alphas alike will need our support. And the men will need your guidance. They're so full of rage, I'm afraid they'll do something stupid if you don't stop them."

"They would never act without my okay," Connor said quietly.

"How am I supposed to know that? You two are in here acting like cubs instead of like the leaders you're supposed to be."

Silence descended on the kitchen.

Finally Connor stood and held out a hand for his brother. Liam's face softened a little as he took it.

"I'm sorry, Ana. I . . . I'm sorry," Liam muttered before striding from the kitchen.

Connor turned to face her and had the decency to look embarrassed. "I apologize for my behavior, Ana."

She shook her head. "Don't apologize to me. What's going on with Carmen? I wanted to see you before I go over there. I need to know your men won't do anything stupid."

"They *won't*. And she's okay. Not like Teresa. She was sleeping when I left her, but I think she'll pull through. I wouldn't have left her if . . ."

In her heart she'd known that, but she'd needed to ask. "What's going on with you and your brother? Why are you fighting like this?"

"Don't worry about it." He shrugged out of his wet shirt.

Her eyes narrowed as he bared his chest. "Are you trying to distract me?"

The corners of his mouth tugged up slightly as he shimmied out of his wet jeans. "Would it work right now?"

"No."

"Then no," he muttered before leaving the room.

Her jaw clenched at his retreating backside. His very firm, sculpted backside. After all they'd shared last night she still felt like he was a stranger to her in some ways. He and Liam had gotten in a fight, and he couldn't even open up to her about that. It was just another reminder that no matter how much she gave of herself to him, he was still holding something back.

Chapter 13

Liam slowed his truck as he and Ryan passed December's bookstore. He could see a few customers inside, and even though common sense told him to keep driving straight back to the ranch, he pulled into one of the empty parking spots along the strip of stores.

"What are you doing?" Ryan frowned as Liam put the truck into PARK.

"I need to make a quick stop."

His frown deepened. "We need to get these supplies back to the ranch."

"I'll just be a second." He had to refrain from snapping at his friend. It wasn't Ryan's fault he hadn't gotten any sleep because he'd been up all night keeping an eye on December's house. Just as it wasn't his friend's fault that guilt ate away at Liam's insides about Alicia, the young she-wolf who had died. He simply couldn't stay away from December.

The need to be near her and, more important, protect her was overwhelming. The animal inside him wanted to take her away and lock her up somewhere safe. She might want to keep her distance from him, but that didn't mean he'd stop looking out for her. His inner wolf had already staked a claim. Now he just had to convince her they deserved a chance.

As he strode inside, he held open the door for two women who were exiting. December stood behind the cash register. Her eyes widened slightly when she saw him but she stepped out and faced him.

"Buying more books today?" Her voice was wry.

"If that's what it takes to get you to talk to me, I'll buy your entire stock." He took another step closer and inhaled her sweet scent. He bet she'd taste as sweet as she smelled. His cock jumped as he imagined running his tongue and teeth across her neck, then dipping lower, beneath her silky top.

She nervously tucked a wayward curl behind her ear. Today she'd pulled her hair back into a ponytail but some of her curls wouldn't stay put. He wanted to reach out and free all that hair. Run his hands through it and—

"Stop looking at me like that," she muttered.

"Like what?"

Her bright blue eyes narrowed. "You know exactly what. You can't keep coming in here to see me."

"Have dinner with me again. Please." He nearly choked on the last word. He didn't want to *ask* anything. The animal inside him wanted to take, dominate and claim.

"I don't know," she hedged.

At least it wasn't a no. "It's just a meal."

"Fine."

"What?"

She sighed. "I'll have dinner with you but only because I know you won't leave until I agree."

The vise that seemed permanently tightened around his chest loosened a fraction. "I'll pick you up here at six tonight."

"Is that a question or an order?" Her eyebrows rose slightly.

He cleared his throat. "Would you like me to pick you up here?"

A small smile touched her lips and she nodded. "Listen. My brother told me a little about what's going on at the ranch. Is everyone . . . are you safe?"

Liam wasn't sure what her brother had told her or how much Parker even knew but he wasn't going to discuss it with December. He might want her but that was still pack business. "I'm fine. You just watch out for yourself." He hated that he couldn't protect her all the time. The need to do so was messing with his head and his relationship with his brother.

If she was mated to him he'd have her under his roof and it wouldn't be a problem. Until that happened, there wasn't much he could do. This mate business was bad news. He'd heard about males going crazy and becoming ultraprotective of their mates, but he'd never imagined the need burning through him would be so powerful. So fucking dominant it was a constant battle between his human and wolf sides. Now that Liam understood the mating frenzy, the fact that Connor had walked away from Ana said a hell of a lot about how much he'd loved her, even back then. Liam didn't know that he'd have been able to sacrifice that much.

She rolled her eyes. "I'm twenty-eight years old, Liam. I'll be fine."

She wasn't fine. Someone had broken into her house and assaulted her. Even the thought of someone touching her, hurting her, made him see red. The predator inside him wanted out. "I'll see you tonight," he said, and grunted before hurrying from the store.

His canines pushed at his gums as his entire body fought the change. This hadn't happened since he was a cub learning how his body worked. He needed to fuck or fight to get this rage out. And he really knew which one he'd prefer to do right now. His cock started to harden as he thought about what it would be like to sink inside December.

As he slid into the front seat of the truck, Ryan let out a low curse. "Damn, Liam. You look ready to kill someone. You all right?"

"Fine. Let's get this stuff back to the ranch." In the back of the truck they had boxes and boxes of bottled water to replace the ones they'd thrown away. Ana had wanted to pick it up herself but Connor had been pretty insistent that Liam take care of this, and Liam understood why. His brother wanted to show they were all taking an active role in helping solve the pack's problems, and after the way Liam had disappeared last night he owed his brother that. The young she-wolf's death had hit the men pretty hard. And he was embarrassed he hadn't been there when it happened. He knew it was biology, but the knowledge that they must propagate their species was ingrained in them. Not through teaching but in their DNA. Losing a female—any female—was always difficult. It was why Liam couldn't understand shifters like Taggart. According to Ana he disrespected the females of his pack, and Liam hadn't forgotten the way he'd been ready to attack Ana that first night they'd arrived. Most male shifters didn't act like that and wouldn't stand to see others act that way.

"What did the human say?" Ryan asked.

"Her name is December . . . And she agreed to have dinner with me tonight." He could only hope for more than a shared meal.

Ryan grinned. "I never thought I'd see the day you got all twisted up over a tiny woman."

"So, how is *Teresa* doing anyway?" Liam knew his

friend had a thing for her, but Ryan had yet to even see her since she'd been bedridden. It was out of character for the other wolf.

The grin melted from Ryan's face. "The same, I guess."

Guilt jumped inside Liam. Just because he was in a dark mood didn't mean he had to take it out on his friend. "I'm sorry, man. I—"

"Forget about it. I get it. Women have that effect."

He grunted in agreement. While he might not understand Ryan's reluctance to see Teresa, he knew the other wolf well enough to realize that there was likely a good reason behind it.

As he neared the turnoff toward the ranch, he frowned when he saw flashing blue and red lights in his rearview mirror. He checked the speedometer. Under the speed limit by a couple miles per hour. "What the hell?"

Ryan turned around in his seat. "You think they know about Alicia?"

Liam shook his head. "I don't think so." He knew his brother better than anyone. Connor would alert the Council of the poisoning and subsequent death, but he wouldn't be jumping on the phone to alert the locals. Didn't matter what Ana wanted. His brother liked to keep his distance from humans. Not because he didn't like humans; he just didn't trust them. Pack business stayed pack business. No matter what.

He rolled down his window as he put the truck in PARK. He gritted his teeth when he spotted December's brother stalking toward him. "Son of a bitch," he muttered.

The sheriff stopped by the door but didn't make an attempt to pull out his pad or write him a ticket. His eyes were narrow slits. "Stay the hell away from my sister."

"What are you talking about?" Maybe this bastard really did have a GPS tracker on him.

"I saw you leaving her store. Stay away from her," he ground out.

"She's an adult." A very sexy one who'd gotten under his skin.

"People in town are starting to talk."

Liam shrugged. *What is this guy's deal?* "So?"

"I don't want my sister labeled as some shifter . . ." He shook his head as he trailed off, but Liam knew what he'd been about to say.

Shifter whore. The term wasn't unique or even clever. But that's what she'd be called by some. He didn't give a shit what people thought but he also didn't want December ostracized. "Is this harassment about a general dislike of shifters or is it just me you have a problem with?" Liam wanted to get right to the heart of the problem. The rage rolling off the sheriff was different from anything he'd ever scented before. The cop's anger was personal.

"Just stay away from December. If I catch you anywhere near her, I'll arrest you."

"For what?"

"I'll come up with something."

"I'm taking her to dinner later, so you might want to check with her before you make plans to arrest her date." Liam couldn't keep the sarcasm out of his voice.

The sheriff took a deep breath and stepped back from the car. "You hurt my sister, I'll fucking kill you."

Liam didn't respond as the man stalked away. He didn't care if her brother didn't like him. He just needed to make sure December did. *One step at a time.*

"Can I give Carmen and Teresa the balloons?" Vivian asked from the passenger's seat of Ana's truck.

"Of course." Ana had taken Vivian with her to the feed store mainly to keep the little she-cat busy, but also because she'd wanted the company. Then they'd stopped at the drugstore because Vivian wanted to get something special. Ana had wanted to pick up the backup water supply but Connor had been insistent that his brother take care of it. She was a little annoyed by that but decided to let it go.

"You really think Carmen will be okay?" she persisted.

"Sweetie, she's going to be fine." Carmen had passed out after imbibing a small amount of silver but she wasn't bedridden like Teresa. For some reason her cousin wasn't faring well, even though it should be out of her system by now. Some shifters just had stronger immune systems than others.

"What about you?"

"Me too. I promise. We're going to figure this thing out." She hoped at least.

"Connor says you're tough." Vivian's voice was matter-of-fact.

Ana frowned as she pulled onto the two-lane highway. That was interesting. "He said that?"

"Uh huh. Before we moved here. He told me you were the most beautiful she-wolf he'd ever met and that you were tough as nails. He said you'd be the perfect Alpha's mate."

Ana didn't know about *that*, but she nodded at the young she-cat's words. Connor wasn't exactly known for being loquacious so it surprised her that he'd opened up to the little girl. Maybe he'd simply told Vivian that so she'd feel less nervous about moving to a new place. Yeah, that was probably it. "You're pretty tough yourself, living with a bunch of wolves for so long."

Vivian rolled her eyes with the typical flair of a ten-year-old. "My mommy always told me that males were the same no matter the species."

Ana swallowed a laugh. "Your mom sounds like she was a smart woman."

"She was. And she was pretty like you . . . I miss her."

"I miss my mom too."

"Do you still cry over her?" Vivian's voice cracked slightly.

"Yeah." She didn't trust her voice to say any more.

"Connor told me it gets easier with time but I don't believe him. I hurt every day. Every day I wake up and there's a big hole in my chest and sometimes my tummy aches so bad I can't eat. I just want to see my mommy's face again."

Fighting the rush of emotions, Ana reached out and patted her head gently. "You'll always miss her. It might not get easier exactly, but some of the sting will fade with time."

Vivian mumbled something under her breath and turned to stare out the window, but Ana didn't miss the few tears that spilled down her cheeks.

Shifter or not, growing up without a mother was hard. Hell, maybe harder for this little one. She was already different from the majority of the population and now she was living with a bunch of wolves. Ana's heart ached. She reached out for her again. "Vivian—"

Her entire world jerked as someone slammed into the back of her truck. She flew forward but her seatbelt pulled her back. The action was jarring but not enough to give them whiplash. A dark green truck with tinted windows had hit them.

Grappling with the wheel, Ana struggled to straighten it. "Great," she muttered. What kind of idiot couldn't drive straight on a two-lane road?

She turned on her blinker, ready to pull off on the side of the road, when the truck slammed into them again.

This is not *an accident.* Her instincts went into overdrive. She gripped the wheel tightly and pressed harder on the gas.

The needle shot up instantly. And the other truck followed.

"Ana?" Vivian's voice shook.

"Sweetie, you need to stay strapped in and do as I say, okay?" She fought to keep her voice calm.

"Okay."

They weren't that far from the turnoff to the ranch. *Protect Vivian.* That thought rang in her mind clearly. If she could just get home, they'd be safe. She would be able to keep this little one alive.

As the needle rose higher, Ana tried to think. In the rearview mirror she could see the silhouettes of two men in the green pickup.

Or they could be shifters. It was impossible to tell without smelling them. A hand reached out of the passenger's-side window. Metal flashed in the sunlight.

A gun.

Ana yanked the wheel, swerving into the next lane. As she did, the back window exploded and Vivian screamed. A loud thud sounded as the radio burst apart.

Her sweaty palms slid against the wheel and her heart raced out of control. *How can this be happening?*

"Stay down!"

When Ana looked at the little girl, Vivian was shifting to her animal form. Her clothes ripped and she cried out as she underwent the change. The little cub jumped down onto the floorboards and curled into a ball.

Ana couldn't blame her. The girl was only ten and her instincts were telling her to protect herself.

Another loud set of pings ricocheted off the interior of the cabin. A sudden pain ripped through her shoulder.

The searing sensation tore through her arm, sending shock waves to all her nerve endings. Blood ran down her arm to her elbow. She knew she'd been shot, and while it burned, it wasn't fatal. Holding the wheel with her hurt arm, she ripped her sweater sleeve off with her free hand. The clenching action only intensified the pain and she cried out. She knew it would be so easy to panic right now but she had a little girl to protect and her animal instincts were taking over. Her inner wolf begged to take over completely and regulate the pain, but Ana focused on the road in front of her.

They weren't using silver bullets or her skin would have started turning gray. She *would* survive this. She just needed to get them to safety.

The little cat cried and meowed loudly on the floor.

"I know, sweetie. We're almost home."

Behind her, the truck swerved into the next lane and started gaining speed. So Ana increased her own speed. *Are they going to run us off the road?*

Connor! She shouted his name in her mind, knowing it was useless. They weren't linked because they weren't bondmates yet.

Shit, shit, shit*!*

Her heart pounded wildly in her chest. They were so close to the turnoff. So close to safety. The other truck shot forward in a burst of speed.

Before Ana could react, it rammed into their side. She struggled with the wheel but it was too much for her to handle.

Swerving off the road, she thought she saw red and blue flashing lights before her truck slammed into a tree.

Then blackness.

Pain streaked through her skull. Ana felt as if one of her horses had kicked her in the head. *Where am I?*

"Stay with me, Ana. Come on, wake up." The voice was familiar. Unexpected.

Ana cracked open an eye and found herself staring into the dark eyes of the sheriff. The driver's-side door was open and he stood there, looking at her with a concerned expression. "What are you . . . ?" She couldn't finish. It hurt to talk.

"I saw what those assholes did. They tore out of here when they saw me." He pulled out a knife and she flinched.

He paused for a moment, then shook his head. When he came at her with the knife she shrank back against the seat. Something in her body was broken and she couldn't defend herself. He likely wouldn't be able to kill her but he could hurt the hell out of her if he wanted to.

"I'm just cutting the seat belt," he muttered.

When the strap snapped free, she tried to move, but he put a gentle hand against her shoulder. "I've called an ambulance."

Panic and a surge of adrenaline flared inside her at the word *ambulance*. She didn't want to involve the locals. She twisted her head around. "Vivian?"

A small cry came from the other side of the truck. Everything was still blurry but things were slowly coming into focus. The sheriff started talking rapidly into his radio, but she ignored him.

"Vivian? Are you okay?"

A paw appeared on the seat; then her spotted head popped up. The front of the truck had been smashed, pushing the dash forward, but it looked like it had created a little cave for Vivian.

"You're okay?" she slurred.

Vivian crawled onto the seat and scooted closer. Despite the pain rolling over her, a sharp burst of relief surged inside Ana. She didn't know how the little cub was unscathed but she wasn't going to question the fates.

"Oh, my God. I didn't realize anyone else was in the vehicle." She turned at the sound of the sheriff.

"Don't touch her," Ana snapped. Talking was using more energy than she had but she didn't want him going anywhere near Vivian. The little cub was scared and could lash out. And if he tried to touch the cub, Ana feared her own inner wolf would take over. If that happened, she might attack the sheriff.

"Help is on the way. And I've called in backup to go after the guys who did this. I recognized the truck."

She didn't want his help. All she wanted was for him to stop talking. She didn't care if he called in backup. Connor was going to go after whoever did this and that terrified her more than anything. Looking down at herself, she saw blood and a ripped sleeve, and she was pretty sure her arm was broken. The pain could be from the gunshot, but instinct told her otherwise.

The sound of a vehicle approaching made her tense. If she could just get out of this stupid, smashed-up truck, she'd be fine.

"Shit," the sheriff muttered and strode away.

"Ana!" *Connor.*

Her eyes closed in relief. She tried to twist in her seat but more pain splintered through her. This time it was in her leg.

Then he was standing there, concern etched in every line on his face. "What happened?"

She motioned with her hand. "Get Vivian out of here. Sheriff . . . called ambulance. Don't want her near here."

"Ana—"

"Do it!"

He muttered something and reached across her to

pick up the small cub. Less than a minute later he was back by her side. "I'm going to get you out of here too."

"Where's Vivian?"

"My truck. Can you lean forward a little?"

She nodded.

"What the hell are you doing? Don't move her. I think her arm and leg are broken," the sheriff said.

"Yeah, no shit," Connor grunted. He slid his arm under her shoulders as she leaned forward.

Twisting to the side, she allowed him to pull her from the vehicle. It didn't matter that she'd heal faster; a broken bone hurt like hell. And she had two.

"Damn it," the sheriff muttered as he hurried to the other side of her. He lifted and held her legs as Connor gently pulled her out.

They laid her on the soft, grassy incline and she finally let out a breath she hadn't realized she'd been holding. Connor crouched beside her and held her as close as he could without jostling her.

"You've been *shot*." Connor's eyes started to darken, as if he'd just realized the extent of her injuries and that this wasn't an accident. An animalistic rage like she'd never seen flared there. And she could smell the change in the air. There was a dangerous darkness to it. Her mate was in battle mode. Ready to kill, regardless of man's or the Council's laws.

Feeling desperate, she clutched his arm. "Don't. *Please*. Just stay with me. I need you." The last three words had an immediate calming effect.

If he shifted and went after whoever had done this, it would cause a war. People wouldn't care who had started it. They'd know only that a shifter had killed some humans. And she knew Connor wouldn't be quick. He'd rip them to shreds and he wouldn't be apologetic afterward.

Some of the natural green crept back into his eyes,

but the beast inside him warred with his human side. She could see it so clearly it scared the holy hell out of her. Thankfully his human side won as he moved closer to her.

"You're going to be okay," he murmured.

"I know." And only because he was there. His presence gave her a profound comfort.

A loud siren blared in the distance. The ambulance was close. And she wanted nothing to do with it.

"They're almost here." The sheriff stood a foot away, staring at the two of them as if they were crazy.

"No, I'm taking her home. She doesn't need your help." His voice was dark and edgy. The sweet way he cradled her was in direct opposition to his angry tone. She soaked it up.

"She's been shot and she's got a couple broken bones. She could have internal bleeding. Or a spinal injury. She needs to go to the hospital. I thought you were her mate," he said disdainfully.

"She'll heal fine without your fucking hospital or doctors," Connor growled at the sheriff but smoothed back her hair gently. "You're going to be okay, Ana. I'm going to get you back to the house and take care of you."

The sheriff ignored him. "That may be so, but she's going to a hospital. I want this documented and I need her statement. Whoever did this isn't going to get away with it."

"Connor. I'll go ... Don't fight him." Something in the back of her mind questioned how Connor had even known she was there, but she brushed it aside. All she cared about was the fact that he was there and holding her. Comforting her. The pain was overwhelming and she needed to block it out. She closed her eyes and let the blackness take her again.

Chapter 14

Connor paced at the end of Ana's bed. Bringing her to the hospital had been a mistake. They could have taken better care of her at the ranch. Vivian wiggled in his arms but he held her tight. They'd already gotten more than a few odd stares when he'd walked through the emergency-room doors, carrying a crying jaguar cub.

The only reason they hadn't called security was likely because he'd been with the sheriff.

Vivian growled and nipped him as she struggled in his arms. She didn't draw blood, but she dug her teeth into his hand hard enough to make him flinch. If it had been anyone else, he'd have punished her. But she was young and he understood what she wanted. He held her up and looked into her big brown eyes. "I'll let you lie next to Ana, but don't jostle her, okay?"

She licked his face.

Shaking his head, he set Vivian down near Ana's side. The young cub immediately curled up as close to Ana as she could without touching her. She was inches away from one of Ana's hands.

Ana's arm and leg were wrapped and bandaged and

in soft casts. In less than forty-eight hours she'd be healed, so it would be pointless to put a hard cast on either injury. The doctors seemed to understand that when he'd explained it, but he was under the impression that they hadn't dealt with many shifters before. Which only made sense. Most shifters avoided hospitals at all costs. For all he knew Ana was the first shifter they'd ever actually helped.

He pulled the chair next to her bed and sat. Every primal instinct inside him wanted to hunt down whoever had hurt her and rip their throats out. But he couldn't leave her. Not like this. When she woke up, he wanted her to see his face.

As if she read his mind, her dark eyes flew open. She looked around the stark white room before settling back on him. "Where am I?"

"Hospital."

"Oh, right . . . What happened?"

"The sheriff came upon a truck trying to run you off the road. He got the plates but he says he thinks he knows who did this to you anyway."

"I remember that part . . . Humans?"

He nodded. A shifter wouldn't have used a regular gun. Or a gun at all. They'd have stalked and hunted her down with much more cunning. The attack in broad daylight was stupid, arrogant. Besides, even the most hardened shifters wouldn't have gone after her with a *cub* in the vehicle. Well, except maybe someone like Taggart, but Connor hadn't scented him in the area. "The bullet is out and you're already starting to heal. I think you freaked the doctors out with that." Shifters might have come out to the world, but they didn't frequent hospitals or flaunt all their abilities.

She glanced down at her body and winced. "I don't care what anyone says; getting shot hurts."

Careful not to disturb her, he reached out and cupped her cheek. Her skin was soft and the pulse on her neck jumped out of control as he touched her.

"How did you know where I was?" Her voice was scratchy.

"I heard you."

She frowned. "That's impossible. We're not bonded."

He shook his head. "It was in my head. Loud and clear. You screamed my name and I got a vision of where you were. It was . . ." *Terrifying*. He didn't say it out loud. He couldn't because he didn't trust his voice. His inner wolf had howled in pain when he'd heard her cry out for him. It had been so brief. Just one word. His name. And she'd sounded so scared he'd felt as if his heart had actually stopped for a moment. It was an incredibly rare thing for those not related and not bonded to be able to communicate. The knowledge only solidified that he and Ana were meant to be together. Even knowing that he'd likely die inside if something ever happened to her couldn't stop the burning need that begged him to bond with her.

She pressed a shaky hand to her sternum and rubbed in small circles, something she did when she was nervous. "Can you hear what I'm saying now?" She stared at him but he heard nothing.

He shook his head. "No, but I know what I heard and saw, Ana. Maybe we linked because you were so terrified."

Her frown deepened. "Maybe."

The door swung open and Vivian growled as the sheriff stepped inside the room. Connor bit back a smile at the little cub's protectiveness. He understood how she felt.

Ana reached down and petted her head, quieting her.

"How are you feeling?" The sheriff ignored Connor and Vivian and focused on Ana.

"Like I got shot," she murmured.

He cleared his throat as if he were uncomfortable. "We've taken two men into custody. They weren't hard to track down."

"Who are they?" Connor blurted the question even though he knew the sheriff wouldn't answer.

"I can't tell you that."

"Do you know why they went after her?" Connor asked.

"Not yet, but they were seen leaving a bar right before your attack. One of them has a history of violence against shifters and people in general. It's possible they saw Ana on the road and this was a crime of opportunity."

This was why Connor avoided towns. Some humans didn't need an excuse for violence. Ignorance and blind hatred were enough. "I assume you're going to prosecute them." Though he wished the sheriff wouldn't. Let the bastards go free. They'd never see another sunrise if Connor had anything to do with it.

He nodded. "This will be considered a hate crime. . . . Listen, I know this might not be the time, but I want to ask you some questions about your neighbors."

Connor stiffened in his seat. "What about them?"

"Have you noticed any unusual activity over there?"

"We're separated by a large section of land. We don't associate with Taggart's pack if we don't have to."

Ana squeezed his hand. He risked a quick glance at her, and it was obvious she wanted to tell the sheriff about the meth house they'd seen. He squeezed back and shook his head. Sighing, she laid her head back against the pillow.

"Is there something you'd like to add, Ana?"

"No." She shut her eyes, effectively dismissing him.

The sheriff rubbed a hand over his face. "I know

something is going on over at his place, but so far I haven't been able to get a warrant and they won't let me on their property. I want to keep my town—your town— safe, but if you won't tell me what you know—"

Connor pushed up out of his chair and stood. "Ana is tired and she doesn't know anything. If you have any more questions, we'll be back at the ranch. We won't be staying here much longer."

"Just tell me this. Was he involved in the attacks on Kaya and my sister?" Sheriff McIntyre said.

Connor ignored the question and strode toward the door. Standing by it, he waited until the sheriff muttered a low curse and stalked out.

He paused by the entrance and turned back to Connor. "I *need* to know. Did that bastard Taggart try to hurt my sister?"

Connor's eyes narrowed a fraction. "If he'd gone after your sister, she'd be dead. So would you, likely. Taggart's a piece of shit but I don't think he's dumb enough to attack a cop's sister." But Taggart *was* ballsy enough to mess with Ana. He wouldn't be a problem for very long. Connor couldn't know for sure if the two humans who'd gone after Ana were involved with Taggart and he didn't really care. The beast inside him wanted blood. And he was going to get it.

Sheriff McIntyre shook his head and strode down the hall. His shoes squeaked loudly across the terrazzo.

"Connor, when can we get out of here? I don't like being in this place. It smells like death." Ana's frustrated voice cut through the air, jerking him out of his thoughts.

When he turned back she was shoving off the covers and trying to sit up. "Damn it, woman. Don't move." He hurried to her side and pressed a gentle hand to her noninjured shoulder. "I'll take care of this. Just give me a few minutes."

She stuck her chin out mutinously, as if she thought he didn't want to get her out of there as much as she wanted to be gone.

He knew the hospital staff would likely fight him but he didn't care. He didn't want her there, exposed, longer than she had to be. That was the problem in mingling with humans. Too many people had access to her. She'd heal better surrounded by her pack anyway.

Ana tried to hide her groan as they pulled up to the gate, but Connor knew she was in pain. He'd taken great care in driving her home but the bumps in the road still had to hurt. The gunshot wound hurt worse than anything, though. He knew because he'd been in her shoes more than once. The wound would burn as if someone had poured scorching lava on her skin.

"Are you sure you won't take any painkillers?" Connor asked as he put the vehicle in PARK. Part of him wanted to force her to. He hated seeing her suffering. The doctor had given him a small supply of pain meds and a prescription to fill later.

"Maybe later," she muttered through clenched teeth.

But he knew she wouldn't. Just as he wouldn't. She didn't want anything to dull her senses. Shifters had a higher tolerance for pain, but she was still hurting. He could see it clearly on her face.

He was surprised the hospital staff had let her go so quickly, but maybe they didn't want to deal with a shifter in their ward. He didn't know or care what their reasoning was. "I've already called and let your sisters know what happened."

"How are Carmen and Teresa?"

"Carmen's better. Teresa . . ." He checked the rearview mirror and stopped when he saw Vivian paying attention. "She's hanging in there."

"I'll see her tonight after the burial ceremony for Alicia. Listen, I don't want to go to the ceremony in a wheelchair." He understood that she didn't want everyone to know the extent of her injuries, but there was no way around it.

She'd been knocked out in the hospital for hours after the accident so her bones were already fusing back together, but it would be a couple days before she'd completely heal or be able to shift to her wolf form.

"I'll take care of you, Ana." How could she not know that? He felt as if years of his life had been shaved off in the past few hours. When he'd seen her bleeding and barely moving in that truck, he'd hardly been able to contain his inner wolf from acting. The need to kill had been overwhelming and it had scared the shit out of him. Being mated had already changed his life in more ways than one. He was so used to being in control of himself, but with Ana around his world had shifted dramatically. It made him wonder how much stronger his need to protect would be when—if—they became bondmates.

As he got out of the truck, Liam yanked open the gate and rushed at him. Before he could respond, his brother wrapped his arms around him and pulled him into a tight hug. "I'm sorry about Ana. We'll find who did this."

Surprised by his brother's sudden show of affection, Connor returned the embrace before stepping back. "Thank you, brother."

"I know I haven't been around . . ." He cleared his throat once but held his gaze. "I'm here for you. If anything were to happen to Ana—"

"It *won't*." Connor didn't like to even say it aloud, let alone think it. "The sheriff said he knows who did this."

"Well, now, so do we. Ryan hacked into their system.

Two men were just entered into the system for driving under the influence, reckless driving and opening fire in a public place. They might not have enough to charge them with attempted murder, so they're hauling them down for questioning. A good lawyer could argue they weren't intending to hurt Ana and Vivian, but just out drunk and joyriding and weren't shooting at anyone. Even if they make the charges stick, they'll still be let out on bond before their trial—if it even gets that far."

"You have names?"

"And addresses. One of them has a rich daddy. I doubt he'll be held long. Probably be out on bail in a day or two."

Connor glanced at Ana through the windshield. Her dark eyes narrowed as if she knew exactly what they were talking about, so he turned back to his brother and lowered his voice. "Don't say anything to Ana. We'll handle this *our* way."

Liam nodded, then looked over his shoulder into the truck. "Want me to drive the truck into the garage? I'll take care of Vivian too. She looks like she's about to bounce off the walls in there."

"Yeah." Connor rounded the vehicle, then opened Ana's door. Walking her to the house would be less stressful on her body than driving her.

"What were you two whispering about?"

"He just wanted to know how you were doing. Now lean forward."

Muttering under her breath, she did as he said. "I know when you're lying."

Slipping his hands under her legs and around her back, he eased her from the truck. She fit against him perfectly. When she laid her head on his shoulder, he had to remind himself she was real. She wasn't lying dead on the side of the road.

"What's wrong?" Ana murmured against his neck, her breath warm and soft.

"Nothing."

He could feel her smile against his neck. "Are you going to lie about *everything* tonight?"

"When I heard that scream in my head I . . ." His throat squeezed painfully tight as he tried to finish the thought. It still baffled him he'd even been able to hear her since they weren't bondmates, but he wasn't going to question the fates. The only thing that mattered was that he *had* heard her and she was alive in his arms.

She didn't need him to. "I'm still here, Connor. And I'm not going anywhere."

The reality didn't do anything to quell his fears. When he closed his eyes all he could see was her in that truck, barely moving and bloody.

"Loosen that grip, buddy." Ana's voice was strained.

Immediately he relaxed his hold. "Sorry."

Once he got her upstairs and into their room, he pulled the covers back and laid her against the sheet and pillows. He wanted to stay with her, but now was the time to act. His men needed answers and to nail down their plan of attack. Someone had gone after an Alpha's mate. *My mate.* Human or not, the punishment would be brutal and swift.

Without bothering to pull the covers the rest of the way down, he stretched out next to her. She would heal. He could see that with his own eyes. But the animal inside him howled. It desperately wanted to ease her pain. "Please take a few of the pills." He pulled out the small packet the doctor had given him.

"It's not gonna happen so just drop it. And you can toss that prescription because I'm not going to be filling it either."

He quieted, knowing he shouldn't upset her at a time

like this. She needed to save her strength. "What do you want me to get for you? I can grab some bottled water from downstairs or—"

"Connor, I just need sleep, and I know there's stuff you need to take care of. Please don't worry about me. As soon as you leave I'll rest."

"I want to stay with you—"

"I understand, Connor. Go talk to everyone, please. They have a right to know what's going on. Too much has happened in the past couple days and we don't want rumors or panic starting. I need to sleep anyway."

Her eyes were drooping low so he knew she was telling the truth. And she was right. He needed to do some damage control. Once word spread that she'd been attacked rumors and fears would grow and spread like wildfire among the pack. He set her cell phone on the nightstand within reaching distance. "If you need anything, call me."

"I'm not going to bug you."

"Promise me you'll call. I'm not leaving the ranch so I won't be far."

Her dark eyes flared for a moment. "You're not leaving the ranch?"

He shook his head.

"Then promise me you won't go after the men who attacked us *later*."

"They're in custody right now."

"That's not a promise." Her voice was wry.

"No, it's not." Leaning forward, he pressed a kiss to her forehead, then her mouth. Her soft lips parted on a sigh and he swept his tongue into her mouth, tasting her sweetness. His cock started to lengthen and shame burned through him at his instinctive reaction. She was injured and laid up in bed. He shouldn't want to jump her.

Somehow he pulled back. "Call me if you need anything," he rasped out before hurrying from the room. At that moment he wanted to tell her how much he cared for her. That he loved her. But he didn't. He wanted her head clear when he admitted it, and if he was honest with himself, he wasn't sure he was ready for her response. If she didn't return his feelings . . . an uncomfortable pain lanced through his chest at the thought.

As he descended the stairs, Liam's voice sounded clear in his head. *Brother, you're gonna want to get out here. Take a guess which dumb-ass shifter has the balls to be cruising up our driveway right now.*

Taggart. Connor didn't have to guess. Tempering his desire to fight, he strode across the yard. Liam and Ryan stood by the main gate and a few of his men were scattered around the yard. Not all of them were visible, though. He might not be able to see them but they were all there. Waiting for his command.

Ready to kill Taggart, if necessary.

Digging his fingers into his palms, he stopped by the gate where his brother stood. Opening it would imply they were inviting him in. That wasn't happening.

"He is one dumb shit." Liam shook his head as Taggart got out of his truck.

Another male followed suit and exited from the passenger's side. No doubt his second-in-command. Connor kept his focus on the tall blond Alpha instead. As far as shifters went Taggart was on the lean side. Almost lanky. Strong, though. Just by looking at him Connor knew why he was Alpha of his pack. Dominance and power rippled off the conniving lupine shifter.

"What the hell are you doing here?" he spit out as Taggart neared him.

"Aren't you going to invite me in?"

Next to him Liam growled deep in his throat, but

Connor motioned for him to back down. He didn't want a fight today. His pack already had enough to worry about without him challenging another Alpha. "State your business, then get off my land."

"Your land? Not long ago this was Cordona property. If Ana's father could see you now he'd roll over in his grave. That proper son of a bitch would hate that she's with a mutt like you. Everyone knows your own father couldn't even keep your pack protected. Are you just as weak as him?"

The taunt about his father sliced through him but Connor forced himself to remain calm. It stung as much as the knowledge that Ana's father actually had despised him, but he doubted Taggart knew that. The other wolf was just trying to piss him off. "Talk or we'll force you off."

Taggart's dark eyes narrowed dangerously. "Fine. You killed one of my men."

"What the hell are you talking about? Are you talking about the *feral* wolf that nearly attacked Ana?"

"Who says he was feral?"

Connor took a step forward, thankful the gate provided a barrier, even if it wasn't much. "You know he was. And the real question is, Why? What shit are you into that would cause one of your own to become feral? You turning humans for sport, or maybe your wolves are into drugs?" Even though he knew the answer he wanted to see Taggart's reaction.

The other Alpha paused, likely wondering how much Connor actually knew. "I have no clue what you're talking about. You killed one of my wolves and you owe me. I'll take a portion of your land as payment. Simple as that."

"Not gonna happen. You got a problem, take it up with the Council."

"I will," Taggart spat.

"Good. They'll be expecting your call. I've already let them know about the feral wolf on our land *and* your illegal activities. If I were you, I'd keep my nose clean, or you might be getting a visit from one of their investigators soon. Or maybe from *the enforcer.*"

Taggart's brown eyes darkened until the whites of his eyes were nearly invisible.

Connor resisted the urge to smile. He'd definitely hit a sore spot. The Council wouldn't necessarily stop anyone from engaging in illegal activities, but they'd make Taggart's life hell if he brought extra heat from the humans. And running drugs was guaranteed to do that. Bringing the enforcer in for a visit was sure to screw up Taggart's little operation. The investigators were usually a precursor to the enforcer's visit. Once Jayce Kazan— the only enforcer in North America—came around, it was time to clean house. Not always, but that's usually what happened.

"You're full of shit," Taggart growled.

Connor didn't answer. Just stared at him and let the other Alpha feel the truth of his words. Taggart could call the Council and try to convince them the wolf Connor had killed hadn't been feral, but in response they'd definitely send down a team to investigate his claims. And when they did, they'd find Taggart's meth house. It would be destroyed not out of a sense of morality, but because it made them easier targets for the humans. Something Taggart knew.

"You tell the humans about my business too?" Taggart asked, not even bothering to deny it now.

He shook his head. "Hell, no. And if you're smart you'll stay away from them." Connor might detest Taggart but he didn't want the other wolf messing with the locals. It would reflect badly on all shifters, and if Taggart hurt Liam's human woman, it would start a war.

"This isn't over, Connor. You owe me."

"If you're smart, you'll walk away right now. That kill was justified and you know it. If you want to challenge me, you know where to find me." Connor let the words hang in the air, but Taggart didn't even pause or acknowledge them.

Taggart nodded at his man and they headed back to the truck.

"You already contacted the Council?" Liam asked as the truck steered down the drive.

"Yep." Something his brother would have known if he'd been around.

"Connor, I, uh, I'm sorry."

He turned to face his brother. "For what?"

Liam scrubbed a hand over his face. "You gonna make me grovel?"

"I'm thinking about it."

"I deserve it," his brother muttered.

"Yeah, you do. So are you with us now?"

Liam nodded, and Connor hated the conflict he saw on his brother's face. "After the burial tonight I'll send one of the guys over to December's to shadow her."

"Send Aiden." Liam's request was immediate and Connor understood why. Aiden was practically a saint where women were concerned.

"I will." They both knew none of the pack would make a move on a woman Liam had claimed, but Connor understood that his brother's inner wolf didn't care about that. Connor hated putting his brother in a position to choose family over his possible future mate but he needed him now more than ever. His men were all well trained and capable, but he and his brother had been living and fighting together for over a century. He didn't trust anyone the way he did Liam. "Once we've found whoever's poisoning the pack, you can—"

Liam clapped him lightly on the shoulder. "I know. We're brothers and I . . . shit, Connor. I'm sorry I haven't been here for you. For us."

Taggart gripped the steering wheel as he and Vince headed back to their ranch. "We never should have gone there."

Vince cleared his throat nervously and a slight trace of fear rolled off him. Taggart savored the smell of it. "We couldn't have known Connor had already contacted the Council."

We. He gritted his teeth at Vince's use of the word. As Alpha, Taggart should have trusted his gut and ignored Vince's request. Lately Vince had seemed bothered by some of the requests Taggart had made of him. It was hard to find loyal wolves who weren't waiting to attack and kill him. He'd wanted to appease whatever bullshit the other wolf was dealing with by approaching Connor and his pack this way.

He should have stuck to the original plan and killed the males of the Armstrong-Cordona pack. It might have caused a stir among the local humans, but when shifters died, they didn't get all up in arms like they would if humans were targeted. And most of the locals wouldn't even know of the new males' existence anyway. They'd just arrived at Fontana Mountain. Hell, the humans would probably rejoice in the death of shifters.

"We'll go after them tonight. Since Connor has contacted the Council it'll only be a matter of time before they send an investigative team or the enforcer to check on us." He fought off a shudder even thinking about the enforcer. He'd met that hulking, scarred bastard once and it was one time too many. Shoving the thought away, he continued. "If we dispose of Connor before then, we don't have a problem."

"What about Ana? If you kill her mate she won't keep her mouth shut."

"I have a plan to keep her in line. If it fails . . ." His shoulders lifted casually. He'd kill her too. He didn't want to but if he couldn't keep her compliant, then she'd become too much of a burden and a liability. Still, he'd get a taste of her before he killed her. After years of watching and imagining her in his bed, writhing underneath him, he'd take what he wanted. Maybe after she experienced what he could offer she'd change her mind about being with him.

Hell, the females of his pack fought to sleep with him. He frowned as he turned down the road toward his place. Yes, once she realized how much he could offer her, Ana would be no different than his females. Hopefully he wouldn't have to kill her after all.

Chapter 15

Even though he hadn't felt it buzz in his pocket Connor glanced at his cell phone to see if Ana had called. After checking on the rest of the females, he'd instructed Noel to keep an eye on her, but he didn't like leaving her. He'd never questioned his role as an Alpha before, but on a day like this he wished he was simply Ana's mate. With no responsibility other than her safety and well-being.

He shoved those thoughts aside when Liam strode into the barn and joined the circle of the rest of the men. His brother nodded once at Connor to let him know the cubs were safe with the women.

"Those humans need to pay for what they did to Ana," Ryan growled before Connor could speak. The anger that rolled off him was potent but unsurprising. Hurting any female went against everything ingrained into all shifters. Well, except psychopaths like Taggart, but he was the exception.

A burst of adrenaline exploded through the enclosed space, emanating from all of the males. The nearby horses sensed a shift in the air and whinnied nervously.

Connor thought of the promise Ana had tried to get him to make. He couldn't stand back and do nothing after his mate had been attacked. Not to mention that sweet little Vivian had been with her. The cub had already been through so much in her short life and he hated how terrified she'd been. His biology demanded retribution. Looking pointedly at Noah, he said, "What else did you find out about the two humans?"

"Felix Carr and Bennett Harrison. Both twenty-nine, both spoiled rich kids. They grew up together and, according to their records, they've both been brought up on charges of sexual assault on more than one occasion. Looks like they work together in that aspect. Real douches, these two."

Connor fought the images playing in his mind. Ana was strong enough to take care of herself against humans, but if they'd gone after her with the intention of injuring her so they could rape her . . . He actually had to shake himself. "Why aren't they in jail?" he asked.

Noah shrugged. "From what I can tell, the parents paid off two victims and there wasn't enough evidence for the third." He cleared his throat and looked at the circle of men. "The last victim was barely eighteen and mentally disabled."

More anger popped into the air like a cluster of fireworks. The scent that permeated was like a rancid mold. Connor's rage was the strongest. "You get pictures of these two?"

Noah grinned. "And addresses."

"As soon as they're released on bail Liam and I will go after them. They'll never hurt anyone else again." The cops would never find their bodies. Sure, they'd speculate that Connor's pack had something to do with it, but they wouldn't be able to prove shit. Something told him the investigation would be closed quickly anyway. His inner wolf and the laws of his kind demanded retribution. There wasn't much worse than going after an unarmed woman and child.

The other men murmured their agreement. While tempers were still high, some of the anger in the room died down.

"There's still the problem of Taggart." As a rule Connor didn't like to attack other packs, but Taggart's was threatening their entire existence. If the humans found out about the meth house and God knew what else Taggart had going on, it would be bad for their kind.

Noah spoke up again. "We don't know that he's behind the attacks in town or that he has anything to do with the poisoning. He's an asshole, but that's no crime."

Connor nodded. "I don't think he's behind the poisoning. That's much too subtle for him. But he is running a meth house on his land. If the Council doesn't take care of it, sooner or later the humans will find out and it will reflect on all of us."

"And he tried to attack Ana our first night here. Did you forget that?" Liam spoke up, his voice heated.

Noah growled deep in his throat. "I didn't forget. I just want to make sure this isn't about revenge."

"What did the Council say?" Ryan asked, interrupting them.

Connor shrugged. "They're not going to do anything about it now. They want to see how it plays out."

"Typical political bullshit. They're just hoping the problem goes away. Or they want *us* to take care of it," Liam muttered.

Connor didn't want to defend the Council but he also understood how short on manpower they were. They preferred their packs to self-govern if possible. Even with their investigators, they had only one enforcer in the States and he was expected to deal with all the problems across the country. Ridiculous, but that's the way it was. Enforcers trained hard, but they were also born into that role. They were alpha in nature, but they weren't Alphas. They were more or less lone wolves and wouldn't want the responsibility of their own pack. They looked out for the greater good of all their kind. Like warriors, they were skilled fighters but unlike warriors, they were much more lethal as fighters in human form. Or at least that was Connor's understanding. The enforcer was more than capable of taking care of Taggart, but he was probably working on something more important than a meth lab right now. "So we'll *make* the problem go away. After the burial ceremony tonight, Liam and Ryan, you two come with me and we'll destroy it. Not a long-term solution but it'll send a message. And it will stop Taggart's money flow for a while."

If they could get the other wolf to leave Fontana Mountain without bloodshed, it would be ideal.

"Taggart will retaliate." Liam's voice was quiet, thoughtful.

"You're probably right. He's already shown he had no problem attacking the Cordona women while they were unprotected. Now that we're here, it's time to make a statement to him that our land is off-limits and we won't tolerate drugs." Considering they'd found a feral wolf on their property, Taggart shouldn't be too surprised when they retaliated.

The others murmured in agreement, but he wanted it to be official. "Let's take a vote, then. Who's in favor of going after Taggart?"

They all nodded.

Just to be safe, he asked, "Any opposed?"

When he was greeted with silence, his inner wolf sighed in relief. He needed his men united in this.

After the men dispersed, Ryan hung back and waited

until everyone had cleared out of the barn. He glanced toward the open door and lowered his voice. "I looked up that stuff you wanted."

"And?"

For a moment he looked uncomfortable and Connor didn't blame him. He'd asked Ryan to check up on Liam's mate. "It took some digging but I found out that Sheriff McIntyre had a younger brother. Died a little over a decade ago. Murdered."

Before he asked the question, something in his gut told him the answer. "How?"

"Lupine shifter attack—the animal was feral. Happened down in South Carolina. Seems the sheriff and his sister saw it happen. Luckily a local rancher managed to kill it before it could kill them too. They moved to Fontana not long after the attack." His voice was grim.

"December *saw* it? Shit. You didn't say anything to Liam, did you?"

Ryan shook his head. "No. Wasn't sure if she'd already told him, and besides, I figured you'd want to take care of this either way."

"You were right to keep it to yourself. Don't tell anyone about this, all right?"

Ryan nodded. "Of course not. How's Ana?"

"She'll heal." But the men who'd hurt her wouldn't. And now Connor wondered if Liam had been holding back that information about December or if she hadn't told his brother. Either way it could be very bad if she had an ulterior motive. Liam was already feeling insanely protective of her, and if she wanted to hurt him she could. In more ways than one.

Liam's palm tightened around his cell until the distinctive click of someone picking up sounded in his ear.

"December's Book Nook." December's voice was

breathy and seductive and wrapped around him like a warm summer breeze.

So much so, he forgot to breathe or speak.

"Hello?"

He cleared his throat. "Uh, sorry. It's Liam."

"Hey. I'm about to close up so—"

"I won't be able to make it tonight."

"Oh." That was definitely disappointment he heard.

"I'm really sorry, December. We're dealing with a lot of pack stuff over here and I can't leave. Believe me, I'd rather be with you than anywhere else."

"Don't worry about it, Liam. I . . . It's probably better this way."

Better? *What the hell does that mean?* "I still want to see you. Once all this sh— *stuff* is settled, I really want to see you again."

There was a long pause and his chest constricted. Finally she spoke but her voice was guarded. "Liam, I like you. A lot. But I don't think you should come into my store anymore. Or call me. There's stuff you don't know about me and things would never work between us. Okay? I can't believe I've let things go as far as they have," she muttered.

"December—"

"Just leave it alone. Leave *me* alone. If you really do care for me, you'll do as I ask."

Before he could respond the phone went dead. He started to call her back but knew it would be pointless. Things weren't over between them. Far from it. But maybe it was better this way. If he couldn't talk to her while he was helping the pack deal with the poisoning problem, maybe it would be easier. Who was he kidding? Being able to hear her voice kept him grounded in a way he hadn't thought possible. Now he'd just worry that much more about her.

Shoving his phone into his pocket, he stalked toward the main house and fought his dark mood. The burial ceremony was soon and there were still things that needed to be done. The last thing anyone had time for was his self-pity.

Ana swung her legs off the bed when she heard the front door open and shut. Testing her strength, she stood and was satisfied when there weren't shooting pains splintering up her body. Her bones had already fused together but she still hurt and would need help getting to the ceremony. Even thinking about another death in the pack made her sick. Her stomach swirled with nausea but it subsided when Connor entered the room.

He frowned when he saw her standing. "What are you doing up?"

"I'm fine. I'll need help getting the whole way there but I'm healing nicely."

"I'm sorry I couldn't stay with you." His voice was ragged.

She took a step toward him but he quickly covered the distance. "Connor, you're the Alpha. I get that. If I've made you feel like you've abandoned me or whatever, I swear I didn't mean to."

He cursed under his breath. "It's not that, Ana. You *never* ask for help. I'm worried that I won't be able to tell when you really do need me. You're too ... too ..."

Too stubborn, pigheaded. Oh, she'd heard it all before from her father. Some days she wondered if he'd have preferred a son to her. She gritted her teeth, waiting for the lecture. "Gonna finish that thought?"

"Too good for me," he muttered.

The softly spoken statement made her jerk back in surprise. "Wait, what are we talking about here?"

His green eyes were shuttered as he turned away and

stripped off his shirt. "I need to change, but then we'll head over there. Liam is helping your sisters with Alicia's body."

"Connor, you can't keep shutting me out like this. I'm not used to asking for help but that doesn't mean you can shut me down every time I ask you a simple question. You won't tell me why you left, you won't tell me why you and Liam have been arguing, you held back the existence of the cubs, you won't even discuss the possibility of *not* going after those assholes who shot me and I have to find out from your brother that he thinks his mate is a human. I know that last one isn't even a big deal, but it's like you don't want to actually talk to me about anything. You just want someone to warm your bed!"

"You know that's not true. And now's not the time." He didn't turn from the open closet door as he pulled a black sweater from it and tugged it over his head.

Anger burned hot and wild inside her and the fact that he passively stood there only stoked the fire more. "Yeah, well, when is the time? You want me in your bed but you don't want me to be your mate in every sense of the word. If you want this thing between us to go anywhere, then you better get used to sharing things with me because I'm not going to be someone you sleep with but get nothing else from."

When he didn't respond, she scowled at his backside. She'd agreed to a lot when he'd come to her ranch, offering his protection. Was it really too much that she wanted him to open up to her a little? Her parents had shared everything with each other and she wanted the same thing. Connor might not love her, but she knew he cared for her. And maybe with time ... She shook her head as traitorous tears pricked her eyes. If he couldn't even open up to her about simple stuff, then they had no future. She shoved all her feelings for him back inside.

He started to take off his pants so she stalked from the room, knowing it would piss him off.

"Ana," he called out.

But she ignored him. Despite the discomfort she hurried down the stairs and grabbed her coat on her way out the front door. Her entire body ached and screamed at the quick getaway she'd just made. She knew she should take it slower and wait for him but right now she wanted him as annoyed as she was. She slammed the door behind her and felt irrationally pleased at the booming sound it made. Before she'd taken three steps, however, she felt the whoosh of the door open behind her and Connor scooped her up in his arms.

She tried to struggle against him but fresh splinters of discomfort coursed through her. Every second that passed she gained strength, but that didn't mean she wasn't painfully sore.

"How do you think it will look if you show up hobbling without my help?" he asked through gritted teeth.

"I don't care how it'll look." She glared at his profile because he refused to make eye contact with her. His jaw was clenched tight and that pissed her off. What did *he* have to be so angry about? He was the one holding stuff back from her. Not the other way around.

"Damn it, woman. Now isn't the time."

"Then tell me when *is* the right time. Keep pushing me away like this and I hope you don't ever expect more than a temporary mating. I will never be your bondmate if this is what I have to look forward to." Her words were harsh and drew the reaction she expected.

He glanced sharply at her. The hurt in his eyes surprised her, however. Still, he said nothing. And that hurt her worse than the physical pain humming through her.

As they neared the field next to the barn, Ana shoved aside her anger at Connor when she saw all her packmates standing somberly around the funeral pyre. "Will you put me down?" she whispered to Connor. She didn't want everyone to see her like this. Now of all times she needed to appear strong.

He did as she asked but didn't remove his arm from around her shoulder. Despite her anger at him she was grateful for his strength and show of unity. No matter what, it seemed she could count on him for at least that. Even though her parents had loved each other, if her mother had disagreed with her father he'd given her the cold shoulder until one of them caved on an issue. Connor was so different in that respect. Leaning against him, Ana wrapped her arm around his waist and used him to support her.

Vivian came to stand by her side immediately. Wordlessly she grabbed Ana's free hand and gripped it tightly. Ana squeezed back, knowing this was hard on the little she-cat even though she hadn't known Alicia. Hell, dealing with death was always hard for their kind, regardless of species. Despite the few angry humans who thought shifters were evil and planned to take over the world, their numbers were so few they were technically bordering on extinction. They were increasing every day, but it was one of the many reasons the Council had decided to come out to the world. For the most part they could now live and procreate without worrying about hiding or moving every couple years. With the advancements of satellites, government agencies becoming more intrusive in civilian lives and even social networks, it had been harder and harder to keep the fact that they didn't age at the same rate as humans a secret anymore. The world was just too connected. Despite their longevity, every time one of them died the grief spread throughout the entire pack with a vengeance. It was another reminder how small in number they were and how fragile their lives could be.

As they all gathered around the funeral pyre where Alicia's naked body was draped in the standard sheer burial cloth, Isabel pulled the burning torch from its stand and lit it under the body. She placed it back in the holder, then went back to stand with the rest of her sisters.

The flames licked high into the darkening sky, painting it a bright orange. Sharp and intense, the colors mimicked the sad yet angry mind-set of the mourners. Despite Ana's desire to stay away from vengeance she knew that once the pack discovered who had done this, blood would be spilled.

One by one each pack member walked up to Isabel and her sisters and gave them comforting hugs and kisses. Their funerals were different from that of humans. No flowery speeches were given, no eulogy. They simply embraced one another and after the flames died down they scattered the ashes of their loved ones. Their bodies burned much quicker and easier than humans. Something different in their DNA. Some thought it was barbaric, but they'd come from the earth and that's the way they returned. With no barriers and no urns used to save the remains.

Ana wasn't sure how much time passed but eventually Connor, Liam and the rest of the males started the process of scattering the ashes.

"I don't know if I can take much more of this," Carmen murmured as she wrapped her slim arm around Ana's shoulder.

Ana pulled her younger sister into a tight hug. "I'm so happy you're all right." She kept her voice a whisper. A trickle of shame surged through her because she was grateful her own sister was alive. It wasn't that she wished her cousin dead instead, but the relief that Carmen was safe was almost overwhelming.

"I'm still weak but better than Teresa." Carmen's voice was just as low.

Ana felt another pair of arms wrap around her from behind and knew it was Noel without looking. "I swear if anything ever happens to you two . . ." Noel shuddered and Ana mirrored the reaction. Her sisters had been her lifeline after their parents died. Even before that, actually. Ana had loved her father but he'd been a hard man and part of her thought he'd always wished for a boy. Whenever he'd gotten into one of his lecturing moods, the three of them had always stuck together.

A piercing scream ricocheted through the air, pulling them all apart. Ana swiveled toward the sound.

It was Isabel. Her face was ashen and she pointed toward the barn. A few of the horses whinnied loudly, and though it was dark Ana could see the outline of at least four wolves. By the time she realized what was going on all the men had moved into action.

Connor rushed at her, his jaw set in a firm line. "Take all the women and cubs back to the main house. I'll send a couple of the males to guard the house, but we'll take care of this."

"We can help." Noel stepped forward.

"Now," he barked.

If Ana hadn't been injured she might be tempted to argue, but he was right. They needed to get the majority of the pack inside. If mass pandemonium followed it would be better if they were all in one place. She wasn't sure what was going on, but if Taggart wanted to separate any of them now would be the time. And she refused to let that happen.

"Come on." She grabbed Vivian's hand and started helping her sisters herd everyone inside.

Connor looked back at Ana as all the women hustled together. He hated leaving her but she was with her sisters. They were all protective and he knew they wouldn't let Ana out of their sight.

The wind shifted and a familiar scent rolled over him. It wasn't Taggart but the wolf he'd visited the ranch with earlier. He was hiding somewhere in the forest. The smell was too distant.

He pointed at Nathan and Aiden. "You two, guard the main house with the women." Then he swiveled toward his brother. "Liam, you're with me. Everyone else, fan out and do what you do best." He didn't need to give more orders than that. His men knew how to handle themselves. It soothed him to have two of his men guarding the house but the wolves here tonight wouldn't get that far. He'd make sure of it.

The seven of them started to fan out while Nathan and Aiden headed for the house. Connor stayed trained on the barn. Two wolves stood by the entrance and something told him there were more inside. Waiting. And definitely more waiting out in the fields.

When it came to numbers, Taggart's pack was bigger than his. For now. That would change soon, though. Not that it mattered. All his guys were trained warriors. And a hell of a lot older and stronger than anyone in Taggart's pack.

Without pause he underwent the change.

His sweater and pants ripped as his bones shifted. The cracking and breaking was painful as always but gave way to a rush of adrenaline. As his bones and joints realigned he growled deep in his throat.

If Taggart wanted to bring the fight to them, that was fine. From a tactical standpoint, home turf was better anyway.

Let's take the two by the barn, he projected to Liam.

My thoughts exactly. Liam howled loudly, sending an eerie vibe through the night air. With the exception of their eye color, he and his brother looked almost exactly alike in wolf form. Liam had the same black coat but his golden eyes glinted dangerously, echoing Connor's own rage.

Connor knew there were other wolves out there watching and waiting, but he had to trust his pack enough to watch his back.

The two wolves didn't move as he and his brother zeroed in on them. Just bared their teeth like inexperienced fighters. He glanced to his left and found Liam directly next to him, ready to attack.

Without having to give any direction to his brother, Connor went for the gray wolf on the left. The fight was over before it started. He could see it by the way the young wolf hopped and danced around like a crazed boxer.

Connor crouched low and started to circle the wolf. Out of the corner of his eye he could see Liam doing the same thing to the other one.

Part of him felt pity because he knew these wolves were following their Alpha's orders, but he didn't feel so bad he'd let them kill him or his brother.

The gray wolf lunged once and Connor darted out of its way. He could hear the sound of its jaw snapping against air. If he could tire the animal out or make him see it was a losing battle, maybe it would run off. Though he doubted it.

Swiveling, he faced off with it again. Behind him the horses still whinnied loudly. Next to him, his brother and the other wolf still circled each other.

Keeping focus he crouched lower and waited for an opening. The other wolf wasn't jumping around as wildly now but still looked antsy. It bared its teeth and lunged at him again.

Connor dodged away and sank his teeth into the animal's side. Not as hard as he wanted, but he drew blood and pulled away fur and skin. The coppery taste in his mouth made his animal side hungrier.

The gray wolf growled in pain and lunged at him again. This time Connor didn't retreat or dodge. He extended his claws and slashed at its face with his paw.

The blow was harder than a punch. Connor had a lot of strength, and unlike regular wolves lupine shifters were more in control of their blows.

When the animal hit the ground, Connor jumped on top of it and bit its neck.

Hard.

It didn't even get a chance to cry out as he broke through its spinal cord and ripped its head off. Instead of piercing his claws through the animal's chest and heart, he preferred taking the head. It sent a message. The acrid scent of blood rolled over him.

He'd sensed the fight in the young animal. It wasn't going to stop until it killed something. Sometimes Connor hated his human side. If he let his animal side completely take over while fighting, there wouldn't have even been a fight. He'd have just killed the wolf without guilt.

A new scent played against his nose. He looked up to see Liam standing over the other wolf. It was decapitated too. Behind his brother two other brown wolves were attempting to creep up behind him.

Down! he projected to Liam.

Without pause his brother dropped to the ground. Using the strength of his hind legs to propel him, Connor exploded through the air and over Liam.

These two wolves were more experienced. No hopping around like maniacs from them. But he had strength and speed on his side. As he hurtled toward one, he turned in midair so that his back legs hit the one on the left and he tackled the one on the right.

Liam growled behind him so he didn't bother turning. He knew his brother had his back and would take care of the second animal.

As they tumbled onto the hard earth he felt the other animal's sharp teeth dig into his shoulder. Rolling away from him, he bit back a howl as his skin ripped away. The rush of pain centered him.

Hard and fast.

That's how he needed to strike this one.

On all fours he squared off with the animal and found it rolling to its feet. Lunging, he threw himself at it and took it off guard. It extended its claws and swiped at him.

Connor endured the pain of the attack as he zeroed in on its neck. Instinct, primal rage and power surged through him as he went for the killing blow.

Its claws dug into his side but he barely felt it. With one giant bite Connor locked his teeth onto the animal's neck. The crunching and snapping of cartilage and bone resounded through the air. He didn't have to finish it off. Connor's bite was so sharp the animal's head was barely attached.

Immediately he turned to find Liam stepping away from the other wolf. Before they could hunt down any more intruders, Ryan ran in from the east field.

He was one of the few wolves that could communicate with them in shifted form. Normally blood relatives and bondmates were the only ones who could communicate and oftentimes even blood relatives couldn't. Ryan was different, though. Connor wasn't sure what it was about the older wolf and he didn't truly care. He trusted him almost as much as his brother.

The perimeter's secure. I killed three wolves. A few escaped but most of our guys killed one or two. They're all headed back as far as I can tell, Ryan projected.

You two head to the main house and make sure the women are safe and Nathan and Aiden don't need backup. Keep it locked down until I get there, Connor ordered.

As they left, he ran through the barn and thankfully didn't scent anything unusual. No wolves waiting to attack later. As he looped back around the outside of the barn he found Noah, completely naked, shouting at an equally naked Erin. Noah held one of the horse blankets and was trying to shove it at her.

Connor hadn't wanted to shift to his human form yet but he braced himself and underwent the change. Shifting back always hurt worse. He didn't have his animal side to block out most of the pain.

It took a moment before he could see straight. Everything in front of him was hazy and blurred. When his vision cleared he stalked toward them.

"What the hell are you doing?"

Erin turned to glare at him—the first real sign of defiance he'd seen in her since they'd found her, broken and bloody, all those months ago. Almost immediately she dropped her gaze to the ground and the timid she-wolf he'd gotten used to fell back into place.

"She was out there fighting!" Noah's voice filled with anger—and fear.

At his words Erin's temper flared to life. "Yeah, and I killed two of them. You shouldn't be yelling at me, Noah. You should be thanking me!"

"You killed *two* of Taggart's wolves?" Connor couldn't keep the surprise—and respect—out of his voice.

"Yes, I did, Alpha." Her words were less heated when she addressed him.

When they'd first found her she'd been covered in a lot of blood and Noah hadn't allowed any of them to see her naked body for long. Before he'd even spoken to the small she-wolf he'd treated her like she was his mate. Since then she'd been so careful about shifting with any of the males present, always keeping her body hidden from others. Now he could see old scars nicking her neck, shoulders, and side. Really, *really* old.

Noah growled low in his throat and Connor realized it was because he was looking at Erin. His assessment might be clinical but the other wolf wouldn't care. As a mated male who understood the protective urge more than most, Connor didn't blame him.

Connor shook his head and grabbed the blanket from Noah. He draped it around Erin's shoulders.

She stiffened slightly at the contact but didn't pull away. "Are you going to punish me?" Her voice was deadpan.

Punish? Hell, no. "You haven't talked much about your past and I haven't pressured you until now. Were you part of the warrior class of your old pack?"

With her jaw clenched tightly, she simply nodded in response.

She wasn't particularly small in her wolf form but she wasn't hulking either, so it surprised him. "Why didn't you say anything until now?"

She swallowed hard. "I wasn't ready."

"And you are now?" Connor asked.

"No, she's not. She's not fighting anyone. This is insane." Noah stepped in between them but Connor placed a light hand on his shoulder and pushed him back.

"If she wants to fight it's not your place to stop her." Connor understood that the other wolf was protective but he also understood that whatever had happened to Erin had stunted her somehow. If she was finally coming out of her shell and was ready to fight again, it would be the best therapy anyone could offer her. He wouldn't stand in her way.

"Really?" There was a light in Erin's eyes he hadn't seen before and he knew he'd made the right decision.

"If you can hold your own I have no reason to stop you. We'll talk about this later, though."

She was silent but her lips curled up slightly at the corners.

Noah started to protest but he silenced him. "Enough, Noah. I don't have time for this. Help me round up the rest of the guys and meet back at the main house. We need to take care of the bodies and do a head count."

Connor knew he needed to get the rest of the guys but he desperately needed to see that Ana was okay. He headed across the main yard. Liam and Ryan were patrolling the house, but he had to see Ana's face. Touch her skin. Make sure she was safe. She might have communicated with him briefly before but that was an anomaly he'd chalked up to her raw fear. When—if— they officially became bondmates the telepathic link would become permanent.

When he reached the front porch he grabbed an afghan draped across the back of one of the rocking chairs and wrapped it around his waist. He didn't mind the nudity but he thought it might make Ana uncomfortable.

As he opened the front door, a scream ripped through the night air. His heart leapt into his throat. *Ana!*

Chapter 16

Ana clutched Teresa's hand as her cousin let out a toe-curling scream. Her back arched and her eyes were open as she stared at the ceiling, but it was as if she wasn't seeing anything. The scream seemed to go on forever but after a few seconds she fell back against her pillow and her eyes fell shut again.

Ana shivered. Whatever was going on inside Teresa, she was in pain. Serious, serious pain. Ana hated that there was nothing she could do for her. The poison just needed to work its way out of her system. If only it would do it faster.

The bedroom door flew open and slammed against the wall with a thud. Connor rushed in, his dark eyes wide with fear. He wore a blanket around his waist and there was blood smeared down his shoulder and side.

Her heart jumped in her throat. She flew at him, mindless of the discomfort that shot down her legs. She was careful not to touch him since she didn't know where he was hurt. "What happened? Are you okay?"

"Most of this isn't my blood. I heard a scream. Are

you . . . ?" He faltered and suddenly looked unsure of himself. "What's going on?"

She spotted Liam and another male in wolf form hovering behind Connor, but when they saw nothing was wrong they turned and disappeared back down the hallway.

Ana glanced back at Teresa. Gloria, one of Teresa's sisters, wiped her face with a damp cloth. "It's Teresa. I think she's okay, though. For now." Okay being a relative thing. She was breathing at least. No matter what they did the effects of the poison would be excruciating. She was like an addict going through withdrawal.

"Where's Dr. Graham?" Connor winced as he pressed a hand to his shoulder.

Alarm pulsed through her. He'd said most of the blood wasn't his but he was too stubborn to let on if he was in pain. "He had to get some sleep and go to work. He'll be back tomorrow, though." The truth was, there wasn't much he could do anyway. They were already doing the best they could to purge Teresa's body of the poison. While it felt like weeks had passed, in reality it had barely been two full days. Her body was simply fighting to survive. Maybe Connor was asking about the doctor's whereabouts for himself. She didn't want to question him in front of Gloria, however.

"I'll send your other sisters in, okay?" she murmured to Gloria, who held Teresa's hand tightly.

Her other cousin nodded, but Ana didn't miss the sheen of tears in her eyes.

Ignoring the uncomfortable sensation in her legs, she strode out of the room with Connor. Her bones had basically healed; she was simply stiff. "Let's talk in private."

He nodded and placed a strong hand at the small of her back as they left the room. Without knocking, she pushed open the door to the room next door and told the other women to go sit with Teresa. They'd been taking shifts so they wouldn't crowd her, but since she was unconscious Ana wasn't worried. As soon as they were gone she reached for Connor, wanting to comfort him. "You've been hurt. What happened?"

He brushed her hand away. "I'm fine."

She jerked back at his rejection. Was it so strange that she'd be worried about her mate?

Immediately his expression softened and he stepped toward her. He placed his hands on her hips and pulled her close. "I'm sorry. It's instinct not to let anyone . . . I'm sorry, Ana."

"And you say *I* don't ask for help," she murmured. She eyed his shoulder and realized it *was* his blood. Thankfully the wound wasn't deep and was already starting to heal.

"It's not that. I want to take care of you."

"Just not the other way around?"

"I didn't say that."

"But you're not denying it either. Why don't you want me to take care of you, Connor?"

"Because . . . I'm afraid of getting used to it." His words were barely a whisper and made her freeze.

She didn't want to touch what he'd just said right now. *Afraid?* Connor wasn't afraid of anything. And something told her he hadn't meant to say the words out loud. Careful not to touch his wound, she smoothed her hands over his chest and stepped closer into his embrace. His grip tightened on her hips and for a moment she fought to think straight. When he'd gone to fight Taggart's wolves she hadn't expected the raw panic that had overtaken her entire body. She was used to worrying about her sisters. That was second nature.

But what she'd felt for Connor was different. Deeper. And a whole lot scarier. The thought of losing him . . .

She simply couldn't think about that. She was supposed to be keeping her distance from him. Getting him out of her system. If he left again, she had to make sure she was free of him. Unfortunately he'd already worked his way into almost all her waking thoughts. "Uh, did you find Taggart? Or did he just send some of his pack?"

His expression immediately darkened. "He wasn't there, but we took out a lot of his guys. He's gonna be hurting after tonight. I'm going to contact the Council in the morning and let them know what's going on. At least so they're aware."

Ana snorted. It's not like they'd do much anyway. Eventually they'd send an investigator down and maybe the enforcer, but these pack skirmishes weren't affecting them nationally and they weren't affecting their relationship with the humans, so Ana guessed they wouldn't be at the top of the Council's to-do list. Since they now had an Alpha to look out for the pack, the Council would want them to take care of things themselves if they could. "You want me to help you patrol tonight?" she asked, even though she knew it would be foolish to try to do so.

"If you weren't still recovering I'd say . . . hell, I'd say no either way."

"Connor, I'm your *mate*."

"Exactly." He kissed the top of her head. "I've got to meet the rest of the males, but I want you to stay here until I come back. I'll probably take this first watch to patrol the property."

She wanted to argue with him but she was in no shape to do any sort of patrolling or even defend herself very well. And even if she wanted to fight, she wasn't part of the warrior class. She knew she could hold her own to an extent or even outrun most wolves, but what was the point in that if she'd only slow Connor down? "Fine, but first I'm cleaning your wound." She clasped one of his hands and tugged him toward the bathroom but he resisted.

"Forget this scratch." His voice was low. Before she could respond he captured her mouth in a hungry, dominating kiss. His lips moved against hers with a hot urgency. Despite everything going on around them, her abdomen clenched and the area between her legs dampened. Moaning into his mouth, she clutched his unhurt shoulder and dug her fingers into his tight skin. The feel of him grounded her, reminded her he was real.

Connor took her face in his wide palms and stepped away. His eyes were dangerously dark and his breathing erratic. "Hold that thought for a couple hours," he rasped out.

"Please take care of yourself." As he left she fought the ache building inside her. Her body might still be healing but it had nothing to do with that. She hated seeing him hurt. Worse, he wouldn't let her take care of him. She understood that he'd been taking care of himself for well over a century but it didn't diminish her need to comfort him. It was probably better this way. She shouldn't get used to taking care of him anyway. With the way things were between them, she wasn't sure what kind of future they had.

Once Connor had gone, she checked on everyone else, then collapsed onto her old bed, where both her sisters and Vivian were already curled up and sleeping. It was a little crowded but she didn't mind. Though she *was* lonely without Connor. More than she wanted to admit.

Her cousins had taken up her sisters' rooms and the guest rooms. No one wanted to sleep in their homes tonight and she didn't blame them. In the morning, once everyone knew what was going on, Ana figured things would return to normal and they'd all feel safer going home.

There was strength in numbers, and if she were honest with herself, she was thankful she had her sisters and cousins to support her while Connor was out patrolling.

Her lips still tingled from his kiss, and with that thought she allowed the blackness of sleep to take over.

Ana opened her eyes as the world shifted underneath her. She found Connor staring at her as he carried her down the stairs. "What are you doing?" she mumbled, and cuddled into his hard body. It was hard to think when he felt so good. So warm.

"It's almost dawn. I just got back in." His voice was a whisper.

She blinked a couple times as they neared their house. "You didn't have to come get me."

He grunted softly. "I don't think I can sleep without you next to me, Ana."

A pleasurable warmth spread through her until his words settled in. *Why does he say things like that when he can't even talk to me?* She rubbed her eyes and stretched as he opened the door to their house. "You can put me down."

He ignored her. Instead he walked to their room, pulled the comforter and sheet back from the bed and laid her gently against the pillow. "How are you feeling?"

"Almost as good as new." She stretched out her legs and lifted her wounded arm to show him there was only a light scar. As if she'd been simply cut, not shot. It would fade by the end of the day. All she felt now was an uncomfortable soreness. Like she'd lifted weights or gone jogging without stretching.

"Good." The word was a low growl as he reached for the button of her pants.

With slow and measured movements he pulled her black pants down her legs to reveal lacy black panties. Before Connor, she'd never thought much about her undergarments. She smiled when his eyes narrowed on the sheer scrap of material covering her. Then she wanted to curse herself for caring that he liked it.

"Lift your arms," he commanded.

Instead of doing as he said, she crossed her arms over her chest. He leaned in close so that their noses were almost touching.

"Lift. Your. Arms."

She wanted to balk at being ordered around but she was too tired to fight. And if she were honest, the dominating note in his voice turned her on. When she lifted her arms, Connor ran his hands up over her hips and snagged the hem of her sweater before lifting it over her head. She had to sit up a little so he could take it off before she fell back against the fluffy pillow. Ana started to close her eyes when Connor stripped off his own shirt.

When he was bared to her she sucked in an involuntary breath. Her original plan to work him out of her system was obviously not going to happen. Every time she saw him without clothes on she wondered if her attraction to him would ever get old. The tight lines and planes of his stomach tensed under her gaze.

Dipping lower, her eyes trailed down the V of his muscles. She swallowed hard as she looked at the bulge underneath his pants, but he didn't make a move to remove them. Instead, he grasped the slim straps of her panties and dragged them down her legs. The feel of his fingers rolling against her skin sent another shiver through her. She felt so exposed in front of him. He hadn't bothered with the lights, but the sun peeked through the windows, bathing the room in a soft orange glow.

"Spread your legs wider." Again with that deep voice.

Her inner walls clenched and she did as he said. Whatever he had planned, she just wanted him to kiss and touch her. To wipe away everything that was going on. At least for a little while. Even though deep inside she feared he'd never open up to her the way she needed or possibly even leave again, right now she just wanted to feel.

Connor stared at the juncture between Ana's spread legs and fought to breathe. He might have already had her but it would never be enough. And he hadn't gotten to taste her the way he wanted yet. That was about to change.

He traced his finger up her slit but didn't penetrate. She jerked under his touch, and the scent of arousal she emanated was almost intoxicating. It reminded him of how much he'd grown to need her in the past couple days and how he'd almost lost her.

Shame filled him at the way he'd brushed off her earlier attempts to get him to open up and then to comfort him. She'd reached out to him and he'd acted like an idiot. It was no excuse but he didn't want her taking care of him; he wanted to take care of *her*. And the thought of opening up to her even on the most basic level terrified him. He'd been without a pack for so long and Taggart's comment about his father not being able to protect his family's pack had struck deeper than he'd imagined. Connor wanted to be strong for Ana all the time, and dwelling on the past or admitting he wasn't good enough for her wouldn't help either of them. He didn't understand why she needed to talk about anything when they were so right for each other. Still, he hadn't meant to hurt her.

Ana scooted down a couple inches, as if she were trying to force his hand. He bit back a smile at her impatience. Shifting positions, he moved so that he knelt between her legs.

Her scent wound around him as she spread her legs farther. Leaning down, he lightly kissed her inner thigh. She trembled under the contact and he didn't bother to hide his groan. When he swept his tongue over her clit she fisted the sheets beneath her.

She was wet and obviously aroused and he wanted to push her over that edge. Seeing gratification on her face was a bigger turn-on than anything else she could do to him. Part of it was selfish, because it turned him on that *he'd* been the one to put that expression there. He dipped one finger inside her and was rewarded when she clenched around him.

"That feel good?" he murmured.

"Faster," she breathed out in a familiar, demanding tone.

She didn't have to tell him twice. Ana was too good for him, and the longer he was around her the more he realized it. It had been unfair to demand that she mate with him, and he couldn't help but wonder if there was some part of him that had demanded it because her father had told him he wasn't good enough for her. Hell, maybe the old man was right. What kind of man would place stipulations on his protection? When she arched her back, he focused on the here and now and her pleasure.

Ana's inner walls tightened around Connor's finger. When he smoothly slid another one inside her, she thought he understood her body better than she did. With a steady rhythm he moved them in and out of her, using just the right amount of pressure to drive her mad.

Though it wasn't hot in the room she felt as if her

temperature had risen a hundred degrees. What he was doing felt incredible but she wanted more.

Needed more.

Through heavy-lidded eyes she watched as Connor leaned down between her legs. Reaching between them, she grabbed on to his head and held tight as he swiped his tongue over her clit.

The abrupt action had her nearly vaulting off the bed. It was quick and erotic. Continuing the steady pace with his fingers, he began a new one with his tongue. He flicked and teased the sensitive bundle of nerves with such precision, her stomach muscles bunched as she prepared to climax. She was almost there. For some reason she couldn't let go of her control.

She knew he wanted her physically but there was so much more she wanted from him. It became clearer to her every second they spent together. She needed to hear him say how much she meant to him. *What* she meant to him. If anything. But he still said nothing. Her idea to get him out of her system had been stupid. She could see that now. She'd let him into her body and life, and if things didn't change between them or, worse, if he left again, it was going to rip her apart.

She closed her eyes and tried to block out those thoughts. After tonight she had to lay down some ground rules for herself. But right now none of that mattered.

She was so close to orgasm, it made her tense everywhere. Her inner muscles fluttered around his fingers with each languid stroke. She just needed to clear her head and let go.

"Touch yourself," he murmured between kisses.

A shiver rolled over her at his commanding tone. She could definitely do that. When he shifted his position to watch her cup her breasts, the fire in his eyes nearly melted her.

The heat coming off him was potent and all consuming, and she loved watching the changing emotions play out in his eyes.

Slowly she strummed her nipples, not only to pleasure herself but to tease him. She liked it when he was as hot and bothered as she was. Right now the look in his eyes told her he definitely was.

"Pretend it's me touching you," he managed to rasp out.

She couldn't hide the small smile at the unsteadiness of his words. As she imagined his fingers and mouth teasing her breasts, he increased his movements. She let out a moan and arched her back slightly as she closed her eyes. Right now was all about the pleasure he was giving her. Everything else faded away.

When he lightly tugged on her clit with his teeth, she jerked at the abruptness but was finally able to let go. Her thighs tightened around his head as her orgasm tore through her with a wildness she hadn't expected.

Using one hand to push back her thigh, he continued rolling his tongue over the sensitive area until she clutched his head, silently begging him to stop. After her climax crested, the extra stimulation was making her weak everywhere.

"Connor." She pulled at him, trying to tug him upward. Her voice was ragged, unsteady.

Leaving his two fingers still buried inside her, he met her mouth with his. Hungrily he ate at her. As they kissed, her inner walls tightened around his fingers once again as another, lighter, tremor curled through her.

Finally she tore her head back to breathe. "Thank you," she murmured.

He dropped a trail of kisses along her jaw and shoulder as he slipped into bed behind her. He pulled her tight against his back, but when he didn't make a move to take off his pants, she frowned.

She shifted her behind against his covered erection. "What about you?"

"Just go to sleep," he whispered against her hair.

"But—"

"Shh. I know you're still sore from your accident and I want this to be only about you. Let me give this to you."

She opened her mouth once, then shut it. If she wanted him to give more to her, she knew she needed to give something too. She could let him take care of her as long as he let her do the same for him.

When he tightened his grip around her, she shut her eyes and sank deeper against him. Later she could worry about the future and the problems facing their pack, but for now she savored his strong embrace.

Ana opened her eyes and frowned at the haziness surrounding her. It was as if she were looking at a fuzzy photograph. She rubbed her eyes and looked around but nothing changed. The edges of her vision were covered in dark shadows. Alarm jumped inside her when she realized she was in the woods.

And naked.

Strange, she didn't feel the cold, though there was a light layer of snow on the ground. Heavier than the last time she was outside. Even with her high body temperature she should still feel the air rushing over her bare skin. When had it snowed so much? Her feet should be tingling from the icy ground. Or at least feeling something.

Why am I naked? *She wrapped her arms around herself to cover her chest and started walking.*

She remembered going to bed with Connor after he'd given her an intense orgasm. Warmth spread through her at the thought of how much time he'd spent between her legs.

Right now she needed to figure out how the hell she'd ended up here and how to get back to him.

She recognized the woods as her own so at least she wasn't lost. She was right in the thick cluster of trees close to the main house.

As she started walking, a mangy, feral gray wolf appeared out of the woods. He was coming right for her. She tensed but he didn't even see her.

Just kept walking. His red eyes glowed fiercely and his fur was dirty, matted and falling off in places. But he brushed by her without a glance in her direction. She shivered and ducked behind a tree, even though he didn't seem to be aware of her existence.

Careful of any protruding sticks or branches, she hurried through the woods until she came to the clearing.

There was a sea of dead and feral wolves. She clutched her stomach as bile rose inside her. The mangy feral wolves didn't seem to be actually seeing anything. They blindly walked among the dead wolves.

As she walked toward the lifeless animals she heard a female cry out. Turning back toward the woods she watched as Carmen clutched her neck and collapsed onto the ground.

Ana started running but she didn't make any progress. "Carmen!" Her heart pounded wildly as she tried to move. She needed to reach her sister. Her legs were like lead.

Suddenly the cold ripped through her and her body became violently aware of the elements. Her sister convulsed on the ground and started foaming at the mouth.

"Carmen!" she screamed again, but it came out as a whisper.

Tears streamed down her face as she tried to reach her.

Her sister's body stilled and Ana cried out in anguish. Why couldn't she get to her?

A warm hand gripped her forearm and everything around her dissipated as if it had never been there. She now stood on the front porch of her house, fully clothed. Matt was there with a grim expression on his face.

He immediately let go of her arm.

"What are you doing here? Where am I?" she demanded.

"You're dreaming." His voice was annoyingly calm.

As if she hadn't just seen her sister dying on the ground. She frowned. "Then how are you in my head?"

"Technically you're in my head. I brought you here to show you this so you understand the danger facing your pack."

"Dream walkers can do that?" She'd always thought she'd known him, but now she realized she didn't know shit.

"Some can't. I can."

"How come you never told me about this?"

He shrugged. "Why would I?"

She frowned at his response, not that she blamed him. Why would he have told her? "Does anyone else know about your ability?"

He snorted softly. "If you're talking about anyone in town, no. My mother knows and so does my . . . former clan."

"In New York? Why did you and your mother leave?" She wasn't sure why she was pushing him, but this was probably one of the weirdest things she'd ever experienced, having someone else in her head like this. She felt like she should know maybe just a little more about him.

He ignored her question. "There's a coyote in your midst."

She didn't care about coyotes. She cared about her sister. "What was wrong with my sister? I need to get to her."

"She's fine . . . for now. What you just saw is a vision of things to come."

"Dead and feral wolves littering my lawn are a vision of what's coming? And Carmen dying?"

"Dreams aren't always literal, Ana."

"Then my sister . . ."

"She needs to be careful. You need to warn her."

"What about the other stuff I saw?"

He shook his head. "If something isn't done about your neighbor and his drug running, the feral wolves will be a reality for our town. They'll sweep through like a disease. People and wolves alike will start dying. Once the first human is killed by a shifter, your entire pack will be targeted. You need to do something about him."

"How do you even know about that?"

"I see many things."

It was hard to digest what she was seeing and what he was saying, and she wanted to make sure she completely understood what was going on. "So wait. These are your dreams or visions, not mine or anyone else's?" *When he nodded, she continued.* "Then who is the coyote in our midst? Who is trying to poison us?"

A dark expression crossed his face. "That I don't know. I have no control over what I see or if my visions are literal or not. I've tried reaching out at night but I can't get into his—or her—head. I'm sorry, but I simply don't know, Ana. His thoughts are too dark, too guarded."

She bit her bottom lip. Connor had told her to stay away from Matt but it's not as if she had a choice since he'd sucked her into his dreams. "My mate told me to stay away from you."

Matt's lips curved into a slight smile. "I figured as much. He cares very deeply for you."

She briefly wondered why he said that, but dismissed it. "What's going to happen to Carmen?"

"You need to warn her to stay away from these woods. I keep seeing her . . . death in my dreams. Warn her to stay inside and to surround herself with your pack."

"And she'll be okay?"

"It doesn't work like that. Sometimes things happen no matter how hard we try to stop them."

"Like fate or something?"

He paused before he said, "Or something."

"How do I know you didn't make me see this stuff? Like, conjure it up?"

His eyes narrowed. "I've shared this with you because I care about your pack and our town. I won't be insulted by you."

She bit her lip. "I didn't mean it that way. I'm just trying to understand what all your dream walking entails."

He started to fade in front of her. "I can't hold the link much longer. Remember what I said."

"But my sister . . ."

The vision in front of her scattered into a ribbon of white smoke.

"Ana. Wake up, Ana." She opened her eyes to find Connor lightly shaking her.

Her heart beat unsteadily as she fought to slow her breathing. She reached out and grabbed his shoulder to make sure he was real. Hard muscles flexed underneath her fingers. "Am I dreaming?"

He frowned. "No. This is real. Are you okay? You were thrashing around and calling Carmen's name."

She sat upright in bed, then reached over him for her cell phone. Snatching it up from the nightstand, she started to dial, but he placed a hand over hers.

"What are you doing?"

"I need to call my sister."

Thankfully he didn't try to stop her. The sun had already fully risen so she wasn't too surprised when Carmen answered on the second ring.

"What's up, Ana?"

"I take it I didn't wake you?"

"Um, *no*. Vivian kicks like a freaking horse. I woke up about an hour ago. This is the last time I'm sharing a bed with that little she-cat."

Ana smiled at her sister's testy voice. Just hearing it soothed her after the nightmare she'd had. "This is going to sound weird, but you need to stay inside today."

"What?"

"I had a weird dream last night about you. Just don't go into the woods. Promise me you won't." She could hear the desperation in her own voice but didn't care.

"For how long? And what if I want to run?"

"Are you really going to give me attitude?"

Carmen sniffed haughtily. "I'm not a child. You can't just order me around without giving me a reason."

"A lot is going on right now, in case you hadn't noticed. Don't be stubborn just because you can. If you insist on being stupid, then take someone with you—one of the warriors. Just don't go into the woods alone. Please, *hermanita*." She rarely used the endearment, but she sensed her sister soften immediately.

"Fine. I promise I won't go into the woods alone."

Ana hadn't realized she was hunched over, but at her sister's words she could feel the tension leave her shoulders. "Thank you."

"I just made a full pot of coffee so if you and Connor want to come over, feel free. If you're lucky I'll cook for you."

"We'll be there in a little while."

As soon as they disconnected Connor plucked the

phone from her hand. "What was that about? What dream?" Concern etched across every groove and line of his handsome face.

"I had an intense dream about Carmen last night." She wasn't sure she wanted to tell him about Matt's presence in her head just yet but she also didn't want to lie to him.

Lying back against the pillow, Connor pulled her with him so that she was snuggled up in the crook of his shoulder. He ran a soothing hand down her back, tracing along the hollow of her spine. Just the feel of him stroking her went a long way to settling her nerves. "Tell me about it, love."

He might not realize it, but when he called her love his voice softened. The sweet way he said it warmed her in a way she couldn't afford to get used to. She quickly relayed the things she'd seen and even though she wanted to leave out the part about Matt, she knew she couldn't. "Matt was in my head. In my dreams. Well, technically I was in his dreams. Or I think so anyway. It was a little confusing. He told me there's a coyote in our midst and we need to be careful. He also said we need to do something about Taggart's drug running. He said that if we don't feral wolves will become a problem for the town, which will become a big problem for our survival. I also saw an image of Carmen . . . dying. It was beyond disturbing." She kept the explanation as brief as possible, knowing Connor would understand her meaning.

Connor stiffened underneath her. "That bastard was in your head?"

She sighed. Of course he would ask about that first. "Connor, if he's warning me to keep my sister safe I don't think he's out to hurt us."

"You don't know that." His voice was a soft growl.

"It's not like I can help that he was in my head."

He sighed and his grip tightened. "I know. I'm not angry at you. I hate the idea of that guy inside your dreams."

"Carmen said she made coffee if we want to stop by." She hoped changing the subject would lighten his mood. It was too early to argue and her dream had really spooked her.

"Sounds good. How are you feeling?"

She shrugged against him. "Better but still sore. I think it'll take another day or two before I can shift."

He kissed the top of her head and smoothed a hand down her hair in a sweet, possessive gesture. "The men who did this are going to pay, love."

That's what she was afraid of.

Chapter 17

"You don't have to do this." Liam spoke for the first time since they'd left the ranch. Connor's brother had been unusually quiet as they trekked through the woods.

"Don't I?" Connor hated the silent accusation he'd seen in Ana's eyes as he and Liam had left the ranch but he couldn't help what they had to do. This was who he was, and someone had gone after his mate. Would have killed her if the cops hadn't come along.

"I'm just saying. The men will—"

"The men won't think less of me if I don't defend my mate?" He shook his head. It was bullshit. Liam knew just as well as he did that as Alpha he had to keep order. Maintain power. Hell, if he didn't go after these guys, he wouldn't be able to look at himself in the mirror. Two rapist bastards weren't going to stop terrorizing women. It would only be a matter of time before they escalated their behavior—if they hadn't already. His beast and human sides felt no guilt.

They were silent as they continued on. Connor's entire body tensed as the typical smells of the woods faded and more civilized scents like vehicle exhaust rolled over him. They'd be there soon. Eventually the pine trees thinned until they stood at a clearing.

"That's gotta be it." Liam set his backpack behind a tree and took off his sweater. He frowned at Connor when he didn't move. "Aren't you going to shift?"

He shook his head. It might be barbaric, but he wanted to feel their bones crunch underneath his fists.

The slight scent of smoke permeated the air. Like someone had let a fire dwindle down to nothing.

According to Ryan both the men who'd attacked Ana and Vivian had been released on bail. He hadn't realized that so many crimes—even violent ones, including those against children—had simple preset bails. It was a wonder humans ever kept anyone locked up. If they couldn't keep these assholes in jail, he wasn't waiting around for them to rape or kill or come after his pack again. Luckily one of the men they were looking for didn't live in a regular neighborhood. His house—which his parents had bought for him—was set on an acre of land.

Liam put his shirt back on and grabbed a small kit from his pack. "I say we go in the back door."

Connor nodded as they started across the backyard. It wasn't fenced in and there weren't many trees, so they had to cross a lot of open space quickly.

Once they reached the back door of the two-story Colonial-style house, Liam got to work with his lock-pick kit.

In seconds the plain white door with the flimsy lock opened.

I'm going to take the upstairs; you take down here, Connor projected as they stepped into the sterile kitchen. White tiles, white cabinets, and even stark white curtains on the small window above the sink. The only sign of life was a sink full of dirty dishes. The faint scent of old pizza and Chinese food lingered in the air. Probably from the trash can.

Ryan had worked his magic and gotten them the layout of the house from county records or something. It gave them a slight advantage but Connor didn't think they'd need it. From what he could scent, the house was empty. They searched it anyway.

Once they'd swept each room and the garage, they met downstairs. Liam locked the back door as they stepped outside into the cold. "His car's still in the garage and the engine is warm."

"Maybe they're at the other human's house," he muttered. They'd come to this house first because it was closer to them and because it was more private. The other guy lived in a condo.

They headed back across the yard. Connor froze when a scream tore through the air. It was muffled but definitely a woman's voice.

He looked at his brother. Without a word they both ran in the direction of the scream—a small, metal shed-like structure about twenty yards from the house.

One of the two wide doors was slightly ajar and a heavy-duty lock hung open on the handle. Connor slipped it off, heaved his arm back and tossed it into the thick grass. When he opened the door farther he didn't want it to bang against the metal.

"What's the matter, whore? Don't want to play with us?" A man's voice.

"Yeah, shifters are good enough for you but not your own kind?" Another man.

"You two are disgusting! The only way you can get a woman is to drug and rape her." The woman sounded terrified but also very pissed.

Since there were no windows they couldn't see inside. Connor motioned to his brother that he was going to open the door farther. *They might have weapons so be alert.*

Liam nodded.

Connor eased the door open just enough to slip through. Liam followed and pulled the door shut. With the overcast sky there was no sun to peek in and betray their presence.

Quickly he drank in the room. Two men had their backs to them and a young woman, maybe in her late twenties, crouched against the wall. Her eyes were wide and she clutched a knife tightly in her hand. Her jeans were dirty and her blue sweater was split down the middle in a jagged tear.

Connor spotted a large cage to his right. No doubt where they'd kept the woman. Against the left wall a flat bench with chains and cuffs was covered in dark stains. The scents of death, sex and blood invaded the air. Who knew how many people these monsters had hurt?

The woman gasped when she saw them. Liam roared and before Connor realized it, his brother shifted form. Bones and ligaments cracked and tore as quickly as his clothing shredded. He'd never seen his brother change so fast.

The two men turned, weapons drawn. One had a knife; the other a gun. Connor dove at the blond-haired man holding the gun.

He fired but the shot was wild, unsteady.

Connor tackled him to the ground. He was vaguely aware of the gun skidding away, but his animal side was threatening to take over. Calling on the strength of his human side he pushed down the beast and slammed his fist into the man's face.

The blond man was surprisingly strong. He took the hit and rolled onto his side before jumping back to his feet.

"Who the fuck are you?" he snarled.

Connor couldn't answer for fear he'd change. If he even said Ana's name or let this man know why he'd come after him, his inner wolf would take over. Not that he cared about killing the guy. He just wanted it to happen on even footing, and that could only be in his human form. Out of the corner of his eye he could see that Liam had the other man backed into a corner. His brother growled and snapped at him but he wasn't attacking. No, he'd leave that to Connor. Liam just wanted to make sure this was one-on-one.

"Felix, what the hell is going on, man?" The man in the corner trembled as he spoke.

Closing the few feet between them, Connor jabbed Felix in the stomach. Hard and swift. The man was in good shape but he grunted at the impact.

Swinging out, he tried to punch Connor, but Connor had speed on his side. Ducking out of the way, Connor delivered another punch. This one harder. The uppercut to Felix's jaw made a crunching sound he savored.

Felix howled as his head jerked back. Rage and something else—lust—rolled off him.

Connor bit back bile as he realized the other man got off on pain. He was actually enjoying this.

Felix's eyes glittered and a taunting smile stretched his bloody lips. "That all you got?"

When Connor didn't respond and instead slammed his bent elbow against the guy's jaw, a healthy dose of fear ripped through the air.

Connor's inner beast roared in satisfaction. He wanted the guy terrified. Wanted the human to know Connor was the fucking boogeyman come to life and he was going to pay for what he'd done.

Lifting his fists to protect his face, the man dodged a blow. "What the hell, man? You want the woman for yourself? Fucking take her!"

Connor struck again. This time he pummeled the man's ribs and he didn't hold back. As Felix tried to deflect the blows a shot rang through the air.

The loud, booming split stilled everything in the room.

The man who'd been hovering in the corner opened his mouth in a wide gasp as he looked down at his chest. Crimson flowed out of a gaping hole directly in the middle of his chest. He lifted a hand to the wound but his eyes rolled back in his head as he slumped to the floor in a bloody heap.

Holy shit. Liam's voice sounded in Connor's head.

He faced the woman. Her hands barely shook, but when she met his eyes he realized she'd never taken a life before.

She swiveled the weapon in his direction. Her pale blue eyes stared blindly so he didn't move. Getting shot wouldn't kill him but it would make him momentarily immobile, and he couldn't take the chance of Felix getting the upper hand. Even if Liam did have his back. This kill belonged to him.

"Oh, my . . . I can't believe . . ." A heavy shudder overtook her as she released the weapon.

It clattered to the floor. Before the human male made the move, Connor knew Felix was going to dive for the gun.

Connor lunged at him.

As the human's fingers grasped the weapon, Connor fell on top of him, pinning him to the ground.

Another shot rang out. A ping ricocheted off the interior wall.

The woman screamed and hit the floor. Connor grabbed the man's arm but he still grasped the weapon tightly in his hand.

Bang. Another shot, then another ricochet.

Something burned the side of Connor's upper arm. Instinctively he let go and rolled onto his back. But before the man could move, Connor raised his elbow and slammed it into his temple. He hit him so hard he could feel the jarring straight to his bones.

The gun fell from the man's hands and his body slumped against the cement-slab floor.

Is he alive? Liam asked.

Connor crouched by the body. No pulse. *Nope.*

When he stood to his full height, the woman backed away until she hit the wall. He held up his hands in what he hoped was a peaceful gesture. "We're not going to hurt you."

Grasping the edges of her sweater, she pulled it together to cover herself. She looked surprisingly calm. "I know."

"How long have you been here?"

"Since yesterday morning . . . I think. What day is it?"

"Wednesday."

"Since yesterday, then. They jumped me when I was leaving the grocery store. My boyfriend is . . . *was* a lupine shifter. Somehow they knew that and wanted to hurt me because of it. I think they were going to try to use me to trap him or something. I heard them talking to someone on the phone—it sounded like their boss—and they were supposed to bring me to him, but I guess they decided they wanted to have fun with me first. I was pretty drugged up when I heard them talking so I can't tell you much more than that."

"So, they killed your boyfriend?" Connor growled.

She snorted as if the thought was ludicrous. "No. I just meant we broke up a while ago. He doesn't even live near here. I don't know how they even know who I am, but they told me I was a shifter whore and they planned to teach me a lesson." At her own words she wrapped her arms tighter around herself and shuddered. "If you hadn't come along I don't even want to think about what would have happened."

"Did they . . . were you hurt?" Despite his desire to leave the police out of this, he knew this woman needed help. Probably medical.

"They roughed me up a little before they left yesterday but they didn't rape me, if that's what you're asking. They sure as hell planned to, though," she muttered.

He cleared his throat and tried to choose his next words carefully. "Why did you shoot the other one?"

"I'm not the first woman they've taken here. They were very explicit in what they'd done to other women and what they were going to do to me." Her eyes glinted defiantly. "I'm not sorry. I don't know what that says about me, but I'm not."

What the hell are we going to do? Liam asked.

Killing them was self-defense. And she's seen us. We can get our stories straight and I'll take the blame for shooting that guy. We've got to call the cops.

"You two should probably get out of here." She bent next to Felix's dead body and fished around in his back pocket until she pulled out a phone.

Liam growled, mirroring Connor's sentiments. "What?"

Her dark eyebrows rose. She stared at him as if he were stupid. "I'm gonna call the cops. You two need to be gone by the time they get here. . . . Where is here, by the way?"

Alarm pricked the back of his neck. This felt too easy. That normally meant a trap. "Why are you so calm about this? And why do you want us gone?"

Her cheeks tinged bright pink. "My last name is Saburova."

The name tickled something familiar in the back of his brain. He couldn't place it though. "And?"

"My father is . . . I'm no stranger to violence. I mean, I've never killed anyone or anything but this isn't the worst thing I've seen. Not even close. Besides, I know what the cops will do to you. No matter what I say or how evil these two assholes were, they'll find a way to blame you somehow. And even if they let you go, people will blame you because of who you are. I don't want that hanging over my head."

"You're a strange human." Connor spoke before he could censor himself.

To his surprise, a grin lit up her bruised face. "And you're bleeding. Get out of here and make sure you take all your stuff with you." She motioned toward Liam's ripped clothing.

Can we trust her? Liam's voice was a low growl in his head.

I think so, brother. "What are you going to tell the cops?"

"That they didn't want to share me so that one"—she pointed to the man she'd shot—"beat his buddy to death. He lost his gun in the process, and when he tried to attack me I shot him."

The story could work, but he didn't like the thought of leaving her to deal with the cops on her own.

As if she had read his mind, she shook her head. "I have no reason to lie and I've been missing long enough that my friends will be worried. I need to call the cops now. And you really need to leave before you get blood anywhere."

His wound was already starting to heal but he nodded. "Fine. If you need anything or get into any trouble, I'm Connor Armstrong and this is my brother, Liam. We just settled at the Cordona ranch."

Her eyes widened slightly. "I've heard of you."

For a human she was surprisingly at ease around them.

And the fact that she'd heard of him and his brother meant she'd done more than just date a shifter. Whoever she'd been with, they must have been fairly serious. "What's your first name?"

She paused for a moment, then shrugged. "Katarina. But since you saved my life, you can call me Kat. I'm a ski instructor—among other things—at Fontana Mountain Resort, if you ever want to look me up."

He nodded and gathered the rest of his brother's torn clothes and one of the bullets. After a quick scan of the small shed, he was certain they hadn't left anything behind. His shoulder burned where the ricocheting bullet had nicked him but he wasn't gushing blood. Still, he looked around and sighed when he spotted a spray bottle of bleach. These fuckers had likely used it to clean up their DNA. He handed the bottle to her. "You know what to do with this?"

She nodded. "I'll tell the cops that one tried to clean up after himself before I shot him. They won't know you were here."

Keeping pressure on the wound, he eased open the door and let Liam out first.

Kat stopped him as he stepped out. "Thank you for saving my life, by the way."

Pausing, he nodded once, then strode after his brother.

Snow was starting to fall in icy flurries. If they hurried, it would cover their tracks before the cops arrived.

She was an interesting human. Liam bounded along beside him.

Interesting and pretty fucking brave.

I hear that, brother. If humans are going after those who hook up with shifters, we might have a bigger problem than we originally anticipated. A touch of alarm edged Liam's voice.

Connor knew he was thinking about his own human,

December, and he understood his brother's fear. *I'll contact the Council* again *and see if they've been having similar problems around the country. Those two men could just be evil assholes acting alone, but she said she'd heard them talking to someone. A boss?* That could mean serious trouble. He'd been contacting the Council a lot lately. That normally went against his nature, but if he wanted his pack to thrive the Council needed to be aware of any and all problems. At least in the beginning.

But the truth was, in the past couple years there had been a growing fear among humans about their kind and vampires. Instead of the rampant terror expected twenty years ago, when shifters and vampires had revealed themselves to the world, it seemed there had been a delayed reaction to knowledge of their existence. Most shifters intermingled among humans on a semi-regular basis, at least to shop for necessities, but almost all vampires still kept their distance. They didn't need regular food to survive so even the interaction of shopping was eliminated. They had their own nightclubs and a startling amount of vampire groupies.

Thanks to things like that, rumors and lies now had a chance to spread and take over, ruling people through fear. There would always be ignorant fools willing to latch on to blind hatred. If there were more people like the two men they'd just killed, they would definitely have a big problem. It wasn't like shifters could go back into hiding.

Chapter 18

Connor put his truck in park and glanced at Liam. "I won't be long."

"I'm gonna head down to December's. She should be open by now." His brother wasn't asking.

"We'll meet back here, then." Connor understood his brother's need to see his human. After witnessing what those monsters were planning to do to that woman—and finding out they might be working for someone—Liam had been jittery and agitated the entire drive to town. At least they'd brought an extra set of clothes.

Liam stepped from the vehicle and slammed his door with more force than necessary. Everything about the quaint downtown was calm today. Soothing holiday music emanated from most of the stores. Couples and families strolled down the sidewalk, wearing winter coats and carrying brightly colored shopping bags. The peaceful scene was in direct opposition to the adrenaline still pumping through him.

Liam strode with purpose down the sidewalk lining the strip of stores on Avalon Street, while Connor had to compose himself before entering Matt and Kaya's store.

A little bell jingled as he entered the gift shop. The scents of patchouli and sage hung in the air. Ana would probably be pissed when she found out he'd visited Matt, but he shoved aside the repercussions. He side-stepped a display of rugs and quilts with geometric designs as he moved through the store. He couldn't see anyone but he sensed he wasn't alone.

"Are you here shopping or is this a personal visit?"

Connor turned at the sound of Matt's voice. He spotted him standing next to a display of turquoise jewelry. "Anyone else in the store?"

"Why? You plan to kill me, wolf man?"

He bit back a growl. "Stay out of Ana's head."

"Or what?"

"Just stay the hell away from her. I don't know what you're up to, but if I find out you had anything to do with these poisonings, I'll kill you myself."

The other man didn't flinch at his words. Without looking at him he adjusted an intricate beaded necklace on a mannequin bust. "I had nothing to do with the poisonings. Don't let your baseless jealousy get in the way of your common sense."

"Jealousy?"

Now Matt looked at him, his dark eyes far too knowing for Connor's taste. "I'm not saying you're jealous of *me*. You love Ana but you're unwilling to tell her. This anger you have with me is misplaced and I think it's something you're already aware of."

Connor's throat seized. He wanted to argue with Matt. Walk away from him. Maybe punch him. But his curiosity got the better of him. "How do you know I haven't told her I love her?"

Matt shrugged but avoided answering directly. "Don't let old fears and insecurities get in the way of your happiness."

Insecurities? Connor started to scoff but held back. It disturbed him that the other man could read him so well. They'd only interacted a few times yet Matt seemed to understand him better than most of his pack. "How do you . . . ?" He caught himself before he finished. He wasn't going to admit anything to this stranger.

But Matt didn't let him off easily. "Call it an educated guess. I know you left Ana before—I've seen it in my dreams. I don't know *why* you left, but I've seen the way you look at her—like she's the best birthday present you've ever received—so you must have had a damn good reason to go. And you act jealous for no reason so I know you're not. Not truly. You're insecure about *something*. My guess is it has something to do with the reason you left the first time."

Connor frowned as he digested Matt's words. He was having a hard time remembering why he'd even come to the store, when one of the dream catchers hanging from the ceiling swayed against a vent. "Just stay out of Ana's dreams," he muttered before stalking from the store.

Liam wasn't at the truck yet so he called Ana. It had been only a couple hours but he already missed her voice.

She picked up on the second ring. "Hey."

Suddenly he felt like an inexperienced, tongue-tied cub working up the courage to talk to the girl he liked. Except Ana was no girl. She was all woman. His woman. "Hey."

"Is everything okay?"

"Yeah."

"Did you— Is it done?"

"I don't want to talk about that." He hated that she even knew where he'd gone that morning.

"Then why are you calling?"

"I just wanted to check on you." *And to hear your voice.*

"Well, I'm fine." Her voice was clipped, distant.

"What's wrong?"

"You mean other than the fact that you went off to kill some humans this morning despite knowing it could hurt the entire pack? And the fact that you won't even talk to me about it?" Now there was no distance. Just boiling anger.

"Damn it, Ana. I'm your Alpha and I'm doing this to protect you. These are my decisions to make. Mine alone."

"So you just want me to fall in line and agree with everything you do?"

"I didn't say that."

"Well, you're sure as hell not denying it," she shot back.

He scrubbed a hand over his face. How had this even started? He'd just wanted to check on her, hear her voice. "Why are we fighting, Ana?"

Her frustrated sigh filled the line. "Because you won't open up to me about anything and I'm sick of it. You and your brother just make decisions, and you don't include me when you meet with the males of your pack. I'm your *mate*. I thought you said we were supposed to be a team. When you first got here you told everyone that if you weren't around they were supposed to come to me. How can anyone believe that when you don't even include me in your stupid meetings! After last night I realized I can't live like this. I can't be mated to someone who won't even talk to me."

Her words pierced him straight in the chest because they were true. He hadn't even thought to include her. He just wanted to protect her. Keep her safe. "Ana—"

"I'm not finished! I only asked you once when you

first arrived, and I think I've been pretty damn patient about waiting for you to come to me on your own. Especially considering your stupid demand that I become your bondmate, without giving me any reason to trust you. We're mated now, I've let you into my bed and I've given all of myself that I possibly can based on what you've given me. Why did you leave all those years ago? And how do I know I can trust you not to leave again? Did you mate with someone else? Did she die? Did you break up? Am I your second choice? Is that what you're too afraid to tell me?" Her voice shook at the last question.

He hadn't wanted to do this now. Or ever. He'd known it was inevitable but he'd still been hoping to avoid this. "I didn't mate with anyone else! It's always been you, Ana. I wanted you fifty years ago, so much it scared me. I went to your father and asked him for permission to take you as my mate. He told me no and that if I mated with you anyway he'd kick you out of your pack forever. That you'd *never* be able to see your sisters, mother or cousins again." Once the confession started, the words just poured from him.

"Liar! My father knew how much I cared for you. He saw how much your leaving tore me up. For all I know you really were just a coward and didn't want the commitment of a mate. If you wanted some stupid, gullible mate maybe you should have chosen someone else instead."

"Maybe I should have!" As soon as the words escaped, he wanted to cut out his own tongue. He didn't mean it. "Ana, I—"

She hung up on him.

"Shit," he muttered. Connor hit his speed dial but it went straight to her voice mail. He tried again. Voice mail again.

He banged his fist against the steering column. He loved Ana. Why the hell had he said that? After all she'd been through and all she meant to him, hurting her was the last thing he ever wanted to do. He projected to his brother. *Liam, whatever you're doing, you better get back to the truck. We've gotta get back to the ranch now.*

It was time to set things straight between himself and Ana once and for all. If he had to face her rejection, he'd deal with it. He loved the stubborn she-wolf and she needed to know.

Liam hurried down the sidewalk toward December's store. After her brush-off on the phone yesterday he wasn't sure he'd get the best reception but he didn't care. Those sick humans had targeted that woman because she'd dated a shifter. Technically he and December weren't even dating but she'd been seen out in public with him. And someone had attacked her in her own home. Someone obviously knew that she meant something to him, even if he meant nothing to her. After what Katarina had said about those men using her to trap her ex-boyfriend, he figured this might be completely about him or hurting his pack. December could just be a pawn in all this—whatever *this* was. After her assault the other night it was obvious she'd landed on someone's radar.

As he entered the store her subtle jasmine scent wrapped around him. The place was empty, though. Frowning, he strode through the store, past the cash register and into the back room. Boxes of opened books filled a couple shelves, and shipping boxes and materials sat on a table in the middle of the room. The back door was slightly ajar.

He knew he was acting stalkerish by rushing into her storeroom unannounced and uninvited. He didn't care. Nudging the back door open with his foot, he peered out. When he saw December tossing a garbage bag into the green Dumpster, he nearly sagged against the doorframe.

Not wanting to freak her out, he inched back, but froze when he spotted a hooded man peering out from behind the Dumpster. December's back was turned to him as she walked toward the store.

Thinking it might be a homeless man, he waited. But when the man slowly crept out from behind the Dumpster with a gleaming knife in hand, Liam shoved the door open.

"Liam," December gasped.

She held a startled hand to her throat, but he rushed past her. Whoever this guy was, he wasn't getting away this time.

Still holding the knife, the guy straightened when he spotted Liam. He started to charge, then thought better of it. Turning, the guy ran a few feet, but Liam didn't give him a chance. With lightning speed he crossed the distance and tackled him to the ground. The knife clattered next to his head.

The man howled in pain as Liam shoved him face-first onto the dirty asphalt. "Get off me."

Liam dug his knee into the man's back and kept his wrists securely behind his back. The man struggled but it was useless. "What the hell are you doing behind this lady's store with a knife?"

"Fuck you," he gasped out.

Aware of December behind him, he half turned. "Grab some packing tape." When she disappeared inside, he slammed the guy's head against the asphalt. "Answer the question or I kill you now."

"You're a fucking animal."

"You got that right," he growled, fighting back his inner wolf. "Now, what are you doing here?" Still holding his wrists, he increased pressure on one of the guy's thumbs, bending it back at an excruciating angle.

He howled in pain again. "Shit, man. I was just following orders."

"Taggart's?" He bent his thumb back farther.

"Who—? No, man. I was just supposed to grab this bitch."

At the word *bitch*, Liam snapped his thumb. He'd only meant to scare him, but this guy wanted to hurt December.

The man screamed again as December ran back outside, carrying a roll of thick tape. Her blue eyes were bright and frightened as she handed it to him. "Liam, what's going on?"

"Go back inside and call your brother."

She stared at him hard. "Liam, your eyes are ... What's wrong with your eyes?" Her voice quavered.

He cursed under his breath and turned away from her. "Call your brother!"

He heard her shoes pound against the ground as she practically sprinted back inside. She was probably more terrified of him than the guy on the ground. He knew what his eyes looked like when he was angry. Right now he was fighting the change. He'd barely managed to leash it. The only thing keeping him in human form was December. He never wanted to scare or hurt her. Unfortunately his dark eyes were likely completely black now, with not a fleck of white showing. He probably looked like a fucking demon to her.

Beneath him the man still cried and whined about his broken thumb. Liam needed to get information out of him before the cops got there. After binding his wrists, he pulled out the guy's wallet. When he tugged the license out, a business card and a couple pictures fell out.

Liam grabbed the guy's hoodie and yanked it back.

That's when he saw the swastika tattoo on his neck. "So you just hate everyone, don't you?"

"Man, what do you want to know?"

"For starters, why the hell were you here with a knife? Who told you to take this woman?"

"He'll kill me if I tell you."

Liam snorted as he flipped over the driver's license and read the man's name and address. "I'll kill you, Mr. William Braun. And everyone you've ever met. Got kids? A wife? You want that blood on your hands?" He'd never kill any innocent women and kids, but if this guy thought he was a mindless killer the power of that fear would get him the answers he wanted. And he didn't have time to waste.

"Adler. Edward Adler. He's the leader of our local group."

Liam grasped his other thumb and twisted. "And that would be?"

"Antiparanormal League. APL."

Liam paused. "That's a real thing? It's not even clever."

"Whatever, man. Just kill me now. When Adler finds out I gave him up, I'm dead. Fucking *dead*."

"Why is he after December? She's the sheriff's sister." *And more important, my mate*. If someone went after her again, a broken thumb would be the least of his worries.

"He wants anyone connected to shifters or vamps taken. I don't know his plans, man. He takes orders from someone else. That much I do know."

Liam filed that bit of information away. "You know two guys named Felix Carr and Bennett Harrison?"

He squirmed against the ground, so Liam dug his knee in harder. "Yeah, I know those crazy assholes. They were supposed to do some bag-and-grab work for Adler with some chick but they disobeyed his orders. Didn't bring her in like they were supposed to."

"And why is that?" Liam already knew the answer but he wanted to see how honest this guy would be.

"They're part of the same group as me but we don't run in the same circles, if you get what I'm saying. I'm no rapist. Adler never should have recruited them in the first place. They don't care about our cause . . ." He trailed off as if he realized who he was talking to.

"So you're not a rapist—you just deliver innocent women to a bunch of crazy radicals. What do you think your boss Adler would have done to her? What the hell's the matter with you? You've got two daughters."

When he stiffened, Liam plucked one of the fallen pictures from the ground. Two young girls with curly blond hair cheesed it up for the camera. He shoved it in his face. "I'm assuming these are yours. Adler's never going to find out about our conversation as long as the cops don't find out either. You got me?"

William nodded, rubbing his face against the ground.

"Say it," he growled. "I don't care what you tell them. Tell them you wanted to rob her or whatever, but if you tell them the name of your boss, I will come back and kill you. I've got your name and your scent. I'll *never* forget it either."

"I won't say a word. I swear."

Another thought settled in his mind. Sirens blared loudly in the distance. Liam's heart rate sped up. "Were you the one who broke into her house?"

He shook his head again. "No. That was Chuck. He's . . . dead. He was supposed to get her and that old Indian woman but he failed. I don't know for sure, but I think Adler killed him for his failures."

When two cop cars zoomed into the back alley, Liam stood and backed away from the guy.

Sheriff McIntyre jumped from one of the vehicles and rushed toward them. "What the hell's going on?"

Liam nodded to the dirty, dark-haired man. "This asshole tried to assault December. That's his knife."

The sheriff jerked back slightly, then composed himself. He motioned to two of his deputies. "Take this guy in."

Liam stepped back as they hauled the guy up. The man howled in pain again.

"What happened to his thumb?" one of the deputies asked as he eyed Liam warily.

"I did that myself." The man avoided looking at anyone and instead focused on the ground, but fear was evident in his voice.

Liam's inner beast roared in satisfaction at the edge of fear he heard. He wanted that jerk terrified. The humans wouldn't be able to keep him for long and he didn't want the cops nosing around the leader of this Antiparanormal League. If the group caught wind that the cops knew who they were, Liam could only imagine what they'd do. Probably leave town and cause havoc somewhere else. Or they'd simply tighten the ranks and become even more careful. Liam planned to make sure that didn't happen. Whatever it took, he and Connor were going to eliminate these guys. Most important, he was going to protect December.

Liam, whatever you're doing, you better get back to the truck. We've gotta get back to the ranch now. Connor's voice sounded loud in his head.

December was almost attacked again. By some asshole that's part of a group called the Antiparanormal League, if you can believe it. I think the cops want me to make a statement, he projected back.

Call me if you need a ride back to the ranch.

Will do, brother. He was thankful Connor didn't give him grief about wanting to stay. Not that he'd expected too much resistance. Not in a situation like this.

"Did you hear what I said?" Parker asked.

"What?"

"You need to come down to the station and make a statement."

Liam nodded and glanced back at December, who still hovered by the back door. She clutched the doorframe. It took all his willpower not to rush over to her and gather her in his arms and comfort her. Either it would embarrass her or she'd reject him. Or both.

"You should have broken more than his thumb," Parker growled.

Liam grunted his agreement. "Listen, whatever our differences, I think it's obvious we both care about that woman. I know a guy in security. The best. I want to have a system installed at December's house and her store. Can you convince her to let me do it?"

Parker muttered something under his breath but nodded. "Yeah, I'll convince her."

Chapter 19

Ana turned off her phone and shoved it into the front pocket of her jeans. With balled fists, she fought her rising temper. She couldn't believe what Connor had just said to her. She knew he'd said the words in anger, but the middle of her chest ached nonetheless. And for all she knew part of him meant what he said.

She opened the front door to the main house and froze when she saw Teresa at the top of the stairs. All thoughts of her argument with the man she loved dissipated.

Her cousin's damp hair was pulled back into a messy knot, as if she'd just gotten out of the shower. She clutched the balustrade tightly. But she was awake. "Hey."

"Teresa." A burst of joy filled her and Ana couldn't get out more than her cousin's name. She flew up the stairs and nearly bowled her over in a giant hug. Before she could stop herself, a stupid sob caught in her throat. Tears rolled down her face as she held on to her. She knew she was probably gripping her too tight but couldn't stop. When Teresa cleared her throat, Ana pulled back. "I'm so glad you're okay. Are you hungry? Why are you out of bed without help? What can I get for you?"

A tired grin lit up Teresa's face. "Calm down, woman. I'm very hungry, and Carmen was here not too long ago. She said she had to take care of something but I thought she'd be back by now."

A thread of alarm wormed its way into Ana's head. Carmen would never have left Teresa if it hadn't been important. Still, it was starting to snow really hard outside. Just like in her dreams. But Carmen had *promised* her she'd stay away from the woods. Pushing down her fear, Ana slid her arm around Teresa's shoulders and helped her down the stairs.

"All the food has been checked, so whatever you want to eat, I'll get for you." She opened the pantry, then the refrigerator and started rambling off what they had.

"Maybe yogurt and an apple," Teresa finally said.

Ana raised her eyebrows. "That's it?"

"To start. I'm not sure what I can keep down. Oh, and some ginger ale." Teresa leaned back in her chair and stretched. Even though her face was tired and drawn, a spark of color had returned.

As Ana set the foodstuff on the table, the front door flew open and Ryan rushed in. He froze when he saw Teresa. "You're awake."

Her cousin's cheeks tinged pink as she nodded.

"I'm glad." There was a hot promise in those two words. Even Ana could hear it. And the lust that came off him spiked off the charts. Ryan opened his mouth as if to say more but he shook his head. "Ana, have you seen Vivian?"

"No. Why?"

"She and Lucas were playing hide-and-seek, and it's been over an hour and Lucas can't find her. He just told me, or I'd have been here sooner."

Ana looked worriedly at her cousin, not wanting to leave her alone. "Will you be all right by yourself?"

Teresa nodded and shooed her away. "Don't worry about me. Go find the little she-cat."

Ana hurried out the front door with Ryan. "Where was the last place he saw her?"

"In the barn. I found faint tracks in the snow leading out the back door, but with the snow falling the way it is, they won't last long."

The snow would also slowly begin to cover the little she-cat's scent. He didn't voice it aloud but Ana knew he was thinking the same thing she was. At such a young age, it could mean death for Vivian if she got stuck out in the cold with no food or shelter. "Who have you told?"

"I rounded up Noah and Erin. They're at the barn, waiting."

"Have you seen Carmen?" she asked as they hurried across the yard.

He shook his head.

She pushed down her growing alarm. Carmen was smart, and Ana could only manage one crisis at a time. And maybe Carmen and Vivian were together.

Once they made it to the barn she started barking orders. "We each take a horse and track in opposite directions. I'll take the west field; you three figure out which fields you want. If anyone finds her, we check in." She fished out her phone and turned it on. The voice-mail icon flashed. Five new messages. She cleared the screen. "Everyone understand?"

When they murmured agreement, she saddled Adalita and rode out. If anything happened to Vivian, she couldn't bear it. The little she-cat had burrowed her way into Ana's heart so quickly it had taken her by surprise.

She dug her heels into Adalita. Her Andalusian immediately increased her pace. The shrill jingle of her phone in her pocket made her heart jump. Maybe someone had found Vivian.

When she saw Connor's number, she almost answered but instead pressed the END button. She couldn't talk to him right now. Not without yelling. *Maybe I should have.* His last words hung heavy in her heart and remained etched in her brain.

She'd been so convinced he would leave her again, so convinced he'd left her for another female, she hadn't even thought of the possibility that he'd asked her father to mate her. For nearly fifty years her father had never said a word.

Her father had been a hard man. A hard Alpha. But he'd been a good leader. Fair for the most part. He had been a little biased against other shifters, though. Not overtly; he just hadn't liked outsiders. Her mother had always said it was because he wanted to protect the pack. But he'd known her feelings for Connor and he'd never forbidden her to see him.

Could her father really have threatened to cut her off from her entire pack if she'd mated with Connor? She pressed a hand to the middle of her chest and rubbed her sternum. Even thinking about that made her want to cry. She'd tried to hide how depressed she was after Connor had left, but her mother and father had known. Hell, her father had tried to mate her to someone else not long after, but she'd adamantly resisted. At the time she'd thought he was trying to help her get over Connor, but maybe she'd been wrong.

None of that changed the fact that Connor wasn't opening up to her. Wasn't letting her into his life. He'd demanded she mate with him from practically the moment he'd arrived. He'd never said anything about love either. Sure, he wanted her but he'd said he wasn't good enough for her. His demands could just as easily be some weird way to get back at her father.

As more thoughts bombarded her, she rubbed her temple. Now wasn't the time to worry about this. A little cub was missing and Ana needed to find her. The deeper she ran into the woods, the more dread filled her. Her horse's tracks were almost covered by the falling snow. She might have a higher body temperature than humans, but it was starting to get really cold. Vivian was so tiny in her shifted form and her coat wasn't very thick. She could freeze to death.

"Vivian!" Her voice carried with the wind, so she paused and listened. When she didn't hear a response she tried again and again until she was hoarse.

At least it was still early afternoon so they had daylight left. She started to shout when her cell rang. Shuddering in her thick coat, she fished out her phone again.

She didn't recognize the number but thought it might be Connor calling from a different line. Despite their argument and her conflicted feelings, she needed to tell him about Vivian. "Connor?"

A familiar male laugh filtered through the line. "Guess again."

"Taggart. What do you want?" she asked through gritted teeth. Hearing his voice now was like alcohol on an open wound.

"I think the question is what do I have that you want?"

Oh, shit. He had Vivian. She heard it in his smug tone. She swallowed back her fear. "What are you talking about?"

He made an obnoxious *tsk-tsk* sound. "I found that she-cat wandering around. It's a dangerous place for such a young one to be out unprotected."

"What do you want, Taggart?"

"I want that piece of land we discussed earlier."

"Fine."

He paused. "No argument?"

She cringed at his question. Maybe she should have negotiated, but this was Vivian they were talking about. What was she supposed to do? "I'm not going to barter for a little girl's life. You want the land? I'll deed it to you."

"Good. I've already got the contract drawn up. Meet me in twenty minutes or I kill the cub."

"I can't be there in—"

"Find a way or she dies. You know I'll do it too. Meet me at the property line, south side. And come alone." He disconnected before she could argue.

Shit, shit, shit! Taggart was dirty enough to use a cub. Considering Vivian wasn't lupine, Ana had a sick feeling he'd have a much easier time killing her if he wanted. Most shifters couldn't kill a defenseless cub regardless of species, but Taggart was a psychopath. She'd already seen how little he thought of females. Why would cubs be any different? She tried calling Connor but it went straight to voice mail. The sound of his deep voice soothed her. He was probably going to be pissed, but she couldn't wait around for anyone to meet her. Taggart didn't make idle threats and she had no doubt he'd kill Vivian if she was late. Then he'd just find another way to get to her until more and more people she cared about died.

"Connor, Taggart just called. He's got Vivian and he wants me to deed a section of our land to him. I've got to do it. I'm supposed to meet him on the south side of the property line in twenty minutes. This is probably a dumb thing I'm doing but I can't *not* go. If you get this, haul ass to the property line, because I have a feeling he's not going to keep his word. I never thought I'd be doing this over voice mail, but in case . . . whatever. I just want to let you know that I—"

Beeeep.

The voice mail cut her off. Probably a good thing. Telling him that she loved him over voice mail was a stupid idea. One she'd definitely regret later. If she survived this meeting, of course. Sighing, she dug her heels into Adalita and took off. Considering the ground she needed to cover, she'd barely make it in time. As she rode across the grass and hard earth she called Ryan.

He picked up immediately. "Did you find her?"

"Taggart's got her. I'm meeting him at the south-side property line now."

"Damn it, Ana. You can't go alone."

"I don't have a choice. He wants something from me in exchange for her and he's going to get it."

"Just wait for us to meet you—"

"Not gonna happen, so please *hurry*." She disconnected and shoved her phone back in her pocket.

Her heart leapt in her throat when she reached the property line. Taggart held a squirming Vivian in his hands and five of his wolves stood next to him, including his second-in-command, Vince. The other wolves were a lot bigger and older than the young wolves he'd sent to attack the ranch the night before. Only he and Vince were in human form. At least he wasn't naked this time.

When she neared them, she dismounted. Her hands trembled as she fisted the reins. "Let the girl go. I'll sign whatever you want."

Taggart sneered as he held Vivian up by the neck. The she-cat meowed and struggled but it did no good. "You'll sign this contract all right. But neither of you are going anywhere."

She'd known he'd try something dirty, but a bolt of fear spiked through her just the same. There were a lot of them and only one of her. From what she could tell, they all looked like warrior-class shifters too. She might be able to outrun them but only if she got Vivian first. "We had a deal." Her voice came out stronger than she'd hoped.

"You're going to be my bitch, Ana. I can smell Connor's filthy scent all over you but I can tell he hasn't bonded with you yet. You're fair game as far as I'm concerned." His voice was deadly.

An icy fist clasped around her chest. "I'd rather die first."

"Once we've bonded you can decide if you want to kill yourself."

"I'll never let you touch me," she spat. The thought of his dirty paws all over her made her want to puke.

"You don't have much say over the matter now, do you?" He pulled out a dagger with his free hand and held it to Vivian's chest.

It looked silver, and while Ana knew the metal itself wouldn't do lasting damage to a feline shifter, a dagger to the heart would likely kill one so young. Vivian hadn't built up a strong immune system yet.

She held her breath and watched him. *What the hell is he doing?*

"Strip."

His command jerked her vocal chords into working. "What?"

"Strip. Now. I'm going to put my scent on you."

"Are you insane?" Terror streaked through her, jagged and fierce. He meant to rape her right now. She'd thought he might kill her or kidnap her, but he wanted to rape her? It went against their nature to have sex with one already marked by another. She might not be bondmates with Connor but his scent on her was strong. Taggart really was twisted. "Connor will kill you. Do you understand? Kill. You. Dead. There's nowhere on this planet you could possibly hide."

He snorted loudly. "We'll see about that. Maybe he'll show up when I'm balls deep in you."

She gagged at his vile words and took an involuntary step back. When she moved, he pressed the knife harder against Vivian's chest. The image seared into her brain. The she-cat meowed a sad little cry, but she didn't even struggle. Just cried.

Ana wanted to reach out and comfort Vivian, but not before she strangled the life from Taggart. "Let the girl go and I'll do what you want."

He laughed loudly, the harsh sound bouncing off the forest. "If I let her go, you'll fight. I'm not an idiot. Now strip, bitch."

"You can't be this stupid—"

He pressed the knife into Vivian's fur, cutting Ana off. With shaking hands, she tugged down the zipper on her jacket and let it fall onto the snowy ground. At least it had stopped snowing. She didn't know why she even noticed or cared. What was about to happen to her was going to be horrific with or without snow. She started to tug off her sweater when he shook his head.

His dark eyes glowed wild and insane. "Forget your top. Just take off the pants. This is going to be fast and hard. By the time your mate gets here, my scent will be on you too. I can't wait to see the look on his face."

Again, bile rose in her throat but she shoved it down. "It's not as if you can make me your bondmate." It wasn't a full moon, something they both knew, but she wanted to stall.

"So? You think Connor will want you after I've had you? Not that it matters. I'm going to kill him when he shows up, but before he dies at least he'll know I had you." His smile grew, wicked and terrifying.

She fought off a shiver that had nothing to do with the cold. "Will you at least turn Vivian away? I don't want her to see this."

Keeping the knife against the feline, he turned her around.

Ana wished there was more that she could do for Vivian but she was out of options. She felt light-headed as she struggled with the button of her jeans. *How can this be happening?* Her fingers clenched into fists. It took all her willpower not to shift and attack. She might not be a warrior but she was still an alpha. Her inner beast demanded she fight, even if she knew she'd lose. Her basest instinct wanted to struggle right to the death. By some magic feat, she lassoed her inner wolf and stayed in human form. If she shifted he'd kill Vivian. No doubt in her mind.

As she started to pull down the zipper of her jeans, a roar slashed through the trees.

Connor.

The sound was loud and eerie and chilled her straight to her bones. She froze and the other wolves did the same.

"What the hell was that?" Vince muttered. A burst of fear jetted off him and the rest of the animals.

Then another noise ripped through the air. Loud, angry howls. And they were getting closer.

"Now's your chance to run, Taggart. Leave now and he'll let you live. You have my word." Ana didn't know if she could control Connor but she could sure try. If it avoided bloodshed—no matter how much the bastard deserved death—she was in favor of it. She just wanted to get Vivian to safety.

"Shit!" Taggart dropped Vivian when she bit into his wrist.

A couple of the wolves made a move for the feline

but Vivian was fast. She ran to Ana and darted behind her feet.

"Uh, boss?" Vince asked. There was no denying the nervous note in his voice or the stench of his fear.

"Get the weapons ready," Taggart growled.

Weapons? Ana's heart rate tripled. Since Taggart's attention was diverted, she bent and picked up Vivian and her jacket. As she scooped the cub into her arms, a dark wolf emerged from the woods.

Not Connor, but Ryan. One by one, six more wolves emerged, growling and snarling. Ryan must have notified them, though she didn't see Liam in the group. Maybe he was with Connor. Her hands still shook as she thought about what had almost happened. She still might die today, but at least she wouldn't be raped by that monster.

Still no Connor. He was coming, though. She could hear and feel him. They all could. The air buzzed with an electric energy.

Ana took a small step toward her horse. "Leave now, Taggart. Before he gets here."

Ignoring her, he and Vince pulled out two big guns. Knowing Taggart, they were packing silver bullets.

"So you're going to fight dirty? So typical," she sneered, unable to keep the disgust out of her voice.

He flicked a quick glance her way, his dark eyes hollow. "Shut your fucking mouth."

Ana glared at him but did as he said. She took another step back toward her horse, and two of the wolves growled at her. Adalita whinnied and put some distance between them but at least she didn't completely abandon Ana.

Stopping dead in her tracks, Ana tucked Vivian under one of her arms. The she-cat didn't struggle or wiggle around. Just meowed. Ana ignored the little one's cries and watched as her packmates stalked across the clearing. Whatever happened today would change everything between the two packs.

Out of the corner of her eye she saw a flash of fur. Then wind rushed by her face, caressing her with an icy breeze.

Before she could blink Taggart flew through the air as two hundred pounds of black fur and muscle slammed into him. His weapon seemed pathetic now as it too sailed through the air. It landed in the snow with a soft thud a few feet away.

Taggart screamed in pain as Connor pinned him to the ground.

All the air whooshed from her lungs as she stared at them. She'd known Alphas were fast but she'd never seen one move *that* fast before.

"Shoot him!" Taggart screamed.

Vince lifted his gun, but Ana dropped Vivian and lunged at him. Preparing for a fight, she clutched at his arm. When he didn't struggle she realized he didn't *want* to shoot Connor.

That put a whole new spin on things. She still held his arm but chose her words carefully. "According to Council laws, they have to fight unimpeded in wolf form. Do you really want to go against our laws? More important, do you *want* Taggart to be victorious? Connor is a good Alpha. A fair one," she murmured. She didn't think Vince was fast enough to shoot Connor anyway but she didn't voice that.

Vince looked back at the other wolves, who moved around nervously in the snow. After a moment he nodded, almost to himself. Jaw set, he faced Connor and Taggart. Connor hadn't made a move to kill Taggart yet and she knew it was because he respected their laws.

"This will be a *Nex Pugna*!" Vince shouted loud enough for all the wolves to hear. A death fight.

"You son of a bitch," Taggart growled.

"Sack up, boss. If you can't do this the right way, you don't deserve to be our Alpha." Vince's voice shook as he spoke. At least he'd stood up to the treacherous wolf, but if his Alpha won, it would be certain death for him.

Ana gained a little respect for the other wolf even though all she cared about at the moment was her mate. They might not officially be bonded but he was hers. She felt it to her core.

Connor circled Taggart as he stripped off his clothes and shifted form with the speed of an Alpha. Connor would have loved nothing more than to rip off Taggart's head when he'd jumped him moments ago, but Taggart was also an Alpha. They had to fight properly. It was the way of their kind, and if he couldn't respect his own laws his pack wouldn't respect him.

When he'd gotten that message from Ana that she was meeting Taggart alone, decades of his life had been shaved off. The thought of losing her before he'd gotten a chance to tell her he loved her made him tremble.

No longer a man, Taggart stood before Connor, a brown-and-white wolf. Hulking and dangerous.

Out of the corner of his eye he could see his wolves and Taggart's pack encircle them. Whoever survived, the victor would be respected. There would be no more bloodshed around here after today, and hopefully never again.

Taggart was already dead. He just didn't know it. Connor should have hunted him down that night he'd arrived and caught him assaulting Ana. It was one of the few regrets he had in life.

But Ana—his sweet Ana, who felt she had to be strong for everyone—had told him not to. He didn't want her watching this, but she was right. She was his mate and needed to see his strength. See what he was capable of.

Keeping his head low, he stalked to his right. With his guys watching his back, he wasn't worried about being flanked.

Taggart also moved to his right, circling him.

They could dodge and dance around all day. The end result would be the same. Connor braced himself for the pain as he went on the offensive.

Taggart started to duck away again but Connor lunged at him. Using all the strength from his hind legs, he launched forward, right at the other wolf.

The brown-and-white wolf snarled but kept its neck down as Connor tackled him. Claws dug into his side and underbelly with ripping agony.

He ignored it. As he swiped at Taggart's face, he extended his claws and slashed one of his eyes. The blinding blow would enrage him, which is what Connor hoped for.

Taggart's actions today were erratic and insane. Connor would never understand why Taggart was so unstable but he didn't really care. The shifter was just plain evil. Trying to kidnap another Alpha's mate was asking for bloodshed.

When the other wolf dug his claws deeper into Connor's belly, he rolled off him and pounced onto his feet a few feet away. Blood dripped down Taggart's face. Connor growled in approval.

The sound must have pissed off Taggart, because he lunged. The strike was calculated, but with his eye damaged his timing was off. As he flew through the air, Connor went for his neck. He missed his target but clamped on to one of Taggart's front legs.

As he did, Taggart's claws ripped through the side of his neck. Letting go of the leg, Connor bit back a growl and dodged to the side, preparing for another attack.

A piercing scream ripped through the air.

His heart stopped at the sound. *Ana.* Before he could process anything, Ana's delicate arms wrapped around Taggart's neck as she tried to tackle him. *What the hell is she doing?*

Taggart snarled, and with a startling blow he swiped at her shoulder with one of his paws, sending her flying.

She landed in the snow with a soft thud but was motionless. Connor saw red. Bloody, crimson rage rolled over him. He wanted to go to her but knew it would be certain death if he turned his back on Taggart.

Lowering himself, he launched at Taggart and slammed his head into the other Alpha. The other wolf jerked back, taken by surprise.

At the same time Connor dug his claws into Taggart's chest. Each time the wolf tried to move, the deeper and deeper he dug into his chest cavity.

The action was too much to bear. Taggart howled and tried to jerk out of his grasp but Connor wouldn't let go. Unlike his regular-wolf counterpart, he had claws. Using his strength, he extended them even farther into the other Alpha's body.

Taggart bit him, pulling away fur and skin from his shoulder.

But Connor held fast. The pain would be worth the victory. *Taggart dead.* He envisioned it in his head. The other wolf would die today.

When Taggart thrashed, Connor didn't give up the opportunity to strike. The other wolf howled as he tried to wrench away once again. In doing so, he exposed his neck.

Connor struck fast and hard.

He tasted fur, skin and blood as he slammed his jaw shut. The coppery liquid filled his mouth but he didn't let go.

As Taggart struggled against his hold, he sliced into Connor's side. Connor felt as if razors had ripped through him but the agony was worth it.

Then Taggart stopped moving. The bottom half of his body wilted against the cold ground. Connor held on for a moment longer, then shook his limp neck before releasing him.

Standing over the dead wolf, he slowly turned in a circle to face the rest of the shifters. The wolves from Taggart's pack dropped to their bellies, and even Vince got on his knees and ducked his head.

Little pinpricks of pain shimmied through him as he stalked toward Ana. He hadn't seen her move, but she'd gotten up and now stood by her horse. She must have only been stunned by the blow.

It was as if small daggers had been embedded in his skin. When he shifted back to human form the pain would be that much worse. But he needed to touch Ana. To feel her soft skin under his fingers. Once he reached her, he shifted to his human form. It was asinine. He knew that. He was injured and would heal a hell of a lot faster in animal form, but he didn't care. His beast and human sides were in agreement for once. They wanted to hold Ana.

And let her hold him.

"*Connor!* What are you doing?" She reached out for him, wrapping her arms around his waist.

A wave of nausea rolled over him as he stumbled against her. "What were you thinking?" he murmured softly against her ear. Jumping into the middle of two Alphas fighting was not only dangerous, but if the Council found out she could face serious repercussions.

"From where I was standing it looked like he'd bitten your neck. I thought you'd— I was afraid he'd— I couldn't stop myself . . ." Her voice cracked as she trailed off.

Using her as support, he held on tight but focused on Vince. Connor's vision was a little blurred but at least he was alive. More important, Ana was safe. "Vince, I'll be at your ranch in two days to discuss the future. Once I've met everyone, some of you will have the option to assimilate, and the Council will place the rest of you elsewhere. I'm coming in peace so I'd better get a peaceful reception. And that meth house Taggart has you guys running better be destroyed by then. If you're into any other drugs or illegal activities, I want to know about it, and it will cease, starting now."

Vince nodded and motioned toward his pack, who kept their heads low and their tails tucked as they walked back toward their property.

Ana buried her face in his shoulder. "I can't believe you killed him." A shudder of relief snaked through her. It was so potent he felt it as deeply as if it were his own body.

"You're sure you're okay?" He pulled her tight, then ran his hands over her face and down her arms. He couldn't see any bruises but that didn't mean anything. He'd smelled Taggart's lust earlier. The thought of Taggart touching Ana made him want to kill the bastard all over again.

"He didn't hurt me. He would have if you hadn't arrived—"

"*Meow.*"

They both turned to find Vivian's head poking out from under Ana's fallen jacket. The little cat shivered and cried once she spotted them.

"Shit." He started to pick her up but Ana beat him to it.

Cuddling the she-cat close to her chest, she wrapped her other arm around his waist. "We need to get you back to the ranch and stop your bleeding."

His strength was fading and he wasn't inclined to argue with her. He motioned to Ryan and Noah to stay with the dead body as he retrieved Ana's coat. He wrapped it around his waist, then started to help Ana mount the horse.

She swatted him away with her free hand. "What are you doing? Get on the horse. I'll walk."

"She can hold us both."

"Connor, you're bleeding and—"

"I'm not going to argue, Ana. Get on the damn horse." He was tired and he just wanted to feel her up against him.

Maybe she understood that, because her expression softened and she let him help her and Vivian up. After they were seated, he swung up and bit back a cry of pain. Riding half-naked in the icy weather wasn't going to help him heal any faster, but he needed to get back to the ranch as quickly as possible.

For now he just wanted to hold Ana. She was safe and alive and that's all he could ask for. As Adalita broke into a trot, he felt as if his insides would shake apart.

Ana twisted in her seat to look at him. "Are you sure you don't want me to bandage you? You've got—"

"As soon as we get back, I promise you can do whatever you want to me. Okay?" She could wrap him up like a mummy if it made her happy. When she turned around he winced as more needles of pain shot through him.

Connor! Where are you? Liam projected.

He hadn't had time to send a message to Liam after he'd heard Ana's voice mail. In truth, he hadn't even thought of contacting him. His wolf had taken over and all he'd wanted to do was find and destroy Taggart. *Taggart's dead.*

Holy shit.

Yeah, he kidnapped Vivian in an attempt to take Ana.
He was still fuzzy on the details but he knew Ana would
explain everything soon enough. She sighed and tilted
her head back against his chest. He didn't care that each
jostle of the horse sent fresh waves of agony rolling over
him. The soft feel of her hair tickling against him can-
celed all that out.

*I'm glad he's dead, brother, but we've got some bad
shit to deal with. Carmen's dead.*

His chest constricted at Liam's words. He couldn't
have heard right. *Carmen?*

*Yep. Teresa's better and was getting worried so she
asked me to go looking for her. I found her facedown in
the snow near the forest line by the house. She has a puncture wound in her neck. She was poisoned. Same as Alicia.*

Who knows about it? Connor asked.

No one yet.

Keep it to yourself until I get back. As his brother's
words sank in, he pulled Ana tighter against him. He
didn't know how the hell he was going to tell her about
her sister. Carmen was one of the sweetest wolves he'd
ever met. And he knew how much Ana loved her. How
much everyone loved her. *Shit, shit, shit.* He'd sworn to
protect her and her packmates and now her sister was
dead.

His heart felt like an iron weight in his chest. Ana
would never forgive him.

Chapter 20

Ana ignored the insistent knocking on the bathroom door. She knew her mate was in physical pain and Noel was in emotional pain. She didn't want to deal with any of them right now. It was selfish, yes. She just didn't care. All she wanted was to curl into a ball and cry until she couldn't cry anymore. Or just block out the fact that Carmen was . . . She couldn't even think the word.

As she sat on the cold tile floor, she leaned back against the cabinet door. The metal knob dug into her back so she pressed harder into it. Not exactly painful but uncomfortable. That's what she wanted right now. Pain and discomfort to distract from her emotional agony.

When the door flew open, the lid on Ana's emotions popped off. "Where I come from, when a door's shut it's for a reason."

Connor stood there, his green eyes darkened with pity. She'd bandaged him hours ago, thankful he was alive and ready to celebrate Taggart's death. Then he'd dropped the bomb about Carmen. She still couldn't wrap her mind around it. Carmen was gone. Really gone.

"What can I do, Ana?" His voice was soft and that only infuriated her more.

"Get. Out." She drew up her knees and wrapped her arms around them.

Still in the entryway, he crouched down so he was eye level with her. At least he hadn't made a move to cross the distance between them. "I'm not going to leave you alone right now."

"I don't want to see you or anyone." Right now her emotions were raw and exposed. Like a live wire lying next to a pool of water. She knew if he stuck around she'd say something she regretted. She wasn't so far gone in her own agony that she wanted that. But she'd lash out if he stayed. Knew it as well as she knew her name.

"Come on, love. It's been six hours. You can't hole up in here anymore."

"I can do anything I damn well please. And don't call me love!" Angrily, she swiped at the stray tears lingering on her cheeks.

"Why not?" Again with the soft, soothing voice.

She didn't want soft right now. "Because it's bullshit. Everything is bullshit," she muttered.

"My love for you is real."

She snorted at his words and still refused to meet his eyes. The floor tiles were more interesting.

That got her a small wave of annoyance from him. Something mean inside her smiled. It wasn't her animal side. No, this was entirely her human self. She was angry and hurt and she wanted someone else to hurt too. "Your 'love' ran away from me fifty years ago."

"I did it for your own good."

"My own good? That's convenient. Maybe you just wanted to sow your wild oats or some other tired cliché." Even as she said the words she didn't believe them. Hated herself for trying to drag him down in the gutter with her. He growled deep in his throat, forcing her to look at him. She glared at his flashing green eyes.

"I wasn't lying when I said your father vowed to banish you."

"I ... I know." She might be hurting but she knew he hadn't lied about that, even if she had accused him of being a liar earlier.

He faltered for a moment. "You know *now*? Or you knew then?"

The questions pissed her off but at least this was better than talking about Carmen. She couldn't bear that. "Of course I didn't know then. I thought you'd left because, well ... whatever. I just thought you'd left because you didn't feel the same way about me."

He sighed and leaned against the doorframe. "What I feel for you ..." He laughed harshly. "I can't even put into words what I feel."

"How about you try?" Her voice shredded on the last word. She was on the edge of breaking down, but she was starving for his reassurance. For him to take away some of the bleak pain burning in her soul.

"You really want to talk about this now?"

"It's as good a time as any."

Connor shook his head and reached out to cup her face between his hands. "I love you, woman. Practically from the moment we met I knew I wanted you. At first I thought it was just physical, but over time ... I love everything about you, Ana. Still, I shouldn't have demanded your submission, and I won't force you into anything."

She jerked her head away. "So now you *don't* want to mate with me?" She wanted to cry again.

"Yes. No. I do, but ... damn it. Don't put words in my mouth. Of course I want you. Why do you think I wanted you to be my bondmate? I didn't want you to be able to walk away from me. It was selfish."

His frustrated tone touched her. Shoved aside some of her pain. She tried to digest his words but something else erupted inside her. She wasn't sure what it was, but she snapped. "So that's why all those years ago you left without talking to me? Without asking me what *I* wanted?"

"I had no pack, not much money. Enough to live on but you deserved better than that. Better than me. My father shamed us when he let our entire pack die like that. What could I have offered you? Not a stable home or pack life like you deserved. Eventually you would have resented me for taking you away from everything you knew and loved. I was doing what I thought was best."

"Exactly. What *you* thought was best. Just like you've been doing since you got here. Is that what our relationship is going to be like?"

"I'm willing to admit that I should have invited you to some of the meetings, but I'm your Alpha. When I make a decision, it's for the good of this pack."

She snorted loudly.

"You doubt me?"

"You left me without asking what I wanted. *And* you went after those humans for revenge."

He growled at her, the sound deep and angry. "I went after those assholes because it was the right thing to do. Do you think I should have forced you to choose between your family and me? Look at how much Carmen's death is—"

She let out a scream and threw herself at him. He didn't fight as she tackled him to the ground. Straddling him, she pounded against his chest. "Don't say that. Don't fucking say the word."

Grabbing her wrists, he twisted and in a few short moves had her pinned beneath him. "Your sister is dead

and I'm *sorry*. I can only imagine how much this is tearing you up, and if I could I'd take away all your pain. But
as far as what happened fifty years ago, I'd do the same
thing again. I loved you too much to make you choose
between your family and me. But I'm not leaving again.
Whatever you think about me, you better believe that.
Whether you agree to be my bondmate or not. I'm not
leaving. Ever."

His words washed away her anger. He did love her.
Maybe she was the one who didn't deserve him. She
couldn't even say the words. She was afraid if she did,
she'd lose him too. Unbidden tears streamed down her
face. First as a trickle, then a waterfall. She couldn't see.
Could barely breathe. As she tried to catch her breath,
she was aware of Connor smoothing her hair out of her
face, then lifting her.

He scooped her up; then suddenly she wasn't on the
hard ground but a soft bed.

"You shouldn't be lifting me." His wounds hadn't
been as bad as she'd originally thought and in a few
more hours he would be almost healed, but she didn't
want him straining.

"Shh." He pulled her back tight against his chest and
continued murmuring consoling words to her. She could
barely comprehend what he was saying; she just knew
the words were said with love.

In that moment, she knew that if he'd asked her to
mate with him fifty years ago, she'd have gone with him.
Without a doubt.

Chapter 21

Two Days Later

"How's Ana doing?" Liam asked as he set his coffee cup on the table.

Connor shrugged because he wasn't sure. "She's mainly slept the past couple days. After the ceremony for Carmen, she—"

He stopped when Noel walked into the kitchen. She had the same hollow look as Ana. Her unique amber eyes were dull and listless. She looked at them for a brief moment, then stumbled toward the coffeepot. Wordlessly she filled a mug, then left the room.

That's how it had been around the entire ranch since Wednesday. Taggart was dead, and even though that threat was eliminated, there was so much sorrow surrounding everyone.

Connor scrubbed a hand over his face. So far no one else had gotten sick, and Teresa was almost healed now. It didn't matter, though. They'd lost two of their youngest pack members. Not just the youngest, but the kindest.

"I called the hospital." Liam's voice broke into his thoughts.

"And?"

"And the reason Dr. Graham hasn't been by is because he's been working overtime. Apparently they had a bunch of overdoses that were brought into the ER last night."

"Hmm." Connor tapped his finger against the table.

"What's that look?"

"Something's been bothering me about Teresa. She should have gotten better a lot sooner."

Liam shrugged. "Her body was fighting the poison. It was only a couple days."

"That's not what I mean. She started healing once he was *gone*."

At his words, Liam frowned. "No one would think twice if he was wandering around the ranch."

"He has access to everything he needs to hurt us. Syringes, silver, our food and water. I thought there was a possibility it was Matt who had tampered with Carmen's food that day. He'd been in the house immediately before she was poisoned, but the doctor was around too. He had access to her food."

"Maybe he was keeping Teresa sick as a reason to stay here."

Connor mulled over the possibility and nodded. "It would be smart."

"I thought Ryan checked him out."

"He did." *But he could have missed something if he wasn't looking for it.* Connor pushed up from the table at the same time Liam did.

They found Ryan in the males' cabin, in the office with his laptop.

Connor didn't bother with small talk. "Where's that file on Dr. Graham?"

Ryan nodded at the stack of files he'd accumulated over the past week. "It's the green one."

Connor flipped it open and he and Liam skimmed over it together. As they read, Ryan interrupted them.

"I did some checking on that Katarina Saburova woman you two saved. Looks like the cops believed her story about the deaths of those two humans. And she wasn't lying about being no stranger to violence. Her father is part of the Russian mob in Miami."

"Keep reading," he murmured to his brother, then looked up. "Why is she here, then?"

Ryan shrugged. "Not exactly sure. I did some digging but wasn't able to find much except some old cell-phone records. Her car's paid off and she lives at the ski resort, as far as I can tell. She doesn't have many bills and only one credit card to her name."

"And?"

"You said she mentioned dating a shifter."

"Yeah."

"It could be nothing, but until about six months ago she was in contact—*daily contact*—with Jayce Kazan."

"She dated *the enforcer*?" *Great*. The Council had been pleased when he'd told them they'd cleaned up Taggart's illegal activities, but if Kazan had been involved with this human, Connor had a feeling they'd be getting a visit from him soon. It wouldn't matter that he and Katarina had broken up. Male shifters still looked out for their own. It was in their nature. And if the enforcer had been involved with a human, he'd want to check up on her after something like this, whether she informed him or not. Connor's pack had nothing to hide, but with all the recent deaths they didn't need more bullshit brought to their doorstep. And Jayce had a reputation for cleaning house first and asking questions later.

"Their phone records go on for about eight months before that. Then one day, nothing. He called her a few dozen times but she never picked up. If they're not talking anymore, then—"

Connor shook his head and sighed. "That doesn't mean shit. You've *met* Jayce. And it sounds like she left him."

Ryan nodded and a small bit of fear trickled off him at the name. Jayce was a scary motherfucker even to the most hardened warrior. He was old too. Probably older than some Council members. If someone had fucked with his woman—or ex-woman, as it were—he'd come sniffing around sooner or later. Connor was betting on sooner.

"Brother, I think I might have found something." Liam's agitated voice brought him back to their current problem. "Look at this."

"Bear attack?" Connor murmured as he read the report on the doctor's father's death.

"Yeah. His mother committed suicide not long after that. What if it wasn't a bear attack?"

Even if it was a simple bear attack the doctor could have a vendetta against shifters for another reason. With his mate in mourning and all his pack suffering, Connor owed the doc a visit. "Let's head to his place now. Ryan, you're coming too."

They parked a few neighborhoods over from the doctor's quiet, upscale neighborhood. Using the cover of falling darkness they made their way through backyards to get to his home. Even though it was winter, his lawn was immaculate. The brick ranch house had a custom-made, Mediterranean-style stone patio, which included a custom-made giant stone fireplace and was offset by a hammock swing. Nothing flashy, but still expensive.

In Connor's experience, people who lived in places like this rarely had alarm systems. Stupid, but true.

"Ryan, can you read me?" he spoke into his earpiece.

"Loud and clear, Connor."

"What if this doesn't work?" Liam murmured as they stalked across the lawn.

"Then we handle it our way." Raw energy hummed through him like an electric current.

His inner beast wanted to handle this one way and one way only, but he couldn't do that to Ana or the pack. He hadn't told her where he was going because he hadn't wanted to upset her. First he needed to know if the doctor really was responsible for the poisonings. If he was ... a shudder rolled through Connor. He just hoped he could control himself enough to follow through with the plan. On the drive there he'd gone over things in his head a dozen times and changed his mind just as many times. Even if the bastard deserved it, Connor couldn't kill him. This guy wasn't a thug or lowlife criminal. He was a respected member of the community. And even if he deserved to die, Connor had to put the good of the pack before everything else. Sometimes he hated being Alpha for that very reason. Right now he wanted blood. Every breath he took was laced with the need for vengeance.

Before they'd reached the patio, one of the French doors opened and the doctor walked out, carrying a snifter of amber liquid. Expensive scotch, by the cedary scent. The doctor didn't even notice them as he collapsed onto one of the cushioned wicker chairs.

"How's that drink, Doc?" Connor asked as he stepped out from behind one of the columns.

The blond-haired man sloshed his drink against the glass table, but then he straightened almost resolutely. Connor could see the knowledge and acceptance of what was to come in his brown eyes.

"Why are you here? Is everything okay at the ranch?"

"Carmen's dead."

He frowned, as if concerned. "I'm sorry to hear that." But he wasn't. The man's eyes gave him away. And he didn't ask what had happened. If he truly cared, it would have been his first question. It was human instinct.

Connor watched him carefully. In addition to the stench of the lie rolling off him, his pupils dilated wildly for a moment before returning to normal. For a human he was quite adept at hiding his emotions. They'd just happened to catch him off guard. "Why don't I believe you?"

The older man cleared his throat nervously.

"You know why we're here, don't you?" Connor asked.

He opened his mouth once as if to say something, then shook his head. "Mind if I smoke?"

"Go ahead."

Liam leaned against the column and Connor sat as the doctor placed a cigarette between his lips with shaky fingers. He wasn't as brave as he let on.

"You were responsible for all those deaths earlier this year." It wasn't a question.

No answer.

Connor's canines throbbed and he clenched his fists together tightly. His claws started to extend, digging into his palms and piercing him painfully, but he reined his rage back in. He had to do this right. "You get any help from the APL?" If the Antiparanormal League had been involved, Connor needed to know.

The doctor blew out a long puff of smoke and actually smiled. Proudly. "I didn't need any help from those backwoods idiots. I did this. All. By. Myself. I would have finished off the Cordonas too if the poison had worked right the first time. Those fools trusted me the entire time they were dying around me. Welcomed me onto their land with open arms." His lips curled up as he stared at Connor.

It took all of Connor's restraint not to strangle him. He kept his voice even, without inflection. He needed to get these answers from him. "Why didn't you try sooner, before we got to the ranch? And why not go after Taggart's pack?"

"I've been traveling too much for work. Just got back from a charity mission in South America a month ago. And Taggart? That fool is gonna bring himself down. One of his 'clients' almost overdosed, and admitted where he'd gotten his meth from. Why bother with him when the law will take care of it? And if not, I'd have gotten to him eventually." Pride laced his words.

"You do charity work yet you kill innocent people?" Connor couldn't wrap his mind around that kind of logic.

"You're not people!" The first sign of real anger popped up as he leaned forward.

"How did it feel to plunge that syringe into Carmen's neck? Or Alicia's? What about the Hippocratic oath?" He gripped the armrests of the wicker chair so hard the sides crumbled under his fingers. He wished it was the doctor's neck.

"I don't have to justify myself to you. You're an animal. An abomination. And I liked watching the life drain from Carmen's eyes. Stupid bitch saw me at the edge of the woods and tried to follow me. She was *easy* to kill."

Snarling, Connor lunged at him, but his brother must have expected it. As Connor jumped from the seat, Liam snagged him around the waist and yanked him back. "Think about the pack," Liam murmured. "If we turn him over to the police, it proves we're not animals and we respect their laws. The world deserves to know what he did to Ana's family. That we're innocent in all this and did the right thing. The long-term effects of this action will prove to people that we can be trusted."

His brother's words computed but took a long moment to digest. His canines—which had fully extended—bit into his lip. He tasted blood and the acridness only made his inner wolf angrier. It wanted death and vengeance. Struggling to breathe, he took long breaths in an effort to control himself. His brother was right. He *knew* that. He just had to make his wolf listen to reason.

The doctor stubbed out his cigarette and stood defiantly. "Do what you came here to do."

The command pulled Connor back from his dark thoughts. This asshole expected to die—and maybe deep down he knew he deserved it. But Connor wouldn't—couldn't. What he did next would show the town what his pack was like. If they wanted to settle here—and raise cubs here—he couldn't have his pack alienated. Or worse. "What is it you expect us to do?"

"What you fucking animals enjoy doing," he spat.

"You don't know shit about us," Connor growled. Though he wanted to stay and argue with the man about who the real monster was, he took a step back. If he stayed any longer he feared he wouldn't be able to control himself. He wouldn't give in to this asshole. Wouldn't prove him right. He was better than that. His entire pack was. And they were the ones who deserved to live peacefully where they belonged.

He looked at his brother and nodded. They'd gotten everything they needed. Wordlessly, they turned and headed back across the yard.

"Where the hell are you going?" the doctor called after them.

Connor didn't respond or turn to look at him. If he

did, he might throw out his resolve and rip the doctor's head off.

Once they reached the truck, he shut the passenger's door with more force than necessary. For how he felt, he was surprised it didn't tear off the hinges.

"We got it all." Ryan put the truck into gear.

They were all silent as they headed into town. The decision they'd made was a risk. Calculated and completely depending on the local cops to do their job. So far the sheriff hadn't exactly warmed up to them and he probably never would, but after Liam had saved the guy's sister, they all figured that would make a difference in how today went down. And Ana had told him after the poisonings that he'd done his job and launched an investigation. He might be an asshole but he didn't seem dirty.

Ryan placed the recording in Connor's outstretched palm as he parked in the police station's parking lot. "I've made a copy in case they don't do what's right."

Connor simply nodded and got out. He received a few curious stares as he entered the two-story building, but he ignored them all.

The Asian woman behind the desk faltered when she looked at him. "Can I help you, sir?"

"Sheriff McIntyre in?"

"Yes, I am."

Connor turned at the sound of the sheriff's voice, then held out the slim black tape. "If you're interested in arresting the man behind the poisonings on our ranch, all the information you need is here."

The sheriff eyed him warily but tucked the tape into his front pocket.

Connor wasn't through. He stepped closer so that only the other man could hear him. "If you don't take care of this, you better believe I will. And you won't like the fallout. Trust me."

Without waiting for his response, Connor left the building. His mate was at home, mourning, and he planned to take care of her tonight. Ever since his declaration that he loved her two days ago she'd been quiet. Most of it had to do with her sister's death, but it still stung. He'd told her he wouldn't force her to bond and she hadn't said she wanted different.

It might slowly kill him to be simply mated with her instead of bondmates, but he'd take what he could get. Tonight he planned to comfort his woman every way he knew how.

Ana eased open the door to the main house. It was quiet but she knew it wasn't empty. Noel and Vivian's scents were strong inside. Carmen's still lingered, triggering too many memories, but Ana knew she was truly gone. Might not want to admit it, but her heart had accepted it.

She'd seen Noel and Vivian at the burial ceremony but she'd barely spoken two words to them. To anyone. They deserved better than that.

Upstairs a faint light shone under Noel's door. She knocked but didn't get an answer. She thought about leaving but opened it instead.

Noel lay on her back, staring at the ceiling. Her dark hair was pulled away from her face. She glanced at Ana for a moment, but just as quickly averted her amber eyes. Without a word, Ana slipped off her shoes and slid into the bed next to her.

"I'm sorry I haven't been over here," she whispered, hating the way she'd avoided her pack and, more important, her only remaining sister.

"You needed to take care of yourself. Trust me, I get it." Noel linked her fingers through Ana's.

Tears pricked her eyes and she didn't bother to swat them away. "I miss her."

"Me too. I can't believe she's gone. It's too surreal. Too . . ."

Noel didn't finish and she didn't have to. Ana understood. They'd lost their parents and now their sister. She tightened her grip on Noel's hand.

"I can still smell her everywhere and I keep expecting her to walk through the door, telling me about her latest crush." Noel's voice broke on the last word.

Her sister curled up on her side and laid her head in the crook of Ana's arm. She tightened her grip and rubbed Noel's back in small circles. When their parents and packmates had died, she'd done the same thing with both her sisters. Just like her mother had done for her when she was sick or upset about something.

When Noel finally drifted off to sleep, Ana slipped out of the bed and headed back to her and Connor's house. She was glad she'd been able to comfort her sister, but she still felt hollow inside and knew that wasn't going away anytime soon. It was dark now and there was a distinct bite to the cool night air.

"Hey." Connor's deep voice startled her.

She swiveled and nearly lost her footing. "Where did you come from?"

"Liam and I just got back from town."

She frowned but didn't comment. If he wasn't going to tell her why he'd gone to town, she wasn't asking. She was tired of drilling him for information.

"Dr. Graham was behind the poisonings. All of them," he said as he fell in step with her.

"What?" she gasped out. *The doctor?* Something in her chest twisted and broke. She'd thought he was their friend. After the first time her pack had been poisoned, he'd been there for them. Or she'd thought he had. "You're sure?"

"I didn't want to say anything until I knew for sure, but it was him. He admitted poisoning your pack two months ago, and he was responsible for . . . for Alicia and Carmen's deaths. We got him on tape and I delivered it to the cops. I'm sure it won't stand up in court or anything, but it'll give them a place to start."

"Why didn't you kill him?" she asked.

His eyebrows rose. "Do you want me to?"

Yes. The word instantly jumped into her head. She knew he would if she asked, but she shook her head. They needed to do things the right way. It would keep the rest of the pack safe from bloodthirsty humans bent on retribution. "No."

Instead of closure or whatever she was supposed to feel, she just felt empty. Alone. Carmen was still gone. Her parents were still gone. Killing the man who'd done this wouldn't bring them back. "I—I want to move back to the main house, Connor."

He jerked as if she'd slapped him, and she realized he'd misunderstood her. She grasped his arm. "With you. I want us both to move back *together*. Maybe if we'd been living there Carmen wouldn't have—"

He wrapped his arm around her shoulders and pulled her tight against him. "That wasn't your fault, Ana. But we'll move back tomorrow. You're right. Noel shouldn't be alone right now."

"And I want to adopt Vivian. Officially. If she'll have us, of course."

His brows knitted together as he held open the front door. "You're sure?"

"Of course I am. I've done a shitty job of taking care of her the past couple days but I think—hope—she'll forgive me." The little she-cat needed to know she had a place with them. Just taking her in wouldn't be enough. Adopting her told the entire world she belonged here. And, more important, it told Vivian this was her home. Her pack.

"She's worried about you, not angry." Connor's deep voice comforted her.

As they ascended the stairs, she bit her bottom lip. They'd danced around talking about anything real for the past couple days—and that was her fault; she knew that. He'd been giving her space but now she craved closeness from him. And she needed to make the first move. He deserved that much. She rubbed her hand down his forearm in an intimate, soothing manner. "How are your wounds?"

Lust rolled off him as he answered. A good sign. "Almost a hundred percent."

She paused by the edge of their bed and tried to formulate her words. "I'm sorry I didn't take better care of you," she murmured. He was her mate—and hopefully he still wanted to be her bondmate. She should have been there for him. Instead she'd shut herself away from the world like a coward. Part of her feared that if she admitted how much she loved him she'd lose him too, but she couldn't live like that. Fear wouldn't rule her.

"You've got to stop apologizing to everyone, love." Without warning he grasped the bottom of her sweater and tugged it over her head.

Lifting her arms, she let him. Didn't even think to stop him. More than anything she wanted his hands and mouth on her. As always, she didn't tire of the way he seemed to devour all of her in one breathless sweep.

"It's a full moon tonight." Her words sucked the air out of the room in one violent whoosh. They could officially bond tonight if they wanted. If not, they'd have to wait another month. If he still wanted her.

His green eyes darkened until they were almost obsidian. "Yes, it is."

"I love you, Connor. After these past couple days, it's all the more clear. I realize I haven't been the best mate but I want to be your bondmate. If you'll still have me." Blood rushed loudly in her ears as she waited for him to say something.

She swallowed hard as Connor stared at her. The man looked like a lethal jungle animal stalking its prey. In an instant his demeanor changed from relaxed to hungry. Her pulse tripped like that of a hunted animal.

Except she very much wanted to be caught.

Instead of pouncing, as she'd expected, he clasped the bottom of his sweater and slowly peeled it upward.

Almost involuntarily, she took a step back. The back of her knees hit the bed, but she couldn't take her eyes off him. It didn't seem to matter that she'd seen his chest before. The man was pure sin in the flesh. All hard muscles just begging to be touched.

Taut, lean lines, and not an inch of fat on him. If it weren't for the scars nicking his chest and ripped stomach, he could have been carved from stone. She moistened her lips as she drank him in.

"If you keep looking at me like that, I'm not going to take my time," he growled.

Her eyes flew up to meet his darkened, predatory ones. An involuntary shiver ran through her.

They stood inches apart and it was all she could do not to jump him. He was waiting for something, though. She couldn't figure it out, but he was looking at her questioningly.

"Are you sure you want this?" he asked.

Sure? She'd never been more certain of anything in her life. She nodded because she didn't trust her voice.

Reaching out, he cupped her face. She could feel the

primal energy humming through him, but his hold was gentle. He leaned in slowly, giving her plenty of time to change her mind.

As if.

His lips met hers, softly at first, then more demanding. His tongue probed her mouth. He tasted like coffee and cinnamon. With each stroke of his tongue, her imagination went wild, fantasizing about what was to come. He'd marked her but the scent would eventually fade. This, however, would never fade. It would unite them for life.

Her hands splayed across his chest. His raw power was tangible. She could feel the energy humming from him and washing over her. Feeling almost drugged with desire, she reached between them and grappled with the button and zipper of his pants.

He chuckled lightly as he pushed them down in a slow, sensuous move before stepping out of them. A shudder rippled through her as she stared at him, and before she could take her next breath, he had her flat on her back. The sheets beneath her were cool, but her body seemed to burn everywhere. Especially when he stared at her as if he'd like to devour her whole.

As she stretched out on the sheets, an unbearable heat built between her legs. But she knew he'd give her everything she craved.

His hands shook as he pulled off her jeans. It surprised her. He never lost control. The thought that she could make a man like Connor tremble was a strange aphrodisiac.

Once she was completely bare before him, she reached out and grasped his hard length. She simply wanted to touch him everywhere. Well, she wanted more than that.

She wanted to stroke. Kiss. Lick.

She wanted to do it all. Words jumbled around in her

head as she tried to get a grip on what they were about to do. In the dim light streaming in from the windows, his body was perfectly illuminated as he moved on top of her. His eyes glittered with barely restrained hunger. He wasn't holding anything back from her now.

"You're perfect. Absolutely perfect, *mo chridhe*," he murmured before taking her mouth again.

She wasn't sure what he said, but whatever it was she wanted to hear it on his lips again. His possessive tone made her toes curl. Wanting to feel all of him, she wrapped her legs around his waist and held on to his shoulders while she kissed him deep and hard. A blistering need surged through her as their tongues and bodies meshed.

Now it was skin on skin.

Aching, sensitive breasts against his rock-hard chest.

Pelvis against pelvis.

He rubbed his body against hers in a sweet caress, and it was all she could do to stop from impaling herself on his rigid length. The more he teased her, the hotter her temperature grew. He was trying to torture her. It was the only explanation.

Deft hands caressed and palmed her breasts. She shifted her hips in an attempt to entice him, but he just chuckled in that maddening way she found she was getting used to. Tonight would be about his domination and her submission.

She traced her fingers down his back until she clutched his backside. His muscles contracted under her touch and his hips automatically jerked against hers. When his penis rubbed against her clit, she dug her fingers into his taut skin.

Breathing erratically, she drew her mouth away from his. She was hot, ready and willing.

His eyes darkened and all traces of amusement left

his handsome face. He knew exactly what she wanted without her having to ask. His head dipped to her ear and he sucked the sensitive lobe between his teeth. One of his hands found its way in between her legs, and she nearly vaulted off the bed when he touched her.

Connor groaned when he felt how wet she was. Ana was absolute dynamite in his hands. He slipped one finger inside her and slowly dragged it against her inner walls. She clenched around him with a long, liquid moan. When he withdrew his finger and clutched her hips, she silently arched her body toward his.

The animal inside him howled in satisfaction. This was his mate. *His.* She was giving all of herself to him. Flipping her over, he grasped her hips tight and pulled her back against him hard.

Tonight there would be no buildup. This was about their unification and so much more. With one thrust he was inside her. She was so tight, he wasn't sure how long he would last. He'd been trying to hold off because he'd known he'd be lost once he was inside her. And this bonding had to go right. He was staking his claim. After tonight there would be no doubt to anyone that she was his.

Her neck arched abruptly. "I'm so close . . ." The whispered words sent a rush of heat coursing over him.

He'd barely stimulated her and she was about to climax. It seemed impossible, but this was what the bonding was supposed to be like. Or so he'd heard.

Moving in slow, steady strokes, he stared at her body beneath his. Her dark hair streamed over her face like a silky waterfall as she ducked her head in submission. Palming her ass, he savored the feel of her smooth skin and the way her body tightened around him.

She milked him tighter, and when he felt her inner muscles contract in quicker successions he knew she was about to fall over the edge.

Like lightning, her orgasm hit hard and fast. Her breathing became more erratic and she dug her fingernails into the sheets beneath her, urging him deeper and faster.

As her contractions started to fade and a sweet, almost whimpering sound escaped her, he let go of his control. There was nothing graceful about his climax. With a loud groan he clutched her hips and emptied himself inside her. He was vaguely aware that he'd probably leave bruises. That pleased him. He wanted to mark her in every way possible.

He came long and hard, spilling himself inside her. As he did, he sank his canines into her neck. Like before, but harder and deeper and this time he drew blood. The small punctures would mark her forever. She let her head fall forward as he marked her.

As she did, he felt a slight burning on the side of his neck. Reaching up, he gently touched it. Though he couldn't see it, he knew a tiny Celtic symbol had appeared on his skin. Deeper than a tattoo, because it came from the inside. It was different for all male shifters, but his father's had been Celtic and his would be too. The pain was short-lived and triumph immediately roared through him. Their bonding was complete. She was his and he hers.

Though his body protested, he gently withdrew from her. Instead of collapsing on her, he rolled to the side as she flipped onto her back. He kept a hand on her stomach as he stretched out next to her, needing to feel her. His hand tightened against her abdomen and she smiled at him. Something she hadn't done in more than two days. It wasn't a big, toothy grin, but a shy, almost reserved one. And it made him lose his mind. No matter what, he wanted to keep that expression on her face.

Silently, she reached up and traced the side of his

neck. Her smile grew a fraction as she ran her finger over his mark. She looked proud, and that touched him in a way he couldn't find words for. Eventually he'd want to see what the symbol looked like, but for the moment he couldn't imagine moving away from her warmth.

"That was amazing." She dropped her hand as she spoke. The words were whispered so low he wasn't sure he'd even heard her right.

With his free hand, he smoothed back her hair and kissed her again. This time it was soft, almost chaste, but absolutely perfect. Wordlessly he pulled Ana closer. His chest and throat constricted as she snuggled deeper against him. She was like warm silk in his arms, relaxed and trusting.

"Any regrets?" he whispered, not wanting to break the intimacy of the moment.

"No way." Her voice was just as quiet as his. "I do need to tell you something, though. It's not a big deal, but . . ."

"What is it?"

"I was never mated. When you first came to the ranch you said you'd heard about my pack and mate dying, and I never corrected you. I . . . I don't know that I'd have ever gone through with it either."

Something warm constricted in his chest. He'd tucked away the knowledge that she'd been mated before him and forced himself to bury it. To know she hadn't been set something free inside him. Something he didn't know had been captive. Connor pushed out a deep breath. "In the interest of full disclosure, I bought your pack's old land in upstate New York. After your father moved it changed hands a couple times, but once I had the money and it was available I purchased it about a decade ago." It wasn't exactly a dark secret but he didn't want to keep anything from her.

She shifted in his arms. "Why?" There was only curiosity in her voice.

"It's where I met you. Since I couldn't have you, being in a place that reminded me of our time together was second best." Living there had occasionally been torture because of that fact.

"What does *mo chridhe* mean? You said it before."

He paused, despite the fact that they'd just bonded and she'd admitted she loved him. Clearing his throat, he forced the words out. "It's Gaelic and it means 'my heart.'" She'd stolen a piece of him from the first moment he'd met the she-wolf.

He could feel her smile against him. "I like it," she whispered.

The animal inside him sighed in acute relief. There was still a lot to deal with in the near future, but he had her by his side. Ana was stronger than even she realized and she was the perfect mate. Perfect for him.

Epilogue

One Week Later

Ana nudged open the front door to the main house with her foot. As she stepped inside, Noel immediately grabbed one of her boxes.

"You guys didn't have to move back, you know," her sister said as they headed up the stairs together.

"Someone's gotta make sure you're eating right." All week they'd been slowly moving everything back. Not that she or Connor had much stuff; they'd just been busy getting the ranch back in order and dealing with mourning pack members. In addition to their own sorrow. Some days it was all Ana could do to get out of bed. She didn't know if moving back into the house she'd shared with Carmen would be better or worse. Probably a little of both.

Ana, can you meet me in the barn? Connor's voice sounded loudly in her head. Now that they'd officially bonded they could communicate telepathically.

"Yeah," she said out loud before she could stop herself.

Noel frowned at her as she set the box on top of two others. "What?"

"Uh, nothing."

"Is Connor talking to you again?"

She grinned and nodded. "Yeah."

Noel mock shuddered. "And that doesn't freak you out?"

"I'm still getting used to it." Somehow Connor could carry on a conversation aloud *and* in his head, but she couldn't do both. *Should I bring Noel with me?*

Come alone if you can.

"I'll be back, okay?" she said to her sister.

Noel nodded. "I'll start going through your clothes."

"Just make sure they end up in *my* closet."

"No promises." Her sister grinned as she lifted a few coats lying across Ana and Connor's bed. It was the first time Ana had seen her smile since Carmen's death.

When she reached the barn she found Connor, Liam and Erin and the rest of the males waiting. Erin was obviously ignoring Noah, the dark-haired wolf who couldn't wipe the scowl off his face. Liam looked just as grim. But Connor . . . when he looked at her, her insides heated up instantly.

Something was on his mind or he wouldn't have called the meeting, but he looked as if he could jump her right then. And she just might let him. Ever since they'd bonded and completely opened up to one another, it was like an invisible wall had crumbled between them. Now that she knew he loved her and didn't have to hide herself, she felt free.

He didn't bother to hide his love for her either. As she approached the small circle, he covered the distance and wrapped his arms around her. When he pulled her into a tight embrace, a low growl escaped his throat, causing her to smile. She could scent his desire and no doubt every shifter in a fifty-mile radius could too.

"Didn't you call this meeting for a reason?" she whispered, mindful of their audience.

He loosened his grasp but there was a promise in his eyes that later they'd be tangled between the sheets—or in the shower. Or on the kitchen table.

"The sheriff called me a few minutes ago." His words had a silencing effect on the small group.

"What did he say?" Liam demanded.

It surprised Ana that Connor had waited until she was present to tell everyone, but it also pleased her.

"They arrested Dr. Graham on suspicion of multiple murders. The murders were going to be charged as hate crimes."

"Were?" Ana asked.

He nodded, his expression grim. "He killed himself in holding."

Ana didn't know whether to feel relieved that her sister's murderer was dead or not. Right now all her emotions were so screwed up. "So what does this mean?"

"Technically the case is closed, but we still have a problem. The doctor was well liked in the community. It doesn't matter that he was guilty of killing twenty-three innocent shifters; some people will consider his death a tragedy. Sheriff McIntyre made it clear he was going to keep this whole thing as quiet as possible, but people will find out why a prominent doctor killed himself."

"We did nothing wrong," Liam spat.

Connor nodded. "Sometimes that doesn't matter. In addition to that we have another problem. After Liam's conversation with that man who tried to attack December, we know the guy is working for someone in that Antiparanormal League. He was just following orders.

Just like the two men who went after Ana and kidnapped that woman connected to the enforcer. There
will likely be more of these people out there, and it's apparent they have no problem going after innocent humans connected to our kind." He cut a sharp look at
Liam and cleared his throat. "December isn't even connected to us but someone knows she means something
to my brother. That's dangerous for everyone we know."

"We need to make a list of all humans we're friends
with or associated with and let them know what's going
on." Ana spoke before she could censor herself. Erin
and the group of males stared at her, but she continued.
"I know *I'd* prefer to keep humans out of our business,
but thanks to the Council the world knows about us. We
just have to deal with it, and we can't let the people who
are actually our friends be blindsided by some hate
group."

Connor's grip on her tightened and she wondered if
maybe she should have kept her mouth shut, until he
spoke. "Ana's right. We don't live in a vacuum anymore.
All of you need to list every single human you know
who supports our kind. I'll let the rest of the pack know,
but I want that list by tonight."

Ana let out a breath she didn't know she'd been holding. His support meant more to her than she wanted to
admit. Okay, maybe she didn't have much of a problem
admitting it anymore. Depending on him was something
she could get used to in a big way.

"What about Taggart's pack? Do we want a bunch of
new males around here who just a couple weeks ago
hated us? Everyone is still reeling from Alicia and
Carmen's . . ." Erin's voice cracked.

In the past couple weeks the redhead had undergone
a transformation. She wasn't as meek or timid anymore.
Decked out in cargo pants, a tight black sweater, and a

dagger strapped to her hip, she looked like a warrior. Well, a petite, very pretty warrior. And she was royally pissed off about Carmen's death. Ana saw it every time she looked at the she-wolf.

"I've already spoken to the Council and to Taggart's pack. Vince—his second-in-command—has been unhappy for a long time. They all have, but were too afraid to get help. Taggart was growing mentally unstable and most of them want to get as far away from here as possible. The warriors and alphas will be dispersed to various packs across the country. There are a few betas who want to stay and we have no reason not to take them in. It's not their fault they had a shitty Alpha. Most of his pack will be leaving with the alphas and his land is now ours."

Once the meeting wound down, everyone started to quietly disperse, with the exception of Erin and Noah, who began arguing almost immediately. Connor stiffened beside Ana. "Looks like I get to play referee again. I'll meet you at the house," he muttered.

Grinning, she nodded. Those two had some serious issues to work through and she was glad she wasn't in the middle of them. She fell into step with Liam as they headed back to the main house.

"Noel said something about cooking for everyone tonight but I can't make it. Let her know, okay?" Liam said.

It would be dark soon so Ana knew exactly where he was going. "Going to spy on December again?"

"I wouldn't have to spy on her if she'd accept my protection." His voice was testy and tired.

"Give her time," Ana murmured.

Liam muttered something inaudible but he scowled darkly, possessively. He got the same determined look on his face as his brother did when he wanted some-

thing. Ana smiled to herself. December might not realize it yet but she belonged to Liam.

As Ana entered the main house, Noel and Vivian
were leaving. "What are you two doing?"

"Taking a break. Vivian wants to ride your horse, and
I got tired of unpacking *your* clothes," Noel softly teased.

"I can ride your horse, right?" Vivian jumped from
foot to foot as she stared at her expectantly.

Smiling, Ana placed a quick kiss on the top of Vivian's head. "Of course. Just don't go too far." There might
be warriors patrolling the land, but she still worried all
the time.

Once inside the house she immediately headed upstairs. If she knew Noel, half of her clothes hadn't been
put up or even made it into her room. When she passed
her sister's room, she saw she was right. A few pairs of
Ana's shoes were strewn across the floor.

Sighing, she picked them up and headed to her
room—her and Connor's room. As she opened her
closet door a strong arm wrapped around her waist. The
man was so stealthy sometimes it scared her. She hadn't
even heard him come up the stairs. But his spicy scent
twined around her now.

Connor nuzzled the side of her neck before he gently
raked his teeth over her skin.

She shuddered lightly. Inhaling deeply, she leaned
back against him. "Referee time over?" she murmured.

"They can work out their own problems," he growled
next to her ear before turning her around to face him.

Immediately she draped her arms around his neck.
"Is that right?"

"Mm-hm. There's something else I'd much rather be
doing." He reached down and grabbed her behind, hoist-
ing her up so that she wrapped her legs around him.

"Me too." Almost before the words were out of her mouth, he'd crushed his lips over hers.

They met each other with the same urgent kisses. Hungry and insatiable yet sweet and gentle, Connor was everything she'd ever wanted in a bondmate. She knew their pack would be facing problems in the near future, but she also knew there was nothing they couldn't handle as long as they stood together.

Acknowledgments

First I have to start off by thanking God for listening to all my fears and for giving me so many wonderful opportunities. Without you, none of this would be possible.

Many thanks go to my dedicated agent, Jill Marsal, for having faith in me even when I didn't. So much gratitude goes to my amazing editor, Danielle Perez, for all her guidance and help in bringing this world to life.

Working as a writer is often a solitary profession, but I've been lucky enough to have the support of some wonderful people. Kari Walker, you are my voice of reason and keep me sane when I need it most. Thank you for always being my biggest cheerleader. I'm so thankful to have a friend like you and mere words can never express how much. Dara Edmondson, I will always be thankful for all our coffee dates, plotting sessions and long distance phone calls. Having a friend like you is priceless. Cindy Roussos, your kind nature never ceases to amaze me. Thank you for freely giving of your knowledge and experience and for just being an amazing friend. So many thanks go to Chudney Defreitas-Thomas, Jax Cassidy and Tracy Truman for being so forgiving of my silence when I'm working on deadlines and for helping me brainstorm anytime I need help. Uncle Carl, thank you for always being available to answer random police procedural questions, and Aunt Selina, thank you for your love and support.

Last, but definitely not least, thanks to my very supportive parents and beautiful sister. I'm so blessed to have such an encouraging family who always fostered creativity. I couldn't ask for a better support system.

Read on for a preview of

PRIMAL POSSESSION

the next thrilling novel in Katie Reus's
Moon Shifter series!

December McIntyre managed to smile at her date as he pulled out her chair for her. Her cheeks hurt from all the fake smiles and forced laughter. She should never have agreed to this date as she'd rather be anywhere else. With *someone* else. But she and Liam had no future, and going out with a random guy was the only way to show Liam *and* herself that she was serious about that.

"Have you been here before?" her date—Mike something—asked. As a tourist from the nearby ski lodge, he wasn't a local of her small mountain community, so it made sense that he'd never eaten at the cozy Italian restaurant.

She nodded. "The *bucatini puttanesca* is really good. So is the *pollo caprese*. Actually, everything on the menu is good." The Russo family had settled in Fontana, North Carolina, decades ago, many years before she'd been born, and Russo Ristorante had become a staple in the mountain town. The locals loved it and so did the tourists. Occasionally they even got visitors from not just Fontana Mountain but from their neighbors, Beech and Sugar mountains.

Almost immediately after they ordered drinks, her date excused himself. He was a broker or something and had to take an important call. Normally that would have bothered her during a date, but she didn't really care about this one. The brief reprieve was fine with her. She wanted to get through the meal, get home, and just go to bed. Going out with this guy had been a colossal mistake no matter how nice he seemed to be. She'd known it the second after she'd said yes. Regret had surged through her, but it had been too late then.

All she could think about was Liam. Liam with his broad shoulders, dark hair, and deep, knowing, coffee brown eyes. When that man looked at her, she got shivers. The good kind. Heat bloomed between her legs when he was around. He didn't have to do *anything* other than train that heated gaze on her and she wanted to melt into his arms. He might have been built like a linebacker, but his hands were gentle. At least the few times he'd caressed her face they had been.

Her image of him was so clear she could almost see him now. In front of her. As she stared into space she frowned. Then blinked. Good God, he *was* in front of her. Walking straight toward her.

"Crap," she muttered. Tensing, she braced herself. She'd thought if he saw her leaving her bookstore — because she'd seen him watching — with another guy on a Friday night, he'd get the hint and leave her alone. If it was anyone else she might think he was acting like some sort of creepy stalker, but she knew him better than that. As one of the few lupine shifters who lived in their town, Liam had tried to warn her about some crazy fanatic group that wanted to hurt humans involved with shifters. At twenty-eight she'd been taking care of herself for a long time — and besides, *they* weren't involved, so there was no reason for some fanatics to come after her.

Should have known Liam wouldn't give up so easily. The maître d' led him and another huge guy directly to the table next to hers. There was a decent amount of space between them, but for the way he was drilling his gaze into her, he might as well have been sitting at the same table.

"Hello, December." Liam's deep, intoxicating voice forced her to acknowledge him.

She flicked a quick look at his dark-haired friend, who cracked a small, almost amused, smile until she glared at him—then she focused on Liam. "What are you doing here?" she asked through gritted teeth. It wasn't for the damn food. That much she knew.

He shrugged as if it should be obvious. "Eating."

She glared at him. "You know what I mean. I'm on a *date*, Liam."

At the word "date" those espresso eyes of his got even darker. Under normal circumstances she might have thought it was the light playing tricks on her, but she knew better. She'd seen him enraged once before when a man had tried to mug her. His eyes had changed then. The whites had almost disappeared, and she'd found herself staring into not-quite-human eyes. He'd later explained that it sometimes happened when his inner wolf wanted to take over. It had scared her then, but not now. She knew he wouldn't hurt her. Not physically. He might be dominating and sometimes too pushy, but he cared for her. In another world she might allow herself to care for him too. But they had no chance, and she wasn't going to risk getting her heart broken and losing her only family due to her involvement with Liam. Especially when anything that happened between them couldn't last. He barely looked thirty, but she knew he was over one hundred years old.

"Get rid of him." He didn't raise his voice, but there was a razor-sharp edge to it.

Maybe his tone should have made her nervous, but it just infuriated her. *He* infuriated her with all his arrogance. "Or what?"

"Or I'll do it for you."

She balled her hands into fists under the table. "You are so ... so ..."

In a fluid, graceful motion that reminded her he was more than human, he stood up and slid into the chair across from her. As if he had every right to do so. He half smiled and her traitorous libido roared to life. Why did the soft candlelight have to play off his features, making him even better looking? "Charming, handsome—"

His smartass response annoyed her even more, but it also allowed her to find her voice. "Arrogant and *annoying*," she said in a loud whisper, barely containing the need to shout at him. "Why would you think on any level of normalcy that it was okay to interrupt my date when I've made it perfectly clear nothing is going to happen between you and me?"

His eyes darkened. "I'm not interrupting. I'm just eating. Or don't you think shifters should be allowed in the same restaurants as humans?"

His words were like a slap. Shocked, she jerked back. She had issues with his kind—issues he didn't even know about—but the thought of restricting someone, anyone, access to a public place was horrifying.

Her dismay must have shown because he cursed under his breath. "I didn't mean that, December. I know you don't think like that."

"Then why'd you say it?"

"Because you're driving me crazy, woman. Why are you out with this loser?"

"He's not a loser."

"He's a fu— loser for leaving you all alone. And he's not me. He'll never be able to give you what I can. I can smell how much you want me even now. Just give us a chance, December." His voice dropped slightly, taking on that sensuous quality that made her legs tremble and heat spread across her lower abdomen.

"Liam, we're—"

"Too different. Yeah, that line is getting really old, Red."

A flush hit her cheeks. "Don't call me that."

"Why not?"

"It's too . . . familiar." Unfortunately, she very much liked the intimate way the nickname rolled off his tongue. And that was bad.

"I plan to get very familiar with you soon, *Red*." He reached out and fingered one of her bright red curls.

Her stomach muscles clenched with need as his knuckles brushed against her cheek. As his masculine, earthy scent rolled over her, she struggled to remind herself why things would never work between them. When he looked at her with those captivating eyes, it was hard to remember her own name.

The sound of a man clearing his throat jerked her back to reality. Her date stood next to the table, looking between her and Liam with slightly narrowed eyes. "I didn't think I'd been gone that long," he said half-jokingly.

"I'm sorry"—*Oh God, what was his name?*—"Mike. This is a friend of mine. And he's *leaving*."

Liam snorted loudly and glared at her. *"Friend?"*

He wasn't going to make this easy for her. Holding her breath, she waited for him to move.

After what felt like an eternity he finally stood. Completely ignoring her date, he looked at her. Anyone else would have said a few polite words or excused himself, but not Liam. It wasn't in his DNA. He wouldn't be civil or polite if he didn't mean it. "This isn't over, *Red*."

Mercifully, instead of sitting back down Liam nodded at the guy he'd arrived with. His friend dropped a bill on the table and they left without even having touched their drinks.

As her date slid back into his seat she blew out a shaky breath.

"Ex-boyfriend?" Mike asked.

She shook her head. "Not exactly. I'm really sorry that happened."

He shrugged but she could see the annoyance in his expression. Not that she blamed him. In his position she'd be ticked off too. When their server came back to take their order, she knew she couldn't sit through a meal with this guy. Seeing Liam had shaken her to her core and had made it clear that she wasn't interested in dating anyone else. Until she could purge him from her system she might not ever be ready. Just knowing he was out there and available made everyone else pale in comparison. After asking their server to give her a few more minutes, she looked at her date. She was ready to bail, but he beat her to the punch.

"You want to leave, don't you?" he asked, his voice wry.

Embarrassment flooded through her, but not enough that she changed her mind. She nodded and pulled her wallet out of her purse. She dropped a twenty on the table. It would more than cover their drinks. "I'm so sorry to have ruined your evening. There's no excuse for my behavior. I know you don't want all the details, and I'm just . . . sorry. Would you mind taking me back to my store?" She'd let him pick her up there instead of at home, mainly because she'd wanted Liam to see them leaving together, but also because she didn't like giving her address out to too many people. Curse of being a cop's sister, she supposed.

"It's no problem and you don't have to pay." He placed a clammy hand over hers. His hands were soft, unlike Liam's calloused, roughened ones. She didn't know what it was, but the sensation of this guy touching her made her feel ill. He tightened his hold slightly, and something akin to fear jumped inside her. Which made no sense. He seemed like a nice man. He'd held open her doors and pulled out her chair and had been perfectly polite. But he wasn't Liam.

Somehow Liam had ruined her for anyone else, and they'd never even kissed. She wanted to curse his name for that. December stood, using it as an excuse to take her hand back. "I spoiled our date. At least let me pay for the drinks."

Mike hadn't attempted to pull out his wallet, so she figured he didn't actually mind her paying. The walk to the parking lot was quiet. Politely, he held open the passenger door of his BMW.

As they steered out of the parking lot, the need to apologize again overwhelmed her. She'd never been so rude to a date before. "I know I said it already, but I really am sorry for messing up your evening."

Without looking at her, he pulled onto the two-lane highway that led back to the small downtown area. His shoulders hitched slightly in a casual shrug. "It's no problem. That guy obviously upset you."

She had started to relax against the leather seat when he continued.

"I don't know why you'd expect anything less when you're associating with animals." The last word dripped with disdain, and there was an unexpected rise in the pitch of his voice.

It took a moment for the significance of his words to register. She'd never said anything about Liam being a shifter. And it's not as if people could tell what they were simply by looking at them. But by the way Mike had said "animals," it was obvious he *knew* what Liam was without a doubt. She frowned at the knowledge. "Excuse me—"

She jerked back toward the door when he suddenly brought his right hand up. She saw the flash of the syringe and reacted. Barely had time to think.

Adrenaline swelled through her as he swung the needle at her shoulder. Using her arm to deflect the blow, her wrist jolted as their forearms collided with a solid thud. He still held the small weapon in his strong grip, but he hadn't managed to pierce her.

A bolt of terror splintered through her veins as she stared at the needle. She wasn't sure if it was poison or some sort of sedative, but whatever he planned to do, it wasn't good. If he knocked her out he could do whatever he wanted. Take her anywhere. The knowledge sent another jolt of fear spiraling through her. Despite the confines of the car, she turned, pressing her back against the door. Then she lifted her leg and kicked out at him. Her winter boots were thick and sturdy and had a two-inch heel that could do some damage. They were still barreling down the highway, and he had to keep his eyes on the road, putting him at a huge disadvantage.

"Bitch," he snarled and tried to stab her leg while keeping the wheel steady.

He missed so she kicked again. This time she twisted completely and raised both legs. The roads were icy and it was obvious he wasn't used to the snow. If he were he'd have already gotten chains on his wheels. His inexperience was probably why he'd attempted to stab her while driving. *Idiot.*

The vehicle swerved across the road and the syringe flew out of his hand. While he grappled with the wheel she kicked out at him again, all fury and anger. This time her booted heel slammed against the side of his face and her other foot shoved the wheel wildly to the left. He grunted and expelled a string of nasty curses as the car bucked sideways, but she didn't care.

All the air rushed from her lungs as they fishtailed out of control. Everything slowed. She heard the sound of a horn blaring in the distance, tires screeching, and braced herself for the impact. For the pain.

On instinct she held on tight and crouched low in her seat. Her stomach shot into her throat as they flew off the road into a snowy, icy embankment. She felt like she was on a roller-coaster ride, except she knew the ending was going to be much less fun. The car spun wildly out of control for what seemed like forever until it skidded to a smooth stop on a bunch of fluffy snow.

Like a miracle, they didn't flip or ram into anything. Mike shook his head and looked around, a dazed expression on his face.

He might be in a state of shock but December knew it wouldn't last long. She had to get out now, no matter how shaky she felt. She was twisted at an odd angle and sitting low so she slowly reached behind her with one hand and felt for the handle. As she did, she unsnapped her seatbelt with the other.

The door swung open and Mike finally realized what she was doing. She fell back into the snow and he lunged at her. But his seatbelt snapped him back into the seat.

Rolling over, she scrambled to her feet and started running. Or tried to. Her boots pressed into the white thickness as she struggled to make it up the steep embankment to the road, away from the forest they'd almost plowed into.

She heard him shouting behind her, but she kept going. It was dark, but if she could flag down a car before Mike caught her she knew she'd be okay. She tripped and fell but clawed at the icy ground and pushed herself back up. Her heart hammered against her ribs and her skin crawled as she fought to get away.

Even though she wanted to look behind her, she didn't dare. It would only slow her down. When her boots touched the asphalt a new burst of energy detonated through her. As fast as she could, she ran along the icy edge of the road. Her coat and jeans were dark, so she prayed anyone driving had their lights on.

She'd only gone a few feet when two bright headlights shone in the distance. Waving her arms around like a madwoman, she continued running. She slipped again and tumbled backward. The ground was icy and hard but she barely felt the impact on her hip.

Her survival instinct told her to haul ass if she didn't want to be killed. Or worse. As she started to push up, strong hands gripped her arms and pulled her to her feet.

A scream tore from her throat. Twisting around she tried to break free until she suddenly recognized Liam towering over her in the darkness. She stared at him in confusion. *Why was he there?* "What are you—"

"What happened? Are you all right?"

Her heart thumped a staccato beat against her chest as she stared into Liam's dark eyes. "Where did you come from?" She started to involuntarily shake and his grip tightened. He was warm and safe.

"I saw you running down the side of the road. What the hell happened, December?"

She frantically glanced behind her, expecting to see Mike running at them, but no one was there. Turning to Liam she opened her mouth but no words came out. Instead, the shaking intensified. She didn't know *what* had happened exactly. It had all been so fast. Suddenly she needed more air. It was as if her lungs had shrunk. She sucked in a deep breath, trying to steady herself, and Liam frowned.

He took one of her wrists, and his frown deepened. "Your pulse is erratic," he murmured.

Of course it was. Her date had just tried to kill her. Or maybe he hadn't wanted her dead. He might have wanted to . . . "My date," she gasped out. "I told him I wanted to leave the restaurant. He had a syringe. He tried to stab me while he was driving and I kicked him and the wheel. I didn't even think about it. We flew off the road and I escaped . . ." She shook her head and turned around again. It was too dark to see how far she'd run. "I don't think it was far from here. I just started running."

Still holding onto her wrist, he looked past her into the darkness. "I want you to stay here with Ryan, okay?"

No! She grabbed his arm. "Who's Ryan?" She felt disoriented and a little confused. And she couldn't stop the chills skittering over her skin.

"I won't let her out of my sight." The male voice from behind her made her jump, but when she turned to face the other shifter, all she saw was compassion in his dark eyes.

Liam hated leaving December, but he hurried down the embankment to find the piece of shit that had attacked her. Other than the fresh smells of the forest, he scented slightly burned rubber and December's date. His canines throbbed just thinking about her out with someone else, and knowing she'd been attacked made his inner wolf almost blind with rage. He'd tried to warn her that members of the Antiparanormal League might target her because of her association with him. Not that he had the kind of "association" he wanted with her. He'd recently discovered that the APL somehow *knew* he cared for her, so they wanted to use that against him or his pack. Or both. It didn't matter that he and December weren't physically involved—or involved at all, really. Which was why he'd been watching her. Even thinking about what might have happened if he hadn't been nearby tonight . . . His inner wolf rattled dangerously, so he shut down those thoughts.

As he neared the car, he frowned when he saw the passenger's and driver's doors open. December's footprints led back the way he'd just come, but there was another set leading away into the woods. He stared toward the tree line, fighting back the primal growl trying to claw its way out of his throat. The key was still in the ignition, the car still running. Leaning over and being careful to take it by the edges, he slipped the key out and dropped it into his jacket pocket. The contents of her purse had been dumped onto her seat. A small makeup bag, a book, and a planner. No wallet.

His most primal side wanted to hunt this guy down and tear him apart limb from limb. Slowly. But he couldn't leave December. Liam still wasn't sure what had happened, but she'd been close to going into shock. If she hadn't already.

Pushing down the need to hunt and protect what was his, he gathered her stuff and shoved it in her purse. He checked the glove compartment to see if he could find some paperwork with an address on it, but he came up empty, so he headed back to the road.

Ryan had already taken her back to the truck. From their silhouettes Liam could see December sitting in the middle of the bench seat and Ryan in the driver's seat. Normally Liam preferred to drive but right now all he wanted to do was comfort her.

She kept pushing him away, but he didn't think she would now. She might try to deny she wanted him, but every time she fixed those baby blues on him, he could see lust and confusion battling inside her. He didn't care that she was human and he was a lupine shifter. Differences like that didn't matter. At least not to him. Obviously some people cared enough to want to hurt her.

At the moment she was vulnerable, and he knew she actually might let him comfort her. Maybe he should feel guilty about taking advantage of her emotional state, but he didn't. He would touch and hold her any way he could.

As he slid into the seat next to her, she immediately scooted closer to him. Reaching out, he tucked a red curl behind one of her ears. Her ivory skin was soft, slightly flushed, and her breathing was still erratic. Brushing his hand against her cheek, he let one of his fingers stray to her pulse point below her earlobe. Still erratic. Not good.

"Honey, look at me." He waited until her eyes focused on him. "Have you called your brother?" He might not get along with the sheriff, but Parker loved his sister and had more resources than Liam did at the moment.

"No. And I don't want to." Her voice shook, but it was still strong.

"Some guy just attacked you. We need to report this."

She stuck her chin out mutinously, but he didn't miss the raw fear that had bled into her eyes. "I'm *not* going down to the station."

He sighed and looked at Ryan over her head. "Go to her store," he told him. Then he refocused his attention on December. "We're still calling him, Red."

"Don't call me that," she snapped.

The burst of annoyance that rolled off her was exactly what he wanted. She didn't seem to be in actual shock, but after what she'd been through, she would be coming down from an adrenaline high. She needed to find a balance. And he needed her to answer some questions. "Where did you meet this guy?"

"Uh, my store. He's just a tourist on a short ski vacation—or he told me he was. I'm sure that was a lie. I thought it would be a harmless date and a way to . . ." Her blue eyes widened as she trailed off.

"A way to what?"

"A way to convince you to leave me alone." She blushed, staining her ivory cheeks a deeper shade of red.

Her words stung. He didn't want them to, but they did anyway. All he wanted to do was protect her. Yeah, they came from different worlds, but it shouldn't matter. His inner wolf growled at him, and in that moment, he hated his primal side. The side that told him to just take what he wanted. His human side cared a hell of a lot more about December to ever hurt her, and he didn't like the turn his thoughts were taking. Steering the conversation in a different direction, he said, "Your purse had been dumped out and I didn't see a wallet. He probably has your address anyway, but you're going to need to cancel your credit cards."

"I don't carry a wallet. I keep my driver's license and credit card on me. Parker drilled that into me years ago. In case I ever got mugged or something. He's really particular about stuff like that." She patted her coat pocket, then frowned, presumably as the rest of his words sank in. "What do you mean he probably has my address? He picked me up from my store."

"You were attacked in your house a few weeks ago." Even thinking about that got his heart racing. If her brother hadn't been there to scare off the guy, anything could have happened.

"Yeah, so?"

"Your date and that guy are probably part of the same organization."

She lifted an eyebrow. "Are you going to start in with that APL stuff again?"

"After tonight, I wouldn't think you'd need as much

convincing. This is a small town, and it's not hard to find out where someone lives anyway." With enough money, anything was possible.

She started to say something, then snapped her mouth shut. A frown marred her pretty face as her eyebrows knitted together in concentration.

"What is it?"

"He said something about you being an animal. I can't remember exactly what it was, but I never said anything about you being a shifter. Still, he *knew* you were. Right after he said that he pulled out the syringe. Then everything sort of went crazy." Shuddering, she wrapped her arms around herself, and he couldn't help it. He wrapped an arm around her shoulder and pulled her tight against him. She needed comforting. Whether she admitted it or not. To his utter surprise, she didn't fight him. For a brief moment she stiffened, then melted against him.

Like warm silk, she sank into his side and buried her head against his neck. Her jasmine scent twined around him, making him dizzy for a moment. The feel of her warm breath on his skin made the ache between his legs impossibly painful. Reaching out his other arm, he pulled her completely against him. The position was awkward for him but he didn't give a shit.

Liam battled his disappointment as Ryan steered into the parking spot next to December's car. He didn't want to let her go. Wanted to keep holding on to her like this as long as she'd let him. But he needed to get her home.

When she realized they'd stopped, she pulled back and frowned.

Sighing, he fished out the car keys from her purse and handed them to his packmate. "Follow me back to her place."

"What do you think you're doing?" she asked.

Liam ignored her as he rounded the vehicle and slid into the driver's seat. He didn't want to move her and he didn't want her driving. She might not be in shock, but she was shaken up pretty bad.

"Liam, what are you doing?"

"What does it look like? We're going back to your place and I'm calling your brother." He'd have already made the call if he hadn't thought it would upset her.

He found it interesting that instead of moving into the free passenger seat, she stayed where she was, in the middle seat. If anything, she actually moved a little closer toward him.

She might try to deny the chemistry they had, but she knew instinctively that he would protect her. December might not even realize it, but her most primal side trusted him. Her desire to be near him proved it. That knowledge soothed his inner wolf. And he would protect her. No matter the cost.